I0612693

Payback

by

David A. Freas

This is a work of fiction. Names, characters, places, and incidents are either the product of the author's imagination or are used fictitiously, and any resemblance to actual persons living or dead, business establishments, events, or locales, is entirely coincidental.

Payback

COPYRIGHT © 2022 by David A. Freas

All rights reserved. No part of this book may be used or reproduced in any manner whatsoever without written permission of the author or The Wild Rose Press, Inc. except in the case of brief quotations embodied in critical articles or reviews.
Contact Information: info@thewildrosepress.com

Cover Art by *The Wild Rose Press, Inc.*

The Wild Rose Press, Inc.
PO Box 708
Adams Basin, NY 14410-0708
Visit us at www.thewildrosepress.com

Publishing History
First Edition, 2022
Trade Paperback ISBN 978-1-5092-4278-8
Digital ISBN 978-1-5092-4279-5

Published in the United States of America

"Rick, are you drinking?"

"Just a couple beers." And six or eight more after these two.

"Why?"

He settled on the living room sofa before he answered. "Because I want them."

"Because?" Ann drew the word out impossibly long.

He took a couple swallows from his bottle. "I feel like it."

"Because of Mary?"

"Yeah, because of Mary."

"And how is getting smashed going to help?"

He drank some beer. "I'll be so blotto, I can sleep like I'm dead all night long and not dream bad dreams about her."

"About a woman you say you have just a casual thing with?"

He hadn't fooled her back in November and wasn't fooling her now. In spite of his insistence there was nothing special between the two of them, Ann had sensed Mary meant more to him than he realized. She'd read him like a book even when he couldn't see the words himself. Denying it now would be foolish. "Things have changed a bit since Thanksgiving."

"Or did you just wake up to what was there even back then?"

He raised the bottle, stopped with it almost to his lips, and lowered it. "I guess I woke up. It took Mary getting shot to wake me. I wish—" He stopped. His mind churned with so many thoughts, he couldn't catch one to say it. He set the bottle on the table by his recliner. "I wish I'd told her how I feel about her."

Other Wild Rose Press Titles by Dave Frees:

Illegal Maneuvers

Dedication

To my parents, Foster and Emma, your love of reading planted the seeds that grew into this story.
To my family, Linda, Laurel, and Colin, your support watered those seeds, helping them grow.

Acknowledgments

My parents, Foster and Emma instilled a love of reading and words in me from my earliest days. That love made me look at books and think I could do better.

My family, Linda, Laurel, and Colin, were my primary sounding board, brainstormers, and surrogate characters when I needed help translating the ideas in my head to accurate words on the page. And they understood that for me taking writing supplies on a vacation was as necessary as clothing.

Marty, Pam, Andi, and Bill believed in me and encouraged me from the start of this journey, when I doubted I'd be good enough to make it to the end. And they called me on it when I delivered anything less than my best. Katie, Jim, Janet, Paula, Thorsen and Neva continue that support.

Pennwriters members – a more diverse group with so much in common doesn't exist anywhere on this planet – have taught me so much in so many different ways that to list you individually would take volumes.

Bob Muller, my beta reader, called me on things I got wrong that I thought I had right and made me smile in the process.

Ally Robertson, Lori Graham, and Rhonda Penders at The Wild Rose Press took a chance on me and, with a massive dose of patience, made a dream continue to come true.

Thank you all for making this book possible.

Prologue

Sunday – April 19, 2015

The dead guy on the sofa, the hint of burned gunpowder in the air, and her weapon in her hand added up to bad. Nausea roiled her stomach. *What had she done?*

Mary Conner honest to God did not know.

"Stop," she said to herself, "Think. Assess." It had been her mantra throughout her career.

She looked at the dead man. Bobby Ed Lukens. He'd sold her son, Sam, the coke that had killed him.

The last thing she could remember was seeing Lukens strut across the lobby. Everything between then and now was gone. No, not all of it. Bits and pieces surfaced.

A shouted accusation. "You killed my son."

Calm denial. "I had nothing to do with that. I don't even know your kid."

"You sold him the dope that killed him."

Heated denial. "Don't lay that on me. Ain't my problem he OD'd." Then a threat. "Get out of here 'fore you get hurt."

Drawing her weapon from her purse.

Two splotches of blood on Lukens's shirt. Had she shot him? She raised her weapon and sniffed. She'd fired it. She checked the sofa, his hands, and the floor around

1

him. No gun in sight. She'd killed an unarmed man.

Panic flooded her. *Had anyone heard the shots? Had they called 9-1-1? Were cops racing toward her?* Her body quivered so violently, she had to drop into a chair before she collapsed, and her heart thundered in her chest. She took in a deep breath and let it out slow. It didn't help. Her panic swelled.

She'd screwed up big. It could mean the end of her career. With Sam dead, all she had was her career. She couldn't lose that.

Her stomach knotted tighter with bitter realization. Saving her career was nothing. She'd killed a man in cold blood, and she'd go down for it. Her future flashed in front of her eyes. Trial. Conviction. Life without parole. It would be a short life. Cops didn't last long in prison.

She doubled over in the chair, her body tortured by fear and horror, tears welling in her eyes. She couldn't go to prison. She had to get out of this. Only one person could help her. A fixer. She scrabbled in her purse for her cell phone. Like a living thing she couldn't hold on to, it squirmed from her hand twice before she lifted it out.

Her hands trembled so harshly, she misdialed the number and had to start over. She misdialed again. Her panic swelled higher. Tears flooded her eyes, blurring her vision. Clenching the phone in a two-hand, white-knuckle grip and pressing her forearms hard against her thighs, she was finally able to tap in the number right.

She listened to the ring and begged, "Pick up. Pick up. Please pick up."

****

Fear held Mary in an iron grip as she waited for

Sergeant Mike McHale. He was taking forever. What if someone heard the shots, and other officers got there before he did? She checked the hall it seemed like a hundred times in the ten minutes since she'd talked to him. Finally, the elevator thunked to a stop and she had the apartment door open before he had a chance to knock.

"What's up?"

She waved him inside. He scanned the room then crossed to the dead man on the white leather couch and studied him for a second. "You know who this is?"

"Bobby Ed Lukens. He sold Sam the coke that killed him."

"He's also one of Joey Day's lieutenants. And his half-brother. Jesus, Conner, what the hell were you doing? Stalking him?"

"Checking on that woman who was beaten up last month in the parking garage on Ninth. She lives here."

"How did that get you in here?"

"I saw him in the lobby and the next…the next thing I knew—" She pointed to the body.

McHale pulled Bobby Ed's body forward by the shoulder. It flopped back against the cushions when he let go. "Let me see your weapon."

She dug her Glock out of her purse with a trembling hand and popped the magazine. It slipped from her fingers and thudded on the carpet. Clearing the round from the chamber, she handed the pistol over. She could sense McHale ogling the curve of her butt and the length of her thigh as she squatted to pick up the round and the magazine.

McHale lifted the Glock to his nose and sniffed the muzzle. He tipped his head toward Lukens. "You capped

3

him?"

"I must have."

He handed her pistol back. She thumbed the round into the magazine, snapped the magazine home, and ran the slide to chamber a round.

"What happened after you saw him in the lobby?"

She dropped the weapon in her purse. "I told you! The next thing I knew, I was here, and he," she pointed to Bobby Ed, "he was there. Just like that."

"What else? There must be something. I can't help you if you won't help me."

"I don't know. I can't remember."

"Think!"

"I'm trying, dammit!" she wailed. A long silence. She shook her head. "I can't remember. Everything after he passed me in the lobby is...gone."

She'd stepped in it deep with both feet. The force had zero tolerance for cops whacking unarmed civilians in cold blood, even if they were drug dealers. And in spite of the fact she hadn't been stalking Bobby Ed, had just happened on him in the lobby, it would look like she'd followed him here and blown him away.

"Can you help me? Can you fix it?" Cleaning up after she'd stepped in it on leave would be a bear.

McHale rubbed his square jaw. "Maybe."

Mary fidgeted with the claddagh ring on her left hand. "With Sam gone, all I have is my career. I...I can't lose that."

"You got a bigger problem."

"I know." Tears welled in her eyes. "I can't go to prison. You know what happens to cops in prison."

"You got an even bigger problem than that. If you'd smoked Bobby Ed during a bust, Joey would have written it off as a cost of doing business. This way, he's gonna take it personal. He's gonna know by tomorrow you did it, and he's gonna send somebody after you."

"Oh, God, no! Please, McHale, you…you've got to fix this."

He scanned the room for a few moments then nodded. "No problem."

Fear loosened its death grip on her heart. She relaxed like she'd just downed a double shot of Chivas Regal, letting out a long sigh of relief. "Oh, God, thank you. I owe you. How can I pay you back?"

"Don't worry about it. We'll work something out."

A shudder raced along her spine, and bile rose in her throat. Other female officers had told her McHale's 'something' for helping them out of a jam was doing the mattress mambo. She forced the bile down. If saving her career meant bumping uglies with him, she would. Once.

"I gotta get some stuff outta my car."

"Hurry! Please. Before somebody calls 9-1-1."

"Relax. I got you covered."

Mary sighed with relief when he returned to the apartment. It had only been a couple minutes but it felt like he'd been gone hours. She pointed to the gym bag he carried. "What's in there?"

"Everything I need to save your hide." He squatted by Bobby Ed's body, pulled rubber gloves out of the bag, and worked his broad hands into them. "Here's your story." He showed her a small automatic he took from the bag. "The scumbag pulled this on you. You fired back in self-defense."

He closed his hand around the pistol's grip. "If you hadn't, he'd have shot you. Like this." He pulled the trigger twice.

Mary cried out in shock and pain as the rounds ripped into her gut. She staggered back, tried to sit on a chair, caught just the edge of the cushion, and slid to the floor. Blood soaked her blouse and slacks, stained the white carpet. McHale stood over her, aimed the pistol at her, and she knew she was going to die. Then he lowered it.

She could feel herself slipping away, a dark gray fog slowly descending over her. Mustering her waning strength, she gasped, "Why?"

He shrugged. "Orders."

****

McHale picked up the gym bag and ambled out. Maybe he should have popped Virgin Mary a third time. Nah, bleeding like she was, she'd be gone in another minute. Too bad he'd never get a ride in her saddle. Oh, well. *Can't win them all.* In the elevator, he pulled a burner phone from his pocket and dialed a number. "It's done, Mr. Day."

He drew his pay from the city. But he worked for Joey Day.

Chapter 1

Monday – April 20, 2015

Detective Rick Lafferty walked out of the morning briefing, his stomach churning. Mary Conner had gone down last night. Captain Marco 'Dee' DeAngelis, his boss in the Philadelphia PD, had choked up announcing it, and Lafferty felt like he'd taken a full jolt from a stun gun.

The aroma of coffee and the smell of pastries from the box next to the brewer churned his stomach even more. Around him, phones rang and were answered, babbled conversations formed a haze of white noise, and people flowed by.

Lafferty heard and saw it all, but was not part of it. None of it was real, none of it mattered. Mary was dead. That was real, that was all that mattered. He shook his head to clear it. Time to get to work. He grabbed a manila folder from the stack on his desk and flipped it open.

Dee had partnered him with Mary when she transferred into the Zero-Seven. Had it really been three years ago? Their first case, he saw she didn't get her gold shield just because she looked good in a skirt. She was a good cop, a good detective. He'd liked her thoroughness, her skill, and her style. From there it was a short step to liking her. They'd become friends, then more than friends. Not lovers exactly, just the occasional no-strings-attached bedmates when the mood or the need struck. They'd had plenty of good times together, both in and out of bed.

Last Saturday had been one of the best. Mary had seemed like herself again, not a sad façade of the vibrant woman she'd been before Sam died. For the first time since that grim day a year ago, she'd been able to talk about him without falling apart. Her lovemaking that night had been different, too. Not a narcotic consumed in haste to blunt the agony of her loss for a few moments, but a slow and gentle sharing of pleasure.

Lafferty didn't like the pain those memories created. To force them away, he focused on the report in the open folder. One sentence into the report, his mind started a litany. *Mary was a good cop. Mary was a good cop.* Too good to be dropped by some dirtbag street dealer in his own pad. She never would have let that happen.

Lafferty shoved away from his desk and crossed to the captain's office. DeAngelis glanced up at his knock and waved him in.

He closed the door behind him. "What can you tell me about Mary getting it?"

"Not much more than I said in the briefing."

"Who caught the squeal?"

"Harter and Pryzlo from the One-Two. They notified IA when they saw it was an 'officer down' situation."

He knew Harter and Pryzlo by reputation. They'd work a case into the ground to solve it. The IA troglodytes were another story. "Who called it in?"

"I don't know. I haven't seen the reports yet. Where are you going with this?"

"She was my partner. I knew her. She was too good

a cop to go down like that."

"You've been on the job long enough to know it only takes a second. Let your guard down, lose focus for an instant, and…" DeAngelis's shrug said *you're gone.*

Lafferty's mind filled with the image of Mary dead. He shook his head to chase it away. "I don't buy that. Not Mary. She wouldn't let her guard down—ever—on the street or off duty."

"Take it easy, Rick. This is hard on all of us. It's hit you harder because you and Mary were…close." His tone said he knew just how close.

Rick wasn't surprised. There wasn't much DeAngelis didn't know about his squad. "One thing has nothing to do with the other."

"Doesn't it? She made a mistake going there alone, Rick, and it cost her. You've got to accept that."

"No. Something is wrong—big time wrong—with her shooting. I feel it. I *know* it." He drew himself to attention. "Captain, I'd like to be assigned to work her case." One good clue, just one was all he'd need to hunt down Mary's killer. "She deserves better than some IA ratfink who doesn't give a damn about her, just wants to clear the paper on her case."

"You know I can't do that. IA handles all 'officer down' cases. Even if they didn't, I couldn't let you work it because of your relationship with her."

"Can you keep me posted on what IA gets on her shooting? Let me read their reports? I have to know what happened, how it went down."

"I'll think about it, but right now, I don't think that's a good idea." DeAngelis leaned back in his chair. "Look, Rick, you've got lots of personal time on the books. Maybe you should burn some." His tone made the suggestion an order.

Frustration and anger rose in Lafferty. But an order was an order. "Yeah, okay, Captain. If you say so."

"I do. Go home and grieve for Mary. Take some comfort from the fact that she took a bad guy down with her."

Rick turned toward the door, his shoulders sagging with defeat.

****

DeAngelis knew what it was like to lose a partner. It had to be tougher for Lafferty, losing someone who was more than a partner. To be a cop in that situation and not be able to do anything but mourn had to be worse yet.

Rick stopped at the door with his hand on the knob. His shoulders squared and he straightened, as if he'd reenergized. Not a good sign. "Rick."

Lafferty turned. "Yeah."

"Don't go getting any ideas. Stay out of it."

"But, Captain, I—"

"Do I need to make that an order?"

Rick's shoulders drooped, and he shook his head. "No."

"Good. Come see me in a day or two." DeAngelis cocked one eyebrow in Rick's direction. "Meanwhile, I'll see what I can find out. Okay?"

Lafferty stared at him for a long moment then nodded. "Okay." He walked out.

DeAngelis picked up the phone and dialed. "Captain Boyer, please."

"Boyer."

"John, it's Marco. How are you?"

They exchanged family news for a few seconds before DeAngelis said, "We need a face-to-face."

"What about?"

"Conner."

****

Mike McHale was in a vile mood. He'd snapped at Joleen, the waitress at Nate's on Taylor, when he'd ordered breakfast and every time she was slow refilling his coffee mug. He hadn't slept well. Visions of Virgin Mary sprawled on the floor in Bobby Ed's place, her clothes bloodied, the pain in her eyes after he'd shot her, had invaded his dreams.

Conner wasn't his first kill for Joey Day. She wasn't the first woman he'd smoked either. That had been a Rushton U. grad student Joey suspected of holding back a gram of the coke she'd muled in from Bogota for him. Suspected, but no proof. Joey told McHale to snuff her anyway as a warning to other mules. He'd cornered her in the basement of her apartment house, shoved a condom packed with lye and cocaine into her vagina and burst it. She'd writhed in pain as the lye burned the tender tissues and the coke set her nerves screaming. It took her an hour to die.

He'd done other hits for Joey. They hadn't bothered him at all. So this one shouldn't, but it did. He ran over whacking Conner for the hundredth time since he left Bobby Ed's apartment. He hadn't slipped up in any way, hadn't left anything there that could point to him or Joey Day. So, why did taking out Virgin bother him so much?

Maybe because she was a cop? He'd never taken out a fellow officer before. Maybe it was the haste. Joey had ordered her taken out on the spot. McHale liked a little time to plan first. Maybe it was that he'd wanted to get into Conner's panties since he met her. He'd tried to get there the regular way more than once, but she'd let him

11

know he didn't have a chance every time. Damn bitch.

Last night would have been different. She'd have owed him, would have been so grateful for him saving her ass that she'd have offered up her sweet bod on a silver platter. But Joey had screwed it by wanting her iced on the spot. And what Joey wanted, Joey got.

That had to be it. He was steamed because Joey had taken away his chance to get between her thighs. He could have doped her up—she was so rattled last night she'd have gone along with anything he said—and stashed her in one of his apartments, kept her buzzed just enough to be compliant, and done her until he was bored with her then snuffed her with a big OD and dumped her body where it'd never be found. Joey might be a little pissed he hadn't put her down right away, but he'd probably have let it pass.

Maybe he should have handed her over to Joey. Let him deal with her. Let him and his *muchachos* pass her around for a couple days. By the time they were done banging her every way possible, she'd be so wrecked he wouldn't want to even touch her. Then he could have put her down without a second thought.

McHale was a cautious man when it came to covering his own butt. He ran over everything he did last night one more time. Nope, no slip-ups. His bad mood eased a little bit. But he still needed something more to clear it away completely.

Time to earn his cop pay. He hated day tour. Too much brass on the street looking over his shoulder. He slugged back the rest of his coffee, pulled a ten from his pocket, and waved it at Joleen. "Hey, sweetheart. Here you go."

When she touched his bill, he jerked it back. "What

time you get off work?"

She tucked a wisp of dark hair behind her ear and mumbled, "Six-thirty."

"I'll stop by your place around seven."

"I can't. Not tonight, please. I…I have plans."

"Lady Coca says change them." Another fall for possession of cocaine would put Joleen Wilson behind bars until she was so old and shriveled even the dykes wouldn't touch her. McHale still had the blow he'd taken off her the third time he'd busted her safely stowed away in his private evidence locker just for situations like this.

She looked at the floor and nodded.

"That's better." He released the bill and strode out of Nate's feeling much better. She'd do what he wanted and like it.

****

"Next time, signal before you change lanes." McHale snapped the ticket out of his citation book and thrust it through the window of the Chrysler.

The driver snatched the ticket and muttered something under his breath.

McHale leaned down and fixed him with a glower. "What did you say, sir?"

"Nothing, Officer. May I go now?"

"Yeah. Take off."

The driver eased into traffic then threw McHale the bird as he drove away. McHale thought for a second about chasing the jerk down and laying more paper on him. Nope. He'd better back off. Word might get back to command he was dumping a load of petty tickets on every clown he pulled over that morning.

Like his first traffic stop. He'd nailed a BMW for running a red. The driver, a Rushton U. snot, had thrown him attitude from the get-go. Took the good mood he'd had when he left Nate's right out of him. He'd buried the punk in a blizzard of tickets.

He eased up but didn't ease off the rest of the morning. A Caddy-wheeling CEO doing thirty-two in a twenty-five zone, a lawyer in a Lincoln not signaling before turning into a parking garage, a Buick-driving minister without his seatbelt buckled, a teen blaring music from his tricked-out Honda. He'd nailed them all, and more. And he always looked hard enough to find at least one more thing to ticket them for.

It wasn't all the BMW kid's fault. Not getting a chance to screw Virgin Mary before icing her still had him steaming. He should have banged her before putting her lights out. Maybe he would have snuffed her while he was banging her. The concept had an arousing appeal. He'd have to try it with the next broad Joey wanted whacked. He hoped she'd be a ripe young college cutie, not some strung-out crack whore.

McHale stopped his cruiser at the corner of Thirtieth and Wilson and snagged a burner cell from his Go Bag. He checked his watch. Twelve-oh-five. Right on time. He thumbed the speed dial button. The phone rang four times before a voice said, *"Buenas tardes."*

"Buenos dias, Mr. Day."

"Mi amigo. The morning paper tells me a police officer was killed last night." Joey Day was laying the Hispanic accent on thick today.

Joey didn't want a comment, so McHale gave him none. Joey was just letting him know he'd checked to see that McHale had done his bidding.

"We are white on this?"

"Si, Jefe." McHale burned a quarter of his Spanish

vocabulary on the answer. Joey liked it when minions like McHale spoke his language.

"Then I am pleased. Very pleased."

"*Gracias, Jefe.*" Half his Spanish shot.

"*De nada.*"

McHale dropped the burner through a sewer grate then drove to Third Avenue and parked in the alley behind Gino's, a bar and grill. Gino nodded at him as he grabbed a stool. He poured a shot of cheap whiskey and set it in front of a rummy anchoring the middle of the bar then poured a double shot of Jameson's for McHale.

McHale slammed back the booze, felt its fire spread through him. Gino asked, "Your usual, Officer?"

"Yeah." He glanced around the bar. "And make it to go."

Gino poured him another double then scurried into the kitchen. McHale sipped this round slowly, savoring its smooth taste. Gino delivered his food fifteen minutes later, popped the cap off a Miller Genuine Draft, and set the bottle next to the food.

McHale gathered up his meal and headed toward the back door. He sensed Gino's eyes boring into his back as he stopped by his wife mopping off a table. "Come out in twenty minutes for my trash."

She stiffened and said in a low whisper, "Please, no, Officer."

"Everything has a price, Rosalie." McHale glanced at a slick-looking guy nursing a beer in a booth, "Gino wants to keep letting drug deals go down," he shifted his gaze to two scantily clad and overly made-up young women in a booth, "and not get busted for pimping, you gotta pay. You got me?"

She stared at him with fear in her eyes. "You said it

would only be a few times I would have to—"

"I could come in here every day to collect. You want that?"

"No." She swallowed hard. "All right, Officer."

"It's Sergeant, not Officer." He pinned a hard glare on the woman. "Don't you ever forget that."

McHale slumped in his cruiser and took a long draw on the Miller before starting on the Italian sausage sub and fries. A dog, his ribs raising lines under his tan coat, trotted into the alley and straight for the trash bags by the dumpster. He nosed them then clawed a hole in one and dug for food. McHale whistled softly to get the mutt's attention then tossed the last bite of sub toward him. The dog approached the scrap and sniffed it warily before gobbling it down then went back to the torn bag. He bolted from the alley when Rosalie stepped through the door.

She plodded to McHale's cruiser slowly, her shame at having to service him showing in her lowered head and slumped shoulders. She slid into the cruiser's front seat. Tears wet her long black lashes. "Please, off—sergeant," she pleaded, "please don't make me do this."

Sometimes the cruelest punishment was the one imagined by the victim, not the one they received. "Do what? I just wanted you to take my trash in." McHale handed Rosalie the basket, empty Miller bottle, and a ten-dollar bill. "Here you go."

She stared at him, stunned, then straightened and smiled. "Thank you, sergeant." She got out of the cruiser and started toward the door.

"Hey, Rosalie."

She looked back.

"Maybe next time."

Her shoulders slumped and her head dropped.

McHale chuckled and drove away.

****

Rick paced his apartment, a fresh mug of coffee in one hand, a lit cigarette between the first two fingers of the other. He hadn't smoked in ten years, and he hadn't given in yet, but each passing second made the chance stronger. He sipped from the mug. He'd already drained the pot once, and caffeine jittered his nerves.

It was better than beer. If he'd started on that, he wouldn't have stopped until he was blotto. He didn't want that. He wanted to be sharp, but that let him think about Mary. He didn't want that either. It hurt too much.

The cigarette had burned down to where heat from the tip warmed his fingers. He doused the butt under the kitchen faucet and dropped it in the trash. He poured the coffee down the drain and rinsed his mug then dried it and set it by the NYPD mug Mary had appropriated for herself a year ago. He hadn't used it since then. It was hers now, would always be hers.

Too many things in the apartment reminded him of her. Maybe he should get rid of them. No. He'd have to get rid of everything he owned. Every damn thing in the apartment—hell, the apartment itself—reminded him of her.

Maybe he should go for a walk. No good. He and Mary had spent hours strolling his eclectic neighborhood, poking their heads into the funky shops and sampling the foods at the UN of restaurants lining the streets.

He flopped in his recliner and rubbed his eyes. He needed to clear his mind of memories and focus on Mary's murder. His mind filled with questions. Who killed her? Why? What was she doing at Bobby Ed Lukens' condo? Had he lured her there? Did it have something to do with Sam's death?

The night Sam died, Mary called him right after calling 9-1-1. He'd raced to her home and stood by her during hours of questions. The detectives who caught Sam's death had done their best to be gentle. Mary had held up throughout the ordeal but when everyone had gone, she'd crashed and burned. He'd held her and rocked her until her tears finally ran out as the sun rose.

Had she traced the coke that killed Sam back to Lukens? Had she gone to his place to get revenge? The coke that killed Sam had Joey Day's mark on the vial. So, why didn't she go after Joey?

Rick stopped that train of thought before it ran away with him. Mary would never take the law into her own hands. If she traced the coke back to Lukens and through him to Joey Day, she'd have handed the trail off to Narcotics Field Unit. They'd have jumped on the info like a hungry man on a free buffet. There wasn't a cop in the city who wouldn't give his pension to nail Joey Day.

A chill sliced through Rick. What if Sam's death had run Mary off the rails? What if she *had* gone gunning for Lukens? He couldn't see that. He could buy her going to his place for a lead on Joey Day, maybe tried a little 9-millimeter persuasion. Was that where it went hinky? Had he distracted her enough to get the drop on her and cap her?

Tears rose in his eyes. He hadn't cried since he was ten. They spilled over, running down his cheeks.

He cried for a long time.

Chapter 2

Just before two p.m., Captain Marco DeAngelis bought a coffee from a street vendor and strolled slowly down Market. He stepped under the arch that marked the entrance to Griffin Park and strolled at an easy pace toward the duck pond. A lean man in a gray suit sat on a bench facing the pond, reading the paper. DeAngelis sat next to him. "John."

"Marco." Boyer folded the paper and laid it on the briefcase at his side. "What's up?"

"How tight is the lid on the Conner shooting?"

Boyer sipped from his own go-cup. "Sealed, locked, and bolted."

"I need you to lift it."

Boyer studied him for a second. "Why?"

"I got a hurting man in my squad."

"Who?"

"Lafferty. He and Conner were closer than most partners, if you catch my drift. I want to give him something to hang onto. Without it, I'm afraid he'll go renegade."

Boyer shook his head. "No can do. He could be our dirty cop."

"I'd stake my shield he isn't. I pulled his jacket and talked to every commander he ever served under this morning. Not so much as a hint of suspicion of anything bad on him."

"That doesn't mean—"

"He's been in my squad since he got his gold shield. I've worked cases with him. He's had a hundred chances to walk money and jewelry out of a crime scene with no one the wiser, and he never did. Hell, John, he won't even take a free cup of coffee from a diner. He's as clean as fresh snow."

Boyer stared straight ahead. DeAngelis knew him, knew he wasn't looking at anything. Instead, he was reviewing everything he knew about Rick Lafferty. Finally, he glanced at Marco. "How high you hoping to lift the lid?"

"All the way."

"I can't go that far, Marco. I'll share what I can."

"Make it something positive so he's not eating holes in himself over her."

Boyer considered his request. "I can do that." He handed DeAngelis a folder from his briefcase. "With a bit more for you."

****

McHale's good mood didn't last long. Shortly after he'd gone back on patrol, a radio call sent him to Fifth and Tyler to direct traffic because a semi cut the corner too close and wiped out the stoplight pole. He hated traffic duty. That was a job for rookie patrolmen, not sergeants. Plus, drivers in this city were morons. They didn't understand clear hand signals. By the time another officer relieved him, McHale was ready to commit ticket mayhem on the next brain-dead ass who couldn't tell the difference between 'stop' and 'come on.'

He grabbed a coffee at McDonald's and sat in his cruiser sipping it. The officer relieving him also passed the word Harter and Pryzlo had caught Virgin's murder.

That wasn't good. There were better detectives in the department than those two, but not many.

Pryzlo was one of those cops with a special feel—almost a sixth sense—for the job from the day he left the academy eight years ago. No learning curve for him. He seemed to have it all down right from the start, as if he'd been a cop since his mama popped him out. One of the youngest detectives ever, he attacked the job with the energy of a puppy at play. Harter didn't have that intuition or zeal, but he was like a dog, too, a terrier chasing a mole—digging, digging, digging until he caught it. If McHale had made any slip-ups chilling Virgin, they'd find it.

He ran through the hit again. Nope, he hadn't done anything that could lead them to him. He'd covered all his bases. So why was the damn thing still gnawing at him like a squirrel with an acorn? Because if any two suits could pin Virgin's murder on him, it would be Harter and Pryzlo. There was always that slim chance someone would sell him out, too. Then he'd be arrested and tried for her murder. And that would drop him in deep, deep shit.

A chill rippled through him. Being tried for killing Virgin didn't bother him. Joey Day's legal eagles would see he beat the rap no sweat. It was the time in jail between the arrest and the trial that scared him. In this city, ugly things happened to people in custody for killing a cop. It would be a hundred times uglier for a cop who killed a cop.

He needed a way to point Harter and Pryzlo in the wrong direction.

****

Rick Lafferty washed down the last bite of pizza

with the last swallow of Coke. The day had dragged on forever, and he still had a long evening of thinking about Mary ahead. He gathered up the box and empty can and took them to the kitchen. He was crushing the pizza box to stuff in the garbage can when the phone rang. "Lafferty."

"Rick, Marco. I'll pick you up outside your apartment in a half hour."

At the District house, he was Captain DeAngelis. Everywhere else, he was Marco or Dee. "Why? What's going on?"

"Just be waiting outside."

That was good enough for Rick. Dee was righteous in his eyes, an opinion shared by everyone in the squad. When you needed him, he was never more than a phone call away. He worked his share of holidays so cops with little kids could spend the day with them, and he caught cases just like every detective. Working with him never left you feeling like you were being tested or he was watching over your shoulder. In the field, he was your partner, nothing more.

Rick was waiting at the curb when DeAngelis pulled up in his Ford Escape and motioned him to get in. As Dee edged the SUV back into traffic, Rick asked, "What's the scoop on Mary's funeral? You know anything?"

"I'll fill you in in a bit." He made a left at the corner. "You had dinner yet? You want to grab a bite somewhere?"

"Nah, I'd just finished a pizza when you called."

"Okay. Tell me about Mary."

"Geez, Dee, you worked with her, you knew her. She was a good cop. She—"

"I know the kind of cop she was, Rick. I want to know about the person."

"She was a good person, too. Smart and funny, and she never seemed to let things get her down. Until Sam." Rick paused for a second then started talking again. "She liked to do the crossword puzzle in the Sunday paper and watching Disney movies. She went on the job to help people and because it meant a regular paycheck, but sometimes things she saw got to her, and she'd weep over the things people did to each other."

Dee shot Rick a raised eyebrow look. "She did? I didn't know that."

"She never let you see it, Dee. She didn't want you to think she was weak. She was afraid, too, afraid the grime we saw would erode her...humanity, would turn her cynical and bitter like so many other cops, and she wasn't going to let that happen. She wore something lacy or frilly under her clothes every day to remind her she was a person first and a cop second. She liked Looney Tunes cartoons. She'd laugh so hard at them, even ones she'd seen a hundred times, she'd get hiccups. She liked hard-boiled eggs on toast for breakfast and milk with her pizza. She'd rather play Scrabble or Trivial Pursuit than see the latest movie. She—" He fell silent as memories of Mary filled his mind too fast to sort out. He shook his head. "It hurts, you know?"

"Yeah. Sounds like you were maybe in love with her."

He shook his head again. "It wasn't like that. It was—" He fell silent again. After a few moments, he said, "Maybe I was."

Dee drove a few more blocks. "I pulled your jacket after you left this morning, talked to every commander you ever had. They all had the same read on you I have—honest, thorough, smart, and good at your job, a straight shooter." He paused as he maneuvered around a double-parked cab. "But they also said you bend some rules sometimes."

"I—"

"I said 'bend' not 'break.' There's a difference. Sometimes, you have to bend the rules. And you have to know when you can't and when you can and how far."

"Where you going with this, Dee?"

"I know when to bend them, too. I'm bending them now. I'm going to tell you some things only five other people know. If I hear them from anyone other than those people, I'll know they got them from you, and I won't bend you, I will personally break you. I want you to understand that up front."

"I got you." Even without the warning, Rick would carry whatever Dee was going to tell him to his grave. "So what's up?"

Dee studied Rick out of the corner of his eye as they waited through a red light. It changed to green and he accelerated across the intersection. "Mary's alive."

"What?" Rick's heart hammered inside his chest.

"She's not dead, Rick. A cruiser was a block away when the call came in. When the unis entered Lukens's apartment, she was still ticking. They got her help ASAP."

"Why'd you tell us in briefing she was gone?"

"She'd taken two in the gut that ripped her up bad. She was in surgery all night, and it was touch-and-go for a while after. After you punched out, we got word she'd made it through."

"Where is she, Dee? I...I've got to go see her." At

that moment, nothing else in the world was more important.

"She's in a coma, never came to after surgery, so she's hooked up to every machine under the sun to keep her going. And we still could lose her. If that happens, do you want your last sight of her to be with her hooked up to all that stuff?"

"I don't care. Where is she?" He'd lied to himself and to Dee earlier. No maybe. He had loved her. That required a re-think now. He did love her, present tense.

"She's somewhere out of the city. That's all I can tell you right now."

"What the hell, Dee? Why can't you—"

Dee sighed heavily. "To keep her safe. We've got a bad apple in our bunch."

"In the D squad?"

"Somewhere in our house. IA thinks Mary was hit because she tumbled onto something that gave the game away. They think whoever did it will come after her again if they know she's alive, maybe finish the job this time. So, officially she's dead."

"How you going to cover that she's not? People will be expecting a funeral in the next few days. If they don't get one, they're going to start asking questions."

"We can hold it up maybe a week, ten days saying the autopsy's incomplete, delayed pending test results, something. After that, if we need to, we'll go to something else."

"This place you've got her, you're sure it's safe?"

DeAngelis nodded. "We've got people with her 24/7. Boyer from IA—"

"IA. Jeez, Dee, you got—"

Dee raised a hand in a 'hold up' gesture. "Boyer and

I go back a long way, Rick. And IA or not, he's a good cop."

That was all Rick needed to hear. If Dee vouched for Boyer, Rick would second it.

"Boyer called in a favor with the State Police. The Staties guarding Mary are from the governor's protection detail and were trained by the Secret Service, the guys who guard the President. Nobody's going to get to her. And Boyer and I—and you—want the same thing: to nail whoever put Mary down. He put his two best cops on her case."

"We got any leads?"

"We know she got it in a condo owned by Bobby Ed Lukens, a shirttail brother of Joey Day and part of his organization. A couple things there don't add up. Like the gun used on her was a crappy .32 auto."

"Doesn't add up how?"

"Cap pistols aren't Bobby Ed's style. Crime Scene Techs found a .45 under a cushion in the sofa he was on and four more stashed throughout his apartment, no peashooters. Plus his prints were only on the .32's grip and trigger, nowhere else. Either he never touched it without gloves on before last night, or it dropped out of the sky into his hand."

Rick stared at him. "A plant?"

"Looks that way. You have any idea what she was doing at Lukens's place?"

"No."

Dee let out a sighing breath. "IA thinks maybe it had something to do with Sam. Like she went there to have it out with him. Could it have been that?"

Rick thought a moment. "Could be, but I don't see it. If she found out anything tying Lukens to Sam, she'd go by the book."

They were back on Rick's street. Dee braked his SUV to a halt in front of his apartment house. "Joey finds out Mary took down Bobby Ed, he'll go after her."

"I know."

"That's the other reason why what I'm telling you has to stay here." He tapped Rick's head. "For her sake."

"Count on it. I won't put her in more danger."

"Good. Anything I hear about how she's doing, I'll pass on to you ASAP. And soon as I know it's safe, I'll let you know where she is so you can go see her."

"Dee, I appreciate this. All of it. More than you'll ever know. I owe you, big. If there's anything I can do…"

"Just sit tight for now." Dee clapped a hand on Rick's shoulder. "And remember what I said about bending rules and breaking them."

****

Joleen had just kicked off her sneakers when a knock rattled her apartment door. She answered it to find McHale standing in the hall. She glanced at the living room clock. Six-forty. "You said seven."

"Guess I'm early. Too bad."

"I need a little time to get ready." Time to down enough vodka to numb her for the next fifteen minutes. She tried to shut the door in his face.

He slapped it open, knocking her down. "I'm ready now."

Joleen scrambled to her feet, staggering off balance. McHale grabbed her arm and shoved her toward her kitchen. She stumbled and almost fell again but managed to keep her feet under her. He followed her into the kitchen. She faced him. "Please, McHale, not tonight."

"Shut up." He backhanded her, snapping her head left. She cried out. He spun her around and slammed her face down onto the cheap table. Fear coursed through her. She'd never seen McHale like this. He always treated her like shit, but he'd never hit her.

Pressing down on her back so hard she feared her breasts would rupture, he flipped the skirt of her uniform over her back. A tug and a rip as he tore her panties off. She steeled herself for what was coming next.

Two minutes later, an eternity to her soul, it was over.

"Thanks for the good time, Joleen." He walked away, leaving her bent over the table. She straightened and faced him. At her front door, he looked back at her and smirked. "We'll do it again real soon."

She sagged against the table. The room shimmied and swayed around her. Her cheek burned where McHale had smacked her. She bolted for the sink and vomited until there was nothing left to come up. Too spent to move, she watched pink traces of blood tinted water swirling toward the drain and whispered, "You are dead, McHale, dead."

She didn't care if she spent the rest of her life in prison. It would be better than life as McHale's sex slave.

****

Rick Lafferty got a beer from the fridge, drained half the bottle in one long swallow, and the rest in a second. The phone rang. He thought about letting the answering machine get it then changed his mind. He grabbed another beer, strode into the living room, and picked up.

"Hey, little brother." Ann. "How are ya?"

He flopped onto the couch and took a swallow of beer. "Okay. How are things up there in the sticks?"

"Quiet. What's new in the big city?"

Another drink before he answered. "Nothing much."

A couple moments of silence before Ann said, "What's wrong?" Her tone of voice said she knew something wasn't right with him.

He wasn't sure he could talk about Mary without breaking down. "Nothing."

"Something is," she said. "Come on. Tell me."

Two answers, three words had given him away. He and Ann shared a bond beyond the normal brother-sister thing siblings have. Separated by less than two years, they'd always been able to sense each other's moods, read each other like a book. They could often con Mom and Dad but never each other. The passing years hadn't changed that.

"Mary—" He paused, took in a big breath and let it out slowly. "Mary got shot last night. Bad. She almost died."

He didn't need to tell Ann who Mary was. After last year's Thanksgiving dinner at their grandparents' house, while the rest of the family watched football, argued politics, swapped recipes, or slipped into a food-induced coma, they had strolled the block. It was their time to catch up with each other, a tradition they'd started Ann's first year in college. Ann had filled him in on the latest feats of his niece and nephew then asked how his love life was. He'd told her he'd been sort of seeing a fellow cop named Mary. She'd kidded him with that old ditty, "Rick and Mary sitting in a tree, k-i-s-s-i-n-g." He'd said it wasn't like that at all, wasn't going anywhere beyond a casual thing. Only it had.

"Oh, Rick! I'm so sorry. What happened?"

"We think—we don't know for sure—she got into

some kind of face-off with the dealer who may have sold her son the drugs that killed him, and it went haywire."

"Oh, my God, Rick. She's going to be all right, isn't she?"

"They say she will be, but—"

"Well, how does she look? Is her color good? Is she breathing okay?" Ann, a nurse, rapid-fired the questions.

He paced the length of his living room. "I don't know. I haven't seen her."

"What? You haven't? Why not?"

"They won't let me. Not yet. The docs say she's in a coma." He paced back.

"When did 'They won't let me' ever stop you? March into that hospital, into her room, and find out."

"I can't. I don't know where she is, except it's some hospital far away from here." He polished off the beer.

Ann caught the shift. "Why?"

"To keep her safe." He strolled into the kitchen for a fresh beer. "The news media here are all reporting her dead for the same reason. We think a dirty cop working for a major drug dealer shot her on the dealer's orders. If he learned she was alive in a hospital here, he'd send someone after her to finish the job." The bottle clinked against another one as he pulled it out.

"Rick, are you drinking?"

"Just a couple beers." And six or eight more after these two.

"Why?"

He settled on the living room sofa before he answered. "Because I want them."

"Because?" Ann drew the word out impossibly long.

He took a couple swallows from his bottle. "I feel like it."

"Because of Mary?"

"Yeah, because of Mary."

"And how is getting smashed going to help?"

He drank some beer. "I'll be so blotto I can sleep like I'm dead all night long and not dream bad dreams about her."

"About a woman you say you have just a casual thing with?"

He hadn't fooled her back in November and wasn't fooling her now. In spite of his insistence there was nothing special between the two of them, Ann had sensed Mary meant more to him than he realized. She'd read him like a book even when he couldn't see the words himself. Denying it now would be foolish. "Things have changed a bit since Thanksgiving."

"Or did you just wake up to what was there even back then?"

He raised the bottle, stopped with it almost to his lips, and lowered it. "I guess I woke up. It took Mary getting shot to wake me. I wish—" He stopped. His mind churned with so many thoughts, he couldn't catch one to say it. He set the bottle on the table by his recliner. "I wish I'd told her how I feel about her."

"Tell her when you see her. Tell her before you say anything else, before you even say 'Hi' to her."

"Yeah. I will." He fell silent for a moment. "If I get the chance. Her docs say she still could die." He felt like his heart was being crushed in a vice.

"Don't think like that. Keep telling yourself she'll make it, and you'll get the chance to tell her." Many silent seconds passed before Ann said, "Rick?"

"I'm afraid I'm going to lose her."

****

Rick and Ann talked for another hour. After she hung up, he sat for a long time staring at the floor. Dee had told him there was a dirty cop in their District house then told him not to do anything about it. He couldn't sit by and do nothing. Not while Mary lay somewhere between dead and alive in a hospital far away, maybe put there by that dirty cop. He got a fresh beer from the fridge and, sipping it, started running the name of every cop in their district house through his mind. He shifted to his desk before he'd gone very far down the list, got a fresh notebook from a side drawer, and opened the center drawer for a pen. A picture stared up at him.

He and Mary at a carnival in Griffin Park last June, the stuffed bear he'd won for her nestled in the crook of her arm, his free hand at her waist. They both smiled widely at the camera, her head on his shoulder, both of them holding long paper cones topped by a cloud of cotton candy, their lips blue from the sticky treat.

Dee had said she still could die. Rick's breath caught in his throat and fear seized his heart. *She can't die, she can't.* Rick said a quick, fervent prayer she wouldn't.

Returning the picture to the drawer, he opened the notebook and marked one page GOOD, one page DON'T KNOW, and one page BAD. He started writing cops' names after giving each a moment's thought as to where it belonged. Finished with the cops in the Zero-Seven, he switched to every cop he knew in the city. He finally wrote the last name and eyed the clock above the desk. 2 a.m. Had he really been at it for five hours? He tipped the last swallow of beer into his mouth. Warm and flat, it hung at the back of his mouth, choking him for a second, before he got it down.

He skimmed over the BAD list. Twenty names.

Thirty under DON'T KNOW. Too many in both. Double that under GOOD. Not enough. He'd start confirming the BAD list in the morning. He rose from the desk then sat again. Taking the picture from the drawer, he paper-clipped it inside the notebook's cover. He dropped the empty bottle in the trash and headed for bed. He knew he'd dream of Mary. He hoped the dreams wouldn't be of her shot, bleeding, and almost dying.

They were.

Chapter 3

Tuesday – April 21, 2015

Rick Lafferty walked into Nate's just after eight the next morning. He slid into a booth and pulled the breakfast menu from the rack at the back edge of the table. A waitress in a pastel pink uniform arrived and asked in a flat voice, "What can I get you?"

He looked up from the menu. Her name badge read *Joleen*. "Coffee, as soon as possible, please. And keep it coming." He carried a major case of tired on him. "Then OJ, two eggs over easy, toast, sausage links, and home fries, please."

The cop in Rick studied Joleen as he gave her his order. Early thirties maybe, about five-seven and thin, maybe one-ten to -fifteen, dark brown hair, lighter brown eyes. Take away the dark circles under the eyes and the drawn look to her face, and she'd be pretty in a girl-next-door kind of way. A little life in her eyes would help, too. She looked worn-down. He spotted the shadow of a bruise under the makeup on her cheek, changed worn-down to defeated, and knocked five years off her age.

She was back in a heartbeat with a white mug of coffee and little jugs of creamer, setting the mug down with a thump and dropping the little jugs on the table.

"Thank you."

He took a big sip of coffee. It was hot and strong,

and he imagined the caffeine going straight into his blood. It didn't really happen that way, but he wanted to think it did. He yawned, rubbed his eyes, and took another swallow of coffee. A memory of a breakfast with Mary at a coffee shop near her apartment snuck up on him. He wished she was across the table from him right now, hoped someday soon she would be. He hadn't realized how much he'd come to think of her as more than a casual companion and occasional bedmate until Dee had said she was dead. He wondered when the shift had really happened.

DeAngelis had called him just after seven to say Mary was holding her own but not out of the woods yet. She still could die. His heart knotted, and a flicker of worry danced in his head.

Joleen set his meal on the table then pivoted away. He said her name, and she came back. "Something wrong with your order?" A tremor in her voice as if she expected to be slapped.

"No." He crooked his finger until she leaned toward him. "How'd you get the bruise on your cheek?"

"I fell."

"No, you didn't." He gave her the stare he'd used on many criminals, a mix of foresight and control that held their gaze until he let them look away.

She couldn't look away either. "My...boyfriend. He...slapped me. He didn't mean to, he just...lost it for a second."

"How many times has he lost it for a second?"

"Ne-never before. And he promised me it won't happen again."

"It will. I can guarantee it."

"It won't." The touch of hope in her voice belied her

words.

"It will. And, next time, he may not stop with a slap." Rick pulled a card from an inner pocket of his blazer and offered it to Joleen. "That happens, you call me."

She slid the card into a pocket on her uniform, shook her head, and walked away.

One day a cop, maybe him, would have to clean up the mess left by the boyfriend who'd never do it again. He shook his head sadly. Why would any woman let a guy knock her around? Why would Joleen let a man smack the life out of her until she looked used up and older than her years? He could never understand it. He couldn't stop it from happening, either. He could only pick up the pieces after it did. That frustrated the hell out of him.

He shook his head again and tucked into his breakfast. He was down to a half a slice of toast and one sausage link when a rough voice said, "Hey, Lafferty! How's it hanging?"

Mike McHale slid onto the seat facing him without waiting for an invite. Rick's meal soured in his stomach. He kept his voice neutral. "McHale."

"Hey that was too bad about Virgin getting popped night before last, wasn't it?"

"Yeah." He hated the nickname other cops had hung on Mary. She'd laughed it off.

"The Slime Squad got anything on it yet?"

Rick didn't like Internal Affairs Bureau any better than any other cop did. But he understood why they were necessary. "They don't share with me."

"I figured they'd keep you in the loop." He turned towards the counter and bellowed, "Hey! What's a guy gotta do to get some service in here?"

A black waitress name-badged Ramona hurried over. Rick wondered where Joleen had gone. Ramona said, "What can I get for you, Sergeant?"

Rick noticed a sneering undertone in her voice when she said McHale's rank.

"Coffee black as you, and get it here quick."

Ramona strode away. Rick asked, "Why would IA tell me what was going on?"

"Conner was your squeeze."

"Where'd you get that idea?"

"Saw you around town with her. Coming out of Argento's one time, Windsor Inn another, going into Captain Nemo's, a couple other places."

McHale's tone made Rick's happy times with Mary sound like quickie couplings in a hot sheet motel. "You following me, McHale?"

"Nah." He flashed a smirk at Rick. "I just get around a lot. See things. Hear things."

Ramona thumped a two-thirds full coffee mug down in front of him. He growled, "About goddam time!" then eyed the low level. "You call that a friggin' cuppa coffee?"

"Sorry, sir. I'll be right back." Ramona didn't seem flustered or intimidated by McHale's attitude.

McHale dumped sugar and cream in the mug and took a noisy slurp. "So what's the story, Lafferty?" He put on a leer. "You doing the bedsprings bounce with Virgin?"

Rick wondered if McHale ever spotted him or Mary leaving the other's house early in the morning. "We had dinner together a few times. Nothing more."

"Don't shit me, Lafferty. You and Virgin were

doing more than having dinner together a few times. You were trying to taste her tonsils in the parking lot at Brews Brothers a couple weeks ago."

They'd been so hungry for each other that night, they'd barely been able to hold back until they got to her apartment. "One time deal. We both had a bit too much to drink, got a little carried away for a moment."

"I wouldn't a minded getting carried away like that with her. Only I'd a carried it a lot further than tasting her tonsils. And more than once. Know what I mean?"

Ramona returned with a carafe, topped off Rick's mug, and splashed more coffee into McHale's. Some landed on the table and McHale's shirt. He snarled, "Watch it, stupid."

"Sorry, sir."

Rick could tell she wasn't. As she strode away, he said, "Honey works better than vinegar, McHale."

"Showing them you're the boss works best." McHale leaned toward Rick. "So what was it like screwing Virgin Mary?"

Rick fought down the urge to drive McHale's nose through the back of his head. "Screwing her?"

"What are you, a Boy Scout? You know." McHale stroked the middle finger of his right hand in and out of the tube formed by the curled fingers of his left. "Humping her. Boning her. Banging her. Whatever you want to call it."

The gesture offended Rick more than the phrases. He bored his stare into the other cop. "You born that crude, McHale, or did you study it in school?"

"I'm just saying any normal man would've hopped her bones every chance he got. You didn't, you were a fool. Or a faggot. I'd had a chance to bang her, I'da been on her a second after she offered. And once wouldn't've been enough."

"Have a little respect for the dead, McHale." Calling Mary dead while she was still alive twisted Rick's mind. "Especially when she was a fellow officer."

"Fellow officer." McHale snorted. "She was a stuck-up bitch. Wouldn't hardly give me the time of day."

"Maybe with good reason." Rick slid out of the booth and dropped a twenty on the table. He stopped Ramona and gave her another twenty. "For Joleen and you."

****

On the sixth floor of Northeast Medical Center, just past the entrance to the Surgical Intensive Care Unit, a short hall jutted to the left. Surgeons and surgical residents used the three rooms on each side—once patient rooms—to grab a few moments of sleep between crises. The last one on the left side of the hall had been re-converted into a hospital room.

Mary Conner lay in the bed, her body from ribs to hips heavily bandaged. IVs in both arms delivered drugs to slaughter any bacteria trying to infect her, suppress even the faintest flicker of pain, keep her body's chemistry in perfect balance, and provide the exact nutrition her body needed to heal. The most sensitive monitors available sat on racks to one side of her bed, tracking everything happening in her body.

Two nurses maintained a constant vigil over her in twelve-hour shifts. They just sat, one inside the door to the room, the other by the head of Mary's bed. They never left the room until their relief arrived, and each team confirmed the other's IDs before one left and the other took over. None of the four ever checked Mary's blood pressure, took her temperature, changed her dressings, or hung new IVs. They weren't nurses.

They were female State Police troopers assigned to protect Mary.

****

"Hi, Janet. You wanted to see me?" Ann Hendershot rapped on the Northeast Medical Center nursing supervisor's open office door and stepped in.

"Yes. I need to move you to Surgical Intensive Care. It's a special assignment. You'll only have one patient in your care."

That struck Ann as unusual, even on Surgical Intensive Care. Most nurses handled a minimum of two patients, usually three. One would be a day at the beach. "Sure. No problem. Let me grab my things from my locker, and I'm ready to go."

Janet said, "In a minute. I need you to work every day until further notice. Will that cause you a problem?"

"Not if I can get my parents to help with my kids."

Janet pointed to the phone. "See if they will."

Ann made the call. Her parents were happy to pitch in for as long as she needed. She hung up the phone. "All set."

"One more question. Do you know Linda Allington and Denise Sholes? Do you have a problem working with them?"

"Yes, I know them, and no, I don't have a problem working with either one."

"Good." Janet stood. "Let's go then."

Five minutes later, they stepped off the elevator on the sixth floor. At the nurse's station, Janet plucked a chart from the rack. Ann reached for it. "Who is it?"

"In a minute." Janet steered Ann into the break

room. A lean woman sat at the table. She wore nurse's scrubs, but Ann sensed she wasn't a nurse. Something about her reminded her of Rick. Maybe it was the way her eyes focused on Ann yet seemed to take in everything around her. Janet closed the door to the room. The woman held out her hand. "May I see your hospital ID, please?"

Ann slipped the lanyard holding the plastic card over her head and handed it to the woman. She studied the picture on the card and Ann for several seconds. "May I see some other ID—like a driver's license—with your picture on it?"

The woman's no-nonsense attitude sealed the deal. She was a cop of some kind. Ann's hand shook as she fished in her purse for her wallet. Why did a cop need to see her ID? What was going on? She worked her license out of its slot and gave it to the woman. She compared both photos to Ann then gave a short nod to the nursing supervisor. "She'll do."

"I'll do?" Ann snapped. "Who are you that you get to make that call?" Why did a cop need to approve her? She glared at her supervisor. "What's going on here, Janet?"

"Calm down, Ann. I told you it's a special assignment."

The woman at the table returned Ann's ID and license. "Every time you need to enter the patient's room you will knock first and show the person inside both IDs. Is that understood?"

"Yes." Ann's senses kicked to full alert.

"You will also be frisked. Do you have a problem with that?"

The woman's flat voice irritated Ann to the breaking

point. "I will if you don't tell me who you are, and what's going on here right now."

"I'm Sergeant Boniface of the Pennsylvania State Police." She flashed an ID at Ann. "Four of my troopers, Caitlin Burke, Janet Langdon, Rachel Newman, and Allison Sheehy are guarding the patient you will be treating. She's alive, and we aim to keep her that way."

"Who am I treating, The governor's wife?"

"Here." The supervisor finally handed Ann the chart.

The name on the front read Miranda Vincente. Ann flipped back the cover, and skimmed the admittance sheet. Thirty-seven-year-old female—too young for the governor's wife—shot twice in the abdomen, stable but comatose post-op, transferred in from Thomas Jefferson Hospital in Philadelphia. Ann paged to the patient data sheet and traced a finger down to the line for occupation. Police detective. Definitely not the governor's wife.

Still… In nursing school at Jefferson, she'd learned hospitals sometimes used phony names to keep a patient's identity secret.

Could it be? Chills slithered down Ann's spine, and goose bumps tickled along her arms. Her heart raced in her chest, and her mouth dried up. Thumbing to the last page, she skimmed the confidential information. She held in the gasp trying to escape and willed her hands not to shake.

Her new patient was Rick's Mary.

****

The blackness lifts. She knows she is somewhere. She doesn't know where. Blackness settles over her again.

****

Joleen sat on a commode in the lady's room. Her arms, wrapped as tightly as she could get them around herself, couldn't stop her shivering. Nothing could. It was easy to be brave when pain and humiliation burned hot and fresh in her and her abuser was gone. It wasn't easy in the cold light of day when the fire had faded and hope held out to her had been snatched back before she could grasp it.

She pulled the card from her pocket and read it again. *Richard M. Lafferty. Detective.* She laughed bitterly, sickly. She'd felt a glimmer of hope when she'd first read it. He wouldn't be like McHale. He was a detective. They were the elite of the Philadelphia Police, better than the rest. Maybe this Lafferty guy could help her get out from under McHale's thumb. Then she'd seen them sitting in the same booth, talking.

McHale had stared right through her when he entered. She was used to it. She didn't exist except when he raped her and maybe for five or ten seconds on either side. He never stopped existing for her, a cancer eating at her soul, and she didn't know how much more she could take before it consumed her. She'd bolted for the lady's room right after he'd entered Nate's and made it just in time to vomit her breakfast into the commode.

McHale would kill her one day, she was sure of it. Or he'd grind her down until there was nothing left. She'd be just as dead as if he'd put a gun to her head and pulled the trigger. She sobbed. She was only twenty-six years old.

"Girl? You still in here?" Ramona called out. She pushed open the door to the stall. "What's wrong, child?"

Joleen wiped her eyes with a wad of toilet tissue and blew her nose. "Nothing."

"Don't tell me nothin', girl. Somethin' is." Ramona was fifty-two, tall and stringy with an almost buzz cut of gray hair. "Why's that man scare you so?"

"Wh-who?"

"McHale, that who. Every time he come in, you get white as a sheet. You been hiding in here ever since he come in today."

"It wasn't him. I got feeling sick and I—"

"Don't bullshit me, girl. I know scared when I see it. You was scared."

"I was not!" Joleen shrieked.

Ramona held up her hands. "Okay. You ain't. Have it your way. Anyway, you can come out now. He's gone."

"Yeah, I'd better get back to work before Nate fires me." She left the stall and flipped Lafferty's card toward the trashcan.

Ramona caught the fluttering card on the fly, glanced at it, and tucked it into her uniform pocket. "Ain't no problem, girl. I covered for you."

"Thanks, Ramona. You're a pal." Joleen leaned over a sink and splashed water on her face. She dried her face with a paper towel, taking some face powder away.

Ramona touched her bruised cheek with a lean finger. "Who put this on you, girl?"

Joleen pulled away. "I tripped in my bedroom and banged into the wall."

Ramona's face said she wasn't buying it. "McHale done it, dint he?"

Joleen held her gaze for a second. She started to shake her head. Tears rose in her eyes, and she nodded.

"Why'd that bum smack you? He got something on you?

44

Joleen nodded again.

"What?"

"I…I can't say."

Joleen shrugged. "Okay." She took a ten-dollar bill from her uniform pocket. "Anyway, Lafferty give me a twenty, said to split it with you. This yours."

Joleen backed away as if the money was a snake coiled to bite her. "I don't want it."

"You crazy, girl? It's ten bucks." Ramona studied her hard. "Why not?"

"Because he's a cop, just like McHale. I saw them talking."

"Talkin' with McHale don't make him like McHale. You dint see the look on his face while he was. Like he was lookin' at a cesspool."

She put a strong bony hand on Joleen's shoulder. "Girl, you need to hear some things. First off, just 'cause Lafferty a cop, it don't make him like McHale. He don't use people." She held up the card. "He give you this, he seen you're hurtin', and he reachin' out to you, offerin' you help. You best take it. Second, you need to get McHale out of your life."

Joleen felt that glimmer of hope again. "Ho-how do I do that?"

"Girl, there's only one way to handle slime like the McHales of this world. You gotta stand up to him. Only way you gonna get him outta your life."

****

McHale scowled at the street in front of his cruiser. Who the fuck did Lafferty think he was, telling McHale honey worked better than vinegar? Pompous asshole, thinking he was better than McHale just because he wore a suit. Probably thought his shit didn't stink, too.

McHale remembered the night Lafferty thought he'd screwed up a drug bust. He hadn't been so high-and-mighty then. He'd been shitting bricks. Big ones with hooks on them. All because he'd lost a key of Jamaican Red from a raid on a heroin packaging operation near the docks. Lafferty'd been in a panic, sweating what would happen to him for losing the kilo. He hadn't even really lost the kilo, the dumb fuck, just couldn't find it. The package had fallen off a table and gotten kicked into a corner. Took McHale all of about ten seconds to find it.

And what was that shit about maybe Virgin had a good reason to snub him? Conner must have been polishing Lafferty's pole. Had to be. The way his back went up—like a pissed-off Rottweiler—when McHale asked what it was like banging her made it a sure thing. Conner was putting out for Lafferty regularly while she wouldn't even give him the time of day. His anger seethed hotter.

Then he laughed. Lafferty wouldn't be getting it any more from Virgin. Two rounds in her gut had fixed that. *He'd* fixed that.

Just thinking Conner's name started pressure building in McHale's crotch. He pounded the steering wheel with his fist. Damn! He should have boned her before whacking her.

A Cadillac in the left lane, turn signal winking, crossed in front of his cruiser, aiming for the open parking spot at the curb. The move fueled McHale's anger. He flicked on the roof lights, stopped with the cruiser's nose overlapping the Caddy's front door, and got out.

"You're blocking my door, Officer." The driver

wore an expensive looking suit, white shirt, and red power tie.

McHale glanced at his cruiser. "Hunh! Guess I am."

"Would you mind moving it so I can get out?"

"You in a big hurry to get somewhere?"

"As a matter of fact, I am." He pointed to the building across the sidewalk. "I have a meeting inside in five minutes."

"Afraid you're gonna be late." To make sure he was, McHale paused at every comma, crossed every t, and dotted every i writing the guy up for an unsafe lane change. It was a bullshit ticket. The Caddy hadn't come within four feet of clipping him.

McHale gave the guy his ticket, got in his cruiser, and backed it clear of the Caddy. The driver bolted from his car and sprinted for the building.

McHale glanced at his watch. Not quite eleven a. m. An hour and a half 'till lunch. Nulty's Diner on Wilson made a stick-to-your-ribs beef stew, served in big bowls with thick slabs of fresh crusty bread on the side. That sounded good. With a humping for dessert. From who? ADA Bartlett's wife? He hadn't done her in three weeks. Miss Vassar Grad was forty-two, but she was still hot and always happy to drop her LaPerla undies for a quickie with him. *Perfect.*

An après-lunch trip to Boston Square went on his agenda.

****

At noon, McHale travelled Forty-third north to Pierce. He parked on the corner with the nose of his car jutting into one lane of Pierce and took a fresh burner from his Go Bag. When his watch read twelve-oh-five, he dialed. Five rings later, Joey Day said, *"Buenas tardes, mi amigo.*"

"*Buenos dias, Jefe.*" Christ, he wished Joey would shitcan the Spanish lingo. And stop expecting him to spew the crap, too. But Joey's money bought a lot of crap spewing.

"I have some news I wish you to relay to Luis Herrera, *mi hermano.*"

"What news is that?" McHale could guess without breaking a sweat.

Joey sighed dramatically. "It appears Luis is experiencing a small accounting problem. His receipts do not always tally exactly with his sales, if you understand me. Perhaps you could enlighten him on the need for fiscal accuracy in his dealings with me?"

McHale hated Joey's artsy-fartsy English speech style as much as the Spanish. Made him sound like some fag professor. He bit his tongue. Joey's money bought lots of that, too. "Of course, *Jefe.* I'll see to it tonight."

"*Gracias.* Your usual fee of course. A moment, *por favor.* I have something to consider."

McHale waited while Joey breathed into the phone for a few seconds.

"You have earned a bonus, *mi compadre,* for your loyal service to me."

"That is not necessary, Jefe. You reward me well." Joey liked a little kowtowing from his employees. Kowtowing to Joey made McHale want to vomit.

"I was thinking of a different kind of bonus, my friend. I have arranged for Darcy to be available next weekend."

McHale's crotch stirred. Darcy Brown, a sexy long-legged brunette, ran one of Joey's nightclubs. But at a snap of his fingers, she'd get on her back or knees for any man he told her to. And she flat out liked sex, the wilder the better. She was Joey's special treat for those who pleased him. *"Muchas gracias, Jefe."*

****

Rick prowled the streets patrolled by District 7 all morning, hunting down officers on his GOOD list, asking them about cops on his other two lists. It had been a fruitless morning. Every uniform he talked to was positive there were cops on the take but none could name even one they knew personally. Or maybe wouldn't name them.

A little after noon, Rick stopped at Gordy's for lunch. He took a stool at the counter and ordered a hot roast beef and cheddar on rye, fries, and chocolate shake. The round-faced waitress said she'd be back in a minute with his shake.

She was as good as her word. Rick drew a mouthful through the wide bore straw and savored the feel and taste of it. Gordy's made the best shakes in the city—always cold, thick, and rich.

Rick pivoted on his stool and ran his gaze over the people in the restaurant. He'd given the place a quick once-over when he entered, now it was time for a slower, more thorough sweep. He didn't spot anybody he knew and faced the counter.

His thoughts jumped to Mary. Was she better? Worse? The same? He hoped better, but figured Dee would have told him if she was. Or if she'd gotten worse. 'The same' would have to hold him for now.

A few moments later, a uniformed sergeant slid onto the stool next to Rick. He had grizzled hair, a bushy gray mustache, and service bars halfway up his sleeve. He tossed Rick a tight nod. "Suit." A uniform's standard greeting to any detective he didn't know.

Rick didn't recognize him from the District house. "Sergeant."

The chubby waitress approached them. The sergeant told her, "Pastrami and Swiss on a sesame bagel, medium Coke, and a coffee, two creamers, two sugars to go."

"Sure thing." She retreated.

The sergeant eyed the soda machine behind the counter. "Hear you've been asking around about cops."

Rick replied, "Where'd you hear that?"

"My men. What's your name?"

"Lafferty."

"You Slime Squad?"

"Nope."

The sergeant gazed directly at Rick. "Can you prove it?"

Rick matched his stare. "Depends on whether you believe what I tell you."

"Trust but verify."

"You know Captain DeAngelis in the Zero-Seven?"

"Marco DeAngelis?" At Rick's nod, the sergeant said, "Yeah."

Rick wrote a number on the back of one of his cards. "Call him. He'll verify me."

"Don't go away." The sergeant got off his stool and headed for the entrance.

Rick's food came. He lifted the top slice. Lettuce and tomato. He'd forgotten to tell the waitress to skip the rabbit food. After picking them off and laying them aside, he spread mustard on the bread's toasted surface and added a dash of salt to the sandwich and several dashes to the fries. He ate a couple fries then took a bite of the sandwich.

The sergeant reclaimed his stool. "Alvarez."

Rick took his offered hand. Alvarez had a firm grip with no macho overtones. He asked, "Why are you asking about cops?"

"I'm looking for ones who skate a little too close to the edge. Or sometimes over it."

Alvarez chewed on that for a second. "Okay. Let's say I know some like that. And let's say I give you their names. And let's say you take down one of them for some reason. That gonna come back on me?"

"No."

"Any chance this thi—" Alvarez stopped as the waitress set his food and drinks at his place. He tugged out his wallet.

"On me." Rick pulled a twenty and five from his pocket, pointed to both meals, and handed the bills to the waitress. "Keep the change."

Alvarez said, "Thanks. Any chance this will go official, and the Slime Squad will get involved?"

"Not if I can help it."

"Word gets out I ratted to them, even indirectly, I'm screwed."

"I'll do my best to keep you clean.

"That's fair."

"So how about some names, Alvarez?"

Picking up the bag and cardboard tray holding his food, Alvarez rose from his stool. "I'll get back to you."

Chapter 4

McHale left Nulty's, his belly full of beef stew and warm bread, and aimed his cruiser in the direction of Boston Square. His cell phone rang as he sat at the light at Tenth and Cleveland.

"It's Davenport. Got a situation I could use your help with."

He was two blocks from a bed-busting romp with ADA Bartlett's hot wife. Shit. "How bad?"

"Could jam a greenie up big if you can't help him out." A rookie patrolman.

That could have bigger benefits down the road than a quick round of 'Slide The Salami' with Heather Bartlett. She'd have to wait. "Where are you?"

"Larch between Second and Third."

"On my way." McHale toggled the roof lights and gunned his cruiser onto Cleveland. On the way, he dialed ADA Bartlett's house and told Heather something had come up and he couldn't make it. She sounded disappointed.

****

"You want a what?" The shriek in Ramona's voice bored into Joleen's brain like the screech of a drill. Ramona's eyes, wide with surprise at Joleen's request, turned hot with anger. "You outta your mind, girl?"

"I-I don't know what else to do."

They were in the ladies' room at Nate's again. It was

the after-lunch lull.

"Girl, I ain't gettin' you no gun. Even if I could, I wouldn't. A gun just gonna give you more trouble than you got now."

"Anything's better than what I have now."

"You shoot a hole in McHale's fat lily-white ass, it's gonna get a whole lot worse than you got it now, believe me. What hold's that man got on you, you want to be killin' him?"

Joleen broke into sobs so hard she leaned against the wall to keep from falling. Ramona pulled her into a big hug and held her while sobs wracked her thin body. When Joleen stopped crying, Ramona wet a paper towel and gently wiped her face. "What did you do that McHale got his hooks in you?"

"I was dating this guy, Bryce." The tale tumbled out. Bryce used coke, never went anywhere without it. McHale pinched them three times while Joleen was carrying it in her purse because the vial would show as a bulge in Bryce's skin-tight slacks. She'd done short terms in the city jail for possession after the first two busts. Bryce hadn't done a day. The third time, McHale told her the amount she was carrying—no more than she'd ever carried—made the charge possession with intent to deliver, and the penalty was a long stretch in the state pen. Then he'd offered her an out.

"Bang him?"

Joleen nodded, and fresh tears filled her eyes again. "I thought it would be just once. Or twice. I could handle that. But it's been going on now for over a year. And it isn't even sex, he just gets off in me—he won't even wear a condom—and leaves." Tears ran down her cheeks again. "I can't take it much more, Ramona." She muffled a sob. "Maybe I'll kill myself."

"Don't do that, girl. You do, and McHale gets just what he wants. He's destroyed you."

"What's the difference? He's destroying me piece by piece now."

"The difference is you worth somethin'. He ain't."

"So what am I supposed to do?"

"I told you. Talk to Lafferty." Ramona pulled his card from her uniform pocket and held it out to Joleen. "Tell him what McHale's doin'. He'll take care of you."

Joleen shook her head. "I can't. McHale told me if he ever finds out I talked to a cop, he'd kill me."

"Then stand up to him yourself, like I tol' you. Tell him you won't be his whore no more. He's a coward and a bully. You stand up to him once—that's all it gonna take, believe me—he'll turn tail, and run like a whipped dog."

"And what if he doesn't? What if he beats me up? Or-or kills me? I need a gun to at least give me a chance of fighting him off."

Ramona studied the young woman for a few seconds then brushed a lock of hair off her face. "You don't need no gun to do it, child. All you need's a knife. You swing a blade at him, and he'll run faster than you can blink. He scared to death of knives."

Joleen eyed Ramona in awe and wonder and a bit of fear. "Ho-how do you know that?"

"McHale had me once like he's got you now."

****

McHale parked his cruiser by the prowl car blocking the alley connecting Larch to Grant. It was an area of warehouses and dead factories. Deeper in the alley, another cruiser sat with its front end folded around the corner of a dumpster. Two officers leaned against its trunk.

McHale started down the alley. He recognized the older cop with the walrus moustache as Davenport and nodded to him as he neared the wrecked cruiser. "What's up?"

Davenport introduced the tall sandy haired young cop staring at the ground next to him as Rynert. "Tell him what happened, kid."

Rynert studied his brogans for another second then raised his head. McHale could see tiredness pulling at his eyes. His moustache was so thin and light, it looked like a smudge of dust across his upper lip. He cleared his throat. "I was, uh…I, uh, hit the dumpster."

"He can see that," Davenport growled. "Tell him the rest of it, kid."

The young cop's face reddened. "All of it, Sarge?"

"If you wanna keep wearing the blues. Otherwise, you're looking at a career as a night watchman at the Schuylkill Mall."

"Shit." Rynert stared at his brogans again and sighed like the weight of the world sat on his shoulders.

McHale said, "Just tell me what happened, kid. We can probably fix it, but I gotta know what happened before I can say."

Rynert nodded. "Okay. I'm on night tour for two weeks. One of the guys on day tour called in sick today so I volunteered to cover his shift. I been working all the extra I can get 'cause I need the money. I'm getting married in a couple months." He wiped his hand down his face. "This is the third double I pulled this week. And my ass is dragging. I pulled in here to eat my lunch and closed my eyes for just a minute, and I must have nodded off."

The young cop paused for a sigh. "Then the radio squawked on a robbery, and I hit the gas. But I must've only been half awake, 'cause—" He waved toward the front of his car with disgust.

McHale nodded and gave the young cop a comforting smile. "Give me a minute to see what we can do." He eyed the front of the damaged cruiser then scanned the alley. A few feet up from the cruiser, a steel door had been set into the brick wall. *Perfect.*

McHale strolled back to the two cops, clapped Rynert on the shoulder, and gave him another smile. "You don't have to worry about a career in night security at the mall."

"I don't?" The younger cop let out a big breath. "Thanks. I owe you one, Sarge."

McHale offered a cold smile. *You don't know how big a one.* "Give us a minute, kid. Okay?" He motioned for Davenport to come with him. A few feet away from the wrecked cruiser, he stopped. "Call it in as wrecked avoiding a civilian."

Davenport gave McHale a doubting look. "What civilian? The kid never said anyth—"

"Leave that to me." McHale walked away.

****

Darcy Brown took her purse from her desk. "Going to the ladies' room."

Gary—head bartender at *Paraiso*, the nightclub she managed for Joey Day—looked up from the liquor inventory in his computer. "Have fun."

She kept her face still, hiding the pain tracing her ribs as she rose from her chair. The burning between her legs was like she'd douched with flaming kerosene.

Entering the ladies' room, she locked the door behind her. She didn't want any early-arriving staff walking in on her.

Setting her purse by the sink, she examined her reflection in the mirror. Time for a touch up. She took a compact from her purse. The stuff cost a fortune but it was the best makeup she'd ever found for hiding bruises. She brushed the powder along the left side of her jaw and under her right eye.

Her companion last night had been a real piece of work. Councilman Ed Rayburn was an ape in Armani, short and squat, with the table manners of a pig at the trough. She should have realized she was in for a rough time by the way he pawed her leg, like he was kneading dough, all through dinner. In the hotel room he didn't even let her undress, just threw her on the bed, tore her dress off, and took her, ignoring her cries of pain as he forced himself into her then humped away.

She didn't mind screwing but almost getting raped was another matter, and she'd told him she was leaving. He'd grabbed her arm, saying she'd leave when he said she could, not before. When she jerked her arm free, he'd popped her in the jaw. She got the bruise under her eye hitting the dresser a second later. She was lucky she hadn't broken her nose or lost the eye.

She unbuttoned the cuff of her blouse and pulled the sleeve up her arm, wincing from the ache even that simple action caused. She'd worn long sleeves to hide the finger shaped bruises on her right arm and a knee-length skirt to cover the ones on her thighs. She hiked her skirt to check them.

She unbuttoned her blouse. More fingertip bruises dotted her breasts. The councilman had mauled them as hard as her thighs and left a bite mark on one as well. Another bruise covered half her left side. As she struggled to her feet after hitting the dresser, Rayburn had punched her so hard, she'd gone down again, gasping for air, each breath so painful she was sure he'd broken her ribs. She was sure at least some were cracked. Anything more than a shallow breath still filled her side with fire.

That punch was the last straw. When she could breathe again, she got to her feet, said she was leaving, and if he stopped her, she'd cut him. He'd laughed until she'd pulled the switchblade from her purse and snapped it open inches from his nose. Having caught his full attention, she offered him a choice. She could leave or cut his balls off.

She'd called Joey on the way to her car and told him what Rayburn had done, knowing he'd make Rayburn pay for it. This morning, the news had reported that Councilman Rayburn had been jumped outside his Colonial Pike mansion in the wee hours of the morning and beaten to a pulp. Good! It served the bastard right for bashing her around.

She buttoned her blouse and tucked it into her skirt. Taking a pill vial from her purse, she shook out two Vicodins and two ibuprofen and washed them down with a cup of water. She needed something more to get through the day. Reaching into her purse again, she took out a contact lens case. She unscrewed a cap and touched a fingertip to the white powder inside then rubbed the coke along her gums.

Unlike most people, Darcy had managed to keep her coke habit in check. She only used it, and only in the minute amount that clung to her fingertip, when she needed a little boost. Like today. Between the Vicodin and the pain filling her body, she'd crash and burn without it. An instant tingle of numbness spread along her gums followed by the bump she needed.

She'd met Joey Day ten years ago as an assistant manager at resort hotel on the Jersey shore. Joey, a guest at the hotel, had hit on her in the bar one night. The sex that followed had been out of this world. The only downside had been the dour-faced men hovering at Joey's shoulders until he led her into his bedroom. They'd hooked up every night until he checked out, the sex always epic. A week later, he'd offered her a job managing one of his nightclubs in Philly for double what she made at the hotel. She'd said yes and moved to the city, where semi-regular mind-blowing sex with Joey had been a job perk. After one especially wild session, he'd asked if she'd be interested in making some extra money helping him close deals with guys by sleeping with them. She liked screwing so she'd said sure, why not.

Joey paid her a thousand bucks every time she banged someone for him. She supposed that made her a whore. But, hey, it was easy money for doing what she'd do for free with a guy she picked up. Why not get paid for it? Especially since she didn't get to pick the guys, screwed whoever Joey sent her. He'd sent her to some real winners, and she'd taken some slaps and punches over the years. Last night was the first time the guy had really clobbered her.

She ran a comb through her honey blonde hair. Maybe it was time to tell Joey she was done banging guys for him. She was tired of being handed out to men she didn't know, tired of doing men she wouldn't pick up no matter how much she needed to get laid, tired of suffocating under a mound of blubber, tired of gagging on B. O. and bad breath, and tired of duds who couldn't get it up with a crane. Mostly she was tired of not having control over what happened when the hotel room door closed, of not being able to walk away when things got nasty, as they had several times. The scene with Rayburn had been the straw that broke the camel's back. She wanted out before next weekend rolled around.

Joey told her she'd be entertaining Mike McHale all next weekend. He paid her four grand each time she spent more than a night with a guy, and some of them had delivered really rocking sex. But not McHale. No way was she going to spend another weekend with him. The man was a pig, a sick pig. Ten grand wasn't enough for one night of the twisted things he expected her to do.

Leaving Joey would never happen. He'd told her once no one ever quit working for him. If they tried, they died, simple as that. He hadn't said it as a threat, just as pillow talk after an exceptionally fantastic screwing. Still, she got the message. He'd kill her if she wanted to stop doing guys. And what would happen when she hit fifty? Or if her beauty started to fade? Would he let her go then? Or would he put her down like an old dog?

There had to be a way. She had to get out. Maybe she could pack up her clothes and a few things she cherished and drive into the sunset. Maybe just blow the city, make it a fast get away. Once she set up somewhere, she could send for the rest of her stuff. What if Joey could track her somehow? Didn't matter where she fled then, he'd find her and kill her.

She dropped her comb in her purse. It landed with the handle sticking up in the opening. She shifted it, and her hand brushed her switchblade. An image of it sticking out of Joey's chest flashed across her mind. No! She couldn't kill someone.

Besides, killing Joey would be suicide. The minute she tried, his bodyguards would blast her, probably would if they only suspected she was just thinking about trying it. She wanted to escape him, not throw her life away. So scratch killing him.

She dipped her finger in the coke again. Just a little more to get her through the day. She wiped the coke along her gums. Picking up her purse, she left the ladies' room.

The image of Joey with her switchblade buried in his chest lingered in the back of her mind the rest of the day.

****

Shortly after 2 p.m., two sharp raps drew Captain DeAngelis's gaze to his office door. Captain Al Greig, commander of the patrol division in District 7, cracked the door and stuck his head in. "You got a minute, Captain?"

Using DeAngelis's rank meant Greig was making an official visit. DeAngelis waved him in. "What's on your mind, Captain?"

Greig, a paunchy man with sagging jowls and a roadmap of veins across his cheeks and bulbous nose, stopped in front of Dee's desk. "Couple of my guys are saying one of yours been questioning them."

"Which one of my guys?"

"Lafferty." Greig propped his hands on his hips. "Something going on I should know about, Captain?"

His repeat of DeAngelis's rank said he was upset. Dee leaned back in his chair and ran a hand over his short dark hair. "Who did Lafferty question?"

"Drake, Margolis, Judson, Styles, a couple others. So what's going on?"

"What did they say Lafferty asked them about?"

"You and me always got along, always worked together. None of the suits-against-stripes bullshit some houses have. Now, one of your guys is grilling mine, and I got no heads-up from you on it beforehand." Greig leaned toward DeAngelis. "What's the story, Captain?"

The third mention of rank signaled Greig was putting time-in-grade seniority into play. Dee returned his hard stare. "What did your men say Lafferty questioned them about, Captain Greig?" Telling him time-in-grade didn't cut any ice.

"Other men in my command."

Sergeant Alvarez's call at noon had given Dee time to dream up a cover story. He hoped Greig would buy the lie but a talk with Rick got added to his agenda. "Lafferty is conducting authorized background checks on specific officers."

"On whose authority?"

"Higher up the chain of command is all I can tell you."

"Would have been nice if you'd given me a heads up."

"My hands were tied. I had orders not to let you know."

Greig eyed him skeptically for a second then shrugged. "You say so."

****

McHale hit a dozen flophouses and homeless shelters before finding the man he wanted. Billy Drummond smoked a shared cigarette with two other upstanding residents of the area in the alleyway by St. Benedict's soup kitchen on Hayes Street. His eyes widened at the sight of McHale. He turned to follow the other two men now bolting for the far end of the alley.

"Don't even think about it, Billy."

Drummond's shoulders slumped, and he faced McHale. McHale beckoned him closer. Billy shuffled forward as if heading for his execution. "What do you want?"

McHale threw a big arm across the thin man's shoulders. "Billy, how's it going, buddy?"

Billy sniffed hard and rubbed his nose. "O-okay, I guess."

Drummond's breath could gag a sewer rat at a hundred yards. "Billy, Billy, Billy. You really gotta stop hanging around with riffraff like those guys." McHale jerked his thumb at the far end of the alley, "You'll pick up their bad name."

"What do you want, McHale?" Drummond tried to break free of the arm across his back.

McHale tightened his grip on Billy's shoulders. "You got a place to stay these days?"

"Got a room over on Colfax. Why you asking?"

"I thought maybe you could use a couple good meals and a warm bunk."

"Nunh-unh." Billy shook his head. "Not interested."

"How long since you had a drink, Billy?"

"Been a while. Couple days at least."

A couple hours, more likely. "I need you to do something for me."

"I ain't taking no fall for nobody for nothing for you."

"Billy." McHale gave his shoulders a squeeze.

"Would I do that to you? No. I'd never set you up to take a fall for something you didn't do. I just want you to say you were at a certain place at a certain time doing a certain thing."

"I don't want nothing to do with it." Billy twisted free of his grip and turned away.

McHale grabbed Billy's arm. "Those hot Rolexes I took off you last year could still land on some detective's desk. Maybe tomorrow. You want that to happen?"

Billy hung his head and shook it. "Nunh-unh."

McHale slapped him on the shoulder. "Then we got us a deal, right?"

"Yeah, okay. What's in it for me?"

McHale shot him a broad smile. "Those Rolexes stay in my private evidence locker."

"I want something up front, too."

"Sure, Billy. Anything you want. Within reason. Name it."

Billy wiped his mouth. "Been a long time since I had a bottle all to myself. Ain't had the money." He licked his lips. "And smokes. I ain't had a cigarette to myself in days."

"Johnnie Walker Red and Salems, right?" He hooked his arm around Billy's shoulders again and led him one step toward the mouth of the alley. "Come on. I'll fix you right up."

Billy resisted. "What do I gotta do?"

McHale slammed him against the wall and buried a huge fist deep in his gut. Billy doubled over and vomited his soup kitchen lunch all over the alley. McHale grabbed the back of his neck in a steel grip, forcing him to stay bent over. "First thing you gotta do, Billy, is never, ever tell me you ain't gonna do something I tell you to. You got that?"

Drummond nodded as he sucked in air. McHale said, "Are we ever gonna have this discussion again?"

Billy shook his head. McHale let go of his neck, and Billy straightened slowly, his arms folded across his stomach, his face scrunched in pain. McHale patted his cheek. "Good boy."

Billy staggered a few feet sideways from the slap then turned. "Wh-what do I gotta do?"

McHale told him.

Chapter 5

Ann Hendershot's heart thumped so hard in her chest she could barely hear the beating of Mary's—Oops!—Miranda's heart through her stethoscope. She wondered if the troopers guarding Mary could hear it too. She feared her every action betrayed that she knew Mary. She'd debated with herself all night about telling them. That she knew Mary shouldn't make a difference, but Ann feared it would, and the troopers would stop her caring for Mary. She would fight tooth and nail if they did. No one would care for Rick's Mary the way she would.

Closing her eyes, she forced her worries away and focused on her patient. She listened to the slow steady beat of Miranda's heart for fifteen seconds then lifted the stethoscope head from her chest, checked her blood pressure and temperature and jotted the numbers in her chart.

"How's she doing?" Trooper Caitlin Burke asked.

Ann closed the chart. "It's not my place to say. You should ask Doctor Nicopoulos."

"Come on, Ann. You know the big shots never tell us working stiffs the whole story. I'd really like to know how she's doing."

Ann gazed at the closed chart and considered Officer Burke's request. She'd initially disliked the troopers guarding Mary for the rigamarole she had go through just to get into the room and do her job. But she'd seen how Caitlin eyed Mary, as if she was were watching over a favorite sister. Guarding her wasn't just a job for Caitlin. She cared about Mary.

"Good. Her vital signs are stable, heartbeat is steady and strong, blood pressure's good, no sign of infection— that's the biggest worry in a case like this—and she's healing nicely. She's got a long road ahead of her, but Dr. Nicopoulos believes she can make a full recovery."

A smile crossed Caitlin's face. "That's what we want to hear. Any idea when she'll come to?"

Ann shrugged. "When she wakes up."

"Now would be nice," Allison Sheehy, the other officer guarding Mary, said, "so we can find out who did this to her." Sheehy, a stocky blonde, didn't seem to take guarding Mary as personally as Caitlin did, seemed to take it as just another assignment.

"I'll check on her again in an hour." Ann stepped into the hall.

Caitlin followed her. "Hold up a second." She pointed a thumb over her shoulder at the door. "How do you know her?"

Panic seized Ann. Had Caitlin found out she knew Mary, if only indirectly? How had she done it so fast? Had Ann given herself away? Would Caitlin take her off Mary's case? She couldn't let that happen. She inhaled a deep breath to slow her racing heart. "I don't. I mean I know what's in her chart, but that's—"

"You know her somehow. I was a nurse for five years before I joined the State Police, so I know how it goes. You're caring for someone you know, and no matter how hard you try to keep it professional, you always act a little different around them."

"I don't treat her any differently than any patient I've ever had."

The gaze Burke gave Ann matched the one her mom gave her when she lied as a kid. A 'you're not fooling me' look. "You do. You come in all business, Ms. Professional, but the minute you get near her you go all soft and cuddly, Ms. Big Sister."

"I'm that way with all my patients."

"Look, Ann, if you have a problem treating Miranda because she's a cop or with us guarding her or it's causing problems with your family or anything about this situation bothers you, I need to know."

"Nothing's bothering me."

Caitlin crossed her arms over her stomach. "Then tell me why you go all mushy around her."

Ann weighed how to give her enough to let her keep caring for Mary but not enough to give everything away. "My brother's a cop. If he was lying in a bed like her," she jabbed a finger at the door, "I would want the nurse taking care of him to care for him the way I'm caring for her. That's what's going on. If *you* have a problem with that, find someone else!" Ann stalked up the hall, hoping her bluff had worked and frightened it hadn't.

"Wait! Ann!" Caitlin grabbed her arm. "I don't have a problem. I'm glad you care so much, and I want you to care for her. But I had to ask. So you really don't know her?"

Ann had heard the deep affection in Rick's voice every time he talked about Mary. He hadn't fooled her one bit, not even the first time he'd mentioned her name last Thanksgiving. He loved her. Ann would do anything—even lie—to keep caring for Mary. For Rick. "No, I have never met her." Not exactly the truth; not exactly a lie.

Caitlin studied her for a second. "Okay." She slipped back into the room.

Ann walked back to the nursing station with her heart hammering in her chest.

****

She hears sounds. She tries to identify them but can't. They are just noise. She tries to focus on them but they fade away as blackness steals over her.

****

Rick cruised District 7, talking to patrol officers, for several more hours. Except for the teaser of a lead he'd gotten from Alvarez, he was no further ahead than when he'd started that morning. At 3:30 p.m., he drove across the city.

The One-Two's house had undergone a refurbishing a year earlier to keep it in line with the revival going on in the area. The old building had the same glow as the rehabbed warehouses and factories stockbrokers and lawyers, artists and actors called home these days. Rick mounted the steps and pulled open the crimson door.

"Lafferty," the desk sergeant called out when he spotted Rick.

"Hey, Tommy."

They exchanged what-you-been-up-tos for a minute before Tommy asked, "What brings you to our humble home?

"Looking to talk to a couple of your suits, Harter and Pryzlo."

"Lemme check." Tommy picked up the phone and dialed. He talked with someone briefly then hung up. "They're finishing up some things, said they'd be down in about fifteen."

****

Just after five that evening, a well-oiled Billy Drummond staggered into the District 5 house and up to the desk. "I am so shorry, ossifer."

The sergeant manning the desk scowled down at Billy. "Yeah? What are ya sorry for, ya rummy?"

Billy grabbed the edge of the desk to keep from falling. "I dint mean to caush that ossi—ochifer— offisher any harm. I hope I dint get him hurt none."

"What officer?"

"The one who crashed his car."

"What are you talking about?"

"I feel real bad about what I done. I dint know he was coming downa alley or I wounna comed out th' door. If he han'ta been onna ball, he'd've runned me down."

The sergeant nodded his head wisely and pointed to the bench along the wall. "You just have a seat over there, and somebody will be out to talk to you in a minute." He picked up the phone on his desk.

****

Joleen thumbed through the tattered notebook in her hand. Somebody in it should be able to get her a gun or connect her with someone who could. She didn't care what Ramona said. A knife wasn't going to save her from McHale. She needed a gun.

So many names in the book were people she'd lost touch with. Names from her high school days jumped out at her, people who'd sworn they'd be close forever. Reading them filled her with melancholy for what had once been.

She glanced around her tiny, crappy apartment and wondered how she'd fallen so far in eight years. From honor student and Winter Formal Queen with a bright, promising future to former jailbird eking out a living waitressing at Nate's and servicing that creep McHale. The bastard wouldn't even use a condom. It was a friggin' miracle he hadn't given her some disease. She wanted to cry.

It was all Bryce's fault. She wished she'd never met him. His dark good looks had sucked her in, and his smooth lines had conned her into believing everything he said. Even after she'd been burned twice for holding his coke, she'd believed him when he said he'd stand by her if it happened the third time. He hadn't, of course. She'd thrown him out of her life after that. He was gone, but the damage he'd wreaked remained.

She shook those thoughts away and refocused on the notebook. The losers she'd met through Bryce could get her a gun, but they'd want way more than she could afford. And it probably wouldn't be any more reliable than they were. She threw the notebook across the room.

She could call Bryce. She still had his number. No. No way would she go near him, risk falling under his spell again. She was so screwed.

****

Right on time, Harter and Pryzlo trotted down the steps from the Detective Squad on the second floor.

Detective One Adam Harter had beaten the minimum height requirement by one-quarter inch back when the police department still had a minimum height requirement. Detective Three Jared Pryzlo fought the urge to duck every time he walked through a door. Harter shaved his head once a month to hide spreading baldness. Pryzlo shaved his face twice a day. The book on the two was Harter hadn't looked at another woman since he'd married his wife thirty-four years ago while Pryzlo ogled every woman who crossed his path. But the grapevine said Pryzlo hadn't looked at another one since he got an eyeful of Harter's youngest daughter, twenty-five-year-old Olivia, six months earlier. It also said Harter wished Pryzlo would go back to ogling.

Rick stood as they cleared the stairs. He knew Harter from working a case with him a few years earlier, Pryzlo only by reputation. It was a good one. He shook hands with both men. "Can I buy you guys dinner or a cup of coffee?"

The two men exchanged a glance before Harter said, "I could go for a beer."

Pryzlo nodded. "Works for me."

Rick said, "Got a place you like?"

"The Long Arm around the corner."

Every District had its unofficial cop bar near the house. In the One-Two, it was the Long Arm. They walked there. Harter opened the door and peered in for a second. "Let's go someplace else."

He led them to the White Horse in the next block. After they settled into a back booth with cold Yuengling Lagers in front of them, he said, "So what can we do for you?"

His raised eyebrow and wry tone told Rick he knew this wasn't an 'I just feel like buying you guys a beer' situation. Rick nodded in reply, "You guys caught the Conner shooting, right?"

Harter nodded. "Yep."

"What can you tell me about it?"

Harter studied him for a second. "Heard a rumor she was more than just your partner. That true?"

"Yeah." Rick didn't offer details.

"Figured we'd be hearing from you if it was. We shouldn't be talking to you since you have a personal tie to her."

"But you're going to?"

Harter sipped his beer. "Wouldn't be here if we weren't. Your captain okay with this?"

Rick rocked his hand in a 'maybe yes, maybe no' gesture. "That why you bailed on the Long Arm?"

Harter nodded. "Too many ears in there right now. So what do you want to know?"

Rick tasted his beer. "Everything."

"Patrol officers responding to a shots fired call reported two people down in Apartment 3-C, the DeSchain Building, 1475 Third Street."

"What time was that?"

"Eight-thirty, give or take a minute or two. We rolled right away. Building isn't five minutes from here."

Pryzlo said, "We arrived at the crime scene at twenty-thirty-seven hours. Found a white male, mid-thirties, deceased, on the couch, shot twice in the chest."

Harter said, "Bobby Ed Lukens. Two-bit drug dealer. Deader than my chances of being named Chief of Ds. Conner's on the floor across from him bleeding all over the place with the unis on scene keeping her alive. Garber's giving her CPR, and Rizelli's pressing a bloody towel against her belly like he's trying to push her through the floor."

Rick pictured Mary bleeding, dying. The image chilled him. "So she was alive when you got there?"

Pryzlo answered, "Yeah."

"How long till the EMTs showed up?"

"A minute or two after we got there." Harter took a swig from his bottle then leaned toward Rick. "Then things got hinky."

"How so?"

"Couple minutes later, two IA toads show up. I knew one of them, Flynn, so I asked how IA got word so fast. He said Garber recognized Conner and notified them per SOP, and they happened to be in the area. You ever know IA to just happen to be anywhere but around The Tower?" Police Headquarters.

"No."

"See? Hinky, right? So I ask Flynn if IA's taking over. He tells me no, we're going to work it together. As a team. Says he and Pryzlo will work the scene while Schmidt and I do the building canvas. Since when does IA work anything with regular guys? See how hinky this thing is?"

Rick nodded his agreement. "The canvas turn up anything?"

"One thing I'll get to in a minute." Harter took a long pull of his beer. "I'm done with the canvas on one, waiting for the elevator to take me to two. Doors open on the EMTs with a body bag on the gurney, so I ask if Conner didn't make it. The one takes a second too long before he shakes his head, says she's gone." Harter drained his bottle and signaled a passing waiter for a refill. "They were just making it look like she was dead."

"How could you tell?"

"She died in Lukens' crib, they'd have left her there 'till the ME pronounced her, and Crime Scene did their thing. And one EMT's pushing down on something inside the bag by her shoulder every couple seconds like he's squeezing it. I tell them I'll escort her out to the ambulance. On the way, I cop a feel where the EMTs been pressing. It's soft and squishy, so I start thinking IV bag. Then, once they got her in the bus, the way they took off, Mario Andretti couldn't keep up with them. You don't do that with a stiff."

"You wouldn't think." Rick took a long slug of lager. "So what did the canvas turn up?"

"Nobody I interviewed heard anything. Schmidt got the same thing. Not surprising since the building's like a hundred years old, and they built them to last back then. All the walls are double-course brick. You could fire a howitzer in one unit, and the people next door wouldn't hear it."

"So the shooter made the 9-1-1 call?"

"Be my guess. Only thing I got off the building canvas was a lady on the second floor, Ellen Shires, said she was coming in maybe eight-twenty, and she ran into someone she thought was a cop in the lobby heading out."

"A cop? She give you a description of him?"

"So-so one. Big build, dark hair, moustache, no glasses, PD ball cap, uniform shirt and pants, but no badge, rank, or name tag. Said he was carrying a small gym bag, black. That was the best she could do." The waiter delivered Harter's fresh beer. He tapped his bottle. "Truth is her dinner probably was as much liquid as solid."

"She was drunk?"

"Not tanked. Just real fuzzy around the edges."

"Even so, that description ring any bells with either of you?"

Harter pursed his lips and stared at his beer. "I know a couple it could."

Pryzlo said, "Half my class at the academy fit that description, even some of the women." He smiled at his wit. Harter and Lafferty didn't.

Rick asked, "Anything else hinky?"

"Lots," Pryzlo said. "Working the scene with Flynn, he didn't hide a thing from me." He nodded toward Harter. "It was just like working with him."

Harter said, "Schmidt was the same way. Like we were all on the same team." He slid his bottle aside. "Until we were comparing notes to wrap things up, and I said what I saw with the EMTs. Flynn says I saw it right, she's not dead, but we should write up our reports like she was. Made it an order but wouldn't tell me why." He pointed a thumb at Pryzlo and himself. "Then he says we can't talk about Conner's shooting with anybody but him and Schmidt. Said we did, we'd be Meter Maids in Collegetown ten minutes later."

He took the bottle back and swigged. "If Conner was alive, why would they want our paperwork saying she was dead? And why announce she was dead at morning briefing? Something funny's going on. You got any idea what?"

Rick shook his head. "Wish I did. Thanks for talking to me." He slid to the edge of his seat. "And risking that IA'd find out."

"Figured saying we were interviewing you would cover that," Harter said. "So how about you answer some questions for us now."

Rick settled back in the booth. "Sure."

"You got any idea why Conner was at Lukens's place?"

"Nope."

"Any chance—I gotta ask this, so don't take offense—she had a habit?"

"None taken." Rick shook his head. "And no

chance. You know her son, Sam, OD'd? She just about lost it when he did. No way she'd be using. Why'd you think she might be?"

"There was a busted coke vial on the floor near Lukens. Techs lifted a partial print of Conner's off the one piece big enough to print. Other thing is she had a folded fifty loose in her purse, like she was making a buy. You sure she wasn't using?"

"Stake my life on it. Maybe she posed as a user to get into Bobby Ed's apartment, got the vial, and things went sideways after that."

"Could be." Harter studied Rick over his bottle as he drained it. "Guess that's all we need. You going to keep this meeting under your hat?"

Rick smiled. "What meeting?"

****

Two sharp raps drew Captain DeAngelis' gaze to his office door. Captain John Boyer stuck his head in. "Got a minute?"

Without waiting for an answer, he entered, shut the door, and strode to Dee's desk. Planting both hands on it, he leaned toward Dee. "You want to tell me what's going on with Lafferty?"

Dee rocked back in his chair. "What's he doing?"

"Running all over the city questioning officers."

"About?"

"If they know any officers who might be dirty."

Dee suppressed a smile. Rick *had* picked up on his 'bend rules, don't break them' hint.

"You put him up to it?"

Dee leaned back in his chair. "You know me better than that, John."

Boyer eyed him for a long moment then nodded.

"Yeah, I do. That's why this is hard for me but I have to ask." He dropped into a chair facing Dee's desk and crossed his arms over his chest. "How much did you tell him?"

"Just what we discussed. Nothing more."

"Then why is he out questioning cops?"

"Because he's not stupid. He put it together. Cop as good as Conner goes down, you know she got surprised. The only one who could get the drop on her is another cop, someone she trusted. The only reason a cop would take her out is he's fronting for Joey Day. If you think about it, Lafferty snooping could work to your benefit."

"How do you figure?"

"Cops develop lockjaw the second an IA officer says, 'Good morning.' Lafferty asking them about dirty cops is going to get you more info than a hundred IA officers asking the same questions."

"Not happening." Boyer stood. "Pull Lafferty's plug. Now, Captain."

Dee's office door rattled a good five seconds after Boyer slammed it.

****

McHale pressed the bar straight up from his chest until his arms were at full extension then lowered it to touch his chest and pushed it up again. The guy spotting him helped him set the bar on the uprights. Ten reps at 300 pounds. And he wasn't even breathing hard. Damn good for a forty-eight-year-old. McHale sat up and growled, "Yeah!"

Buddy's Gym was no Planet Fitness or Gold's Gym, wasn't even close. Cheap gray carpet, white painted walls, and harsh fluorescent strip lighting masked the building's former life as a transmission repair shop.

Buddy's had no Stairmasters or Nordic Tracs or exercise bikes. Nothing but lots of bars and plate, exercise benches and squat racks, and a perpetual odor of sweat and testosterone.

The guys who worked out at Buddy's favored sweatshirts with the sleeves ripped off at the shoulder and sweatpants with the legs lopped off mid-thigh. They pumped iron every other day, working one area of their body in the morning, another in the afternoon, a third in the evening, grunting as they forced out one more rep or lifted five more pounds. Their bodies bulged with huge, hard muscle under blue-black tribal tattoos. They had jobs as bouncers and bodyguards and things they didn't talk about, even with their girlfriends.

McHale wiped the sweat from his face and broad chest. He stripped down the bar and returned the plates and bar to the storage racks. He drank three cups of water from the cooler in the corner before moving to the curling bench. A half hour and two exercises later, he lapped twice around the perimeter of the gym to cool down, and headed for the locker room behind Buddy's office.

The envelope on the top shelf of his locker hadn't been there when he'd changed into his workout clothes. He opened it and slowly riffled the money inside. Ten used hundred-dollar bills. A grand for icing Virgin Mary. Joey's standard pay. He still wished he'd banged her before capping her. He closed the envelope and buried it in the bottom of his gym bag then took out a syringe, alcohol swab, and vial. He drew a one cc dose into the syringe and injected it into his thigh. Just enough steroid to help speed recovery from his workout, not enough to turn him into a 'roid freak like some of the guys at

Buddy's. He dropped the syringe and vial in his bag. Then he headed for the showers.

In his car, McHale lit a Marlboro and considered how to spend the evening. Dinner first, that was a given. He was always famished after a workout. A steak maybe. A place on Fairbanks served twenty-four-ounce sirloins. Or maybe a surf and turf. That sounded better. Then a woman. Later.

He had the little matter of Luis Herrera to attend to first.

Chapter 6

Rick had been home less than ten minutes when his phone rang. He answered it, and Dee said, "Meet me outside in five."

Rick's stomach knotted. "Did something happen to Mary?"

"Just meet me outside in five."

Rick really wanted to stay home, heat a can of soup, and put his feet up. But when Dee called, he ran. "Okay."

Dee pulled up in his Crown Vic as Rick trotted down the steps from his apartment house, slid onto the sedan's passenger seat, and pulled the door closed. "What's the latest on Mary?"

Dee rejoined the flow of traffic. "Same as yesterday. Her doc says that's a good sign. If trouble's gonna come, it'll come the first day after surgery."

Rick turned in the seat. "Dee, she's not..." He took in a breath. "Paralyzed or anything, is she?"

"No." Dee glanced his way. "I'd have told you up front yesterday if she was."

"When can I see her?"

"Give it a couple more days. Okay?" Dee slowed to let a car into line. "She keeps going the way she's going, the docs are gonna start unhooking some of the machines they've got her on. Maybe she'll be out of the coma by then, too."

"I gotta see her." Rick heard the plea in his own

81

voice.

"I promise you, soon as it's okay, you will."

That was good enough for Rick. "So what did you want to talk to me about?"

"Couple things. Mary's surgeon said both slugs hit her at a steep upward angle. Entered several inches below her navel, lodged high in her back. One of the lab guys got playing around with her shooting, doing a reenactment of how it could have gone down. He figured out the shots were fired from somewhere around Mary's knees and from only a couple feet away."

"So her shooter was kneeling or squatting close to her when he popped her?"

"Yeah. And the rounds Lukens caught were almost straight-on shots."

"So the angle's wrong for Lukens shooting her from the couch. And for her shooting him while she was kneeling on the floor. So there definitely was somebody else in Lukens' place."

"Yeah. The lab guys matched the rounds that hit Mary to the .32 in Lukens's hand. Got a couple prints off the magazine that aren't Lukens's." He stopped at a red light. "Come back to a Jwakeen Phillips, got a rap sheet for mostly minor stuff—drug dealing, B and E, assault with intent, public drunkenness. Name ring any bells with you?"

"No. He known to run with Lukens or Joey Day?"

"Narcotics doesn't know him, so I'm guessing no. Criminal Intelligence Unit says he's a peripheral in the Monarchs." A hanger-on, an errand boy, expendable.

"He have an alibi for when Mary got shot?"

"Criminal Intel is looking for him. No luck so far." The light changed, and Dee crossed the intersection. He fell silent for the length of the block. "Rick, Mary could be in serious trouble, could lose her job, could maybe even face some jail time. The rounds in Lukens came from her service weapon, and the magazine was two short of a full load."

Rick caught the gravity in Dee's tone. He'd suspected that, he just hadn't wanted to believe it could be true.

"And Lukens's clothes had gunpowder residue and some light stippling, putting her gun only a couple feet away when he got capped. It looks like Mary went there and executed him."

Rick's blood iced. Mary could end up in prison. That could be a death sentence. She could survive getting shot only to get shanked in the slammer.

****

After dinner, McHale headed to a dingy two-room apartment he rented in a tenement on the edge of a bad neighborhood. In a room furnished only with a sleeping bag atop a mattress on the floor, he changed into black shirt and cargo pants, laced up dull black paratrooper boots with crepe soles. He pulled a black watch cap over his hair then slid thin black leather gloves and a can of mace into the leg pockets of the pants.

He locked both deadbolts, marched down two flights of stairs stinking of grease, urine, and mold, and along the trash strewn first floor hall to a back door. From there, he walked a reeking alley to Adams Street and turned right. Two blocks along Adams, he entered the equally vile alley leading to Cherry Street and stopped. After a few seconds wait, he pulled the watch cap's mask down over his face and worked his hands into the gloves. He started slowly down the alley, placing each footstep with care. Halfway to Cherry, he crouched behind a dumpster and studied Luis Herrera.

Luis sat on an upturned milk crate near Cherry. When a car pulled to the curb and flashed its dome light, he strolled over and leaned down. After a brief exchange of words, he returned to the alley, stuffing money into the pocket of his jeans. Deeper in the alley, he retrieved a small packet from a cardboard box between two dumpsters and returned to the car.

It looked like a slow night on Luis's turf. Over ten minutes, he only made only one sale. McHale waited. Fifteen more minutes passed before a white BMW pulled to the curb and the driver flashed his dome light. Herrera talked to the passenger then got two packets from his stash and returned to the car. The passenger snatched the packets from his hand, and the driver took off in a squeal of tires. Luis aimed a kick at the car's shiny flank, missed, and fell on his ass.

McHale smiled inside his mask. Luis's evening was about to get a whole lot worse. Pushing to his feet, Luis stomped into the alley spewing Mexican curses. McHale rose from his crouch, pulled the mace can from his pocket, and stepped toward him.

The spray hit Luis square in the face. He cried out and slapped his hands over his burning eyes. His foul breath almost gagged McHale when he drove a fist hard into Luis's gut. The little man dropped to the paving and sucked in air. He eyed McHale looming over him then slowly got to his feet. "What the fu—"

"You got a little accounting problem, Luis." Up close, Luis had greasy black hair and an acne-ravaged face. McHale popped him one in the chest and sent him sprawling.

Luis jammed a hand into his pocket as he scrambled to his feet, pulled out a pocket pistol. McHale grabbed his wrist with one hand and raised the can of Mace with the other. Luis turned away from the mist, and McHale used his momentum to twist Luis's arm behind his back then slammed him face first into a wall. "Drop it, Luis."

Herrera didn't. McHale bent the arm higher until Luis gasped with pain, then wrenched the gun from his hand and dropped it. He jerked Luis's head back and smashed his face into the wall again. "You were short last Friday, Luis."

"A guy stiffed me, man," he said through broken teeth, blood dripping from his mouth.

"Tough titty." McHale whipped him across the alley.

Herrera hit the wall and fell to his knees. "It's the truth, man."

McHale hauled him to his feet. "You're short. Mr. Day don't like people shorting him. Pay up now."

"I-I don't got it, man. Ain't nobody buyin' t'night." Luis's voice carried the high whine and tremor of fear.

McHale liked that. "Wrong answer, Luis." He slammed Herrera against the wall and hammered two hard punches into his ribs.

Luis groaned in pain. "I-I can have it tomorrow. I will. I promise."

"Too late." McHale drove a fist into Herrera's nose, breaking it.

"*No mas!*"

McHale rammed a rapid flurry of punches into Herrera's body and face, hitting him full strength with every blow, each one bouncing Luis off the wall. The third one to his face dropped Herrera to the paving, out cold. McHale patted his body down for the wad of bills he knew Herrera had, found them, and stuffed them in a pocket of his cargo pants. He took a step away then whirled back and drove a heavy boot once into Herrera's face and once into his side.

He scooped up Luis's pistol and stowed it in another pocket in his pants. A few feet from the Adams Street end of the alley, he pulled out a burner and dialed. "Luis Herrera had a little accident, Mr. Day. He won't be able to work for some time."

"I am sorry to hear that. Does Luis have enough to cover his medical expenses?"

"No, *Jefe*. He was mugged and his money stolen." McHale's pay for roughing up the beaner. "But that's all they took." *Your precious heroin is still there.*

"*Muy bien.* I will see that someone delivers him to the hospital and keeps his equipment safe from thieves. I will also see that word of his plight is passed to his associates. Perhaps they will take up a collection for him." Joey barked a cold laugh and ended the call.

McHale pulled Luis's pistol from his pants pocket. It was a Ruger LCP, a quality weapon that might come in handy in the future.

On his way back to his apartment, an idea popped into McHale's head. He hiked four blocks east and one north to a convenience store. Five punks clustered around the pay phone outside, blocking access. McHale said, "Move."

"Fuck you, ma—"

McHale grabbed the teen by the throat and hoisted him off the ground. He snatched a second punk the same way. The rest split into the darkness. McHale carried the two behind the store and pitched them into a rancid dumpster.

He called District 22 on the far side of the city. Muffling his voice with his hand, he said, "Tell the cops looking into that lady cop getting wasted to look at her husband. He did her."

He hung up fast, wiped down the phone, and walked away.

****

Rick Lafferty entered his apartment and dropped his sport coat on the couch. He grabbed a beer from the fridge, twisted the cap off, and took a swallow. He'd just taken a second one when his phone rang.

"Hi, little brother."

"Hey, big sis. Two calls in two days. What's the occasion?"

"Nothing major. I just wanted to see how you're doing."

"Better since we talked last night. Thanks."

"That's what sisters are for."

"All we did last night was talk about me. I never asked about you. Things still going good with Alan?"

She'd started seeing a childhood friend several months earlier, a year after her dentist husband had dropped dead of a heart attack at forty-two. "Real good."

Her tone said he should let it go at that, shouldn't pry for more. "So how's work?"

"Same old, same old, for the most part. But I started working a special assignment today." She paused for a second. "It's a police woman—shot twice."

Rick's gut clenched. That was too close to Mary. Why would Ann tell him she was treating a patient almost identical to Mary when she knew how torn up he was over her?

No, it couldn't be. What were the odds that of the hundreds of nurses at Northeast Medical Center, his sister would be the one taking care of the woman he loved? Not quite sure he could believe it possible, he asked, "Mary?"

"Unh-hunh."

"How is she? Is she all right? Is she gonna make it? Come on, Ann, tell me."

"I will, Rick, but you have to listen to me a minute first." She sighed. "I'm not supposed to tell anyone I'm taking care of her. I'm only telling you because I know how much you're hurting. You cannot tell a soul what I tell you."

"Lips zipped" He mimed pulling a zipper across his closed lips even though Ann couldn't see it. The oath from their younger days to keep each other's secrets from their parents came easy to him. "Now give. How is she?"

"Doing better than expected for what she's been through. She's healing well and there's no sign of infection. The only negative—and it's not a big one—is she's still in a coma. The body does that sometimes so it can focus all its energy on healing. She's going to recover unless something goes terribly wrong. And at this point, I don't know of anything that could."

Rick let out a sigh of relief then panted for a few seconds. He'd been holding his breath while Ann updated him. "Thanks, sis."

"My pleasure."

"If you get the chance, could you tell her—" What he hadn't told her. "Tell her I love her, and I'll see her soon."

****

She hears the sounds again. This time she can make them out as voices. She can't make sense out of them before blackness swallows her again.

****

McHale took a sip from the glass of Glenlivet in his hand while he sprinkled food in the fish tank. A dozen goldfish thrashed the water in a feeding frenzy. The grand Joey had paid him for smoking Virgin Mary was locked in the safe in his bedroom along with four of the six hundred he'd taken from Luis Herrera. The rest had a new home in his wallet.

He kicked back in his recliner, swallowed more whiskey, and shook his head. The uneasy feeling about killing Conner just wouldn't go away. He lit a cigarette and ran through everything he did one more time just to assure himself he hadn't slipped up anywhere. He hadn't.

Oh shit! The woman he'd passed in the hallway. Not really a slip-up, just one of those things that happen. Her coming in as he was heading out was something he couldn't plan for or control. She was pretty buzzed at the time, so she might not remember him. Still, if she ever put his presence and Conner's shooting together it could be trouble. It was a loose end, and McHale didn't like loose ends.

He had a photographic memory regarding people. The woman in the hall had been five-six or -seven, stick thin, long face with brown eyes, straight nose, and a small thin-lipped mouth. He pegged her age at early fifties, her styled and frosted dark hair saying she was trying hard to hold the line on aging. Her movements had been sudden and jerky, maybe from the booze. McHale suspected she moved that way sober, too, one of those high-strung, uptight broads.

He weighed what to do about her. Nothing? That was the easiest course, but possibly the most dangerous to him. Kill her? Extreme, but safest for him in the long term. A good beating? It might put the fear in her enough to seal her lips for good. First, he needed to know what she remembered. Then he'd know how hard to come down on her.

He'd have to follow her tomorrow, find a place he could brace her in private, find out what she knew. He couldn't do that on duty. He called the District house. "Hey, Jimmy, it's McHale. Do me a favor: leave a message for day tour I won't be in tomorrow. I got some bad grub today, I think at that new gook place on Arch. I've had the trots all afternoon. I thought I was over it, but it just flared up again. Gotta go." He hung up.

He belted down the last swallow of Glenlivet and headed for his bedroom.

****

Rick had just gotten into bed when his phone rang. He grabbed it up on the second ring. "Lafferty."

The voice on the other end said, "Swinton, Orchak, McHale, Rooney."

"Alvarez?"

"Yeah." The line went dead.

****

In the alley between Cherry and Adams, blood seeping from ruptured blood vessels inside Luis Herrera's skull swelled the subdural hematoma pressing on his brain. The rising pressure burst more blood vessels and crushed others flat. Denied the blood it needed, his brain short-circuited, and his body thrashed with convulsions. The convulsions stopped as his brain died. A last breath trickled from his lungs.

Chapter 7

Wednesday – April 22, 2015

Rick Lafferty woke a half hour before his alarm was due to go off, his body stiff from sleeping on the couch all night. He hadn't wanted to go to bed, didn't want to sleep, didn't want dreams of Mary shot and bleeding on Bobby Ed's floor attacking him there. In the wee hours of the new day, sleep had overpowered him and dreams had come. They hadn't been the bad ones he'd expected and dreaded. They'd been replays of happy times with her. He took that as a good omen.

In the shower, Rick rethought his approach to hunting Mary's killer. Yesterday, he'd run around the city like a kid playing Blind Man's Bluff, blundering from here to there with no plan. He needed a better way to search. By the time he stepped out of the shower, he had it.

His cell rang as he was rinsing the last bit of shaving cream off his razor. He sprinted to the bedroom and snatched it off the dresser. "Lafferty."

"It's Harter. You got a couple minutes for Pryzlo and me this morning?"

"Sure. This about Mary?"

"Yeah."

"When and where?"

"Mug and Bagel on Madison as soon as you can

make it."

"Give me twenty minutes."

****

McHale parked his car across the street from Bobby Ed Lukens' building. The light gray Impala sedan—a retired unmarked a friend had refurbished to almost new condition—never garnered a second glace. He settled in the driver's seat to wait, lit a cigarette, and aimed his gaze at the apartment house's front door.

His two-week rotation on day tour would end the day after tomorrow. Then three days off—over a weekend, no less—then back on night tour full-time. No brass around meant he could do things for Joey if the city was quiet. That didn't happen on weekends. Night tour on weekends was a whole 'nother story. Talk about working in a zoo with the animals in charge.

The stick-thin woman he'd encountered in the lobby after icing Virgin scampered down the front steps of the DeSchain building. She wore a dark brown dress under a light tan overcoat, had a purse strap hooked over one shoulder, and carried a thermal lunch tote in the other hand. She trotted toward the parking lot on modest heels, got into a white Honda, and headed south on Fourth. McHale gave her a two-second lead then pulled out behind her.

She drove carefully, sticking to the speed limit, signaling each turn, and stopping on the first sign of yellow. McHale followed her on autopilot, his thoughts on Darcy and things he'd do to her in the three days he had her. The sky was the limit. Darcy was a friggin' sex junkie.

On Twelfth between JFK Boulevard and Vine Street, the woman entered a parking garage and took the sloping ramp to the third level, parking her Honda in the closest stall she could get to the elevator. McHale nosed his car into a slot across the way several cars down from hers. She strode to the elevator on sharp, fast steps. He waited a few seconds then followed her, heading for the stairwell next to it. She glanced his way as he passed her. If she recognized him from the lobby of her building, she didn't show it.

McHale sprinted down the stairs and was waiting on the street, staring at on-coming traffic as if watching for someone, when she stepped out of the garage. He let her get to Vine then tailed her two blocks south on Twelfth and three west on Arch Street to the Franklin Building. He followed her across the plaza surrounding the building to the front doors and got on the same elevator with her. She got off on the eighth floor, hurried down the hall to a glass door lettered Jarmann Financial, and let herself in. McHale glanced through the door as he passed. The woman had dropped her purse and lunch tote on a desk angled to half face the door and was getting settled in behind it.

Back in the lobby, McHale tracked down a security guard. The blubber tub looked one heartbeat away from a stroke. McHale flashed his badge, and asked how many entrances the building had. The guard told him the one on Arch Street and a fire door to the alley. On the way back to the parking garage, McHale dialed a number on his cell. When a sleep-thickened voice answered, he said, "Rynert. McHale. I need you to meet me on the third level of the parking garage between JFK and Vine ASAP."

"Geez, Sarge, I can't. I just got off shift an hour ago, and I'm dead on my feet here."

"Remember that little jam you got in the other day? I did you a favor then, you do me one now. Unless you're tired of being on the job. I hear the Oak Park Mall is looking for a third shift security guard."

Rynert let out a long sigh. "Okay, Sarge. I'll be there."

"That's what I like to hear. Tell you what, I'll even make it worth your while. Say six hundred cash for a couple hours easy work? Cash that won't show up on your W-2. You can buy your wife something real nice with it on your honeymoon."

"That case," Rynert said, his voice brighter, "I'm in. Just gimme some time to get cleaned up and get some coffee in me. What do you want me to do?"

"I'll fill you in when you get here. Third level of the parking garage on Twelfth between JFK and Vine. I'm in a gray Impala."

"Be there in twenty. I'll be driving a red Jeep."

"No rush. Long as you're here by eleven-thirty. And wear soft clothes."

"You got it. And, hey, Sarge? Thanks."

McHale settled in his Impala to wait for Rynert. His thoughts turned to Virgin. The whole damn thing with her stuck in his craw. He didn't like the rush job Joey wanted on her hit. He didn't like the nagging feeling he'd slipped up somehow, had left some clue in Bobby Ed's apartment that pointed right at him. He especially didn't like Harter and Pryzlo catching the case.

He pushed those thoughts away. They returned as fast as he pushed them away. It was like a toothache, nagging him and driving him friggin' nuts.

****

Harter and Pryzlo sat at a table when Rick entered

the coffee shop. Five minutes after placing his order at the counter, tray holding two paper-wrapped bagels and a jumbo coffee in hand, he joined them. Harter nodded a greeting as Rick took a seat. He unwrapped his first egg and sausage on a sesame bagel. "What's up, guys?"

Harter said, "What do you know about Conner's ex, Sam's father?" A half-eaten poppy seed bagel with cream cheese and a drying tea bag rested on the wrapper in front of him.

"Not much. Why are you asking?"

"Tip came in we should take a look at him." Crumbs on Pryzlo's plate said his breakfast had been ham, egg, and cheese muffins. He held a cup of heavily creamed coffee in his hand.

"Anything there?" Rick bit into his sandwich.

"Too early to tell," Harter said. "We just got the tip this morning. So, what can you tell us about him?"

"His name is Dennis Foster. They met at City College her freshman year, had been dating about a year when she got pregnant. They got married soon after that. It lasted five years before she showed him the door."

"You know why?" Harter asked.

"Different priorities, according to Mary. Dennis liked spending money but wasn't keen on earning it. And he was more into spending it on himself than his family. Sam would need food and diapers, Dennis would buy himself a shirt. Or he'd blow half the rent money on a pair of speakers. Mary had to hit her folks up more than once for help keeping a roof over their heads. And Dennis never paid much attention to Sam unless it was convenient for him. Mary took it as long as she could, then booted him out. He shaped up a little bit after that, trying to get her to change her mind and give him another chance, tried again after she filed for divorce—too little too late both times in her book."

"The divorce amicable?"

"I guess you could call it that." Rick shrugged. "Mary said Foster didn't seem to care one way or the other, just didn't want her to leave him."

Harter sipped from his cup of his tea. "She have a hard time with him as far as alimony or visitation rights?"

"Right from the start he was shaky on alimony. Missed a few, weeks late on others, shorted her money sometimes. Always had some lame excuse why. He skipped out on Sam's visitations quite a lot, too."

"That ever get better?"

"After she took him to court. When the judge learned how far in arrears he was, he set some stringent requirements for Dennis, including steady gainful employment and an attachment on his wages for what he owed her. He stayed on top of it after that, but he still bailed on his time with Sam as often as he took him."

"How much was he paying her?" Pryzlo asked.

"She never said." Rick took another bite of his sandwich.

"She never said, or you aren't saying?" Pryzlo's tone demanded an answer.

"She never said. And I never asked. It was none of my business." Rick fixed the young detective with an icy stare while he slowly chewed the bite, swallowed, and drank more coffee. "You got a problem with me, Pryzlo?"

"Yeah. I don't think you're telling us everything you know. And I want to know—"

Harter shot a glare at his partner. "Cool it, Jared."

Pryzlo kept his eyes on Rick. "I want to know why. And I want to know why you're sticking your nose in our case. You an IA puke who thinks we don't know how to do our job?"

"Jared, shut up. Not everybody lies to you, and every cop you don't know isn't IA." Harter sighed. "Sorry, Lafferty. He gets a little carried away sometimes."

"Yeah. We've all been there. Pryzlo, Conner was more to me than just another cop. Way more. You get what I'm saying? You think I'd hold anything back, knowing something I tell you might help you find her shooter?"

The young detective held his stare for a moment, looked away for a second, then looked back. "No. I guess not."

"Then let's move on."

"Good idea," Harter said. "You ever meet Foster?"

Rick nodded. "At Sam's viewing."

"What was your take on him?"

"I didn't think much of him. He didn't seem too broken up over his son's death at the viewing, seemed—" Rick took sip of coffee while he hunted the right way to describe Foster's attitude, "more concerned what people would think of him."

"Any trouble between him and Conner there or at the funeral?"

Rick unwrapped his second bagel. "Before Sam's viewing started, he tried to talk her into them playing the mourning couple reunited by the tragic loss of their son. Mary said no way. So he stood at one end of the casket, playing the grieving father to the hilt, while she stood at the other end being a truly grieving mother."

"That the only incident?"

"Outside the funeral home after Sam's viewing, he was on her again about giving him another chance, going on about how he'd changed, how he still loved her, how his life was the pits without her, how losing Sam made him realize what was important in life."

"How did Conner react?" Pryzlo asked.

"Told him to take a hike."

"What did Foster say to that?"

"Nothing. He just stomped off. I was there, waiting to take Mary home at the time. I think he picked up on me being more than a friend. And he wasn't too happy about that either."

"That the end of it?" Harter asked.

Rick shook his head. "He sang both songs again at Sam's funeral. Mary gave him the same answer."

"He take her brush off any better the second time around?"

"No." Foster's words that night snapped into Rick's mind, and he straightened suddenly. "He said someday she'd regret leaving him."

Pryzlo glanced at Harter. "I think we need to talk to Dennis Foster."

Harter nodded agreement.

Rick said, "I want to be there when you do."

****

Rynert showed up at eleven-twenty in tan slacks, a blue-striped white shirt, and blue blazer. "So, what do I have to do, Sarge?"

"Keep an eye on a woman who works in the Franklin Building on Arch." He described her. "Check out Jarmann Financial on the eighth floor soon as you get over there so you know who I mean. She's on the desk right inside the door, you can't miss her. She comes out, follow her, but don't let her catch you at it."

"Sure thing, Sarge."

"I got some things I gotta do gonna tie me up for a couple hours. Soon as I'm free, I'll relieve you. You know who you're watching?"

Rynert recited the description McHale had given him.

"Good. Any security people at the Franklin hassle you about hanging around, tell them it's an undercover op. They want details, tell them they can talk to me when I get back. You got that?"

Rynert nodded. McHale handed the young cop three of the hundreds he'd taken off Luis Herrera the night before and fired the Impala. "I'll give you the rest when I get back."

McHale got to the corner of Polk and Fifteenth just after noon. At twelve-oh-five, he dialed Joey Day on a new burner and waited through three rings before Joey answered. "*Buenas tardes, mi amigo.* How are you today?"

"Fine. How are you, *Jefe*?"

"I am excellent, as always. You are keeping things safe on the streets of our fair city?"

Great. McHale hated when Joey was in a chatty mood. He wished Joey would just cut to the chase, keep things short and sweet. Less chance of a tap on Joey's phone—McHale was sure somebody had one—leading back to him somehow. "As always."

"That is excellent. It is a sad thing, the crime in our wonderful city. I was informed this morning that a Luis Herrera was found dead in an alley off Cherry, killed in a robbery."

Oh, shit. The little beaner died. McHale ran through beating Luis. He hadn't hit him any harder than he'd hit other guys Joey wanted worked over. He wondered if killing Luis had pissed Joey off, and his blood ran a little cold. A pissed-off Joey Day was an ugly man. With his mouth going suddenly dry on him, he said, "I am sorry to hear that, Jefe."

"As am I." Joey let out an over dramatic sigh. "Sadly, his death will probably never be avenged, his killer never punished."

Relief coursed through McHale. He was safe. Joey had written Luis off as no great loss. He probably had a half-dozen *muchachos* ready to take over Herrera's spot. But there was a warning in Joey's words. If McHale ever turned on him, Joey would throw him to the wolves and write him off as quick and easy as he'd written off Luis.

"But life goes on. I wonder, *mi compadre*, if you might be in the vicinity of the docks this evening?"

"I can be, *Jefe*."

"Around eleven, the authorities might find something…mmm…shall we say interesting going on in the warehouse on Pier 7."

So Joey had been tipped one of his rivals was getting a shipment. McHale wondered who and what the shipment was. Didn't matter. Joey wanted the rival screwed, and McHale would see they got screwed. What Joey wanted, Joey got. "Thank you for the information, Jefe."

"*De nada*. I am always happy to assist the forces of law and order." Joey chuckled a mirthless laugh and hung up.

McHale dropped the burner in the sewer and returned to his cruiser, shaking his head on the way. He had to clear out all the shit about Darcy and Virgin that had been running through his head. He had planning to do. At least Joey had given him an early enough heads-up that he could plan the best way to screw that rival big. Better than the ten-second lead-time he'd given him on whacking Conner.

There he went again, thinking of Virgin. McHale shook his head again. He really had to get her out of his mind. And the best way to get one woman out his mind was banging another. He'd had to skip Heather Bartlett yesterday. But not today. He didn't care if the Commissioner himself had his stones in a crusher. He was taking care of his own stones with Heather.

He called her from a pay phone outside a mini-mart and said he'd be there at one. She said she couldn't wait to see him.

****

Lafferty tapped lightly on Captain DeAngelis's door. "You sent me a forthwith?" An order to report immediately.

Dee waved him in and pointed to the seat facing his desk. "Boyer tells me you've been running around talking to cops. That true?"

He could lie to Dee but he wouldn't. "Yeah."

"After what I said the other night about bending rules and breaking them?"

"I couldn't just sit by, Dee, and do nothing. Not while her shooter's still out there."

Dee eyed him for a moment. "I'd do the same. But since Boyer made a stink about it, you have to back off." He rocked back in his chair. "Reprimand over. Did you turn up anything?"

Lafferty smiled. "Some names twitched my

antenna."

"How many are we talking about?"

"Twenty." Lafferty tore a page from his notebook and passed it to DeAngelis.

Dee leaned back in his chair and rubbed a hand over his short dark hair while he read the list. "You like any of these guys better than others?"

"All about the same."

DeAngelis nodded and scanned the list again. "This many will be tough." He handed the list to Lafferty. "Pick five or six. They don't pan out, we'll go from there."

Rick checked several names then handed the list to Dee.

"Swinton, Orchak, Leroux, Parks, Rooney. I'll pass these on to Boyer, see what he says."

"Thanks, Dee." Lafferty stood. "Any word yet on Jwakeen Phillips?"

"Nada." DeAngelis tossed the list on his desk. "Rick? I need to ask you something. Was Mary clean?"

"Yeah. Why?"

"There was evidence at Lukens's place she was making a buy."

"I heard. Harter and Pryzlo told me about her fingerprint on the coke vial and the fifty in her purse. She was clean, Dee, I'd swear to it on a stack of Bibles. Her idea of getting high was giggling herself silly over a movie. And stoned in her book was two glasses of wine."

"I had to ask."

"I know, Dee."

"Where are you off to?"

Rick gripped the doorknob. "Same as yesterday. Working the streets, talking to cops."

"Be careful. Don't let what happened to Mary cloud your thinking, don't end up like her."

"No way. I'm not gonna be lying on a slab in the morgue while some other suit tells her how we got the guy who shot her. I'm gonna be there to tell her myself."

****

Heather Bartlett stretched languorously in her king-size bed and let out a throaty mewl of satisfaction, the afterglow of great sex still heating her body. She'd be sore and bruised in the morning, but it would be worth it. She'd gone almost a month without a hot, fast humping.

McHale fastened the top button on his shirt and grinned a smirk at her. "You are one great fuck."

"You, too." She wasn't lying. McHale's 'lay down and spread your legs' brand of sex was a refreshing change. She could play her personal trainer's inane seduction games and fulfill her doorman's endless fantasies, but sometimes, she just wanted to screw.

"See you 'round." McHale left her bedroom.

Heather waited until she was sure he'd left the apartment then got out of bed. Crossing to her walk-in closet, she eased the slightly opened door a little wider, reached in, and touched the STOP and REW buttons on the tripod-mounted video camera inside. The doorman had rigged up a switch that started the camera recording when she touched the lamp on the table by the bed.

Heather gathered her scattered clothes and the buttons McHale had popped yanking her Versace blouse open. She'd have to take it to her seamstress for repair. Her silk panties were ripped beyond saving. She tossed them in the trash, the rest of her clothes in the hamper, stepped in the shower, and scrubbed the scents of sex off her body. Her husband's sensitive nose could sniff out a change in the brand of soap she used from across the room. She couldn't let him smell another man on her. It would mean the end of the luxuries his income provided. She wasn't about to lose them.

She slipped into fresh LaPerla underwear and a maroon silk robe. Later, she'd put clean sheets on the bed, dab Edward's favorite perfume on all her sensitive spots, and slip on the tight white Chanel dress that sent his libido into overdrive. Dinner would be late tonight. Very late. Getting it on with one of her lovers always made her hot for him. If he only knew…

In the bedroom, Heather popped the DVD out of the video camera and crossed to the armoire facing the bed. She pulled opened the doors, switched on the player and large screen TV, and slipped the disc into the player. She couldn't remember if this was a fresh disc or an old one. Not that it mattered. She liked reruns as well as instant replays.

She settled on the bed, took the remote from the drawer in the bedside table, and hit PLAY. The empty bedroom filled the TV's screen for a moment until she and Kirk, her trainer, enter the frame.

She strips Kirk naked and pushes him onto his back on the bed. Then she kneels between his spread legs and lowers her head to his crotch. When she has him fully aroused, she stands, opens the maroon robe, climbs onto the bed, and straddles him, moaning as he enters her. Fifteen minutes later, they both lay limp as dishrags and gasping for air. In the next hour of video, he takes her twice more, leaving them both thoroughly spent and satisfied.

The eight-month-old video had Heather panting as furiously in her bed as she was on the disc. She had to admit that Kirk, aside from his silly seduction games, was an incredible lover. And once was just a warm-up for him. Maybe she should shift him to the top of her list of afternoon treats.

As soon as they rose from the bed, she hit FAST FORWARD and cleared thoughts of him from her mind. She didn't want to miss a moment of today's performance with McHale. When the picture changed to black, she hit PLAY. Moments later the picture appeared.

She walks to the bed, McHale behind her, then sheds the maroon robe and turns to face him.

Heather let out a shocked gasp.

McHale shoves her down onto the bed, drops his pants, pushes her legs apart, grabs her hips, and pulls her onto his erection. The bed rocks in time with his fierce thrusts.

She hurled the remote at the TV, screaming, "You bastard! You goddamn bastard!"

McHale was screwing her twenty-one-year-old daughter, Ashlee.

Chapter 8

Captain DeAngelis answered a call from Boyer at a little after two.

"Got your message. What's up?"

"Got some names for you to look at. I may have found some jokers in our deck."

"You or Lafferty?"

"Me." No way would he put Rick on a hot seat. "You want them or not?"

"Give me their names."

DeAngelis figured he'd try for a home run. He read the list Lafferty had given him.

"That's a lot of jokers in one deck."

He'd asked for too much.

"You leaning toward some more than others?"

Dee read the five names Lafferty had checked.

"I'll see what I can do."

****

McHale spotted Rynert sitting on a bench outside the Franklin Building, his nose buried in a paperback, a coffee from a snack shop down the street in his hand. He looked up from the book as McHale approached. "She still in there, kid?"

"Hasn't come out except for lunch. Did that shortly after one." Rynert pointed to a cluster of shaded benches on the left side of the building. "Carried a tote over there and ate. A sandwich, a yogurt or maybe pudding, and a bottle of water. About one-thirty, she packed up everything in the tote, got a large coffee with two creams, two sugars from this place," he raised his own cup, "down the street, and went back inside."

"Security try to roust you?"

"Yeah. I told them what you said to. They said they'd talk to you."

"You did good, kid. Thanks. I'll take it from here." McHale pulled three hundreds from his wallet and handed them to Rynert. "Here you go."

"Thanks, Sarge." Rynert fingered the C notes. "You need more help involving these, I'm your man. But not right away. Okay? I gotta get some rest. I really am dead on my feet."

"I'll keep that in mind, kid." He slapped Rynert's back. *You'll help me even when they aren't involved, no matter how tired you are, whenever I need you. Because I own you, boy.*

Rynert slipped the hundreds into his pants pocket and stood. He nodded toward the Franklin Building. "Why are we watching her, Sarge? What'd she do?"

"Just keeping her safe." He winked. "That's all I can tell you, kid."

"Gotcha." Rynert grabbed his book and coffee and strolled away whistling.

McHale shook his head. Kids. He settled in and started thinking. Maybe he wouldn't have to take the woman out of the game. It depended on how much she remembered about the night he'd whacked Conner.

"Excuse me. Officer?" A blocky guy nudging sixty with short salt-and-pepper hair and wearing a light gray suit strode toward him.

"Yeah?"

The guy stopped by the bench and eyed McHale. "I'm Keefer, head of security. May I see some identification, please, Officer?"

"Technically, it's Sergeant."

Keefer said, "Sorry. Sergeant. May I see some identification, please?"

McHale wanted to tell Keefer to buzz off then thought better of it. The last thing he needed was the guy raising a stink and jamming him up. He pulled his badge wallet from his hip pocket, flipped it open, and held it up. Keefer studied the badge and card identifying Michael Francis McHale as a duly sworn Philadelphia police officer for a moment then said, "Thank you, Sergeant. Something going on with one of our tenants I should know about?"

"Not that I know of."

"Then you mind telling me why you and your associate have been warming that bench all day? And why your associate followed an employee down the block and back?"

"Can't. It's an undercover operation."

"Involving Ellen Shires?"

So that was her name. "I can't reveal who's involved either."

"You are way off base if you think Ms. Shires is involved in anything illegal." Keefer gave a snort of laughter, showing bad teeth. "She'd break out in hives if she tried to cross a street against the light."

"We weren't told if it was somebody working here or an outsider. My partner's young and green and got a little carried away trying to cover all the bases." McHale gave Keefer a men-of-similar-experience look. "You know how that is. They sometimes make honest mistakes from over-enthusiasm. I'll set him straight."

Keefer nodded. "I do. I was on the job out of the Three-Eight, did my twenty, and got out five years ago. Anything else you can tell me about this supposed illegal activity?"

"No. Sorry. Wish I could. Word we got was something was supposed to go down," McHale glanced at his watch, "before now." He shrugged and stood. "Must have been a bum lead. Good. I can call it a day. 'Bout time. Another minute on that bench, and my butt'd be dead."

Keefer laughed again. "They aren't comfortable for a reason. It keeps the vagrants from moving in." His expression changed to serious. "The department usually gives me a heads-up before they plant an officer at my building."

"Sorry. The thing came up kind of fast. Somebody dropped the ball letting you know. I'll see it doesn't happen again."

"Appreciate it. You going to be back here tomorrow?"

"Don't know at this point. Sorry if we upset Ms. Shires in any way. Please apologize to her for us."

Keefer nodded. "She is a bit cranked up. I'll smooth it over for you." Marking the building as his turf.

"Thanks. You seem pretty on the ball, Keefer. Maybe we should have just told you and let your people handle it." He stood. "I could a spent the day at home, getting my ashes hauled by the wife."

"You got the whole rest of the day."

McHale shot him a smile. "I do, indeed."

Walking back to the parking garage on Twelfth, McHale silently cursed. Just his luck the Shires broad worked in a building with an on-his-toes head of security. He shut his anger off after a minute. He could adapt. He hadn't gotten this far in life being rigid. Hell, the only way to get ahead in this world was to be flexible, go with the flow, grab opportunities when they popped up, and bend the rules when you had to.

Walking toward his car, McHale flipped open his cell phone and dialed. When someone answered, he said, "I need an apartment number, Wendell. Ellen Shires, 1475 Third Street."

A moment later, Wendell Osborne said, "Apartment 2D."

McHale settled into the front seat to wait. The Shires broad would come back to her car sooner or later.

****

Joleen entered her apartment and kicked off her shoes, flopped on the sofa and let out a groan. Her feet were killing her. Nate's had been hopping all morning and she hadn't had a chance to sit down all shift. She rested a moment then sat up and massaged the worst of the ache from her feet.

The only good thing about being that busy was the tips. She figured she had about fifty bucks. She dumped the wad of bills she pulled from her uniform pocket on the coffee table, straightened and sorted them. Seventy-eight dollars! She let out a whoop of joy. She had the rent covered. There was a time when she would drop that much on a blouse or a pair of jeans just because she wanted it. Those days seemed like a lifetime ago.

She fished in the pocket again and pulled out the card that cop had given her yesterday. *Richard M. Lafferty.* She'd hoped all morning he'd stop in. He hadn't. If he had, she would have told him about McHale and his hold on her. Maybe Lafferty would throw her in jail on the coke thing. She didn't care. Anything was better than life under McHale's thumb.

She remembered Ramona's other advice on how to rid herself of McHale. *Swing a knife at him, afraid of knives.* She wasn't sure that was the answer. If it was, she wasn't sure she could do it. What if she killed him? Could she live with it? What if she only hurt him? That scared her. He'd kill her for sure then. He'd hurt her bad first then he'd kill her. He'd never come right out and said it, but he'd made it clear if she ever crossed him in any way, he would.

It could be months until Lafferty stopped in Nate's again. Months of servicing McHale any time and way he pleased and always with the final degradation of cleaning him after he'd finished. She didn't know how much longer she could endure it. Joleen's stomach knotted, and fresh tears rose in her eyes.

Ramona's way was all she had. Joleen rose from the couch and walked into the kitchen. She opened a drawer, pulled out all six knives, and laid them on the table. She looked them over and selected the longest one, an eight-inch all-purpose one. She tested the edge. Dull, dull, dull.

In her bedroom, a memory of a spring day spent there stirred in the back of her mind. She and Bryce had never left her bed, had made love half a dozen times with cool breezes washing over them from the open window. Bryce had been her best lover ever. None of the other men she'd slept with had even come close. If only he didn't have that damn coke habit... Why did everything good have to have a bad with it?

She rooted in the closet. Finally, tucked way back in the left corner of the shelf, she found the small rectangular box she wanted. She'd laughed the day her dad had given it to her. What good were a whetstone and light oil to a girl heading off to the big city? You never know, he'd said. She'd been tempted to leave them behind when she'd headed to the city to seek fame and glory. Now she was glad she had them.

She took the stone and oil to the kitchen. Placing a few drops of oil on the stone, she spread them evenly over the surface with her fingertip. Then she drew the knife's blade along the stone and back in slow, smooth strokes, flipping it at the end of each pass.

As a child, she'd always wanted to be with her dad, do what he was doing, learn anything he wanted to teach her. She remembered the feel of his big hands on hers, guiding them as they slid the blade across the stone, honing it. Joy had filled her when she got the 'feel' of holding the knife at just the right angle with just the right pressure to create the perfect edge.

Fifteen minutes later, she tested the blade with her finger. She smiled. Her dad had taught her well.

****

She hears the voices again. They are tinny and warped as if spoken through a can-and-string telephone, and she can't understand the words. The blackness enfolds her.

****

McHale got out of his car, stretched, and checked his watch. Five-oh-eight. How long did the Shires broad work? He hoped to God she wasn't meeting friends for dinner or spending the evening shopping. He took a slow amble along the row of cars to work the kinks from his spine then got back in the Impala.

She showed fifteen minutes later. Her heels popped

the concrete like the crack of a kid's cap gun as she strode to her Honda. McHale waited until she'd backed out of her stall to start his car and until she'd gone around the corner toward the exit ramp before following her.

Shires took the same route home she'd driven that morning with a stop a few blocks from her apartment. She entered a market, came out after ten minutes with a not very full bag in her hand, and hit the State Store two doors down. She returned to her car a few minutes later carrying a tall paper bag McHale guessed held a bottle of wine. Depositing her purchases on the passenger seat, she started the Honda and drove away.

McHale let two cars pass before he pulled into traffic behind her. He nosed his Impala to the curb by a fire hydrant as Shires hit her signal to turn into the DeSchain Building's lot. A minute later, she scurried around the corner of the building, up the front steps, and inside.

McHale let another minute tick by. He reviewed the plan he'd developed outside the Franklin building, weighing it. A new plan formed in his mind. Yeah, that would work even better, would solve the problem of the Shires broad once and for all.

He popped the Impala's trunk lid, opened a black gym bag, and took out a tie and dark blue blazer. He worked the tie under his collar and tied it then shook the wrinkles out of the blazer and slipped it on, draping it to hide the 9mm Glock clipped to his belt on his left side. Opening a small locked case, he eyed several leather folders holding fake badges and IDs before selecting one identifying him as an agent of the Federal Security Administration. It didn't exist. Tucking the folder into an inside jacket pocket, McHale headed for the DeSchain

Building.

He entered the vestibule a step behind a thin guy carrying a briefcase. The guy fished a set of keys from the pocket of his dark suit, unlocked the inner door, and stepped into the lobby. McHale caught the door before it latched. The man headed for an elevator. McHale strode across the lobby toward the back of the building and the fire stairs.

He exited onto the second floor and strode to Apartment 2D. He knocked. A moment later, the Shires broad opened the door a crack. "Yes?"

"Ellen Shires? Agent Brewster. Federal Security Agency." McHale flashed the phony ID. "May I come in and speak to you for a moment, please?"

"Ye-yes. Of course."

****

Rick Lafferty unlocked the door to his apartment and stepped inside. He'd prowled the east side of the city after leaving Dee's office, talking to every cop he spotted—scores of them. He'd asked the same questions until it had gotten to the point where he didn't have to think to ask them. They came from his mouth automatically, like words on tape. He chuckled softly. Maybe he should have put them on tape. It would have saved a lot of wear and tear on his vocal cords.

He didn't have much to show for his time and effort. A couple names crossed off his list of possibly dirty cops was all. Still, it was more than he had that morning.

He grabbed a beer from the fridge, twisted the cap off, and took a big swallow. The day had been warmer than usual for this time of year, leaving him hot and parched. The cold brew on the back of his throat was heaven.

His phone rang. He strolled into the living room and answered. Dee said, "You have your TV on?"

"Nope. Just got in."

"Turn it on." Dee's voice crackled with anger. "Channel Eleven. Five-thirty news."

Rick snatched the remote from the table by his chair and jabbed the button. The weatherman, a beefy guy with impossibly black hair, was talking about warm fronts. "What am I looking for, Dee?"

"Keep watching. You'll see," Dee snapped. "Call me back when you do."

Rick dropped into the chair. He'd never heard Dee so irritated. Whatever Dee wanted him to see was major serious. Rick raised the beer bottle to his lips and noticed his hand was shaking. A knot formed in his gut, and the beer soured in his stomach. Only one thing could have Dee that upset. Mary.

He set the unfinished beer on the end table, sat forward in his chair and focused on the TV. Time seemed to crawl. After the sports and a pair of commercials, anchorwoman Lisa Cortez appeared. Glistening black hair, golden-brown eyes, brilliant white teeth, slightly dusky skin, she was hot enough to capture the male audience's attention, but not so hot, she'd be dismissed as just a pretty face.

In a serious yet seductive contralto voice, Cortez said, "Recapping our lead story, Action News has learned that Detective Mary Conner, the police officer shot two days ago, did not die as first reported. A source close to the investigation into her shooting says Detective Conner is currently being treated for life-threatening injuries at an undisclosed location outside the city. WCBL will continue to cover this breaking story. Be sure to tune in to Action News at eleven for a complete update."

"Shit!" Rick reached for the phone. As he touched it, it rang.

"You see it?" Dee snapped.

"Yeah. Dee, what the hell happ—"

"Did you give that out?" Dee's voice said he was out for blood, and the spilling would be copious. God himself couldn't save the cop who blabbed about Mary to the media.

Rick snapped back, "No way would I do that."

Seconds of silence before Dee blew out a heavy sigh. "Sorry, Rick. I know you wouldn't." He sighed again. "We need to get to the bottom of this. How quick can you be down here?"

"Ten minutes. Fifteen max."

"Make it ten."

Rick raced out of his apartment.

Chapter 9

"Who all knew Mary survived?" Lafferty asked.

They were in Dee's office. Harter and Pryzlo were there, along with Flynn and Schmidt from IA, when Lafferty walked in. The IA men had, as usual, grabbed the only two chairs in DeAngelis' office. The detectives leaned against the wall. Dee sat behind his desk.

"Us." Dee drew a circle in the air, indicating the six men in his office. "Garber and Rizelli, the first officers who responded to the 9-1-1 call. The EMTs who transported her. The ER staff at Jefferson. The LifeFlight crew."

"Christ!" Rick snapped, "That's half the friggin' city!"

"More like twenty-five, thirty people, max," Harter said. "And we can narrow it down to less than that. WCBL said their info came from inside the department. So we can rule out the EMTs, ER, and LifeFlight people."

"No, we can't," Flynn, a lean, dapper, graying man in a navy suit, said. "'A source close to the investigation' is a bullshit line to hide where they really got the info. Anyone who had any contact with Conner that night could have blabbed to the press."

Harter shook his head. "We can cross off the EMTs at least. They took her to Jefferson, that's all. They won't know what happened to her after that."

"They could have heard from the ER people and passed it on." Flynn slashed the air with a finger. "Nobody gets a free pass on this. They all get a visit."

"Hold on a second." Dee raised his hand. "I think Harter's right. We can put the EMTs at the bottom of the list. They're the least likely to know Conner's still alive. If we come up dry with the others, we'll go after them."

"Makes sense," Flynn said. "Let's divvy up the rest and go at them. Who gets what?"

"Harter, Pryzlo, you take the LifeFlight people," Dee said. "Lafferty and I will take Garber and Rizelli."

"We'll take them." Schmidt pointed to Flynn and himself. He was a stocky guy in his thirties wearing a subdued green-and-gray plaid sport coat and gray slacks. He had cold eyes. "They endangered a fellow officer and that's our turf."

"We don't know that they did. You two brace them and, innocent or not, they'll figure they're in hot water for something and clam up. Lafferty and I will talk to them. You and Flynn take the ER people."

"No way. We're taking—"

Flynn cut him off with a wave. "We'll take the ER staff."

"They work on a team basis at Jefferson," Dee said, "and the team that treated Conner is on duty tonight. That goes for the LifeFlight crews, too, Harter, Pryzlo. Everybody know what they're doing?"

The five men nodded.

"One last thing," Flynn said. "Let's not go off half-cocked here, thinking this was done with malicious intent or for personal gain. For now, let's work from the premise this leak was just a slip of the tongue, a simple mistake. It turns out any other way, we'll come down on them hard. Any questions?"

"I have one," Lafferty said. He eyed Flynn and Schmidt. "I want to know how you guys got on her shooting so fast."

Flynn glanced at Dee and got a nod in return. He took in a deep breath. "We heard chatter that Conner took her son's death hard. Made us think she might go off the deep end, so we've been kind of keeping tabs on her. Not a close watch, just any time her name comes up, even if it's only for a parking ticket, we get called. When we heard her name and Lukens's in the same breath, we thought maybe she'd gone vigilante."

DeAngelis said, "Tell him the rest of it."

Flynn thought for a second. "This does not, I repeat not, leave this office. Narcotics Strike Force has a mole in Joey Day's outfit. He's learned Joey has some cops in his pocket, but hasn't been able to pick up any names, only that one is Joey's main enforcer, does all his hits. Our guy heard Joey order Conner taken out, but not who he sent to do it. He got word out to Strike Force, they passed it on to us. We were rolling on it before Rizelli and Garber called it in."

"For all the good it did her," Lafferty said.

Flynn lowered his head at the rebuke and nodded. "We got there too late to prevent it. But her being alive works to our benefit."

"How so?" Lafferty demanded.

"Our mole thinks Joey sent his go-to guy to put the whack on Conner. Whoever he sent, she can ID him. We get him, we got a starting point to clean house of cops in Joey's pocket. And maybe bring Joey down in the process."

"Where does Ma—Detective Conner stand in

relation to Lukens?"

"We aren't gonna jam her up over icing him, if that's what you're worried about. Far as we're concerned, Lukens getting taken off the board is no great loss. If push comes to shove on her dropping him, we'll make it a righteous shoot."

Lafferty gave each of the IA officers a hard gaze. "I have your word on that?"

Schmidt glowered. "You saying we're lying?"

"I'm saying I don't trust you."

Dee said, "I have their word on it, Rick. Any other questions?"

All five men shook their heads.

"Let's roll, then." Dee stood. "Rick, a word?" He waited until the others had vacated his office. "You're sitting this one out. You can observe, but that's all."

"Dee—"

"Boyer's orders."

****

"Ma'am, did you notice any unusual activity in your building the day before yesterday?" McHale had already run through the general crap—name, age, occupation, how long at this address, and the rest—with Ellen Shires.

"There was a lot of noise late in the evening, starting around a quarter to nine or so." She took a hefty sip of the red wine in her glass. "It lasted a half hour or so."

"Do you know what was going on?"

"Not until a police detective knocked on my door and told me two people had been shot on the third floor and asked if I'd seen or heard anything earlier in the evening."

"Had you?"

"I hadn't. I'd been out with a friend." She took

another slug from the glass. "We'd made plans to see a play downtown, but I had a bit too much to drink with dinner and started feeling woozy so I came home. I'd been here about an hour when the detective knocked on my door."

"And about what time did you get home?"

"I didn't look at my watch, but I would say around eight-thirty."

"Do you remember if the detective asked you if you saw anyone leaving the building around that time?"

"Who did you say you were with again?"

"Agent Baxter of the Federal Security Agency."

"I've never heard of it."

"We're new and very hush-hush. Did the detective ask you if you saw anyone leave the building around the time you arrived home?"

Another swallow of wine before she answered. "He did."

"You're sure of that?"

"Yes, positive. I had pretty much shaken off the light-headedness by the time he knocked on my door. And he asked me a lot of questions before he got to that one. By then, I was quite clear-headed."

"What did you tell him?"

"That I did see someone, and I described him to the detective as best I could. I couldn't give him much. I was really feeling very out of it when I passed him in the hall."

McHale pulled up an encouraging smile. "I'm sure you can do better for me."

Shires offered a shy, pleased smile in return. "Let me see if I can remember exactly." Her brow furrowed in thought, and she'd almost drained her glass before she said, "He was a policeman in uniform. And he had on like a baseball cap, with the police—what do you call it?—shield, on the front."

"I believe the proper term is patch, Ma'am."

"Patch, then. And please, call me Ellen, Agent Brewster."

"Okay. Do you remember his name, Ellen? He would have had a badge on his shirt here." He placed his hand over his heart, and hoped like hell she didn't remember.

Another second of furrowed-brow thinking. "No, I'm sorry, I don't."

She'd just saved her own life. "What else can you tell me about him?"

"He was I would guess in his forties and tall. Could you stand up, please?"

McHale looked at her, puzzled, then rose. Shires stood, too, and looked him over top to bottom. "I'd say he was about as tall as you."

She motioned for him to sit. "He had a husky build similar to yours, too. I didn't really notice his hair under his cap but his eyes were gray."

Or maybe not. "Anything else you remember about him?"

"Shouldn't you be writing all this down?"

McHale forced out a self-effacing smile. "I have a very good memory, Ma—Ellen."

"I wish I did. I have to write notes to myself on everything." She tipped the last swallow of wine down her throat, rose, and waved her glass at him. "I could use a refill. Are you sure you wouldn't like some?"

"I would, but I can't. I'm on duty."

She sauntered toward the kitchen, putting a swing in

her hips and glancing over her shoulder at him on the way. She wasn't a bad looking broad up close, not bad at all for forty-six. And something about her said it wouldn't take much to get her in the sack.

He'd pass. McHale liked his women young. Thirty-five was his upper limit—with a few exceptions. Heather Bartlett was one. Partly because she was an ADA's wife. And because she was still prime at forty-three. Hell, she looked thirty and screwed like she was twenty. Virgin was prime, too. He'd have waived his age requirement for her.

Ellen Shires strolled the living room on the same walk that carried her out. She took a big sip of wine as she sat and tossed him a coy smile. "Now, where was I?"

"Describing the man you saw leaving the building as you came in."

"Oh, yes." Another sip. "Let's see. Eyes, height, build, hair, clothes. I covered all that, didn't I?"

"Yes, ma'am."

"Did I tell you he had good coloring?"

"Coloring?"

"Yes, coloring. He had a nice tan as if he spent a fair bit of time, but not too much, outdoors. He wasn't dark leathery brown like a construction worker nor pasty-toned as if he spent all his time indoors."

"Anything else you can tell me about him?"

"Let me think." Several more sips of wine seemed to help. "Yes. He had on boxy black shoes with thick soles. My father used to call them Brogans. And he—the man, not my father—carried a black bag like a gym bag, too."

McHale faked a thoughtful expression for a bit. "Okay, I think that's everything, Ellen." He stood.

"Thank you for your time. You've helped me a great deal."

"It was my pleasure. Can you tell me what happened the other night, who was murdered? Someone said one of the people shot was a police officer."

"I wish I could, Ellen, but I can't. As you've probably guessed by the agency I work for, it's a national security matter. Speaking of which, I must ask you not to talk to the local police again about the murder. We've taken over the investigation. If the police approach you, refer them to my agency." He took a card as phony as his ID out of the holder and laid it on the coffee table. "There's our number." He took a step toward the door.

"Um…Agent Brewster, have you had dinner yet?" She gave him a doe-eyed look. "I'm not making anything fancy, just a hamburger for myself. I have plenty. It's no trouble to whip up a couple for you, too. I turn out a pretty mean hamburger, if I do say so myself."

"I appreciate the offer, Ellen, and I'm tempted, but I can't. I have a few more stops to make before I quit for the day. I'll grab something later."

McHale left her apartment and trotted down the stairs. Damn. The Shires broad, tanked as she was the night he'd snuffed Conner, had described him to a T. And she'd been too buzzed tonight to realize it or remember his name. Thank God for small favors.

In his Impala, he took a fresh burner from his Go Bag and dialed. When someone answered, he said, "Let me talk to the boss."

Seconds later, Jose Diaz said, "What is on your mind, my friend?"

"I crossed paths with a friend after making that repair Sunday night." Burner phones were supposed to be untraceable, but McHale didn't want to risk it.

"Do not speak in riddles, my friend." Evidently Joey didn't care if the cops or the feds had a tap on his phones

"We have a minor problem. A woman saw me leaving the building after I did the repair."

"That is unfortunate, my friend." Joey's voice was colder than dry ice.

No shit, greaseball. Time for a little brown-nosing. "I know, and I'm sorry, *Jefe*. But it couldn't be helped. It's one of those things you can't control. Had I tried to avoid her, she would have known something was wrong."

Joey drummed his fingers on some hard surface. It sounded on McHale's cell like four-round bursts of gunfire. "That is true. It was the best course of action at the time."

"There's more. I just talked to her and learned she gave the detectives a pretty accurate description of me. But she didn't connect me with the guy she saw."

"That is indeed good." A moment's silence. "However, that does not mean she will not make the connection at some point in the future. We need to see she does not." Another silence. "You are with her now?"

"Just left her a few minutes ago."

"Why did you not insure right then she would never remember?"

"Because, *Jefe*, she lives in the same building. Three murders in the same building in two days gets cops riled up, and they start looking at things harder than they usually do. We don't need that."

"That is true. How do you suggest we ensure her continued lack of memory, my friend?"

McHale let out a breath. Joey was unhappy, but not

with him. If Joey was asking his opinion, he didn't plan on fixing the problem by eliminating McHale. "Perhaps a mugging would be the way to go."

Another brief bout of silence followed by a sarcastic laugh. "That would be unfortunate, would it not?"

"It would, *Jefe*."

"Tell me what you can about this woman, my friend."

He described Ellen Shires. "She works in the Franklin Building on Arch, a place called Jarmann Financial on the eighth floor. She drives a white Honda and parks in a garage on Twelfth between JFK and Vine. She got there today a little before eight and left around five-ten. Both times, there weren't any people around. That might be the best time and place to do it."

"Yes, I believe it is. Perhaps her mugger will go too far and she will die, and he will steal her pretty little Honda. That would be too bad, would it not?"

"It would indeed, *Jefe*. And it would be a bad idea."

"Why is that, my friend?"

"For the same reason silencing her right now is one."

"*Si*. That is true. We have, however," Joey's voice chilled again. "a more distressing problem, my friend, relating to this matter."

McHale stiffened in his seat as if he'd just been buried in ice. His hand clamped the cell white-knuckled tight. "What problem?"

"It appears the repair I asked you to make Sunday night did not correct the problem completely."

One minute Joey's telling him don't speak in code, a minute later he's doing it himself. *Jesus, Joey, make up your frigging mind.* "What are you saying, *Jefe*?"

"The bitch is not dead!" Joey shouted. "They are saying on the news she did not die. They are saying she was taken somewhere and is being treated."

McHale swallowed dryly. That couldn't be. Absolutely could not be. Conner had been bleeding all over Bobby Ed's white carpet and sucking her last breaths when he left. She had to be dead. "The problem was fixed, *Jefe*. She was two seconds from checking out when I left."

Joey's voice returned to calm. "Now just who am I to believe, my friend? You or Lisa Cortez on the news? You are not of my blood. She is. She would not lie to me."

Joey Day had a big-as-a-whale blind spot when it came to Lisa Cortez. If Lisa reported Joey had been shot in the heart, he'd clutch his chest and fall over dead. "Are you sure she's not just reporting a rumor, *Jefe*?"

"I have confirmed it with others."

Oh, shit! He'd dropped the ball big time. Last night, he'd killed the guy he shouldn't have, two days ago he hadn't killed the woman he should have. "But, *Jefe*—"

"I do not want buts. I want her dead," Joey screamed. "Dead! Do you understand? Dead! That *puta* must pay for what she did to my brother."

Brother, my ass, McHale thought, you'd sell Bobby Ed out in an eye-blink to save your own hide, Joey. Time to do a little ass kissing. "Yes, *Jefe*, I understand."

"Do you?" Diaz inhaled deeply and let the breath out slow as if the burden was almost too heavy to bear. "It is a matter of honor. She has insulted my family by killing my brother. That insult must be avenged."

You want your friggin' family honor avenged, do it yourself. Yeah, like that would ever happen. Joey didn't do jack shit himself, probably even had someone wipe his ass for him. Any avenging of honor to be done would be done by someone else. And if McHale wanted to keep on breathing, he'd be the someone doing it. "I'll take care of it, *Jefe*, I promise."

"Yes, you will, my friend." The cold tone returned. "Do not fail me this time."

****

Rick listened from Observation while Dee questioned officers Garber and Rizelli in District Seven's interrogation room or pit. They'd just taken the corner onto Third when they'd taken a call about shots fired, the address a block away. They'd found Mary alive and done everything they could to keep her that way until the EMTs took over. They swore up and down, on a stack of Bibles, and every other way possible they hadn't said a word to anyone about Mary Conner being alive. They had both assumed she died when they saw EMTs wheeling the body bag out of Lukens's place, had stared flat-out floored when Dee told them she was still among the breathing.

After an hour, Dee let the two officers go then joined Rick in the observation room. "What's your read on them?"

"They're not the leak."

"I agree."

The door opened, and Harter stepped in. "Got someone you're gonna want to talk to." He pointed through the one-way mirror. Pryzlo led a fair-skinned man in a dark blue jumpsuit decorated with multiple patches into the pit.

Dee asked, "Who's that."

"Carl Yonick, LifeFlight nurse."

"What's his story?"

"Get to it in a minute." Harter pulled a notebook from an inner pocket of his suit jacket and flipped it open. "Four people on each LifeFlight crew. The one that flew Conner out was Dave Bridge, pilot, Melissa Cole, co-pilot, Yonick and Brenda Young, Registered Nurses. Bad news is they knew Mary was on the job. Word got passed from EMTs to ER to OR to Post-op to the flight crew."

"Is there any good news?" Dee asked sourly.

"Flight crews never talk to the media about anything ever because of HIPAA rules—they apply to everyone on staff, and it's worth their jobs to break them—and they maintain they didn't do any different with Conner. It rang true."

Dee nodded toward the interrogation room. "So why's Yonick here?"

Harter put on a 'people never cease to amaze me' expression. "You gotta hear it for yourself." He pointed to the 'pit' again. "He's all yours. Pryzlo and I are heading back to St Luke to help Flynn and Schmidt question the ER staff."

Harter left the observation room. When Dee didn't follow him, Rick asked, "You going to find out what the guy has to say?"

"In a minute." When that much time had elapsed, Dee pushed off the wall he'd been leaning against. "Ready?"

"For what?"

"To talk to Yonick."

"But Boyer said—"

Dee shot him a grin. "What Boyer doesn't know won't hurt him."

They entered the interrogation room. Rick closed closing the door and leaned against it while Dee took a seat facing Carl Yonick. Patch pockets on the arms and chest of his jumpsuit bulged with pens, pencils, notebooks, a small flashlight, and stuff Lafferty couldn't identify. Neither he nor Dee said a word.

Yonick's gaze darted from one to the other for several moments. He licked his lips. "Am I in some kind of trouble here?"

"That depends," Dee said, "on what you did."

"Nothing. I swear."

"Those other two detectives didn't haul you down here for a tour of the building. They had a reason. Let's hear it."

Yonick stared at the table and worked his jaw for several seconds. "First, you gotta promise me what I tell you won't get back to Jefferson. I need the job."

"I can't promise anything until I know what you're talking about."

Carl ran his tongue over his lips. "I've been, uh, seeing this woman who works at WCBL. She's a researcher there. The morning after we flew that cop out, I met her for breakfast before she went to work, and she asked me if anything interesting happened on my shift, and I told her we took a gunshot victim to NEMC."

A black rage rose in Rick. He lunged across the room and yanked Carl out of the chair. It tipped over and hit the floor with a bang. Rick shoved Carl against the wall hard. "You stupid son-of-a-bitch! Why didn't you just take out a full-page ad in the *Inquirer* and tell the whole damn world you flew a cop out?"

Carl stared at Rick wide-eyed with fear and swallowed hard. "I-I di-didn't tell her we flew out a cop.

I s-swear I didn't. I just sa-said we transported a gunshot victim to NEMC. She must have put it together with that cop getting shot on her own."

Rick jabbed his finger into Carl's chest. "It still came from you to start. You put a cop in a killer's crosshairs. She dies, I'm coming after you."

"Rick," Dee said softly. "Back off."

Rick jabbed the finger into Carl's chest again. "I will hunt you down. There isn't a place you can go, I won't find you." And again. "You got that?"

Carl nodded, never taking his frightened eyes off Rick.

"Rick. Back off," Dee repeated louder.

Lafferty jabbed Yonick one last time. "You got that?"

"Yeah! Yeah! I got it! I got it!"

"Lafferty!" Dee grabbed his shoulder. "Back off. Now!"

The menace in Dee's voice penetrated Rick's anger. He released Yonick and stepped back. Turning away from the nurse, he took in and let out a deep breath and raked his fingers through his hair.

Carl muttered, "Asshole," as he pushed away from the wall and strode to the door.

Dee blocked his path. "Sit down! We're not done."

Carl stopped and glanced back, his eyes wary.

Dee pointed to the chair. "Sit!"

Carl sat and flicked a jittery glance at Rick.

"Step out, Rick."

He hurried into Observation.

Dee glared at Yonick for several seconds. "You're worried about losing your job over telling your sweetie you flew a cop out? You've got bigger things to worry about. You put an officer's life in danger. If anything happens to that officer, we can charge you with aiding and abetting and conspiracy to commit murder for starters. And we can come up with more on top of that. You're looking at many years —maybe life—in prison. You want that?"

Carl swallowed hard again and shook his head. "No. No way."

"Then you better get in front of this now and help us out here."

Carl wiped his hands hard down the legs of his jump suit. "I swear I didn't tell her it was a cop. All I said was we took a gunshot victim to NEMC. I didn't say anything that gave away her being a cop. I didn't even know for sure she was, had only heard rumors."

"We find out different, you are in a world of trouble. You understand that?"

"Yeah. Yeah. I swear on my mother's grave that's all I told her."

"What's your girlfriend's name?"

"Cor-Corinne. Corinne James."

"And she works at WCBL?"

"Yeah. Only she's not there now. She works days." The words tumbled out of Carl's mouth. "She's at home. Foxcroft Terrace, apartment 12H."

"Okay. If you think of anything more you might have told her—or even think you *might* have told her— you let us know as soon as you think it. You got that?"

Carl swallowed and nodded. "Yeah, yeah, sure. Ca-can I go now?"

"Yeah. Get out of here."

Yonick bolted from the room. Moments later, Dee entered Observation. "You go off on someone we're questioning like that again, and you're off that case that second. That clear?"

Rick nodded. "I'm sorry, Dee. It's just…I lost it for a second."

"And left yourself wide open for a brutality charge. You realize that?"

"Yeah."

"Don't lose it again. And next time I tell you to back off, stand down at once. Don't make me repeat it, or you're on suspension."

Rick nodded again.

"This case is tough on all of us. You more than anyone else, but you can't let it get to you. You're not doing Mary—or yourself—any good if you do. I'm cutting you more slack than I should, but you need to pull yourself together, Rick, and keep it together until we solve this."

"I know." Rick ran a hand through his hair again. "I will. I promise."

"You'd better. Once we wrap this thing up, you want time off to be with Mary, I'll okay as much as you want."

"Thanks, Dee." He stared at the fluorescent lights in the ceiling and cycled through a deep breath. "I think about her all the time. I wonder how she's doing. And I worry something will go wrong, and she'll die."

"I told you she's doing fine. She's got a long road ahead of her, but she's getting better. She's not going to die."

"I keep thinking somebody will get to her and…and kill her."

"We aren't going to let that happen."

Chapter 10

Mike McHale eased his Impala to a stop in an alleyway between two warehouses a block away from Pier 7. His watch read 10:55 p.m. The shit would hit the fan in twenty minutes or so.

Cops never busted a drug deal at the get-go. They waited until the action was up and cranking good before hitting it. Drug deals never started on time anyway. The principal dickheads spent the first ten minutes strutting and posturing attitude at each other before getting down to business.

So figure twenty minutes, a half hour before the boys in blue blew the doors off this one. McHale settled in to wait. He shook a Marlboro from the pack, lit it, and took a deep drag.

The heavy thump of a gonzo car stereo beat his ears seconds before a light blue Ford Explorer rolled past the alley. McHale slid out of the Crown Vic and walked to the street.

The SUV cruised the block, U-turned at the corner, and stopped in front of Pier 7. Four punks got out. A wave of pounding heavy metal music blasted out with them. Two punks took up flanking positions on the big roll-up door of the Pier 7 warehouse. The other two entered it through a door next to the roll-up.

McHale stepped back into the alley's shadows as another vehicle entered the street a block away. A gleaming black Ford Expedition and a graffiti-splattered cargo van, blue smoke puffing from the tailpipe, passed the alley. McHale stepped forward again.

The Expedition pulled to the curb. Two men and another blast of heavy metal got out. The big door in the Pier 7 warehouse clanked open, the van and Explorer rolled inside, and the door rattled down behind them. The Fords gave it away. These were Donny 'Deuce' Doucette's boys. So that's who Joey wanted taken down.

Headlights washed the street from the opposite direction. A gray Mercedes Benz sedan, a battered tan Chevy van, and a white Mercedes SUV approached Pier 7 and slowed. The two Benzes stopped close to the warehouse, and the van backed up to the big door. Four black men got out of the gray Mercedes along with a thundering wave of rap. The driver of the white Mercedes trotted around the car and opened the back door. A lanky black man got out. Roosevelt Ames.

McHale smiled. Oh, this was rich! Joey Day had scored a major coup. Rosie Ames and Deuce Doucette— his two main rivals—taken down in one shot.

The big warehouse door cranked up, and the van backed in. Two of Rosie's men joined Deuce's men by the door. Everyone else followed the van into the warehouse.

McHale glanced at his watch. 11:10 p.m. Showtime soon.

Five minutes passed. The only sign of life on the street was the four men guarding the door on Pier 7. McHale wondered if he'd misunderstood Joey about where the buy was going down. It was that damn accent of his. Joey laid it on so friggin' heavy sometimes, McHale couldn't understand his own name when Joey said it. He wished Joey'd cut that crap out. It led to mistakes, the kind that got people killed.

A Dodge van crept down the street at a hesitant pace as if the driver was lost. It slowed to a stop in front of Pier 7. The guards on the roll-up door took a step toward the Dodge, reaching for guns under their jackets. Before they could draw them, they jerked then collapsed into twitching heaps on the street. Tasered. Black-clad men bolted from the van, grabbed the fallen guards, and heaved them inside. The van pulled away as the side door slid shut.

Police vehicles rolled quietly toward Pier 7 from every direction. They stopped in an arc facing the warehouse. A SWAT team bailed out of another black van and hit the warehouse like a pack of feral dogs. Muted shouts came from inside the building. Muffled cracks followed. Short bursts from automatic weapons.

McHale had been on dozens of these raids. Inside the warehouse, cops and gangsters would take cover behind whatever they could find, pop up to fire a few rounds, duck down to avoid return fire.

An hour later, it was all over. Rosie Ames, Deuce Doucette and their men were marched out to a waiting paddy wagon. Seven men came out on stretchers. Three went into ambulances, the other four a morgue van.

McHale got in his car and backed down the alley to a cross street. Five blocks away, he dialed a fresh burner.

"*Mi amigo!*" Joey answered. "You have good news for me?"

"Rosie and Deuce and a dozen of their people just had a very bad night."

"I am sorry to hear that." Joey's voice didn't hold an ounce of sorrow. "Perhaps I should send them a sympathy card. No?" He laughed his mirthless laugh.

McHale laughed along. When both stopped, he let a few silent seconds lapse. "May I make a suggestion regarding the problem we discussed earlier, *Jefe*?"

"Of course, *mi hermano*! I am always ready to hear your counsel."

McHale took in a deep breath and let it out slow. He was on thin ice here. "I think we need to go slow on fixing it."

"No! I want it solved at once!"

"Hear me out, *Jefe*."

Silence. McHale's heart raced. People had died for suggesting things Joey didn't like.

"I will listen." Delivered in a tone that said listening to McHale for five minutes would consume all of Joey's energy for days to come.

"If we move too fast, we could make bigger trouble for ourselves."

"What kind of trouble?"

"Solving this problem the way you propose so soon after Bobby Ed's death will raise suspicions, and that will not be good for us." McHale stopped for a red light. "To do it safely will require some planning first so it doesn't turn around and bite us on the ass."

"That is true, *mi amigo*. What do you propose we should do?"

"The main problem was only a heartbeat away from not being a problem when I left Bobby Ed's. It's only a problem now because it's on life support. It still could possibly go away on its own with no action on our part."

"That leaves things to chance, *mi hermano*. I do not like leaving things to chance. I did not get where I am today by leaving things to chance. I control things."

"I understand that, *Jefe*." He lit a Marlboro. "But I think waiting a day or two would be wise."

"No! I will not wait! I want the problem fixed! I want it gone! I want the bitch dead."

"Fixing it now will be extremely difficult, *Jefe*. People will be watching, and right now, they will be watching very closely." The light changed. and McHale gunned the Impala through the intersection. "In a few days, boredom will start to set in, they will be tired and not as alert, and getting to the problem to fix it will be easier. Give it a day or two. Let things calm down. That gives us time to think things through before we make a move. We may even get lucky, and it will fix itself by then."

Silence. McHale's heart hammered. He'd pushed things further with Joey than he ever had before. The silence stretched out to almost a minute. Cold sweat bathed McHale. His days could be counted on one finger. It all depended on whether Joey listened to reason or his own over-inflated machismo.

Finally, Joey chuckled. "I am in an expansive mood today, *mi hermano*. I will give you three days. But no more. If it does not fix itself by then, you will fix it."

McHale's heart started beating again. "Of course, *Jefe*."

"While we wait your three days, I think you should visit the Northeast Medical Center for a checkup. I like my people to stay healthy."

So that's where the department had stashed Virgin. Joey wouldn't suggest he drive two hours north and west from the city for a test he could get done in the city. McHale wondered how Joey had gotten the information, decided he didn't want to know. "You're right, *Jefe,* I am overdue for a checkup."

"Of course I am right. I am always right. You said you had thoughts on the other problem, too?"

"I think we should go slow there for the same reasons, maybe even slower because that is not as big a problem. And when the time comes to fix that problem, a different solution than the one you proposed would be wise."

"What do you suggest?"

"An accident. A simple accident that could befall anyone. A careless driver, not paying attention, running a red light as she crosses the street. Perhaps as she walks from the parking garage to where she works."

A few more seconds of silence before Joey said, "Yes. A good idea. *Bueno*. We will do it your way, *mi amigo*. But in three days, I want that other problem solved one way or the other. Three days. No longer. You will remember that." Joey hung up.

****

Rick opened the door to his apartment and stepped in. After he'd manhandled Carl Yonick, Dee had suggested he call it a day. It carried the weight of a direct order. Even if it hadn't, Rick would have gone along. Constant worry about Mary had started to drain him.

He glanced at the answering machine as he passed his desk on the way to the bedroom. No messages. Good. He didn't feel like chatting with anyone.

He opened the bedroom closet door, reached in, and stopped with his hand gripping a hanger. He'd caught the faintest whiff of Mary's favorite perfume. He wondered where it came from, wondered if maybe he'd just imagined it. He'd been thinking of Mary all the way home. He sniffed hard. No, he hadn't imagined it. It was real.

He pawed through his closet, seeking the source. A white blouse on a hanger at the end of the rod. For a moment, he couldn't remember how it got there. Then he did. Several months ago, an accident with spaghetti sauce had stained the blouse she wore. By the time they drove to her place then back downtown, they'd missed a concert they'd really wanted to see. The next week she'd put the blouse in his closet so she'd always have a spare.

He held the fabric to his nose and inhaled the fragrance deep and hard, like a cokehead doing a big line after a long dry spell. It usually reminded him of spring and walking hand-in-hand with her through Griffin Park. Tonight it only caused a deep, wide ache, and tears gathered in his eyes.

He missed her. God, how he missed her. He wanted to be with her, to hold her hand, to whisper in her ear that he was there, and everything was going to be all right. If he couldn't do that, if he could just see her. That would do. If he could just see for himself she was still alive.

He'd asked her the name of her perfume a dozen times in the past then could never remember it when time came to buy her a present. Like some brain-dead ass, he'd stood at the fragrance counter, his mind a blank, with the clerk giving him that 'just like a man' eye roll. Then he'd vowed to write it down for next time. But he never did.

Rick hung up his blazer, stripped to his skivvies, and threw the rest into the laundry bag. He pulled on a pair of exercise shorts and a tee and grabbed a beer from the fridge. He had just cracked it when his phone rang.

"Hey, little brother." Ann, again. "I'm just calling to see how you are."

He flopped into his recliner. "Not good."

"Why? What's wrong?"

"The news media announced Mary's alive."

Ann gasped. "Do they know she's here?"

"They haven't said so, just that she's not here in Philly."

Ann sighed with relief. "That leaves hundreds of places she could be. Pittsburgh, Erie, Allentown, Harrisburg. The odds are stacked against them finding out she's here."

"Or they could find it out in the next minute. Then they'll broadcast it, and the punk who ordered the hit on her will hear it, and he *will* send people after her. Ann, let the cops guarding Mary and hospital security know and make sure they all understand how serious this is."

"I will, Rick, I promise. First thing tomorrow morning."

"If they get to her, if I lose her—" His heart felt like it was being crushed in a vice.

"Rick! Stop talking like that. Stop right now. That is not going to happen. No one is going to get to her." Her words were sharp, delivered in a 'listen to me good' tone. Then it softened. "Talk to me about Mary. Tell me about her."

Rick took a long swig from his beer. His mind was a maelstrom of chaotic thoughts—good and bad—about Mary. One by one, the bad thoughts swirled away until only the good remained. Then he started talking. He told Ann everything he'd told Dee about Mary and more. "We do the silliest things. Fly kites in Fairmont Park, or try to. Watch cartoons on TV. Window shop. Go to carnivals. Last fall we hit the Renaissance Faire in Manheim."

"You?" Ann asked. "At the Renaissance Faire?"

"Yep. Hard to believe, isn't it? I actually kind of liked it."

"Liked it, or liked being there with her?"

No point in denying it. "Being there with her. Being anywhere with her. Doing anything with her. Oh, man, Sis, it's so…special. Special doesn't even cut it. Fantastic, maybe?" He paused a second. "Yeah, fantastic. It lights me up like you wouldn't believe. Everything's better. Food has more flavor. Desserts are sweeter. The sun's brighter. Sunsets have more color. I know that sounds silly, but that's how it is."

"It's not silly."

"And rainy days—you know how I hate them—are great with her. Sometimes we do nothing, just kick back and relax, and even that's a blast."

"You love her, don't you?"

"I do. God, Sis, I do." He sucked in a hard breath. "And I'm afraid I'm going to lose her."

He could let go with Ann, could stop being the tough cop, could be little brother to her big sister. Sobs punched the air from his lungs.

****

She hears the voices again, understands they are saying words but doesn't know what they mean. She tries to hang onto them but the blackness takes them away.

****

Foxcroft Terrace filled the block on Thirty-Third Street between Van Buren and Aspen. Captain DeAngelis pushed through the front door and crossed the tiled lobby to a waist-high counter. Behind the counter, a stocky bald man watched him approach. His face broke into a wide grin. "Marco DeAngelis! As I live and breathe! How are ya, Dee?"

He extended his hand, and Dee shook it. "Doing good, Steve. How 'bout you? You working here now?"

Steve O'Malley had a ruddy complexion made sallow and bluish by the security monitors set into his side of the counter. "Twenty-two-hundred to oh-six-hundred three nights a week. A little padding for my pension. What brings you here?"

"I need to talk to Corinne James. She in?"

Steve checked a three-ring binder in front of him. "Yeah. Been home since five-thirty-four. This official business?"

"No. Just need to ask her some questions about an incident she may have witnessed. What kind of tenant is she?"

"Polite. Always says 'hi' when she signs in. Hang on a sec." O'Malley gazed toward the door "Good evening, Mr. and Mrs. Traynor."

A well-dressed sixty-ish couple—the man in a suit, the woman in an evening dress—stepped to the counter. O'Malley set the binder in front of the man. "Here you go."

The man signed the book, he and O'Malley wished each other good night, and the couple walked toward the elevators. O'Malley turned back to Dee. "The James woman. Takes care of her place. Calls as soon as a problem pops up, doesn't let it go for weeks, nice when she calls, no screaming fits 'cause maintenance isn't there in a second."

"How about visitors? She get a lot?"

"About as many as the other tenants. The ones I see don't twitch my antenna, if that's what you're asking." Steve picked up a phone. "You want me to let her know you're coming?"

Dee shook his head. "Just point me to her apartment."

He lowered the phone. "Apartment 12-H." He pointed across the lobby. "Take the elevator to 12, turn left then left. Her place is on the right."

"Thanks, Steve. Take 'er easy." Dee headed for the elevators.

"You, too. You need my help with anything, dial 9 on any phone."

The hallway on 12 was painted a light tan, the door to each apartment a different color—rose red, deep brown, pale blue, dark green. Corinne James's door was maroon. Dee thumbed her buzzer, heard its muted ring inside. A minute passed. Nobody called out, "I'm coming."

Dee held his ear to the door and gave the buzzer several jabs. Still nothing. Dee's cop-gut stirred then settled. No answer was no reason to assume the worst. No reason to assume nothing was amiss either.

Dee fished his cell phone out then realized he didn't know Foxcroft Terrace's number. He remembered a house phone in a wall niche by the elevators. He retraced his steps, lifted the phone, and hit nine.

"Front desk. This is Steve. May I help you?"

"It's Dee. You sure the James woman is home?"

"She hasn't signed out, so far as I know she is. Why? Isn't she answering?"

"Nope." Dee checked his watch. Ten-thirty. "Would she be in bed this early?"

"I wouldn't think so. She's a night owl, she told me once never goes to bed before one."

Dee's cop-gut stirred again. "Can you ring her unit,

tell her I want to talk to her, have her open the door to me?"

"Buzz you back in a couple minutes."

Two minutes later, Steve stepped off the elevator, a ring of keys in his hand. "She's not answering." He marched to Corinne James' door, unlocked it, and pushed it open. "Holy mother of God!"

In her trashed living room, Corinne James lay face down amid the shattered remains of a glass coffee table, her head in a puddle of clotted blood.

Chapter 11

Thursday – April 23, 2015

McHale blew by a truck chugging up a long grade on the Interstate 80. Cruise control held his Impala at a solid eighty, fifteen over the posted limit on this hilly section. The Fraternal Order of Police sticker on his rear window was his 'Get Out of Jail Free' card on a speeding ticket.

Another hour to Marshville. He wasn't sure where the medical center was in the town, but it couldn't be too hard to find in a burg of 10,000. He cracked his window an inch and lit up a Marlboro.

Talking Joey into letting things with Virgin ride for a few days had been a smart move on his part. It got him time to plan a fail-proof way of removing her. The 'fix it now' job Joey had wanted at Bobby Ed's place had put them in the bind they were in now. Joey had let his ego— not his brain—call the shot that night. The beaner was smart in lots of ways but dumber than toad shit in others. He'd never learned planning was the key to a successful operation. And on-site intel was the key to planning.

That's what this three-hour trip to a hospital out in the boonies was all about. He needed to see the place's layout before he could even start to plan a sure-fire hit on Virgin. He had to find out where she was and how to get to her, what stood between him and her, and how to get away after he'd iced her.

Scouting the place would be a snap. There'd be hundreds of people traipsing the halls. He'd be just one more. Even if somebody remembered him, nobody would connect the guy wandering all over the place today with Virgin getting her brains splattered all over her room a few days from now.

Shipping Virgin to the last outpost of civilization had been a bad idea. Since the brass were keeping the whole thing low-key, he doubted they'd ask the State Police for help. Maybe they had fellow officers guarding her. They'd need six to ten cops minimum. No, he'd have heard from friends if that many cops had suddenly disappeared. And he doubted the Backwater PD had the bodies to spare.

That left Hicktown Hospital's security people. Rent-A-Cops most likely—losers who couldn't cut it on any PD—or old coots retired from the local PD working security to make ends meet. Neither would have the chops to handle something like protecting someone with a target on her back. Getting by them would be easier than getting laid in a whorehouse.

At the next exit, McHale took the off-ramp and stopped at a McDonalds. He hit the head and bought a large coffee with cream and sugar to go from a stocky girl at the counter. Back in his Impala, he checked the map. Forty miles—say a half hour—to the Marshville exit.

****

Rick's phone rang as he finished knotting his tie. "Lafferty."

"It's Harter. We got a line on Conner's ex. You said you wanted to sit in. We're heading there now."

"Where? I'll meet you."

"We'll swing by your place in five. Be waiting outside."

"Deal." He snugged his tie against his collar, clipped his weapon and badge to his belt, and grabbed a light gray blazer from his closet. He had one foot out his front door when his phone rang again.

"It's Alvarez."

"What can I do for you, Sergeant?"

"Had a greenie come to me this morning needing advice. Said he got into something that struck him hinky. Sounds like it maybe ties into the thing we were talking about the other day. You got time to hear him out?"

"Not right now. Can it hold 'till this afternoon?"

"Guess so."

Rick didn't want to waste his time chasing a unicorn. "What's he saying?"

"You need to hear it from him."

"Give me a clue."

"It involves one of the names I gave you. And a gold skirt." A female detective. "The one who had a real bad day the other day."

Mary. "What's your read on this greenie, Sergeant?"

"Hard worker, listens to what he's told, tries to do the job right. Not the fastest jet on the carrier but a good kid." Alvarez paused a second. "I think maybe he got off track, realized it, and came to me to see how to get back on."

A horn blew two long beeps outside. Harter and Pryzlo.

Dee needed to be in on whatever the rookie officer had to say about Mary. "Bring him to Captain DeAngelis' office at one o'clock."

Rick hung up and sprinted out of his apartment. Not wasting a second on waiting for the elevator, he raced down three flights of stairs, dashed into the street, and jumped into the back seat of a double-parked beige Crown Vic.

"About damn time," Pryzlo growled as he gunned the Ford away. "We don't have all damn day."

"Sorry," Rick said. "Phone call caught me on the way out."

"It happens." Harter aimed a glare at Pryzlo. "Cool it, Jared."

"So what do you have on Dennis Foster?"

"Lives in a basement apartment on Seventeenth near center city." Harter pulled a small shrug. "Rest we'll find out when we talk to him." He twisted in the passenger seat to face Rick. "So, were you and Conner getting along okay?"

"What are you getting at?"

Pryzlo accelerated hard up an on-ramp to the Franklin Expressway. "What do you think he's getting at? He's asking if you two had any fights recently, maybe a big falling out over something. Maybe she was showing you the door?"

"You accusing me of shooting Mary?"

Pryzlo whipped into the fast lane and tromped the accelerator. "You wouldn't be the first guy to snuff his honey for dumping him."

"And I'm not the latest one, Pryzlo."

Harter said, "We're not accusing you of anything, Lafferty. We're just asking questions, trying to find out what happened to her. We need to know where you stood with her. So, did you two have any arguments lately?"

"Did you and Mrs. Harter have any? Or you and

149

Olivia, Pryzlo?"

His ears reddened at Olivia's name. So the rumor mill had it right. "We're not talking about us, we're talking about you and Conner, Lafferty," Pryzlo snapped. "Answer the question."

"Yeah, Mary and I've had disagreements," Rick said. "And, yeah, we had them lately. But they never went beyond differences of opinion, never got to the argument stage let alone anything more heated." He leaned forward in his seat. "Listen and listen good. I'd give anything to have been in Lukens' apartment the other night so I could have taken those two rounds instead of Mary. That answer your question of where I stood with her?"

"We had to ask. Okay? You know the drill." Harter raised his hand in a placating gesture. "No offense meant."

"Offense taken. Change the subject, or let me out here and now."

"I gotta ask you one more question, and you know what it is."

"Yeah. You want to know where I was Sunday night. Did things around home most of the afternoon. Grabbed a hoagie for dinner at the deli down the block from my place around six, watched TV and read until eleven, and hit the sack. And, no, no one can vouch for that. The last person I saw was the lady at the deli who made my hoagie."

"Ask you one more question without you taking my head off?"

"Depends on what it is."

"You talk to Conner at all that day?"

"Not during the day. Called her five or six times

after I got home, got her answering machine each time. Tried her cell a half dozen times, too. Every one went straight to voicemail. She probably had it shut off. She hated the thing, only had it because the job demands it."

A vague worry had stirred in him when she hadn't called him back by nine. She should have seen his messages by then and called him. Maybe she hadn't seen them. No. She always checked them first. He'd pushed the worry away, telling himself it was worry over nothing. She was running late and would call him as soon as she got home. Still, the worry had lingered like a bad meal in his gut and he'd called her again.

Had she been shot by then? If he'd reached her earlier, could he have saved her from the bullets that almost killed her?

"Know her plans for the evening?"

"Saturday, she said she was going to do some things around her apartment, laundry, dishes, things like that on Sunday. Chasing down Lukens wasn't on the agenda."

****

"How bad is she, Doctor?" Captain DeAngelis asked.

The surgeon opened Corinne James's chart. "Two skull fractures, neither one serious, although there is no such thing as a minor skull fracture. Numerous lacerations to her face. Broken cheekbone. Fractured radius and ulna in her right arm. Broken left clavicle and several cracked ribs on both sides. Also some bruising to her lungs and liver, so we're monitoring her for internal bleeding."

They were outside a cubicle in St. Luke's ICU. Dee studied Corinne James in her bed. Her face was a grotesque swollen purple mask. A cast covered her right arm, and inflatable clear plastic gloves immobilized both hands. Machines monitored her, and a ventilator breathed for her.

"In thirty years of trauma work, I've never seen anyone this—" The surgeon paused, searching for the right word, "brutalized. Whoever did this to her did it to inflict pain. Every finger on her left hand was broken. You ever break a finger, Officer? The pain is tremendous for such a small area of the body. All the bones in her right hand were broken, too. Somebody stomped on it wearing a heavy boot." He shook his head. "Bastards. About the only thing they didn't do was sexually assault her."

Thank God for small favors. Dee was sure Joey Day was behind the James woman's beating. He'd seen what Joey's boys could do to women, like the Rushton grad student found in her apartment house basement five years ago. She'd suffered a long time in a lot of pain before a huge dose of coke exploded her heart. Dee was sure Joey'd had her iced—she'd been muling dope for him, that had to be behind it—but he hadn't been able to pin her murder on Joey or any of his boys. It still rankled. Dee wasn't going to let Joey get away with it again.

"Let me know when I can talk to her."

The surgeon flipped the chart shut. "Maybe tomorrow."

****

She hears the voices again. It sounds like two women talking but she can't make any more sense of the words than before. She slides into the blackness again.

****

McHale took the Marshville exit. A big sign at the end of the ramp pointed the way to Northeast Medical

Center. Two traffic lights later, he was in the center of town. A few blocks beyond that, an arrow pointed left. When the light changed to green, McHale made the turn onto Hospital Drive. How friggin' cutesy was that? The road curved right as it rose. He almost stopped the car as he rounded the bend.

NEMC sprawled across the hilltop and jutted high into the sky. Jesus! He sure hadn't expected a place this size. With parking to match. There was more macadam around the place than around the city's AmeriBank Stadium and MLK Arena combined. There was even a damn motel on the property.

It made sense. This wasn't the big city with four teaching hospitals, three major medical centers, six specialty and twelve general hospitals, none more than ten minutes away. Out here in the back of beyond, this was it, Jack. Probably wasn't another place like it for two hundred miles.

A blue-and-white chopper thwopped across the sky, slowed, and disappeared behind the tall central section of the main building. McHale made a left onto Clinic Avenue. What was next? OR Street? Surgery Lane? Post-OP Avenue? Christ, these people were inane.

He wheeled his Impala into a stall in the North Lot and strolled down to a kiosk by a road. The shuttle bus he boarded there wound its way through the maze of parking lots and around buildings, making a stop it seemed every fifty feet. McHale was ready to explode long before it finally pulled up at the main entrance. He kept his temper in check. He needed to be just another Joe, there to see an ailing loved one. He'd worn clothes—olive slacks, a yellow polo shirt, and brown loafers—specifically chosen to blend in. Nobody would remember him ten minutes after they saw him. In the lobby, the other bus passengers took off in all directions like rain running off a car's hood. McHale paused to get his bearings.

"May I direct you somewhere?" a white-haired sparrow of a woman at the information desk asked.

If Virgin was anywhere in the hospital, it probably would be in some sort of Intensive Care Unit, probably a Surgical ICU. From a post-op ward, he could probably find his way or get directions there. So, post-op was a place to start. "Uh...yeah. My aunt's a patient here. She had her gall bladder out yesterday."

"Then she'd be on Floor Six in the post-op wing." The woman pointed a gnarled finger. "Go down this hall to the elevators just past the Out-Patient Pharmacy and take the B or C elevator to Six. When you get off, turn left then take the second right to the post-op wing." She offered him a thick brochure. "Here's a map in case you get turned around."

"Thank you."

Two nurses waited by the bank of elevators on their way back from a java run, lidded Styrofoam cups in their hands. One was yapping about a movie she'd seen the night before. McHale waited until she tapped the four button before he said, "Six, please."

The elevator stopped on three, and a pair of doctors got on. One was telling the other about an investment opportunity too good to miss. Figures. Pulling in a zillion bucks a year as docs wasn't enough, they always had to be looking for ways to rake in more.

McHale tuned them out by skimming the brochure. Jackpot! Surgical ICU was on Six, too, a right instead of a left off the elevators. He'd bet good money Virgin was there.

McHale scanned the rest of the brochure. Kee-rist! This was one seriously big-ass place. They had everything here, even some things he'd never heard of. What the hell was cardiac ablation? And bariatrics?

The docs were still discussing how to get richer when McHale got off on six.

****

Rick hammered a clenched fist on Dennis Foster's apartment door.

Mary's ex answered a minute later wearing yellow and blue striped boxer shorts and a red tee decorated with a faded, cracking iron-on of some never-made-it-big rock band. His eyes were puffy, and his voice blurry with sleep. "Yeah? Wha'ya want?"

Harter held up his shield. "Like to ask you a couple questions about Mary Conner."

"My ex?" Foster ran his hand through a tangle mess of curly black hair with a salting of gray. Stubble shadowed his pale face. "Yeah, sure. Why not? Go ahead."

"How about we do this inside?"

"Whatever." Foster stepped back.

Rick followed Harter and Pryzlo into an apartment that was one step up from a pigsty. The only sharp thing in the place was a high-end stereo system filling an entertainment center on one wall. Giant speakers sat in each corner, and several smaller speakers rested on shelves and end tables around the room. Rick bet his upstairs neighbors loved it when he cranked that baby up. Foster dropped into a maroon leather recliner spot-patched with duct tape. Harter and Pryzlo took a green plaid sofa. Rick shifted magazines off a purple chair so he could sit.

"Gimme a minute to wake up here. Had a late night last night." Foster rubbed the heels of his palms against his eyes. "So what's this about Mare?"

Harter opened his notebook. "When was the last time you saw her?"

"Why are you asking?"

"Just answer the question," Pryzlo said.

"Uh, a year ago at my boy's funeral."

"Not since then?" Harter asked.

"No."

"You're sure that was the last time you saw her?"

"Yeah, I'm sure," he said, his voice testy.

"How about before that?"

"Maybe a couple weeks before then. The last time I picked up Sam for the weekend."

"How do you and she get along?"

"We don't. Haven't really since Sam was a baby." Foster stared at Rick.

"Something bothering you, Mr. Foster?" he asked.

"I know you from somewhere." He stared at Rick for a few more seconds then shook his head and shrugged.

"How do you and Mary not get along?" Harter asked.

Foster shrugged again. "Different takes on life. Mare took it way too serious, never really got a kick out of it. She needed to lighten up. Life should be fun, not a drag. You gotta live it happy

"That why you two divorced?"

Foster worked his hand under the tee and scratched his chest. "Yeah, I guess mainly that was behind it." He looked at Rick again. "I know where I know you from.

You were at Sam's funeral. Mare was leaning on you, didn't want nothing to do with me."

Rick let the accusation in Foster's tone wash over him. He wasn't about to defend standing by Mary to this dork.

Foster shifted his gaze to Harter. "Why are you asking me all this stuff about Mare?"

"She was shot a few days ago."

"No shit?" Foster shook his head slowly. "Hunh! Isn't that something."

"You didn't know anything about it? Didn't read about it in the paper?"

"I don't read the paper. Nothing but bad news in it. Too much of a bummer to read that stuff day in, day out. Puts you in a blue mood. Who needs it? She going to be okay?"

"I'm sorry. She's dead," Harter said.

"Damn." Foster shook his head. "She'd stayed with me that wouldn'ta happened. I told her all that serious stuff would get her one day."

"Where were you Sunday night?" Pryzlo asked.

"That when it happened?" Foster looked at the three cops. "Hey, whoa! You think I did it? Wasn't me."

"So where were you Sunday night?"

"Working."

"Where?"

"At Gems."

"The club up on Boyleston." Pryzlo said.

Harter shot his partner a venomous glare. Rick was pretty sure Harter suspected Pryzlo had taken Olivia there and wasn't happy about it. Gems had a rep as a club where things got wild a lot and bad too often. Officers had been called there numerous times to quell disturbances, and more than one drug bust, knifing, and shooting had gone down in the parking lot.

"Yeah," Foster said.

"From when to when?"

"Uh, little after six until about three Monday morning."

"Doing what?"

"Tending bar in the Topaz Room."

"You leave at any time?"

Foster shook his head. "Place was hopping for a Sunday night. We were stepping all night long. I barely had time to run to the pisser."

"Anybody at Gems vouch for you being there all night?"

"Yeah. Steve, the owner, and Brad, the guy bartending with me. And this chick, a new waitress—uh, Ginger—I left with."

"This, uh, Ginger have a last name?" Pryzlo asked, sarcasm in his voice.

Foster shook his head. "Didn't get it. Got her phone number. Will that do?"

"Yeah," Pryzlo said. "Get it for us."

Foster rubbed his eyes again then scrubbed his face. "Let me think a minute where I put it." He scanned the room as if expecting a pointing arrow to light up. "Gotta be in my wallet. Lemme go get it for you."

He pushed out of the chair and scuffed along a short hall, running his hands through his hair. Rick followed him to the bedroom. An overflowing basket of dirty clothes occupied one corner, and the air held a slightly gamey smell.

Jeez, what a swell place to bring a girl for romance. Every time Rick merely suspected there might be a remote chance Mary would spend the night, he'd clean his bedroom top to bottom and put clean sheets on the bed, even if he'd just changed them the day before. He wondered how Mary ever hooked up with Foster, wondered what she ever saw in him. There had to be something, but damned if he could see it.

Foster swiped at the clutter on a battered dresser. "It's not here. Where the hell—must be out in the living room."

Rick tailed him back to the living room, Foster pawed through a mess on the coffee table, excavated the wallet from under a tattered magazine. "Here it is." He fingered through the bills in it and pulled out a wrinkled Gems receipt with a number scrawled on it.

"I'll take that." Rick snatched it from his fingers.

"Hey, come on! I want to keep that."

"Relax." Rick copied Ginger's number into his notebook and handed the paper back.

Foster eyed the three detectives. "That all you want? 'Cause I'm draggin' here, gotta get some more shuteye. I'm on six to two again tonight."

"Just a few more questions about Mary," Harter said. "You said you didn't get along with her. You two fight a lot?"

"Nah. Well, yeah, a lot, kinda, before she kicked me out. I tried to get her to see life didn't have to be all serious all the time, that it could be a blast if she'd let it. She didn't want to hear it, just kept going on about bills and responsibility and all that shit. I gave up. It wasn't worth the hassle. Fighting all the time gives you too many bad vibes, puts a real damper on your good mood." Foster pulled a small shrug. "'Sides, there's other women out there, lots of 'em, looking to have fun. Why try to hang on to Suzie Serious when she don't want you?"

"So you haven't fought with Mary recently?"

"I barely talked to her. We never had much to say to each other after the divorce. And I told you I haven't seen her since Sam's funeral."

"Not even over alimony?" Rick asked.

Foster covered his face with his hands and leaned back in his chair. "Oh, man. You know about that?" He dropped his hands and sat up. "Okay, look. I got behind on it right after the divorce, and she was on me about it big. But it wasn't my fault. I couldn't find work. I got a job and got square with her on it, have been ever since."

Rick leveled a disbelieving gaze at Foster. He held Rick's stare for a moment then looked away and ran his hands through his hair. "Okay. Sometimes I was late or a little short, and I missed a few. But I always made it up."

"How'd you feel about your son's death?" Harter asked.

"I wish it hadn't happened, but gone's gone, man. Nothing you can do about it, you know. You move on."

"You blame Mary for Sam's death?"

"Nah. I mean maybe a little. She'd-a impressed on him a little harder how bad that junk is, maybe he wouldn'ta tried it."

Rick fought down the urge to slap Dennis Foster around the block. "Did you ever talk to him about how bad drugs are?" Anger filled his voice.

Foster shook his head. "No way. I didn't want to rain on his parade. That was Miss Straight-Laced's job."

Once around the block wouldn't do it. Twice, maybe. Not slapping him. Kicking him every step of the way. With steel-toed shoes.

"Mary ever say anything to you about anybody giving her trouble or threatening her?" Harter asked.

Foster snorted. "I told you we didn't talk much. She could barely stand to give me the time of day. She wasn't about to tell me her problems. I didn't want to hear them anyway. I don't need that bummer."

Chapter 12

"So nobody came in while you were on the desk?"
Dee asked. He and Steve O'Malley sat in a coffee shop
across the street from Foxcroft Terrace.

Steve took a sip from the mug the waitress had just
set in front of him. "Just the usual. Residents coming
home from a night out, like the Traynors. Two delivery
guys, one from Happy Buffet, a Chinese place on Spruce,
and the other from Capelli's, the Italian place on Twenty-
ninth. They're both regulars, come in almost every night
I'm on." He slugged back more coffee and rubbed a hand
over his face. "God, I'm tired. Wasn't for this thing with
Miss James, I'd be hunkered down in bed, sound asleep
now."

"Me, too." Dee massaged his eyes. "I haven't been
up all night on a case in five years. That's why I became
a Captain, so I didn't have to do this shit."

"I hear ya."

Dee took a long drink of his coffee. "Delivery guys
sign in and out every time?"

"They do when I'm on the desk. Everybody is
supposed to. I don't know if the other guys make 'em."

"I didn't sign in last night."

"There's exceptions. Like police. That case, we put
a note in the sign-in book that an officer entered the
premises. Or if one of the regular delivery guys comes in
lugging a big order, we let him sign the book on the way

out."

"Any way to find out if somebody signed in yesterday and never signed out?"

"Check the log books."

Dee sipped more coffee and thought. "Any way somebody could sign out but not leave the building? Any place they could hide in the lobby?"

"There's a restroom off the lobby for our use." Steve paused for a sip of coffee. "We aren't supposed to, but sometimes we let a delivery guy use it if he asks. I suppose somebody could go in there, wait 'till the coast was clear, then slip out to wherever he wanted."

"Any way somebody could get in or out other than through the lobby?"

"Only other doors to the outside are fire doors, and they can't be opened from the outside, just by the crash bars on the inside. That sets off an alarm in the lobby, the fire house on Spruce, and at the One-Five on Thirtieth. So they didn't get in or out that way."

Dee drained his cup. "Let's go see what your security cameras can tell us."

****

Rick snapped his cell phone shut. He'd talked to Ginger—her last name was Archer—who'd confirmed she had indeed spent the night with Dennis Foster. If her looks were half as sultry as her voice, she was one hot dish. Rick climbed into the unmarked, shaking his head in amazement. Foster must have some kind of special talent to get a babe like her to climb in the sack with a slob like him.

Pryzlo and Harter strode out of Gems a few minutes later. Harter was saying something that had the younger man bristling. They opened the doors and Pryzlo said,

"—adult, she can do what she wants."

"Not while she's living under my roof, she can't."

They got in and Harter slammed his door with extra vigor. He turned to face Rick. "Dead end. Owner showed us Foster's time card. Punched in at four-fifty-one p.m., out at three-twenty-three a.m."

"Co-worker backs up Foster's version of the evening," Pryzlo said. "Steady business at the bar right up to last call at one-thirty. Neither one left the bar for more than five minutes all night. No way he could make it to Lukens' place and back that fast."

"Ginger alibis him, too," Rick added. "Says the two of them went back to her place and played grope and poke until dawn."

Harter fired the unmarked's engine. "So, where to now?"

Rick said, "Drop me off at my place."

****

"There!" O'Malley shouted. He pointed to the two figures that had just appeared on the monitor. Dee and O'Malley were in the security office behind the reception desk in Foxcroft Terrace. They had spent the last half hour reviewing video from Corinne James's floor.

Watching videos of people coming and going had lulled DeAngelis. His eyelids were getting heavy, his thoughts drifting to his plans for the coming weekend. O'Malley's shout had snapped him back to the here and now. He focused on the video. "I see 'em."

O'Malley let the DVD run. "Two males, possibly Hispanic, in what appear to be police uniforms. They knock on Miss James's door at," he touched the pause button, "Five-fifty-six p.m."

Dee said, "Let's see if she lets them in or they force

their way in."

O'Malley hit play. Both men gave it their full attention. O'Malley said, "Looks like she let them in."

"I'm not so sure. Go back and play it slow."

O'Malley did. The slo-mo replay confirmed it. Corinne James had seen the cops at her door and unhooked the safety chain. They shoved in, closing the door behind them.

"Let's see how long they're in there," Dee said.

O'Malley tapped the Fast Forward control on the DVD deck. Dee started drifting off again, his thoughts turning to the weekend ahead. Gina would be surprised when they got to the inn in the Poconos. Angry, too. She'd told him she didn't want a big fuss made over her forty-fifth birthday. So he was making a little fuss. Her anger would evaporate when she saw the ruby and gold ear—

"Here we go." O'Malley stopped the disc and backed up a few frames. "Coming out at seven-forty-six p.m. Christ! They beat on her for almost two hours."

O'Malley plucked the logbook on the counter behind him. He snapped through several pages then ran a thick finger down the entries on the page he'd stopped at. "Okay. Here's Miss James signing in at five-thirty-four." He slid his finger further down the page. "Son-of-a-bitch!" He stepped to the office door, yanked it open, and bellowed, "Chris! In here! Now!"

Chris stepped into the little room. "What? What's up?"

He was a beefy man DeAngelis guessed to be in his late twenties. O'Malley jabbed his finger at something in the logbook. "Tell me about this entry."

"Like it says: Officers Otero and Mercado to see

Miss James on twelve," Chris answered. "They told me to not let her know they were on their way up. What's the problem?"

"Describe Otero and Mercado."

"Both Hispanic. Otero was about five-ten or eleven, one-fifty to one-sixty, black hair, brown eyes, early thirties, mustache, looked like he was really ripped. Mercado was shorter, maybe five-seven or eight, bulked to the nines, went two-forty, two-fifty easy, black hair, black eyes, younger, scar on his cheek. What's the big deal?"

"The big deal, doofus," O'Malley growled, "is that the badge number Otero gave you is my old badge number."

Chris gave a shrug. "So he's got your old number. What's so bad about that?"

"When you retire, the force retires your number, like the Eagles retired Reggie White's jersey."

Chris swallowed. "You saying they weren't cops?"

"Give the man a cee-gar," O'Malley said. "You signed them in at five-fifty-six p.m.?"

"If that's what it says in the book."

"When did they leave?"

"I can't remember. Lemme see the book." He took it from O'Malley and scanned then reversed it so O'Malley could see the place he'd marked with a finger. "I marked them out at seven-forty-nine."

"You didn't make 'em sign out like you're supposed to?"

"They ran past the desk on their way out, said they had to respond to a call, so I did it for them."

"It didn't strike you as odd they were up there for almost two hours?"

166

He shrugged. "Maybe they had a lot of questions to ask her."

"They weren't asking her questions, they were beating the crap out of her."

Chris sank into a chair, held his head in his hands, and muttered, "No. No. No." He gazed at O'Malley. "Am I gonna get fired for this?"

"If I have anything to say about it."

****

Ann left Mary's—there she did it again—Miranda's room and started up the hall toward the nurse's station. She still hadn't told the officers she knew Mary. She probably should. She couldn't risk it. They'd replace her if she did. She wanted to take care of Mary, had to take care of her, for Rick's sake. Better to keep her mouth shut. No, she had to tell them. Should she tell both Caitlin and Allison? No, Ann decided, if she told them at all, she'd tell Caitlin in private.

Wrapped in her thoughts, she bumped into a man at the end of the hall. Mary's chart slipped from her hands and thunked on the floor. "Oh! Excuse me!"

"No problem," a deep voice rumbled. Quick as a cat, he picked up the chart and flipped it closed. "Here you go."

She took it from him. "I'm so sorry! I wasn't watching where I was going."

He loomed over her by a good six inches. Steel gray eyes, short dark brown hair, a square face with a strong chin split by a hint of a dimple. "Run into me anytime. I won't mind."

She'd heard lines like that before. Dressed in green slacks, a yellow shirt, and tan blazer, he looked like a regular Joe, but Ann got a strong 'bad boy' vibe off him.

She knew that vibe well. She'd dated her share of guys carrying it until she'd realized 'bad boy' was a synonym for 'bad news' and switched to decent guys. That hadn't ended so well either. She took a step back from the man before her. "Can I help you with something?"

"Uh, well, yeah, maybe you can. I think I got turned around somehow. Man, this place is confusing. I'm looking for the post-op ward. My aunt had her gall bladder out yesterday."

"Yes, it can be confusing, but you're not that far off track." She pointed along the hall. "Go back past the elevators then take the second right. That will take you to the post-op area."

"Much obliged." He sauntered away on sure steps.

His eyes lingered in Ann's mind. It wasn't their color. It was the way he used them. Even though they appeared to be focused on her, she'd sensed they'd taken in everything going on around him, too. They were like Rick's eyes. Like Sergeant Boniface's. They were a cop's eyes.

Something else about the man bothered her. It wasn't that he was a cop visiting the hospital. Cops had aunts who had gall bladders out. Ann stepped behind the nurse's station and racked Mary's chart. She stood there for a few moments trying to pin down what about him didn't seem right. It came to her.

Except for that 'bad boy' aura he'd let show right after she'd run into him, he'd projected an image of innocence, almost naiveté. It didn't go with his cop's eyes. That's what didn't add up about him. He was trying too hard to appear innocent. She wondered why. She'd have to think about it, maybe ask Rick about it when she talked to him again. One thing she should do is alert hospital security to him. She picked up the phone.

"Code Orange, Cubicle nine. Code Orange, Cubicle nine."

Ann dropped the phone and ran, the urgency in the page driving all thoughts of the man from her mind.

****

She hears different voices speaking the words. One is deeper, a man's voice. She has to make sense of the words. The blackness drags her down before she can.

****

Rick spotted Sergeant Alvarez as he entered the Oh-Seven's house. The sergeant had a tall sandy-haired young cop with him. Alvarez introduced him as Patrolman Keith Rynert then asked, "So, how come you want us to do this in front of your boss?"

"You said it has something to do with that thing we talked about the other day. He's in on that, too."

"Okay."

Rynert cast worried glances between the two men. "Am I in some kind of trouble here?"

"Nah, kid," Alvarez answered. "Not if you tell them what you told me."

"DeAngelis is square, Rynert," Rick added. "He won't jam you up over something you didn't do."

They started up the stairs to the detective's squad. Rick glanced back at the patrolman. "You look about bushed."

Rynert nodded. "Pulling all the overtime I can get. I'm getting married in a couple months, and I'm trying to get some money ahead so me and Kathy can have one blowout honeymoon. Can't do it on my base pay alone."

Alvarez said, "Take some advice from an old married man. Don't blow all that money on the honeymoon. Save some of it for when you get back. You'll be payin' bills from now 'til the day you die."

They crossed the squad room to the captain's office and Rick knocked on the door. Dee, the phone to his ear, gave them a 'wait one' sign. A moment later, he hung up the phone and motioned them in. Alvarez and Rynert stopped at the door when they spotted two other detectives in the room. Alvarez fired a glare at Rick. "IA. I should-a known. Come on, kid. We're outta here."

Dee said, "Hold up a minute, Sergeant. No one's looking to jam you or the patrolman up. If we were, we'd be having this conversation in the pit. Information is all we're after. None of what you tell us will be used against you."

Alvarez eyed him for a second. "Your word?"

"My word."

"Second I suspect otherwise, we're gone."

"Fair enough." Dee introduced Flynn and Schmidt then waved Rynert and Alvarez into seats facing his desk. He leaned back in his chair. "Okay, so what do we have here?"

"Tell him, Rynert," Alvarez ordered.

The young patrolman swallowed hard a couple times then told them how he'd fallen asleep in his cruiser while on his lunch break, how the radio call had startled him awake, how he'd crashed into a dumpster, how he'd called Davenport who'd called McHale.

Flynn said, "You nod off because you're working a lot of OT, Rynert?"

"Yes, sir." He repeated his marriage and honeymoon plans. "Am I in trouble for that?"

"Doing it too much isn't good for you. It gets you tired. and tired leads to mistakes that can get you killed.

All the money in the world's no good if you aren't around to spend it."

"I read you, sir. Thank you."

"So what happened after McHale said he'd take care of you?" Dee asked.

"He left, and I resumed patrol," Rynert answered. "Then he calls me yesterday morning, says he wants my help watching some lady. I told him I was bushed, needed to get some sleep. He said I didn't help him, wrecking my unit would come back on me, and I'd lose my job. He didn't exactly come right out and say that would happen, but he meant it."

"Do you remember exactly what McHale said?" Dee asked.

"Yes, sir. 'Remember that little jam you got in the other day? I did you a favor then, you do me one now. Unless you're looking to change jobs. I hear the Oak Park Mall needs a third shift security guard.' I didn't want to get kicked off the force, so I said I'd do what he wanted. Then he turns around and says he'll pay me six hundred cash for doing it."

"Did he pay you?" Rick asked.

"Yes, sir, Detective. Three hundred when I showed up, the rest when he came back a couple hours later. All in hundreds."

"Did he tell you the name of the woman you'd be watching?" Dee asked.

"No, sir. But I found it out when a security guy from the building where she worked gave me static about hanging around outside it."

"You remember it?"

"I wrote it down." He took a notebook from his back pocket and paged through it. "Ellen Shires."

The name rang a bell. He glanced at Dee, whose expression said he'd recognized the name, too. Flynn and Schmidt had the same expression. Dee pulled a folder from a desk drawer and flipped through copies of the IR-10s, Investigation Reports, the IA detectives had provided. "That's the tipsy woman you and Harter interviewed the night of Mary's shooting, said she saw a man dressed as a patrol officer leaving the building."

Schmidt nodded. "That's right. I just drew a blank on the name. What did you do with the money McHale paid you, Rynert?"

"Here." He laid a plastic bag holding six hundred-dollar bills lay on Dee's desk. "I don't feel right taking it. I mean I did when McHale gave it to me, and I can sure use it, but later I got to thinking about it, and it felt funny, like something wasn't right about taking it." He paused for a deep breath. "Like somehow it would come back to bite me."

"Rynert," Flynn said, "you keep thinking like that and I'm never going to come knocking on your door."

Dee exchanged glances with the other detectives then said, "Step outside for a minute, Patrolman, but stick close. We may want to talk to you again."

After Rynert left the office, Dee asked Alvarez. "What's your take on Rynert, Sergeant?"

"Not the sharpest blade in the pocketknife, like I told him," He pointed to Rick, "but he's a good kid. He listens and he learns. He'll be a good cop with a little more experience under his belt. I can see him making sergeant some day."

"You think he's shining us on with this story he's telling us?"

"Nah. He doesn't have it in him. He gave you the

straight scoop."

"He wrecked his cruiser because he was asleep like he said, why isn't he on suspension?"

Flynn said, "Davenport wrote it up as Rynert wrecking it to avoid hitting a civilian, Billy Drummond. McHale had to be behind that. He says shit, Drummond squats and strains. And McHale and Davenport are pals from way back. So, Rynert called Davenport when he wrecked, Davenport called McHale to get Rynert clear, and McHale saw a way to get his hooks into a greenie and jumped on it."

"If Davenport's Rynert's sergeant, why'd he come to you about this thing with McHale?" Schmidt asked Alvarez.

"I was his training officer after he got out of the academy. I know Davenport, and I don't quite trust him, so when Rynert got posted to the Four-One, I told him he ever had any problems with the guy, he should come see me."

Dee's face took on a thoughtful expression for a moment. "You think Rynert could handle being our eyes and ears around McHale?"

"Don't know. He's never done anything like that." Alvarez scratched his chin for a moment. "Yeah, I think he could, but you want to go that way, I think you better let me handle him. No offense to any of you guys."

"Rick?" Dee asked. "What do you think?"

Dee always asked his men for their input. It was one more thing that Rick admired about his boss. "Makes sense." He nodded toward Alvarez. "He knows Rynert better than we do."

"Okay. Let's get Rynert in here and set it up."

"Before we do that, you want to tell me what's going

on here?" Alvarez asked. "You want me helping you with Rynert on this thing, I need to know what's going on."

"Sergeant, why don't you and Rynert go get some coffee in the break room."

Chapter 13

McHale climbed into his Impala, leaving his door open so the built-up heat could escape, and lit a Marlboro. NEMC was Grade-A friggin' huge. That was good. Bigger place meant more people. More people meant the chances of everyone knowing everyone else were zip. He could get in, get Virgin, and get out with the odds heavy in his favor no one would pick out that he didn't belong there.

McHale pulled the brochure the lady had given him in the lobby from his inside jacket pocket and thumbed through it to the map for the sixth floor. Okay, there was Surgical ICU nurses' station with patient rooms in three sides of a square around it. He traced a thick finger down the hall from the elevator to the short hall opposite the nurses' station. The map labeled the rooms and hall 'Staff Area' but the nurse had carried a chart. Why would she take a chart to a staff area? She wouldn't. Charts were kept at the nursing station when they weren't being used in the patients' rooms.

McHale wondered how current the brochure was. He flipped it over. Printed at the bottom on the back were the words ©*2003*. So it was out of date. Those rooms had probably been a half dozen different things since then. Hell, hospitals remodeled the way a woman changed her mind. It never stopped.

A tingle scurried up McHale's arms, down his spine,

David A. Freas

and across his back. He knew it, he Goddamn knew it! Staff area, my ass! Those were patient rooms. And Virgin Mary was in one of them. He as good as had her.

Getting to Virgin would be a piece of cake as long has had a good cover story. The staff uniform at NEMC seemed to be no uniform at all. He'd seen nurses in everything from starched whites to scrubs and doctors in everything from suits and ties to jeans and polos. Anything he wore wouldn't merit a second look from anybody.

But he didn't need to pose as a doctor. He could claim he was a cop come to question Mary. The Rent-A-Cops would probably buy it since it was sort of true. He *was* coming for her, just not to talk to her. Hell, maybe one of them would even hold the door to her room for him. Wouldn't that be something, helping him kill the woman they were supposed to protect?

A feeling of power surged through McHale. He'd get Virgin, and nobody could stop him. By the time they figured out what he was doing, it would be too late. She was as good as gone right now.

He still had to find out which room Virgin was in. After dinner, when the place was clogged with another round of visitors, would be the time to do that. He'd plan out the hit on the way home. His watch said he had a good six hours to kill until he could go back to the sixth floor. He dropped his cigarette on the pavement, started his Impala, and drove away from NEMC. At the traffic light, he flipped open his cell phone and dialed.

Joey answered on the fourth ring. "Yes, my friend?"

Thank God he wasn't into the Spanish lingo shit at the moment. McHale didn't need that crap right now. "I will need two days to correct the information you have

176

on file."

McHale hated the long silence that followed. Joey Day's silences were like a fuse on a cheap firecracker. They could lead to an explosion or sputter out to nothing. McHale held his breath, waiting to see which one this would be.

"Two days? *Muy bien.*"

So much for canning the Spanish lingo. Oh well, it was good while it lasted.

****

Sergeant Alvarez took a seat facing Flynn across Captain DeAngelis's desk. "I assume you were checking me out?"

"Unh-hunh," Flynn answered.

"I cleared or I wouldn't be in here? Right?"

"Clean and green."

Alvarez nodded. "So what's the play?"

"Detective Mary Conner was shot a few nights ago, we think possibly by a dirty cop." He told Alvarez the rest of it except that she was alive.

When he finished, Alvarez didn't say anything for a long time. "You think McHale's her shooter?"

"Could be. Could be someone else. Too early to say one way or the other yet."

"So why are you focusing on McHale?"

"Right now, this thing Rynert brought us is the best lead we've got. The cop Shires saw leaving the building could be McHale. If he is Conner's shooter, he could be keeping tabs on Shires to shut her down if she comes to us. Plus he's on the list of maybe dirty cops you gave Lafferty here the other day. You got a better somebody in mind?"

"Nope. Thing is I've known McHale a long time,

worked with him out of the Two-Two from oh-one to oh-four. He wasn't no saint, but a good cop, one you could count on when things went sideways."

"This isn't a witch hunt for McHale, Alvarez. It's a hunt for whoever shot Conner. I'm going to bring that man down even if it's the Commissioner himself." Flynn jabbed the desk to stress each word.

"Like I said, McHale's no saint but killing another cop...I don't see him doing that."

"You gave Lafferty McHale's name as possibly dirty. Why?"

"Eight years ago, I'm second tour patrol sergeant in the Four-Six. I'm in a bar watching the Super Bowl. Patrol sergeant I know in the One-Six sits down next to me, asks if I could use some extra dough. You know anyone on the job that can't? So I ask what do I gotta do, thinking maybe it's some off-the-books security gig. He beats around the bush a bit then tells me McHale sometimes asks him to route patrols away from certain areas in his district, takes care of him when he does. Asking cops to stay away from a place sounded to me like he'd gone dirty."

"You have any idea why or when he crossed over?"

"I lost touch with him after I transferred to the Four-Six in oh- five, so I can't say for sure. I heard through the grapevine he was due promotion to patrol sergeant in oh-six but got stiffed for it. Rumor was a captain on the promotions board had a beef with McHale over something that happened a few years prior. Maybe that did it."

Alvarez stood, stepped to the windows, and stared out for a few seconds. "I don't like bringing down a brother officer." He pointed to the glass. "It's us against them out there. We take one of our own down, it's one less on our side." He paused for a beat. "I like dirty cops even less than the mopes out there." He was silent for several seconds then exhaled a hard breath. "Okay. I'm in. Rynert, too. What do you want us to do?"

Flynn motioned to a chair. "Have a seat. You think Rynert can keep his feet on the straight and narrow?"

"He could-a kept that six hundred McHale gave him, could-a really used it. He turned it over to you instead. That answer your question?"

Flynn nodded. "You're going to be Rynert's contact. Rynert is to do anything McHale asks him to—within the law, of course—report it back to you, and you report it to us."

****

Rick's cell rang as he unlocked his car. The voice on the other end said, "You have time for a cup of coffee? Pot O' Brew on Culver in ten minutes?"

Blaine Crowell covered the police beat for the *Inquirer*. Rick had met him ten years ago on one of his first cases as a detective. Blaine had passed him a tip that helped him break the case. They'd formed a mutually beneficial but wary friendship, trading morsels of information ever since. "I can do that."

Seated at a table in the coffee shop fifteen minutes later, Rick took a sip of his coffee. "What's up?"

Crowell, a chunky man with dark ginger hair and bright blue eyes, wore a faded denim shirt, black jeans, and battered running shoes. Rick had never seen him in anything else. Crowell pulled a notepad from a hip pocket and opened it. "What's the latest on Detective Conner?"

"Investigation's still on-going."

"I know that. What's new since yesterday?"

"Talk to our Public Information Officer."

"I did. He told me, quote, the investigation into the shooting death of Detective Mary Conner is on-going, unquote. Come on, Rick, give me something more."

"Can't help you this time. I'm not involved in the investigation."

"Okay, you can't help me with that; maybe you can on something else. I'm gathering information for a follow-up story on her, a companion piece to run as a sidebar to the article on her funeral. You know when that will be?"

Rick shook his head. "Last I heard, coroner hasn't yet released her body."

"You worked with her, right? She was your partner? What was she like to work with?"

"Good detective. Dedicated. Hard working. Knew her stuff."

"Other detectives get along with her?"

Rick sipped coffee. "Yep."

"What was she like as a person?"

"Where are you going with this, Blaine?"

"Would she have gone to Lukens's place to whack him for causing her son's death?"

"No. She'd have worked within the system, would have helped the detectives handling Sam's death any way she could to bring Lukens down legally."

Crowell downed a slug of coffee. "Even if they were getting no traction on it? She wouldn't get tired of waiting for the wheels of justice to grind Lukens up, wouldn't grind him up herself?"

"Even if."

"Word I'm hearing is her slugs punched his ticket.

And his punched hers, only the piece he used wasn't his usual cannon, was a lightweight piece. Like it was a set-up. Care to comment on that?"

Rick grabbed his coffee cup and stood. "This conversation's over."

Crowell raised his hand. "Hold on, Rick. Calm down. That's not where I'm going."

"Better not be. I told you she wasn't that kind of cop." Rick sat.

Crowell raised a hand. "Sorry. So is it true about the rounds that took Conner and Lukens out?"

"That's what the forensics say."

"So what really happened in Bobby Ed Lukens's apartment?"

"The detectives handling the case are still trying to sort that out."

"What do you think happened?"

"I wish I knew." He couldn't keep the frustration out of his voice.

"Okay. Back to the original topic: What was Conner like as a person?"

Rick considered for a minute then chose his words with care. "Complex like every other person, had strengths and weaknesses like everyone. But she never put on a front. What you saw was what you got. You didn't have to guess where you stood with her."

"Where did you stand with her?"

"Got along fine, never had any problems."

"Outside work as well as on the job?"

"What are you getting at?"

"Saw you two having dinner a few times."

Rick wasn't surprised Blaine knew about him and Mary. "Probably because we were working a case and got hungry."

"You looked real cozy for a pair of cops working a case. You didn't look dressed for work, either. More like people on a date. Spotted you coming out of the movies a time or two as well. You working then, too? Somebody rob the concession stand of its popcorn?" Crowell smiled at his lame humor. "Or was something else going on with you and her?"

Rick waited a moment before he answered. "All right. We were dating. Started off casual, just someone to see a movie or have dinner with once in a while. Found out we liked being with each other. Might've become something more if—" he paused a second, "if she hadn't died."

"I'm sorry, man. I was just curious. None of that will be in my story." Crowell held up his hand again. "My word."

"I know." One of the first rules they'd established was personal lives were off limits. Another was information had to flow both ways each time they met. "What do you have for me?"

"Joey Day knew about Lukens getting it minutes after it happened." Crowell had sources on both sides of the thin blue line.

"How'd he find out so fast?"

Crowell shrugged. "None of my sources knew. Question: Would Conner, if she heard Lukens had a hand in her son's death, confront him about it? Not kill him, just confront him?"

Rick thought for a moment. "Yeah, I can see her doing that. Why are you asking?"

"Okay, say that's what she did, only it went off the rails somehow, and she dropped him. She's got a stiff on her hands, so she called a fixer in the department to help clean it up. Only the fixer she calls is in Joey's pocket. He tells Joey she's whacked Lukens, Joey says whack her."

"Could have gone down that way. But it makes no sense. Conner was no threat to Joey."

"Joey does a lot of things that don't make sense. Except to Joey. One time he had his boys lay a beat down on his Princess for not laughing at something he said."

Beating his main girlfriend for that was sick. "Good point. So, does Day have any cops in his pocket?"

"I've heard anywhere from twenty to a hundred."

"You know any names?"

Crowell tipped the last of his coffee into his mouth. "No. Sorry."

"Get some for me."

"Do my best."

Rick stood. Crowell grabbed his arm before he took a step. "WCBL ran a story last night that Conner's alive. My editor reamed me a new one wanting to know why I didn't have it. Level with me, Rick. Off the record, if you want. Is Conner alive?"

His trust of Crowell only went so far. Rick sat again, stared at the table, and took a few deep breaths. He remembered how he'd felt when Dee announced Mary's death and tried to make his expression now match the gut-wrenching twist that hit him then. He looked at Crowell and shook his head. "She…she died in Bobby Ed Lukens's apartment."

****

Darcy Brown's ribs still hurt every time she breathed, and her bruises had ripened to ugly purple-black. She'd needed an extra heavy layer of concealer to hide the ones on her cheek and chin. Joey Day's enforcers had made Councilman Ed Rayburn pay for punching her out but, bottom line, the beating she'd taken was Joey's fault. He'd sent her to that animal.

She dropped her pen on her desk and closed her eyes. The image of her switchblade jutting from Joey's chest had stayed with her since yesterday. She leaned back in her chair and rubbed her eyes as if that would erase it. It didn't.

"You okay, Darce?" Gary asked from his desk facing hers in the office at *Paraiso*.

She sat up. "I just have something on my mind."

"Want to talk about it?"

She wished she could. Asking his help to escape Joey's clutches wasn't like asking about updating the menu, something they could kick around over Scotch on the rocks. And while she liked Gary, she wasn't sure how far she could trust him. If she told him she was tired of being Joey's 'Employee of the Month' award, he might take it to Joey. She couldn't risk that. She shook her head. "Thanks anyway."

"You change your mind, I'm here." He pushed back from his desk and stood. "Need to run a few errands. Be back in an hour or so."

"Take your time. No rush." His absence would give her time to think without interruption.

As soon as he left, the feeling she'd never escape Joey descended on her full force. Her heart raced, her hands shook, and nausea roiled in her stomach. She willed it away with slow deep breaths. Calm again, she strolled out to the club floor, poured three fingers of Glenlivit into a rocks glass, and returned to the office.

At her desk again, she sipped the Scotch and

thought. To be honest, she was partly to blame for the fix she was in. She could have said no when Joey first asked her to sleep with guys he sent her to. But sex was sex, she liked screwing, and getting paid to do it was icing on that cake. Not anymore. Picking up a guy of her choosing and banging his brains out was one thing, going to a hotel room and humping some guy because Joey said to was altogether different.

Rayburn bashing her around the other night had been the last straw. She had to get out of being Joey's whore. Had to. She just had to figure out how.

Running was out. Joey would find her wherever she landed. Saying no the next time he ordered her to service some guy was out. She'd seen firsthand what he did to people who refused him. A waitress at *Paraiso* who rejected his advances one night was gang-raped in her apartment two nights later by thugs she was sure he'd sent. Maybe she could talk him into letting her stop. Not likely. He used people and things until he'd sucked them dry. He wouldn't let her go until she was used up.

No, the only way she'd get away from him was to kill him. There was no way around it. That stopped her for a second. Could she really kill someone? Just anyone? No. Someone who was sucking the life out of her, who would kill her in a flash if she defied him? She had to!

The how was easy. Her switchblade. She had never stabbed anyone, just the threat of a blade to the gut—or lower—had saved her hide a few times. She would have to stab Joey to save it this time. She took it from her purse and spent several seconds idly snapping the blade out and retracting it. The image of it buried to the hilt in Joey's chest filled her mind.

Now she just had to figure out how to turn that image into reality in a way that wouldn't get her killed, too. That would be the hard part. It would take planning. She couldn't leave anything to chance, would have to lay out every step she needed to take from right now to what she'd do once Joey was dead.

Darcy took a tablet from her desk and started jotting notes.

****

Hearing the apartment door open, Heather Bartlett called from the den, "Is that you, Ashlee?"

"Yeah, Mom," she yelled back. "I just stopped in to get some clothes."

Heather took a deep breath. This was not going to be nice. "Could you come in here for a minute first?"

"Sure." Ashlee, twenty, blonde, green-eyed, almost as tall as Heather, appeared in the doorway, Fendi purse slung over one shoulder, Porsche Design sunglasses pushed up into her hair. Her Rushton U. tee molded to her young body and bared a narrow strip of toned flesh, jewel winking from her pierced navel, above tight low-rise jeans barely hanging on her hips.

Heather bit back the urge to tell her she looked like a tramp.

"What's up, Mom?"

Heather reminded herself to stay calm and patted the sofa facing the big screen TV. "Come here. I want to talk to you about something."

Ashlee rolled her eyes in 'what now?' irritation as she sauntered in then plopped down next to her mother. "Okay. I'm here. Talk."

Heather thumbed the remote, and the video of McHale screwing Ashlee on her bed played on the TV.

Her daughter didn't seem the least bit shocked by the scene. Her own calmness vanished, and she screeched, "How could you?"

"How could *you*?"

Forcing calmness into her voice, she said, "I don't know what you're talking about."

"You fucked him, too."

Heather raised her hand to slap Ashlee, stopped herself at the last moment. "Do not use that word in this house."

"That's what you did, Mother, you fucked him. Him and Kirk and Bret every chance you got."

How could Ashlee know about them? She couldn't. "I did no su—"

Ashlee fixed her mother with a cool stare. "I know all about the camera in your bedroom closet and your video collection."

Oh, God. Heather was stunned into silence for a moment. "We're not talking about me. We're talking about you."

Ashlee shrugged. "So I fucked him. What's the big deal? It's not like I'm a virgin. Wake up, Mother. I lost my cherry in tenth grade."

She stopped the disc. "The big deal is he's old enough to be your father."

"Would you rather I was doing Kirk or Brad? I could really get into doing Kirk." She waved her hand as if she'd burned her fingers. "He is *hot*!"

"Stop it! I don't want you screwing—" This was turning too antagonistic. Heather tried a more conciliatory tone. "I'm not trying to run your life, Ashlee." She pointed to McHale on the TV. "I just want to understand why you'd do *that* with a man like him."

187

"Why do you do it with him?"

Because she liked his no-frills screwing. She couldn't tell Ashlee that. It hadn't been the reason she'd let him do her the first time but it was one reason she let him continue. "I…I have no choice."

"Neither do I, Mother."

"What do you mean? What are you talking about?"

"That accident I had two months ago, when I hit that car? I was drunk." She pointed to the TV. "He was the cop who showed up, and he gave me a Breathalyzer test. I blew point-one-one. He said he had to arrest me for DUI, and Dad could be fired if he did. I was scared. I didn't want to go to jail and make Dad lose his job. I didn't know what to do. He said he didn't want to jam me up or cause Dad trouble so he'd write it up as just an accident and not say anything about me being drunk if I'd do something for him."

Heather aimed a finger at the image on the TV. "That."

Ashlee looked away. "Unh-hunh. It was just that one time, Mom, that's all he wanted."

Heather shook her head then took her daughter's hands. "Listen to me, honey. It won't be just one time."

Ashlee looked at her mother, stunned. "But he said—"

She shook her head again. "I don't care what he said. He'll be back, wanting you to, demanding you do it again and again. And do more. Trust me, he will."

Ashlee pulled her hands free. "Like he does with you?"

Heather froze for a moment then nodded.

"What did you do, Mother?"

She gazed across the room for a moment then

sighed. "Your father and I," she paused, "we like to smoke a joint once in a while at the cabin. About a year ago, I bought an ounce for up there. I usually hid the baggie under the seat, but I was in a hurry that day and stuffed it in my purse. On my way home, he pulled me over for running a red light and saw it when I got my license out. He said it was over an ounce, enough to charge me with intent to deliver. If you think your drunk driving arrest would have ruined you dad's career, think what my arrest for possession with intent would have done. So I did what I had to do."

A little white lie. She'd sized up McHale as a cop willing to trade favors. Always in the market for another lover, she'd hinted she'd be willing to do something for him if he made the arrest go away. He'd snapped up the bait.

"Does Dad know about you and him? Or the others?"

"No." Heather took her hands again and squeezed them. "And you can't tell him."

"I won't." She smiled. "If you want to get it on with guys other than Dad, I'm cool with it." Her smile vanished. "But I expect the same from you in return."

"I don't care who you sleep with, honey, as long as you're careful. But I won't let a sleazeball like him," she pointed to the TV, "have his hooks in you for the rest of your life."

"I don't want that either, Mom. Once was okay, but bumping bodies with him whenever he wants? Ugh!"

"He won't do it again." She'd let him screw her all he wanted to keep her secret safe. She would not let him screw Ashlee again. Ever. "I'm going to stop it."

"How?"

"Leave that to me." As Ashlee left the den, Heather picked up the phone and dialed the number of an old lover.

Chapter 14

Captain DeAngelis sat at his desk. He hoped he hadn't made a mistake bringing Alvarez and Rynert into the Conner investigation.

Alvarez had been a cop a long time, and his rep was solid. He'd passed the detective's exam but opted to stay in uniform, saying he preferred working the streets, passing his wisdom on to new officers. That didn't guarantee he was clean. He could be dirty as hell. In this city, more uniform officers than plainclothes ones were arrested for corruption. Still, Dee was inclined to think Alvarez was a righteous cop.

No, the big question mark was Rynert. A rookie patrolman who hadn't learned all the ropes yet, who didn't know all the traps out there, was easier to lead astray. First year officers were paid forty-one-five a year, so the temptation to pocket some of the mountains of cash lying around a drug bust or take a hefty bribe from someone to look the other way was strong. On the other hand, Rynert had come to Alvarez when McHale's job seemed hinky to him.

Against that was Rynert's newness. Dee wasn't sure he was up to an undercover assignment. He seemed eager to take it on but had no experience in UC ops. Dee wondered if he had the finesse to do it. One little slip could put Rynert in a world of hurt. Dee wasn't sure he wanted to expose the young man to that danger.

Making decisions like that was why the city paid him a captain's salary. Time to make them. After he let his thoughts loose to sort themselves out. Dee leaned back in his chair and laced his hands behind his head.

Maybe Rynert could pull it off. The two best undercover cops Dee had ever met were the last two he would have picked as ace UC operatives. One looked like Richie Cunningham on *Happy Days*, the other like Father Mulcahy on *M*A*S*H*. Keith Rynert looked like he was a high school sophomore, so maybe—

The phone cut into Dee's thoughts. He rocked forward and answered.

"Officer Davis from the Three-Six, Captain. You have a BOLO on Jwakeen Phillips, want to talk to him? Just picked him up on a shoplifting beef. We got him here in our holding pen if you're still interested."

Finally. "We are, Davis. I'll send one of my men down." Dee cradled the phone, opened his office door, and called Rick's name.

****

After a McDonald's lunch, McHale spent the afternoon in a park by the river on the edge of Marshville. He paced the bank for hours, flinging stones into the Susquehanna, his mind locked onto this whole thing with Virgin. It had stunk at the start, and it didn't smell any better now. His street smarts were sending out all kinds of warnings it was bad news. He shoved them away a hundred times, but they came right back.

Maybe this wasn't about icing Virgin. Maybe his street smarts were warning him the roof was about to fall in on Joey, and he should pack his bags and get the hell out of Dodge before it fell on him, too. He had enough socked away that he could live a good life for a long time and never work a day of it. If he set up camp in some low-rent Caribbean nation, he could live like a king. Hell, better than a frigging king.

Trouble was if he split and the roof didn't fall in, there wasn't any place in the world far enough away for him to be out of Joey's reach. He knew too much for Joey to let him leave. Guys who tried that ended up with a .22 slug pulping their brains. He'd pulped several himself over the years.

Maybe he could retire. Yeah, right. Nobody retired from Joey's organization with a fat check and a gold watch. Joey's retirement plan was a knife to your heart and your body dumped in the Schuylkill River. He'd done a few of those, too.

He could always burn Joey himself. He had enough on the beaner to put him away for a couple lifetimes. But that could backfire on him. Even from prison, Joey could hire muscle to put him in the landfill. And the evidence that could put Joey behind bars could land him there, too. Where, again, Joey could hire muscle to ice him.

Offing Joe was an option. Yeah, if he wanted to run a suicide mission. Joey's goons would ice him before he got two feet away from his corpse.

No, if he wanted to live long enough to spend all that money he'd made, he'd have to cut and run in a way that wouldn't piss Joey off. Or one that would make coming after him more trouble to Joey than it was worth.

Maybe he was overreacting. Had to be. Yeah, he was just seeing monsters under the bed. How much fight could Virgin put up a couple days after taking two in the gut? None. Hell, whacking her would be a piece of cake.

He whipped a last rock across the river. It skipped halfway to the other shore before sinking in the water.

He checked his watch. Time for dinner then back to the hospital.

****

Dee's phone rang again as he returned to his desk. "Marco? Hi!"

The voice unleashed a memory from summer twenty-one years ago. He was twenty-seven, a patrolman two years out of the academy when he changed a flat tire for her. She was twenty-two, slim, rich, fresh out of college, and hot. Lord, she was hot. And available if he was interested. He was. Their affair raged like a forest fire for a year. He'd ended it when he'd found out she'd been engaged to a lawyer even longer, and was marrying him in a month. But the memory lived on. "Heather?"

"One and the same." Her silky alto voice stirred images of wild trysts in hastily rented hotel rooms.

They exchanged how-are-yous before he asked, "What can I do for you?"

"Can we meet for a drink sometime this evening?"

They'd crossed paths several times over the years. She'd dropped a hint each time she was still available if he still was interested. He was but passed anyway, especially after Gina entered his life. He wouldn't throw away what he had with her for a quickie tumble with anyone, not even Halle Berry. Still the chance for another wild romp with Heather had been a big temptation each time he'd seen her. It would be an equally big one now. "What for?"

"I need a favor."

"I can't fix parking tickets," he said in a laughing tone.

"It's not a parking ticket. And it's not for me."

The gravity in her voice caught his full attention.

"What's up?"

"I need help with a jam Ashlee's gotten into."

He'd always wondered if Ashlee was his child, her birth coming not quite nine months after the end of their affair. "If it's some sort of legal trouble, you should be talking to Ed about it, not me."

"It's not a legal problem. And Ed can't help me."

"I'll see what I can do but no promises."

"You're the only one who can help. It's...a police officer, a patrolman, is taking advantage of her. He has to be stopped before he takes advantage of other women."

"Who?"

"No. Not on the phone."

"Then come down here and te—"

"No. Not there either. Somewhere else. Please?" She sounded desperate, pleading.

"Okay. When and where?"

"Hotel Atwater. At six? Or would seven be better?"

"I don't think that's a good idea." He loved Gina totally, but he wasn't sure he could resist another chance to do the mattress mambo with Heather Bartlett at the Atwater. Many of their afternoon trysts happened there.

"Then name a place, anyplace you want. Please? For Ashlee's sake?"

"Ah...the Hilton on Filmore." That was safe. They'd never hooked up there. "Six is fine. Can you give me a hint who we're talking about?"

"I'll tell you everything tonight. I promise. Thank you, Marco, Thank you."

As Dee hung up the phone, he wondered if he'd made a foolish mistake.

****

Jwakeen Phillips was nineteen, lean, and hard muscled, with a sparse soul patch on his chin and an elaborate crown tattooed on his left forearm. No MONARCH in the banner below it meant he hadn't earned full membership in the gang. He sprawled boneless in the chair across the table from Lafferty and Officer Ed Davis in the Three-Six's pit and threw a sneer at Rick. "Whatchu wan' wit' me, big bad detective man?"

"Need to ask you some questions."

"You 'terrogatin' me 'bout a shopliftin' beef, must be 'cause," he sneered at Davis, "Deppity Dawg here be afraid to be alone wit' me."

Davis, a mountain of muscle twice Jwakeen's size, fixed him with an icy stare. "You couldn't scare me with a bazooka pointed at my head, punk."

"Oooh." Jwakeen held his hands chest high and fluttered them. "Big man."

"Shut up, shithead, and listen for once in your miserable life. That shoplifting beef can go away, you help us with something else."

"Don't need it to go away. It's a bogus beef, an' you know it. I was gonna buy that bling for my old lady, jus' took it outside to scope it inna sunlight."

"Without asking the owner first," Rick said. "That's theft. This isn't going away, Jwakeen."

Phillips slid another inch down in his chair and shrugged. "You say I did the crime, I can do the time."

"Can you do life without parole? Or ten years on death row waiting to ride the needle?"

Phillips shot upright in the chair. "What? Life? On a shoplift beef? What you smoking,' man? Most I gonna do is a nickel, max."

"On the shoplifting beef, yeah. Snuffing a cop gets you life. Your age, that could be a long time. Or a short one if you get the needle. The DA's leaning that way."

"Whoa! What cop you talkin' 'bout?"

"Detective Mary Conner,"

"I ain't killed no lady Five-Oh. Don't be hanging that on me."

Davis snarled, "We got your fingerprints on the gun that dropped her. That makes you 'it' for her murder. Bet they already got a nice big needle waiting for you at Stony Point." The maximum-security prison in the western part of the state, home to the worst criminals.

"I'm tellin' you, man, I dint do her. May-a been my iron, but it wasn't me poppin' no caps."

"Yeah," Davis sneered, "and I'm the tooth fairy."

"Lis'en ta me! I...dint...shoot...no...lady...cop. I don't got my iron no more. 'Nother Five-Oh took it off me a couple weeks ago. Check it out. It be sittin' in your property room."

"When exactly did this officer take your piece?" Rick asked.

"Was a Tuesday, couple weeks ago." Phillips glanced at the ceiling. "The 'leventh, maybe?"

Rick and Davis exchanged glances then Davis left the room.

"So how did this officer taking your piece go down, Jwakeen?" Rick asked.

"Man, I'm just chillin' down by the river under the Hoover Street bridge, sittin' in my ride, lisenin' to tunes, not doin' nothin' wrong. This cop rousts me, say he after some dude what ripped off a mini-mart an' he thinks it's me done it. I tell him it ain't. He say he don't believe me, drags me outta my ride, cuffs me to the railing, searches my car. Then he say he be wrong, sorry, takes the cuffs off, an' splits. I get back in my ride, and my iron's gone."

"Just like that, hunh? Rousted you and took your gun?"

"I'm tellin' you, man, it's the troot."

Davis re-entered the room, sat next to Rick, and delivered a small headshake. Phillips said, "See? I told you I dint off that cop. Couldn't have 'cause that Five-Oh what rousted me took my iron."

"Tell me another one, worm, I need a good laugh," Davis growled. "No guns vouchered into the property room this month."

"What? That Five-Oh what took it must have kept it."

Rick stared at Phillips until he started to fidget then glanced at Davis. "You ever hear such a cockamamie story?"

Davis shook his head. "Not since my kid's one about how his mom's vase got broken."

"Know what I think, Jwakeen? I think you had a beef with Detective Conner, set her up with a phony meet, and offed her. Then you tossed your piece, and now you're covering your ass with this bullshit story about some cop taking your piece."

"I'm tellin' you, man, he took my iron."

"Where were you Sunday night, Jwakeen?" Rick asked.

"Maurice's."

"The titty bar on tenth?" Davis asked. "Anybody vouch for you being there?"

"Him an' one-a his bouncers."

"Why would they remember a loser like you?"

"Maurice took 'ception to me showin' my

'ppreciation to one-a his fillies by squeezin' her bootie an' tell her what a fine fox she was. Told his muscle to show me the door." Jwakeen made a fist. "I laid one in his eye, show him he cou'n't do that to me." Phillips looked away and worked his jaw for several seconds. "'Bouncer popped me upside my head a couple times and threw me out."

"Tell me about the officer who took your gun," Rick said. "What was his name?"

"I 'on't know. He didn't formally innaduce hisseff."

"Every officer wears a name tag on his uniform," Davis snapped.

"He dint have on no uniform. He was dressed all in black, like some ninja dude."

"So how did you know he was a cop?"

Phillips shot back, "I know fuzz when I sees them. Had fuzz smell on him, too."

"What did this officer look like?" Rick asked.

"He was a big dude." Phillips pointed at Rick. "Tall as you." He pointed to Davis. "Built like you. Tell you somethin' else about him. That guy is one bad dude."

"Bad how?" Davis asked.

"Word on the street be he work for Joey Day."

****

Ernesto Salazar sat in a stolen Ford Focus on the first level of the parking garage at Twelfth Street and JFK. The scrawny sixteen-year-old puffed on a Newport, bobbing his head in time with the salsa music on the lame factory radio. He wished he was in his brother Enrico's tricked out Mitsubishi Lancer, listening to the same tunes on its two-grand stereo. But Enrico had said use this car, so Ernesto did. Just like he kept his eyes glued to the doors to the street like he'd been told to. Whatever it took.

This was gonna be his day. He was finally gonna get his chance to prove he was a man to Enrico. And to Mr. Day. He'd been waiting for his chance ever since he was twelve, and Mr. Day had said it was okay for him to start hanging with Enrico at the clubhouse on Sesame. He'd done some things for Enrico and Mr. Day since then, but they'd been just kid stuff. This was the big time, and he was gonna do them proud.

He'd just about pissed his baggy jeans yesterday when Enrico hauled him in to meet with César Molina. Mr. Day's chief lieutenant had said Mr. Day had a job for him if he wanted it. He'd said yes, sir, Mr. Molina, just like he'd heard Enrico say it. Mr. Molina had said Mr. Day wanted some lady taken out, was he up to it? He'd said anything Mr. Day wants, I can do it. Mr. Molina said if he did good, it could earn him a place in Mr. Day's organization. He'd said he wouldn't let Mr. Day down.

After Mr. Molina left, Enrico had laid it all out for him, how Mr. Day wanted this lady run down, all the details right down to where to dump the car after he'd taken her out her. But that night in his bed, Ernesto had thought running the lady down was lame. He could come up with something better, a way to really prove himself to Mr. Day, to show him he could count on Ernesto to do things right the first time. He laid awake a long time figuring out how he'd do it.

Enrico had taken him to the garage that morning, early enough that they could see the lady arrive and where she parked her Honda. Ernesto didn't know why Mr. Day wanted her dead. That wasn't his concern. Mr. Day said do it, so he would. Once the lady got on the elevator, Enrico had him go through two dry runs on the street just to make sure he had the plan down straight in his mind.

At four, he'd picked up the Ford at the clubhouse, but instead of going straight to the parking garage on Twelfth Street like Enrico had said to, he'd swung by Enrico's crib and taken the MAC-10 from under his bed.

Ernesto lifted the edge of the jacket thrown on the passenger seat and darted a glance underneath. The gun was still there, ready to go. He wanted to be sure nothing would go wrong. He wanted to do this thing right for Mr. Day.

He checked the dashboard clock. Almost five-thirty. He lit another Newport and shifted in the seat, trying to get comfortable. Man, this waiting was a bitch. But he'd wait 'till next Thursday to show Mr. Day he could be a good soldier. And he was sure Mr. Day would appreciate him making sure the lady was taken out even if it wasn't the way he said to do it.

Moments later, the lady he'd been told to watch for came through the doors from the street and got on the elevator. Time to earn his stripes. Ernesto started the Ford, backed out of the stall, and headed for the third level. On the way, he hit the button that dropped the passenger window.

He stopped just before making the turn that would take him past the woman's car then leaned forward in the seat to keep an eye on the elevator. He slipped the MAC-10 from under the jacket and cocked it. A minute later, the woman got off the elevator with a bunch of other people and walked toward her Honda.

Party time. Ernesto took his foot off the brake and let the car roll forward. Steering with his left hand, he held the gun just below the open window until he was alongside the lady. He raised it then and pulled the trigger.

The MAC-10 bucked and jerked in his hand, sending bullets flying everywhere. A half-dozen punched holes in the Fusion. The gun's vicious kick and ear-crushing chatter scared the hell out of him, as did fifty red hot casings bouncing around the interior. He dropped the gun. Time to get out of there and tell Ernesto and Mr. Day the good job he'd done. He stomped the gas pedal to the floor.

The tires spun then bit, and the car shot forward. Ernesto jerked the wheel left to make the corner. The tires slid on the slick concrete, and the Ford plowed into a big Dodge pickup, shoving it into a Buick sedan.

Chapter 15

Dee spotted Heather the moment she entered the bar, and his breath hitched just as it had all those years ago. She still had that air of elegance, grace, and polish, and that something extra that drew the eyes of every man in the room to her. She smiled as she neared his booth, and his pulse quickened. He couldn't deny he still had the hots for her, but he'd made promises to Gina he would not break.

She slid into the booth. Her dark dress emphasized her fair skin, ash blonde hair, hazel eyes, and lithe curves. "Hello, Marco."

Only she could make hello sound erotic. He gave a quick nod. "Heather."

"A Dubonnet Cocktail, please," she said to the waitress who had come to their booth. As the girl hustled away, she said, "How have you been?"

"Good." He sipped his McNaughton's and water. "So what's up with Ashlee?"

"No how are you? No long time, no see?" She covered one of his hands with hers. "You haven't changed a bit, Marco."

"You, either."

Except for some faint age lines around her eyes, she hadn't. Same shoulder-brushing pageboy hairstyle, same full desirable lips, same captivating hazel eyes. And that same whisper of availability. He realized that was what drew every man's eyes to her, that aura that five minutes from now, they could be in a room upstairs, tearing each other's clothes off. It was drawing him in now as it had all those years ago. He slid his hand from under hers.

"Are you and Gina still together?"

"Yeah." The best reason to resist Heather's allure and his growing desire to have her again. He forced lusting thoughts of her away. "Tell me about this jam Ashlee's gotten into."

The waitress delivered her drink. Heather waited until she backed away then took a small sip and set the glass down. "She had a bit too much to drink one night a little while ago and got in a fender bender. The responding officer—"

"How much too much?"

"She blew point-one-one on the Breathalyzer. The officer said he had to arrest her and that it could destroy Ed's career with the DA's office. She was terrified of going to jail and costing her father his job."

Dee made the leap. "The officer said he could make it go away in exchange for something from her?"

Heather took a sip of her drink and nodded.

"Sex?"

Another nod. "What else would a cop want from a twenty-one-year-old girl to make a drunk driving charge go away?"

"Maybe a way to gain access to you? Or Ed? Maybe about a case he's prosecuting."

She shook her head. "He would have no reason to want to get to me. And why would he want to get to Edward about a case he's working on?"

She wasn't telling him something, he could sense it. "To stop it before it got to trial. Nothing like having something on the DA to make the charges go away. Or maybe something in the case could leave him open to prosecution, and he did it to save his hide. Or he could be dirty and doing it for whoever's got him in their pocket."

"Edward doesn't deal with drug dealers or gangs. He handles white-collar crimes like embezzlement and insurance fraud."

"Cops get involved in those, too. Who was the officer who stopped Ashlee?"

Heather shifted her gaze to over his left shoulder and took a long sip of her cocktail. "She didn't get his name."

"It's on the accident report. He gave her a copy." Dee waited a few moments then said, "Who was he, Heather?"

"I don't know." A quick glance at him then away before she spoke.

He took in some of his drink, let it rest on his tongue. What she was hiding clicked in his mind, and he swallowed. "Yes, you do. He jammed you up like he did Ashlee."

"No, he—" She took several sips from her drink as she gazed around the bar for a time. She set the glass down and stared into it for a minute then nodded.

"How?"

She put her hand over his again. Her voice was low and urgent. "You can't tell a soul. It would ruin everything for me if Edward ever found out." She squeezed his hand. "Promise me you won't tell anyone? Please! Promise me." She pinned him with those enchanting hazel eyes and rubbed her hand lightly over his. "I'll do anything you ask, any time you want, anywhere you want, if you promise not to tell him. Right now, if you want. And you know it will be good."

There it was, the come-on he'd been expecting since she slid into the booth. He was tempted—it would be *very* good—but giving in would cause far more damage than the pleasures of her body were worth. He slid his hand from under hers. "You don't have to do anything. I won't tell him. I promise." He'd done far worse things than keep a secret or two with nothing in return. "Let's hear it."

She withdrew her hand and fiddled with her diamond for a moment. Then she told him about being stopped with a small amount of pot by the same cop who stopped Ashlee. He said it was felony weight and arresting her could cost Ed his career but he could make it go away if she slept with him.

Dee wondered who had really made the offer. If she'd sleep with him to keep something from Ed, how far would she go to avoid arrest and save his career? If she'd truly been offended by the cop's offer, she could have reported him to someone in the police department or told Ed and let him handle it through the DA's office. Dee was willing to bet she'd made the offer.

Confirmation of what he'd long suspected she truly was, a woman who used men for her own ends. Well, she'd made that bed and she could lie in it. He wouldn't help her out of it. Her daughter was another story. He still harbored the vague suspicion she was his. "If I'm going to help Ashlee, I need his name, Heather."

"McHale. Sergeant Michael McHale."

****

McHale paid for his dinner and walked to his car. He didn't want to go back to NEMC. He didn't like to hit a place he was casing twice in the same day. But he had to get this done today. Tomorrow was Kill Mary day.

This was starting to feel like another rush job. Two days was no time frame to set up a hit like this. What was Joey's big hurry anyway? It wasn't like Virgin was gonna split for Bermuda tonight. She was going to be out of action for a long time.

Had to be Joey letting his cojones run his brain again. Going for right-now revenge for Bobby Ed hadn't been the smart way to do things. This wasn't either. Joey needed to cool it, let things die down a bit, then go after Virgin when the time was right.

McHale got to NEMC a little after six. The parking lot was so jammed, he had to leave his car in a lot halfway to frigging Outer Mongolia, and the shuttle bus, when it finally showed, was SRO. He spent the long slow journey to the hospital pinned between a rotund woman who'd bathed in Emeraude and an old man who smelled of stale cigars.

He took a crowded elevator to the sixth floor. As the mob shuffled out, he shuffled with them down the hall past the nurses' station. Three women and a man worked behind the counter. He didn't see the nurse he'd bumped into that morning.

Good. He'd read her as one sharp cookie. She wouldn't have bought the 'I'm lost' line a second time. He got the feeling, too, she'd sensed he wasn't what he claimed to be.

As the others peeled off into patient rooms, he continued on to the corner of the short hall where he'd run into the nurse this morning. There, he pulled off a loafer and tipped it over his upturned palm then angled his head as if looking for a pebble in both, but his eyes were on the hall. It appeared unused with dimmed overhead fluorescents and closed doors. Maybe he'd been wrong. Maybe Virgin wasn't in one of those rooms.

He set his loafer on the floor. As he slid his foot in, a door at the end of the hall opened, light from inside the room casting a skewed rectangle on the floor. A nurse stepped into the hall. The door closed as she started toward him, carrying a chart.

He should try to get a look at the name on it, see if it matched the one on the chart he'd knocked out of the other nurse's hand that morning. Bumping into her had been an accident, and he hadn't seen which room she came out of. He knew which one this nurse left. Maybe he could bump into her and make it look like an accident, too. The same name would confirm his gut feeling Virgin was in the room.

It would take timing. He'd take a few steps past the hall then turn back, and crash into her.

"Sir."

"Yes?"

The nurse was only a few feet away, the chart clutched to her chest. "There are no patient areas in this hall, just treatment and therapy rooms."

"Oh, sorry." He flicked a glance past her. A slim bar of light still showed under the last door on the left.

"Are you visiting a patient?" Her nametag read DENISE. Like Ann, the nurse this morning, she was mid-forties, average height, and with an air that said she'd been at it a while.

"Yeah, my wife's great Aunt Hannah. I was supposed to meet her—my wife, not her aunt—here. Maybe I got it wrong," he shrugged an 'I'm just a hapless male' gesture, "and I'm supposed to wait for her in the lobby."

"Maybe you just got off on the wrong floor. What's your wife's great aunt in for? Did she have an operation?"

"No, something with her heart, I think."

Denise motioned toward the nurses' station. "Let's see if we can find where she is." She stepped behind the counter and laid the chart on the raised front. "What's her last name?"

McHale glanced at the chart. The name in the ID slot was Miranda Vincente. Damn. Virgin wasn't in the room after all.

Wait a minute. hospitals in the city had aliases they used for people who didn't want it known they were in there. One alias was a different first name with the same first letter as the patient's real name and Vincente for a last name.

He gave Denise a lame smile. "You know, I hate to admit it, but I'm drawing a blank. It's some sort of Polish name with lots of cees and zees and wyes in it."

"Well, let's see if we can find her just by her first name." Denise clicked the mouse by a computer terminal.

"Thanks for the offer, but I'll save myself a ton of grief if I just go back to the lobby and find my wife." He strode to the elevators, his lips shifting into a grin. He had Virgin now for sure.

Miranda Vincente was Mary Conner.

****

Rick Lafferty entered his apartment and threw his sport coat on the couch. He took a beer from the fridge, twisted the cap off, and took a swallow. He'd just taken a second one when his phone rang.

"Hi, little brother."

"Hey, big sis. Three calls in three days. What's the occasion?"

"I wanted to see how you're doing."

"Better. How's Mary?"

"Doing better, too. Her heart rate, breathing, and temperature are all where they should be, and there's no sign of infection. The only down side is she's still in a coma."

"Is that a bad thing, her still being in a coma?"

"It would be better if she wasn't, but it could be that her body's done it so it can focus all its energy on healing, which is good."

Rick let out a breath. "Thanks, sis."

"My pleasure. Rick—" She fell silent.

He sensed something bothering her. "What's wrong?"

Silence from Ann. He waited.

"We have Mary in a room away from other patients. When I came out one time today, I ran into a man at the end of the hall her room is in." A pause. "I think he was a cop."

"What made you think that?"

"Something about him. I think it was his eyes. They were like yours when we talk, focused on me but taking in everything going on around us."

"Why would a cop bother you?"

"I don't…I just…I got the wrong vibe off him."

"Why? What did he do?" A cold band squeezed Rick's heart. "Did he say he was looking for Mary, ask for her by name?"

"No, nothing like that. He said he'd made a wrong turn getting off the elevator. It's easy enough to do, but I don't think he was lost. I think he was trying to find

Mary."

"What made you think that?"

"Nothing he did. I just got a real creepy feeling off him."

"Did you get a good look at the guy? Can you describe him?"

"Around our age, solid build, about as tall as you. That's the best I can do."

"How about race? Hair color? Eye color? Any scars or other identifying marks?"

"White." Ann paused. "Medium brown hair. Gray eyes. No scars I could see. Oh, and he had a small dimple in his chin."

Rick ran down his mental list of cops he'd flagged as dirty. Ann's description took maybe half of them out of the play. He'd have to update Dee on that. "Okay, tomorrow, you need to tell the cops guarding Mary and the hospital's head of security about the guy."

"I will, first thing. I promise. I don't want to lose her any more than you do."

****

She has to figure out where she is. She knows she's in a bed, but where? The sharp tang in the air is familiar but she cannot pin it down. She feels the blackness creeping over her and tries to will it to stay away.

****

McHale eased his Chevy onto the exit ramp, glad to be back in the city. His day in Dullsville had been a real ton of fun. Jesus, how could people live in a place where nothing was happening? The leading cause of death had to be terminal boredom.

Still, it hadn't been a wasted day. He had Virgin cornered. It was just a matter of when he put the crosshairs on her and pulled the trigger.

On the drive home, he'd planned how he'd do her. He'd made a few false starts and run into a few dead ends before he got a workable plan in place. It would take a little fine-tuning to be sure, but in rough form, it seemed solid. He intended to take the full two days Joey granted him to make it absolutely failure-proof. If Joey didn't like it, tough shit. He wasn't gonna botch taking Virgin out this time.

He stopped at the light at the end of the ramp. God, he was glad to be back in the city. He checked his watch. A little after nine. Too early to put the night away. But what to do?

Getting laid was always a good choice. He wouldn't have minded a round or two with either one of the NEMC nurses he'd run into. Especially the first one. Okay, she was probably on the far side of forty, but she was a real cutie. He could get into doing her. Maybe after he'd smoked Virgin, he'd go for it.

That didn't help him tonight. He ran through a list of women he could drop in on this time of night. He decided he didn't want much, just a quick humping before he headed home for a big Scotch. One name jumped out at him. Joleen.

She'd gotten lippy with him last time. Not a smart move for a broad whose future freedom was in his hands. Maybe she needed a reminder of that.

McHale got back on the Expressway. He took the next exit for the Swedetown area of the city. Five blocks and one turn later, he parked near Joleen's apartment. Her lights were on. Good.

The more he thought about it on the way there, the madder he got about her attempt to refuse him the other night. She really needed to learn her place in his world. He had a full-blown mad on when he pounded on her door.

****

Joleen sat sideways on the couch, her feet resting on the cushion, and massaged her burning calves. She'd worked a split double and her legs were killing her. It hadn't been all bad. Her tips had been good, and Nate had paid her time-and-a-half for covering Cindy's evening hours. He'd told her to take tomorrow off, too.

She closed her eyes and leaned her head against the thick arm of the couch. She couldn't remember the last time she had a whole day off. It had to be at least four or five weeks ago. A whole day with nothing to do. Well, almost nothing. Her apartment could use a good cleaning.

No way. She was *not* going to waste a day off cleaning. No alarm clock tomorrow, either. She'd sleep until she was good and ready to get up. Then what? A picnic? Yes. She'd pack a lunch, grab one of the books she hadn't read yet, and spend the rest of the day—

Hard pounding on her door startled her. She limped to the door, her legs protesting each step, and put an eye to the peephole. Her blood iced. McHale. What was he doing here? Why was he back so soon?

"Open up!" he bellowed over his fist thumping her door.

She glanced in the kitchen. Her knife lay on the table. Might as well be on the moon. Maybe if she didn't move, he'd go away.

"Open the hell up, Joleen! Now! I know you're in there!"

The longer she stalled, the worse his rape would be.

She undid the deadbolt lock. "Give me a second."

"Hurry up! I haven't got all night!"

She unhooked the safety chain. The second she twisted the doorknob, McHale shouldered it open, knocking her off-balance. She staggered back to stay on her feet. "What do you want?"

"What do you think?"

A pinpoint of white-hot rage formed in the center of her chest.

He spun her around and shoved her toward the kitchen. "Get in there." He pushed her again. "Move!"

She stumbled into the kitchen. Maybe, just maybe. She staggered a step sideways to block pulling the sharpened knife under her as he bent her over the table. McHale leaned over her, and in a cold voice, whispered in her ear, "Next time I knock on your door, you better have it open before the third one. Don't, and I will hurt you bad. You got that?"

She nodded as best she could with her head mashed against the table. He straightened and slid his hand to the middle of her back. The knife and her hand pressed into her chest, making it hard to breathe. McHale gathered up her skirt and ripped her panties off. Rage filled her.

McHale's hand left her back to pull his zipper down. *Now*, she told herself. She whirled around, swinging the knife as she straightened. He jumped back and the blade slashed through the space where his belly had been a second ago, the tip slicing his shirt. His face was white, his eyes wide. "Jesus! What the fuck's wrong with you?"

Ramona had been right. The bastard was afraid of knives.

Joleen held the blade at waist level. "Don't come near me again. Ever!" She thrust the knife toward him.

"Do it and I'll cut your balls off!"

He raised his hands, palms out. She stepped toward him. He backed away and licked his lips. "Joleen, hey, think what you're doing here."

"Get out!" She jabbed the knife at him. "Get out!"

He backed up another step. "Okay. Okay."

"Get out! Get out! Get out!" She lunged at him with the knife each time, driving him back another step.

"I'm going. I'm going." He backed to the door, reaching behind him for the knob, his eyes locked on the knife in her hand.

Joleen stabbed the knife at his gut. "Get! Out!"

McHale opened the door and fled.

"And don't come back." She slammed the door behind him.

Elation filled her. She was rid of the bastard for good. She could get on with her life, maybe even rebuild it from the tatters it was in. She raised her fisted hands overhead and shouted, "Yes!"

The knife slipped from her hand and thudded on the carpet. Had she really driven McHale from her life? Or had she just signed her own death warrant?

She stumbled to the couch and curled into a fetal ball.

****

McHale sat in his Impala and waited for his hands to stop shaking, his heart to stop racing, his breathing to slow down. He'd only ever been that scared twice before in his life.

His second year on the force, a greaser got the jump on him in an alley. He froze when the blade came at his gut and, if his partner hadn't blown Tacoboy away, McHale would have gotten sliced and diced but good.

215

He forgot about the incident for ten years until that black bitch, Ramona Jefferson, pulled a blade on him when he cornered her for another payment. She owed him for letting a diamond tennis bracelet stroll out of Harbison Jewelers on her legs. One flash of the knife in her hand that day and he'd backed down like some candy-ass and never messed with her again.

Fear faded and anger took over. A knife! Joleen had pulled a knife on him! How did she know a blade scared the shit out of him? Had to be Ramona told her.

Anger shifted to cold rage. He'd deal with both of those bitches, teach them you don't screw with Michael McHale, not without paying big. He'd get to Ramona in due time, but Joleen was gonna pay first. Defy him then draw a knife on him? She'd gotten way too big for her britches and needed to be smacked down hard. And soon.

He dialed her number. The moment she answered, he shouted, "You are dead, Joleen. Fucking dead!" and snapped his phone shut.

He fired his Impala, yanked the shifter into Drive, and smoked the tires all the way to the corner.

Chapter 16

Friday – April 24, 2015

Rick Lafferty leaned into his hands braced on the shower wall and let hot water stream over his head and down his body. He hadn't slept well, leaving him stiff.

A dream had woken him at four a.m., the image from it hanging in the back of his mind like a shape just visible in a fog. It had to be something important or it would have vanished when he woke. He'd thrashed around in bed trying to pin the image down until his alarm rang at six-thirty. He'd shuffled to the kitchen and started coffee brewing before heading for the shower.

Standing under the water wasn't getting him anywhere. He pushed off the wall and grabbed the shampoo. As he lathered, the image that had eluded him for so long popped into sharp focus in his mind. A phone. What did it mean? Rick was in the middle of shaving when he figured it out.

He raced to work, trotted straight to Dee's office, and burst in without knocking. "Dee, I had a thou—" The expression on Dee's face stopped the rest on his tongue. "What?"

"Ellen Shires got killed last night."

Rick dropped into a chair facing the desk. "Where? What happened?"

"Kid by the name of Ernesto Salazar, sixteen,

dropped her in the parking garage at JFK and Twelfth just before five-thirty last evening."

"Shit!" Rick ran his hands down his face.

"Shit is right." Dee pulled papers from the pile to his right and read. "Breyer and Walsh in the Oh-Two caught the squeal. Salazar fired fifty rounds from a MAC-10 at Shires, killed her and three others, wounded six more, four seriously, and shot up half a dozen cars including the one he was in."

"How did Breyer and Walsh manage to nail him?" Catching the shooter in a drive-by was rarer than finding gold in a donut.

"More by luck than management. He crashed into another car trying to get away, knocked himself out. Car he was driving was stolen."

"Big surprise there. What do we know about this Salazar kid?"

"He's in the system for some juvie beefs— shoplifting, vandalism, drug possession, and the like. Criminal Intel says he's a hanger-on with Los Lobos, Joey Day's crew. His brother, Enrico, is a blooded member."

"You think Day's behind killing the Shires woman?"

"That'd be my take."

"Wasting Shires was Ernesto's final exam to join the Lobos?"

"Yeah, only he failed the final. You started to say something when you came in. What's on your mind?"

"I got to thinking last night about Mary's shooting. Nobody in Lukens' building said they heard the shots. So who called it in?"

"Good question. I don't know if Harter and Pryzlo

ran that down." He picked up his phone and dialed. "Detective Harter or Pryzlo in the house?" He waited. "Harter? Marco DeAngelis…I was wondering did you ever find out who called in Conner's shooting?…No, I was just curious who made it….If you would, I'd appreciate it. Thanks." He hung up. "Harter says they're working on it. Anything else?"

Rick said, "Back to Salazar. What's he saying about smoking the Shires woman?"

"Nothing so far. After he was released from the hospital, Breyer and Walsh let him stew overnight in a holding cell. Breyer called me a few minutes ago, said Salazar wants to talk. Walsh's pretty well wired inside the force, knew Shires was tied into Conner's shooting. He said we could listen in while they question him. You interested?"

"Hell, yeah. Let's go."

****

Like every interrogation room in every District house in the city, the Oh-Two's 'pit' had gray walls, a gray tile floor, and harsh overhead lights glaring on battered gray metal chairs and a scarred gray metal table.

Rick and Dee stood in the observation room next door, studying Ernesto Salazar through a two-way mirror. Walsh and Breyer stood with them. Breyer was a lean black with close-cropped black hair and a thick moustache. Walsh was tall, stockier, and older, with wavy gray hair and gold-framed glasses.

Ernesto slouched in a chair in the pit, a cast-covered forearm resting on the table. He was a thin kid with light olive skin and coal black hair, long black lashes any girl would kill for, and deep brown eyes. Several small cuts marked his handsome young face and a white plastic brace spanned his nose. Next to him sat a well-built middle-aged man in an expensive charcoal suit, white shirt, and dark blue tie with gold fleur-de-lis. His thick black hair appeared freshly barbered, and a heavy gold Rolex circled his wrist.

Dee said, "M. Donovan Nesbitt's his lawyer?"

"The one and only," Walsh answered in a gravelly voice. "Says he was retained to represent Salazar."

"By who? Joey Day?"

"Probably." Walsh shrugged. "You guys good to go?"

"All set," Dee answered.

A few moments later, Walsh and Breyer entered the interrogation room. They took seats across from Salazar and Nesbitt. Nesbitt said, "I'll make this short and sweet. My client has nothing to say to you," in a rumbling bass.

"He told us he did."

"He was in error in that regard."

Salazar added, "Yeah, I don't got nothin' to say."

Walsh studied Salazar for a moment. "You don't want to talk, that's fine. Just listen. Here's where you stand, kid. Forget about the six cars you shot up and the damage you caused to a municipal facility." He swept his hand across the table as if brushing them aside. "We don't need them. We have you cold on four counts of murder, ten counts of attempted murder, and ten counts of assault with a deadly weapon. You're going away for a long time, son."

Nesbitt snorted. "The most he'll serve, gentlemen, is five years at Rockford Hall." The juvenile detention center north of the city. "Or at worst, Elm Grove." The state juvenile correction facility.

"Wrong, Counselor. He's going to Stony Point. For

the rest of his life."

"My client's a juvenile, sixteen years old. And this is his first felony offense. The court will never send him there."

"Oh, yes, they will. Special circumstances attach to the charges because he used a banned assault weapon to murder four people and seriously wound six more—who could still die. He'll be tried as an adult, and he'll do adult time."

Salazar sat up straight. "What? Whad'ya mean—"

Nesbitt put a hand on his cast. "Quiet. That will only happen if you get a conviction, Detective."

"It's a slam-dunk, Counselor. We got the car he used, we got the gun he used, we got his fingerprints on both, we got slugs from that gun from ten people, and four eyewitnesses who put him at the scene, pulling the trigger on that gun."

"Let me tell you what your life's gonna be like at Stony Point," Breyer said in a rich baritone. "They love fresh fish up there, especially a pretty boy like you. They're gonna snatch you up the minute you walk through the door."

"I ain't no boy." Salazar puffed out his chest. "I'm a man!"

"You won't be there. You'll be some lifer's bitch, sucking his cock or taking it up your ass every time he says bend over."

"Anybody tries, I'll cut it off. I ain't no man's bitch."

"You will be. Six guys three times your size will hold you down and do you, and you'll take it and like it. Or they'll beat the shit out of you until you're begging them to let you be their butt buddy. Either way, some lifer will own you and he'll loan you out to anybody he wants a favor from or owes a debt to or just for the hell of it."

Salazar paled under his olive skin.

"That's enough, gentlemen," Nesbitt shouted. "This interview is over!"

"What interview, Counselor? We're just informing Ernesto here of what his future holds. When the lifer who owns you gets tired of you, Ernesto, he'll trade you to another con for a pack of cigarettes, and you'll be that con's bitch until he tires of you and passes you on to someone else. That's gonna be your life at Stony Point until you rot away from AIDS—you'll get it for sure from some con who does you—or get a shiv in your gut for dissing the wrong badass."

Walsh said, "That's if the DA doesn't seek the death penalty." He looked at Nesbitt. "Special circumstances allow that, and he's seriously considering it. Right?"

Breyer nodded and Walsh shifted his gaze back to Salazar. "Know what that means, kid? They strap your sorry ass down and stick a needle in your arm and shoot poison in your veins until your heart blows up."

Fear filled Ernesto Salazar's eyes, and he swallowed hard.

Nesbitt said, "What can we do, gentlemen, to take special circumstances off the table, send this back to juvenile court? Give this young man a chance to turn his life around."

"The DA might be willing to drop special circumstances," Breyer said, "if your client tells us everything he knows about the incident at the garage including who ordered it and why."

"I ain't no rat. I ain't sayin'—"

Nesbitt leaned toward Salazar and whispered in his ear. Salazar chopped air with his good hand. Their whispered conversation continued for a minute before both men faced Walsh and Breyer. Nesbitt said, "Gentlemen, my client is willing provide everything he knows regarding the shooting at the municipal parking facility in exchange for dropping special circumstances. And he will plead guilty to four counts of murder and to the wounding of other individuals if he is assured of incarceration in Rockford Hall or Elm Grove. Do we have a deal?"

"That's up to the DA. Let's hear what your client has to say."

"No dice, gentlemen. Deal first then my client talks."

Breyer said, "No dice, Counselor. Talk first then your client gets a deal. The DA won't approve one until he knows your client has something worthwhile to offer."

"That's unacceptable, gentlemen. My client must have guarantees in place before he says word one about events at the municipal parking facility."

Walsh said, "Talk to the DA."

Nesbitt had another whispered conference with Ernesto then stood. "I will. In the meantime, you are to have no conversations with my client outside my presence. And now, if you will excuse us, I wish to consult with my client in private."

"Sure thing, Counselor."

Breyer and Walsh stood and started for the door. Breyer sang, "Stony Point, here he comes," to the tune of "California, Here I Come."

"Hey! Come back!" Ernesto shouted with panic in

his voice. "I tell you everything I know 'bout whackin' that woman."

Breyer and Walsh stopped, Walsh with his hand on the door handle. Nesbitt said, "Ernesto, be quiet!

"Ain't your ass on the line. I gotta do what I gotta do. Go way. Leave me alone."

"Ernesto, I strongly advise you not to say a word without me here to protect you."

"You gonna protect me at Stony Point?"

"Trust me, Ernesto, you kick me out, you will go to Stony Point." Nesbitt pointed to the detectives. "I'm the only one who can keep them from sending you there."

"I don't want you round here no more."

Nesbitt picked up his briefcase and got to his feet. "As you wish. But I strongly urge you not to talk to these men without legal representation."

"And I strongly urge you to get your ass out of here, lawyer-man."

Walsh jacked his thumb at the door. "You heard him, Counselor. Hit the road."

Nesbitt eyed at the young man for a second or two, shook his head, and walked out.

"You want to know 'bout that lady, I tell you."

Walsh and Breyer returned to the table. Breyer said, "The counselor's right. You really shouldn't be talking to us without a lawyer."

Ernesto shot glances at one then the other. "I don't care, man. I'll tell you all 'bout whackin' that lady, but first, man, you gotta promise me I don't go to Stony Point. I don't want some guy stickin' his cock up my ass."

"That's up to you, Ernesto," Walsh said. "You do right by us, we'll do right by you."

He thought that over for a bit then nodded his head. "Okay. See, my brother Enrico, two days ago he takes me to meet with this guy what says he wants a hurt—"

"What guy?" Breyer asked.

"I ain't sayin.'"

"Don't bail on us right outta the gate, kid. You gotta name names if you want us to help you. Otherwise, you're on the road to Stony Point."

Salazar looked away for a second. "César Molina."

****

Ann stopped at the door to Mary's—She had to stop that!—Miranda's room. She'd gone through another restless night, the guilt over hiding her connection to Mary through Rick eating at her. She'd left home in the morning determined to tell all, then plead her case for being allowed to care for Mary. "Caitlin, could I talk to you in the hall a minute?"

"Sure."

Outside the room, Ann's determination fled as the fear she'd be taken off the case reasserted itself. She'd keep her connection to Mary secret, only tell Caitlin the other thing on her mind. "I had something happen yesterday I think you should know about. I ran into a guy—literally—at that end of the hall yesterday morning who said he was going to the post-op ward but got turned around. Denise had something similar happen to her, too, on second shift."

"People getting lost around here's easy."

"Well, yeah, but I got the feeling this guy wasn't lost." She pointed to the door, "I think he was really looking for her."

"What made you think that?"

"Not any one big thing, just little things. Like I

dropped this," Ann raised Mary's chart a few inches, "when I ran into him. When he picked it up, I'm sure he read the name before he handed it back. And he looked past me while he was telling me about getting lost, as if he was trying to find out what was going on in this hall. And I got a bad feeling off him. That's what really made me think he wasn't lost, was really looking for her."

"What happened to Denise?"

"Almost the same thing. He was standing there," she pointed to the far end of the hall, "like he was going to come down here. She said this wasn't a patient area and asked if he was looking for someone. He said his wife's aunt who was admitted for a heart problem, but she had the same feeling I did that he was more interested in what was going on in this hall. When she offered to help him find his wife's aunt, he couldn't tell her the aunt's name."

Caitlin took a notebook and pen from her smock. "Describe him."

"Tall, maybe six–one or –two as a guess, husky build. In his forties. Gray eyes, short medium brown hair, moustache, a square face with a dimpled chin."

"What about his clothes?"

"Yellow polo shirt, tan sport coat, olive slacks, brown loafers. That's the other thing that gave me a bad feeling about him. Denise described the same guy, right down to his clothes. Don't you think it odd the same man would tell two different stories?"

"Definitely."

"There's one more thing. I think he might have been a cop."

"What made you think that?"

"Mostly his eyes. I told you my brother's a cop. This guy had the same kind of eyes as him. Even though they're focused on you, they're taking in everything around you. You and Allison do it, too."

Caitlin smiled. "Goes with the job."

Ann pointed to the door. "If she's in danger, if that guy's after her for some reason, I thought you should know about it."

"She is, and we should. Thanks for filling me in. Now I need you to do two things for me. I need to talk to the nursing supervisor, and I need Denise's phone number."

"I'll get right on it."

****

She recognizes the sharp tang in the air and knows where she is. In a hospital. Why is she in a hospital? She tries to think. She recalls leaving her car and locking it. The film of her life stops there, cut off as if snipped.

****

Two hours later, Lafferty, DeAngelis, Breyer, and Walsh gathered at the break room table in District 2's house. Rick said, "So Molina recruited the Salazar kid to whack Shires."

"On Joey Day's orders," Breyer said. "Molina's his right-hand man. He doesn't fart unless Day tells him to." He pointed to the pastry box on the table. "Help yourself."

"Only Salazar screwed up big time. Joey wanted Shires run down. Instead, Salazar takes her and nine others out with a MAC-10. Talk about overkill." Rick snagged a pineapple Danish and took a bite.

"Trying to show Joey he's got cojones."

"Joey won't like that," Walsh said.

"The question is why did Day want the Shires woman iced?" Breyer asked.

"It's gotta tie in to Conner's murder," Dee said. "Shires lived in the building where Conner got it, told Harter she saw a guy leaving who could have been Conner's shooter."

Walsh sat up in his chair. "She give Harter a description?"

Dee pulled out his notebook. "A big guy with brown hair and a moustache, no glasses, cop uniform, ball hat with a PD patch on the front, and carrying a black gym bag. That was the best she could do."

"Not much to go on. Lotta cops fit that description. She get a name?"

Dee shook his head. "They didn't talk, she just passed him in the lobby. Be happy Harter got what he did. She told him she was a bit buzzed when they crossed paths."

Walsh tapped a pencil against his palm. "So Day's got a cop in his pocket."

Dee said, "Probably more than one."

"According to someone I know as many as a hundred."

The other cops in the room digested that for a minute. Breyer took a sip from a Styrofoam cup of coffee. "Just because Shires said the guy's a cop, doesn't mean he is."

"Doesn't mean he isn't."

Rick said, "We haul Molina in, he going to give us anything?"

"Attitude," Breyer said. "I worked Criminal Intel for a while. We pulled Molina in I don't know how many times on things we knew—*knew*—Day was behind, sweated him in the pit for hours. He'd sit there and not say boo, just give us the dead-eye stare."

"Maybe you didn't offer him the right incentive to talk." Dee put the last of an éclair in his mouth.

"He'd give up his little sister before Joey. Hell, he did. She's Las Lobas. They did a smash and grab at Delgado Jewelers four years ago where the owner got shot, but Joey for sure was behind it. Owner told us Molina had been in the day before offering 'protection' and said he saw Day's Caddy parked up the block right before the Lobas hit him. So we grab Molina and lean on him for hours about it, say we know Joey's behind it. Finally, he says, 'Serafina, she done it.' He and Joe are free men while she's three years into a dime in Johnson City." A ten-year sentence.

"Molina ever visit Serafina?" Rick asked.

"Every week, according to the visitor logs," Walsh said.

"Maybe that's the incentive to offer him," Breyer said. "Johnson City's ninety minutes from here. Harpsville is all the way up by Erie, gotta be at least nine, ten hours each way. And it's maximum security."

Walsh smiled. "Be a shame if she did something that got her transferred there to serve out the rest of her dime."

"We've gotten off track here," Dee said. "The question is how do we get to Joey for Conner's shooting?"

"Easy. We drag Enrico Salazar in, offer him a choice. He gives us Joey or he and Ernesto go away for a long time."

Breyer stood. "I'll get a BOLO out."

****

"Answer me, Enrico," Joey Day said in a cold voice.

"I swear, Mr. Day, I told him to do it just like you

told me," Enrico answered through split, swollen lips and smashed teeth. Blood from his crushed nose dripped off his chin and splashed on concrete. "I don't know why he—"

"César."

Molina slammed a big fist into Enrico's broken ribs. Salazar screamed in pain. He stood naked on the basement floor of the clubhouse on Sesame. He had no choice. His hands were shackled to hooks in floor joists overhead.

"Do not lie to me, Enrico."

"I'm not lying, Mr. Day, I swear on my mother's grave."

"*Su Madre* was a *puta*, fucking men for five dollars."

"No, she—"

Joey flicked his hand. "César."

Molina buried a fist in Enrico's gut. Enrico sagged against his restraints. Molina slapped his battered face several times then threw a bucket of water on him. Enrico shook his head and got his feet under him.

"Where did your son of a *puta* brother get the idea he could do as he pleased instead of following my orders?" Joey bellowed. "Where? Did you tell him?"

"I swear to you, Mr. Day, no. I told him to do it just like you said. Showed him how. Twice. Had him do it twice, too."

Joey Day sighed. "Yet he did things his way! How is that possible?"

"I don't know, Mr. Day. He, he must have thought you'd be more impressed—"

Joey Day put his face inches from Enrico's and roared, "I am not impressed! I do not like people who do not listen to me! Even worse, your scum of a brother managed to not fix the problem I asked him to fix! He made it worse! I do not like people who fail me!" He backed away. "César."

Molina swung a booted foot into Enrico's swollen testicles. His scream echoed off the basement walls.

"Do you know where your scum of a brother is now, Enrico?"

Enrico shook his head slowly.

"He is with the police! That could cause me problems, many, many problems."

"He won't talk, Mr. Day. He is loyal to you. He will not turn on you."

Joey Day shrugged. "I cannot chance it."

"No, Mr. Day, please. He's only sixteen. He made a mistake. That was wrong. Please, I beg you. Give him another chance. He won't mess up again."

Joey Day pursed his lips and scanned the empty basement for many seconds. "Perhaps you are right, perhaps he does deserve another chance."

"Thank you, Mr. Day, thank you. He won't let you down again. I promise."

Joey Day strode to the stairs. He stopped and stared at Enrico. "Still, someone must pay for his mistake, however." He started up the stairs. "César."

Molina picked up a knife. Enrico screamed until César plunged it into his heart twenty minutes later.

Chapter 17

Joleen hummed as she brushed her hair. McHale was out of her life. She was no longer his unwilling whore. And despite his promise to kill her, she would no longer live in fear of him. For the first time in a long time, she felt like a girl again. Her face in the dresser mirror looked younger, too. The dark circles were fading from below eyes that were bright and happy for a change.

She waltzed to her closet. Jeans and a blouse or a dress for her picnic? She wore that idiotic pink uniform all the time at Nate's. Jeans it was. She glanced out the open window. Sunny. A warm breeze drifting through the screen brushed over her. No, no jeans. A summer-like April day deserved a summer dress. She pawed through the few she had. The light blue one. Perfect. And white sandals.

She slipped them on then pranced into the living room. Scanning the books on her shelf, she paused to consider each title until she spied John Grisham's *The Street Lawyer*. She'd had it for a long time but had never read it, even though he was her favorite writer. She tucked it next to the blanket in her tote, looped the straps over her shoulder, and left her apartment. Oops. Sunglasses. Couldn't forget sunglasses. She dashed back into the apartment to grab them.

Walking down the street in the sunshine was like walking on air. It had been too long since she'd had a day like this, a day totally for herself. Her first day free of the cloud of McHale hanging over her, raining on her. Even the dank reek of the mid-block alley couldn't taint this day. She tipped her head back and smiled at the heat of the sun on her face.

Nothing today was going to be routine. She wasn't going anywhere near Nate's. She wasn't going to think about McHale. She wasn't going to dwell on what her life had become. She was going to look ahead, not back.

She felt like skipping. Why not? She did, all the way to the corner, stopping only because the light was red. She took in a deep breath and let it out with a happy sigh. The light changed, and she trotted across the street on springy steps. A man on the corner said, "Miss?"

"Yes?"

"I just want to tell you seeing a pretty young woman smiling and as carefree and happy as you has made my day."

"Why, thank you!" She executed a small curtsey then entered Sol's Deli. After ordering a turkey and ham hoagie with everything, she gathered a bag of ridged chips, and a bottle of Coke. This was her day, and she was going to enjoy it to the max.

Sol said, "Pretty as a picture you are today, Joleen," as he rang her purchases. "It is good to see you smiling. It makes you beautiful. And it is good for you, too." He waggled a finger. "Take it from this old man."

She stowed her lunch in the tote. On the sidewalk, she skipped a few steps then stopped. She wanted to drink her Coke, not wear it. She strolled the sidewalk on long easy strides, her arms swinging, her hips swaying. A man passing the other way wolf-whistled. She spun around and flashed him a big smile. In spite of all she'd endured from McHale, and maybe because of how worthless and trashy he made her feel, the stranger's admiration make her heart float.

A second later, a police cruiser pulled into the curb, and the driver's door opened. Her blood iced, and her mind screamed *McHale! He's coming to get me!* She froze, ready to turn and run. The driver got out. He was young and fresh faced and didn't look much older than her. He gave her a smile, touched his cap in a salute, and said, "Morning, miss," as he passed her.

She shook her panic away. Not all cops were McHale. She forced him from her mind again. He was out of her life and not going to ruin her day. She made herself take a few light steps then the sun and her freedom and her light heart took over, putting real spring back in her stride. She glanced back. The young officer stood watching her as if he'd never seen a girl in his life. She smiled, and a goofy expression filled his face.

She sauntered the paths of Griffin Park, seeking the perfect place for her picnic. She was in no rush. This was her special day. Everything was clicking. In five minutes, she had her perfect spot by a giant maple.

She spread her blanket half in, half out of its shade, knelt, and laid out her lunch and book. Leaning back on her elbows, she angled her face to the sky and let the sun's warmth wrap around her. She closed her eyes and breathed slowly, savoring the smells of flowers and pine and grass. She let them and the chirp of birds, the squeals of children, and the barks of dogs take her back to her childhood, back to before Bryce and his coke had made a mess of her life, before McHale and his abuse had battered her soul.

She sat up, unwrapped her sub, and opened her

chips. She held the Coke at arm's length and twisted the cap. The soda made a sharp *Pffft!* And foamed only a little. She screwed the cap off and swigged. The fizz and cold felt good in her mouth and throat.

She picked up her sub, took a bite, and opened *The Street Lawyer.* She gagged on the food in her mouth, almost spit it out. *For being stand-up! Bryce,* graced the flyleaf. That's why she'd never read it. The creep had given it to her after she'd taken the second fall for his coke. *Thanks a ton, Bryce, you worm.*

Screw him. He was out of her life now, couldn't mess with it anymore, and she wasn't going to let memories of him ruin her day. She paged to Chapter One.

****

Dee pulled his Taurus into traffic. "I got some bad news, Rick. Our—"

"About Mary? She's all right, right?" He cracked the car's window to let in some air.

"Yeah. She's fine. But Narcotic's UC guy in Joey Day's organization got word to them that Joey ordered another hit on Mary. And he wants it done by this weekend."

"Shit, Dee. When is this gonna stop?"

"Soon. Look, the Staties guarding her are some of the toughest cops I've ever met. Think momma bears guarding cubs, and Mary's their cub. They aren't going to let anybody get to her. Especially after Boyer gives them this new info."

"You say so, Dee, I trust you."

"I also heard from Boyer about those names you gave me. He read all their jackets. Some of them skate a little close to the edge, some of them have been in trouble with IA, but none of them came up dirty. He even had another IA cop review them, and he agreed."

"We need a break on this, Dee. 'Cause I'm getting nowhere fast."

"I think I got one." He wheeled the Taurus to the curb. "Let's grab some lunch."

Seated at a booth in Minnie's Luncheonette, their sandwiches before them, Rick asked, "So what do you have, Dee?"

"In a minute. You got anything for me, first?"

"Maybe. I've been thinking about Mary getting shot. I don't have it all worked out in my head yet, but I'm getting there."

"Let me hear what you got."

"Okay. Mary goes to Lukens' place to confront him about Sam. Maybe he pulls a piece on her, maybe she just loses it for a second. Either way, she caps him. That puts her in a big jam. So, what's she do?" He bit into his hot ham and cheese.

"Call in a fixer to unjam her."

Rick chewed fast, swallowed. "Right. Every cop knows a cop who's good at making bad go away. What if the fixer Mary called was in Day's pocket?"

Dee considered as he chewed a bite of his chicken salad. "Could be."

"The other thing I've been thinking is the whole thing with Mary's shooting smacks of a rush job."

"How so?"

"Lukens was a big-gun guy, right? Nothing but .45s in his crib. Yet Mary got shot by a cheap-o .32. Why didn't the guy who popped her use one of Lukens's pieces? It's like Joey wanted Mary taken out right then and there, leaving him no time to plan, so he grabbed the

.32 because it was handy."

"Does sound like a rush job." Dee drank some Pepsi. "Mary's hit doesn't match Joey's style, either. He orders somebody iced, it's a clean hit— one shot to the head— or he has the guy tortured for a while then kills him painfully. Mary wasn't tortured and she took two in the belly. And usually Joey separates his hits from whatever set him off by a week or more to make the connection between the two less obvious. Harter and Pryzlo haven't found anything linking Mary and Joey Day except for Lukens."

Rick slid his plate aside, waved the waitress over, and ordered a slice of blueberry pie. She scurried away, and he said, "So what's this break we got?"

"Last night an old friend reached out to me for help with her daughter. The girl had an MVA a couple months ago while DUI. The responding officer gave the girl a choice: get hit with the full book for the crash and DUI or put out for him. The daughter chose option two."

"Be a hell of a thing to find out your daughter was doing."

"If Katie ever did that, I'd kill her. First for the DUI, then for doing that to get out of it. There's more to the story. A year or so back, the same officer caught my friend holding less than an ounce of weed, claimed it was enough to charge her with possession with intent."

"And offered her the same deal as the daughter."

"Bingo. But that isn't all. Daddy-slash-hubby is a big man in town. As in an ADA."

"Geez, Dee. You think the cop jammed up the daughter and wife to get to him?"

"Could be. I'm looking into it."

"So who's the cop getting freebies from your friend

and her daughter?"

"McHale."

****

"You like Grisham?"

Joleen shrieked and jumped, dropped her book and almost her sub as well. She pressed her hand over her heart. "You scared the daylights out of me."

"Sorry, miss." The officer she'd passed near Sol's squatted on the grass in front of her, his hat in his hand. He had carrot-red hair and a ton of freckles across his face. He stripped off his sunglasses, revealing warm brown eyes. "I should have cleared my throat or something to let you know I was here." He smiled, showing a chipped incisor, and handed her the book. "But, as wrapped up as you were in this, you still probably would have done the same thing."

She smiled back. "Probably."

"So do you like Grisham?"

"My favorite. Do you like him, too?"

"Darn close to the top of my list." He pointed to the book. "This the first time you read that one?"

She nodded. "I've had it a long time, I just never got around to reading it."

"It's a good one. You'll like it." He seemed suddenly uncomfortable. "I, uh, hope you won't take this wrong, think I'm coming on to you—well, maybe I am, kinda." A shy smile curled his lips, and a blush reddened his face and ears. "But after I saw you on the street earlier, I couldn't get you out of my mind. I've been looking all over the park for you. I had to meet you."

She almost laughed until she felt her own blush rising. "Well, thank you…?"

"Offic—" He shook his head. "Sorry. Tim. Tim

Morris." He extended his hand.

After a moment's hesitation, she shook it. "Joleen Wilson. Nice to meet you, Tim."

"Same here, Joleen. I like that, it's a real nice name. So what's—" He pointed to the blanket. "May I?"

A chill ran through her, and she hesitated again. What if McHale had sent him? What if Tim's come-on was just to catch her off-guard? What if McHale was waiting nearby to kill her for swinging that knife at him last night? She forced those doubts away.

Not every cop was like McHale she told herself again. What if Tim was just what he claimed to be, a guy who couldn't stop thinking about her? It had been a long time since a man talking to her had blushed like a teenager. That made her think his words were honest. Wasn't she entitled to having a guy attracted to her? She was due a little of that. If it blew up in her face tomorrow, so be it. Today she was going to enjoy time with a guy who had to meet her. "Sure."

Tim sat on the blanket. "So, what's your favorite Grisham book?"

****

Caitlin Burke had her hand on her Sig Sauer when she cracked the door to room five just wide enough to peer out. Allison Sheehy had backed against the wall to the right of the door at the knock and drawn her weapon. Dr. Cyril Nicopoulos stood in the hall, his driver's license held up next to his NEMC badge. Caitlin compared both pictures to his face carefully then said, "Okay," and stepped back, opening the door.

Nicopoulos entered, and she said, "Arms straight out from your sides please, Doctor."

"Is this really necessary?" Nicopoulos sighed,

raising his arms.

"Yes."

"Every time?" Nicopoulos asked with annoyance.

"Every time." She did a quick pat down of the doctor's stocky body. "Clear."

Allison slid her automatic into its holster beneath her nurse's smock.

Dr. Nicopoulos bustled to the bed and spent the next ten minutes examining his patient, checking her IVs, and noting the readings on the monitors in her chart. He tapped his pen against the page for a moment then scribbled some notes.

Caitlin asked, "So how's she doing, Doctor?"

Nicopoulos closed the chart. "I really can't discuss—"

"Come on, Doctor. She's a fellow officer. You'd tell one doc how another doc's doing, wouldn't you?"

"As a professional courtesy." Nicopoulos tapped his pen against his palm a few times. "Your point is made. Without going into details, she continues to do better than I expected. Much better, considering the extent of her injuries and the length and complexity of her surgery. But she's not out of the woods yet. She could develop complications that will delay her recovery. I can't say they will happen, I can't say they won't. I can say, barring anything unforeseen, she will make a full recovery."

"That's great!" Caitlin said.

Allison asked, "What about the coma? We really need to talk to her, Doctor."

Dr. Nicopoulos tucked his pen in his smock. "That bothers me. She should have come out of it by now. It could be she is metabolizing—breaking down—the anesthesia much slower than the average person, although I've never seen anyone stay under this long."

"So when's she gonna come out of it?"

Nicopoulos shrugged. "Ask God. He knows. I sure don't."

All three jumped at the sudden harsh screech of the monitor alarm. Mary thrashed on the bed. Nicopoulos lunged toward the wall, slapped the red button on the intercom, and snapped, "Code Orange, room five. Code orange, room five."

****

She is choking, gagging. Something is lodged in her throat. She tries to cough it out but can't. Had she inhaled a snake? She calls out. Are the people with her deaf? She claws at her neck. Can't they see she's choking? Her body arches and thrashes and pain and panic fill her. Suddenly the thing choking her is sliding up and up, sliding, sliding, sliding out of her mouth. Then it is gone and air fills her lungs. She relaxes and blackness covers her.

Chapter 18

Rick unlocked the door to Mary's apartment and stepped inside. Flynn from IA had said they hadn't searched it for clues to why she'd gone to Lukens's apartment, they weren't looking into 'why,' only what happened after she got there. He had to know for his own peace of mind. Had she finally snapped over Sam's death? His heart cramped. Why hadn't she come to him?

He stood inside the door for a minute with his eyes closed, taking in the unique smell of her home. A hint of her perfume in the air triggered a flood of memories. They weren't erotic or even romantic. They were simple day-to-day things. Scrabble games and *Forrest Gump*. Gin rummy marathons and long talks. Saturday morning cartoons and Sunday morning breakfasts.

Rick let the memories play out then stepped to the middle of the living room. He did a slow pivot, taking in everything yet focusing on nothing. He didn't know what he was after, waited for inspiration to strike. Maybe he wasn't looking for anything, just wanted reassurance she would be back here one day, and they would do those simple things again.

He stepped into the kitchen. Another memory hit him. The first time they'd cooked a dinner together, they'd constantly bumped into each other and gotten in each other's way. And laughed about it every time. He opened all the drawers and glanced in all the cupboards, shifted things around, peered behind boxes and canisters, stirred through a drawer of cooking tools. Nothing. He turned to the paperclipped page in a small, thick spiral bound notebook on the counter by the fridge. A shopping list, each item crossed through by a single line. He thumbed through earlier pages. Older shopping lists. He closed the notebook.

She had notebooks and scratchpads everywhere, jotted notes to herself constantly. He'd kidded her about it. She'd confessed if she didn't write things down, she forgot them, but rarely consulted her notes after she'd written them. The act of writing the note was enough to fix the item in her memory.

A quick sweep of the bathroom. A disk of birth control pills and the usual OTC drugs in the medicine cabinet. Shampoo. Deodorant. Toothpaste. Cosmetics on the counter by the sink. He'd chided her about them, saying she didn't need them. She'd said he'd change his tune the first time he saw her unpainted. The first morning he had, he'd sung *She Don't Know She's Beautiful*. She'd tossed a pillow at him. A scratch pad on the toilet tank had Q-tips, floss, and conditioner written in it.

Rick felt like a voyeur going through the chest of drawers and closet in her bedroom. Her perfume was strongest here, its scent squeezing his heart with longing and fear. Memories of intimacies in this room started to overwhelm him before he reined them in. He checked the bedside tables. Odds and ends in the drawers including two foil wrapped condoms. She'd said she trusted him but he'd insisted on using them until he could get tested and show proof he wasn't a bearer of vile diseases. A slim notebook in one drawer was half full of names, phone numbers, and reminders. The last two were 'pick up dry cleaning' and 'get car serviced.'

Her car. He wondered where it was. In the basement garage of her building? Or still parked somewhere near Bobby Ed Lukens's place?

He closed the notebook, dropped it in the drawer, and shut the drawer. In the living room, he pawed quickly through magazines on the coffee table. Vogue, Newsweek National Geographic, Smithsonian. An eclectic collection reflecting Mary's open mind.

The secretary's desk in the corner held unpaid bills, a checkbook, a savings passbook, and a Month-At-A-Glance planner noting bill due dates, birthdays, and anniversaries. On the next page, Mary had edged the block for his birth date and printed his name in caps followed by two exclamation points, all in red. The best birthday present she could give him—the only one he really wanted—was her home again.

Folders holding paid bills and insurances, taxes and warranties filled the top drawer of the two-drawer wood file cabinet next to the desk. The second drawer held catalogs from a dozen different places. Behind a divider, notebooks labeled with the names of cases she'd worked had a home. She started a new one with each new case. He shuffled through them. Ones they'd worked together jumped out at him, raising little flickers of memory. He didn't spot any with Joey Day or Bobby Ed Lukens on the cover. He dropped them all back into the drawer.

Rick closed the file drawer and checked the desk again. No notebook. He checked the desk's cubbyholes to make sure he hadn't missed it. He hadn't. He opened the center drawer. A cellophane wrapped six-pack of new notebooks inside plus two loose ones. He checked the end tables flanking the couch, the coffee table, and the table inside her front door. No notebook on any of them. He dug out his cell phone and called Flynn.

"Yeah, there was one," Flynn answered when Rick asked about a notebook in Mary's purse. "Nothing in but notes to herself. 'Dry cleaning, Tuesday,' 'laundry detergent,' 'gift for Rick,' things like that."

Ouch. "You find one in her car?"

"Never looked at it. Never looked *for* it, to be honest with you. No reason to."

"Thanks." He hung up and returned to Mary's bedroom, opened the third drawer in her bureau, and fished under the sweaters until his hand closed around the second set of keys to her Toyota. After a long wait for the elevator to rise to the third floor, he rode it to the basement garage. Mary's slot, marked by a big white 31 high on the brick wall, was empty. He did a slow scan of the garage. No green Toyota Camry.

****

"I have two small tasks for you to perform, *mi hermano*."

McHale stood in an alley between Harding and Fifth. It smelled like a men's room. An uncleaned men's room. McHale suppressed a sigh. "*Si, Jefe*."

"The first, *mi amigo*, is this. Ernesto Salazar has fallen into the clutches of the authorities. It appears that he has done a truly horrible thing to an innocent woman in a parking garage."

He'd heard about the shooting at morning report. "I thought we had agreed to let that matter lie for a few days, Jefe."

"I decided we could not."

McHale wanted to wring Joey's neck. Why hadn't

the dumb shit waited like McHale told him? His friggin' short fuse was going to blow them all up.

Joey let out a 'weight of the world on my shoulders' sigh. "Sadly, it was handled in a way I did not authorize. Also, I am concerned that perhaps Ernesto may have told tales out of school, so to speak."

Great. Joey was in faggy English professor mode.

"Ernesto is young, and I can be—what is the word? Um—magnanimous and overlook this one small mistake he has made. I do not however tolerate disloyalty. If Ernesto has been loyal to me, I will see that his stay in the hands of the authorities is brief. Make sure Ernesto understands this emphatically."

Translation: Tell Ernesto to keep his mouth shut or die.

"Also I wish you to inform him that his brother Enrico has, alas, met with a terrible end. I wish you to see he gets both messages this afternoon."

"I'll take care of it." McHale knew just the guy to palm it off on. "And the other thing?"

"Some of my associates will be removing some thing I no longer need from my house tonight after sundown. I would like you to see they are not interrupted."

In other words, keep the cops away. The house was Joey's club on Sesame. Any time he wanted something removed from there, it was the body of some slug who had really pissed him off. And it would be gruesome.

Who the hell had Joey killed now? Not Joey. César Molina. Joey never got his hands dirty offing anyone. That was César's job. And McHale's. He'd bet dollars to pennies the thing Joey no longer needed was Enrico Salazar.

Typical of Joey. Send a message to Ernesto by killing Enrico. Sometimes, the beaner acted with all the subtlety of a wrecking ball on a greenhouse. McHale gazed at the sky and shook his head. Oh, well. He wasn't paid to like Joey's decisions, just carry them out. "*Si, Jefe*. But may I ask a small favor?"

"I am listening."

"Could we delay removing that item until late in the evening? I have something I need to handle first, and I don't know how long it will take."

Silence. A minute ticked by on McHale's watch. Joey decided to kill someone in a second, but it took him ten minutes to decide what cereal to have for breakfast.

"Yes, *mi hermano,* I can do that. Will eleven o'clock suit your schedule?" Joey's sarcasm could burn holes in steel.

"Yes, *Jefe*. That is most gracious of you. *Gracias*."

"Think nothing of it. You are my best man. What kind of boss would I be if I did not take my employee's needs into account? I will make arrangements. What progress are you making, *mi amigo*, on the repair I asked you to perform?"

"Another day or two at most."

"See that it does not go beyond that."

****

Rick drove slowly past the DeSchain Building. If Mary went there to smoke Bobby Ed, she wouldn't have parked out front. She wouldn't have parked six blocks away either. One block out in all directions from the DeSchain building gave him a nine-block square to search. Second to Fifth Street, Oak to Church. He started cruising.

After checking the garage under Mary's building,

he'd returned to her apartment and dug the title to her Camry from the file cabinet. He'd called the impound lot, giving the bored clerk the VIN. Two minutes later, the clerk informed him no vehicle with that VIN was there.

Rick figured the easiest way to spot her Camry would be to try the remote on each green one he found and watch for the flash of head and taillights. He got lucky with the first one he spotted, parked on Third at Garfield, the cross street below the DeSchain building's block.

Rick dumped his Mazda in a slot further down the block and walked back to Mary's car. Four parking tickets huddled under a wiper. The slugs in Parking Control had to be the laziest bums on the force. Slap four tickets on a car and never think to run the plate to see if it was hot.

Rick thumbed the remote again and the locks popped. He opened the door but couldn't get in until he shoved the driver's seat back. He could never grasp how Mary, at five-ten, could drive the car with the seat almost against the steering wheel.

He checked the console storage compartment first. Napkins, a petrified pack of gum, and compact binoculars. The glove box held the owner's manual, city and state maps, and broken sunglasses. While he was leaning that far over, he checked the pocket on the passenger door. A small first aid kit. The pocket on the driver's door held an auto expense book with a pen in the coils, gloves, and a small spiral bound notebook also with a pen in the coils.

He flipped through a few pages of the logbook, skimming the entries. Every service she ever had done to the car was there in her neat printing. He dropped the logbook into the door pocket and flipped back the notebook's gray cover.

03/16 1241h lft D/Sb bl Fd Tbrd ELC9225 1404h whrs OFP 1523h 16/Brch/17 1b f ALHS 1524h ofb 1605h dfd 27sls 10p/6wp/11MJ rtb

03/17 1359h lft D/Sb bl Fd Tbrd ELC9225 1509h 23/Wshngtn/24 2b f ECVT 1513h ofb 1615h dfd 35sls 12p/6wp/17MJ rtb

03/18 1410h lft D/Sb bl Fd Tbrd ELC9225 1515h 35/Lm/36 2b f WWHS 1525h ofb 1547h dfd 19 sls 8p/3wp/8MJ rtb

A whole page filled like that. Some of it made sense. 02/17 was a date obviously. D/Sb could be the DeSchain Building, and Bl Fd Tbrd ELC9225 could be a blue Ford Thunderbird, license ELC9225. Mary skipped vowels in words when she took notes. So Brch was Birch, and Wshngtn was Washington—street names. The two-digit numbers were likely streets, too. 16/Brch/17 meant Birch between 16th and 17th. The four-digit numbers were military time. The rest he'd have to work on.

The next page held more of the same. He thumbed through the notebook. Maybe a half dozen pages filled with the same cryptic notations, the last one last Friday. What the hell did they mean? In the pit of his gut, Rick knew it wasn't good. He closed the notebook and tucked it in his jacket pocket.

As he unlocked his own car, a piece fell into place. HS was High School. He aimed another mental slap at his head for not seeing more instantly. So ALHS was Abraham Lincoln High School and WWHS was Woodrow Wilson High. But ECVT? Oh hell! Emmett Cotterman Vo-Tech.

David A. Freas

Rick got in his car, started the engine, and maxxed the AC. He opened the notebook and skimmed the first page again. Another piece made sense. The Vo-Tech was on Washington between Twenty-second and Twenty-third. So the streets were ones near high schools.

03/19 1402h lft D/Sb bl Fd Tbrd ELC9225 1522h 48/RsvltD/49 1b f MRHS 1527 ofb 1558h dfd 25sls 7p/5wp/13MJ rtb

03/20 1405h lft D/Sb bl Fd Tbrd ELC9225 1528h CtyA/MLK 1b f HSPA 1531h ofb 1603h dfd 22sls 5p/6wp/11MJ rtb 2006h ora 2058h 66/Wlnt/67 JD 2206h rtb

MRHS was Monsignor Ryan. But what was HSPA? It hit him a second later. High School of Performing Arts. He did a quick count. Ten different schools.

He could guess at some of the entries. MJ of course was marijuana, so *p* stood for pills of some kind and *wp* meant white powder, probably coke.

It all fell together in a very general way. Whoever Mary had been following was selling drugs outside ten high schools at the end of the school day, hitting each one randomly in a two-week loop. Smart thinking. The same blue T-bird parking near the same school at the same time every day would arouse somebody's suspicions eventually.

But who was she following?

****

Ann Hendershot adjusted the oxygen mask over Mar—No!—Miranda's face. Under the guise of checking the fit of the mask, she leaned close to her ear and whispered, "Rick loves you."

At the words, Mary's heart rate jumped from fifty to fifty-seven, her breathing from thirty-two to thirty-nine.

"What did you just say to her?" Allison Sheehy asked.

Had she heard Ann's words? "What? What are you talking about?" Ann hoped she sounded confused.

"You said something to her, and the readings on her monitor just went crazy."

"They did," Caitlin Burke said. "Everything went up. What did you say to her, Ann?"

Ann inhaled a deep breath and crossed her fingers behind her back. "Just what I tell all my patients: that I promise I'm going to help them get well. That may have made the readings on her monitor go up, but they do it sometimes for no reason with a patient in a coma." She gave Caitlin a 'Go ahead, challenge me' look.

She stared back for a second. "I've heard it happens that way sometimes, Allie."

Ann couldn't read what Caitlin was thinking. Was she agreeing with Ann? Or letting Ann know she was lying?

Allison said, "So that…seizure or whatever she had this morning didn't hurt her?"

"It wasn't a seizure." Ann looped her stethoscope over her neck. "You noticed how it passed as soon as Dr. Nicopoulos pulled the breathing tube?"

"Yeah."

"She was fighting the tube, trying to breathe on her own. That's a very good sign. She's trying to come out of the coma."

"So when's she coming out of it?"

"I wish I could say. I'll be back in an hour to check on her again."

****

A dull ache fills the space just below her ribs. The

pain is strange yet familiar. She'd hurt there before, but when? The memory comes. She was seven and climbing the oak in her grandparents' back yard with her brothers and cousins. She lost her grip reaching for a higher branch, fallen, and landed hard belly first on a lower branch. Her stomach had been black and blue for a week after.

She is too old to be climbing trees now. So why does her stomach hurt? Did Dennis punch her again like the morning she reamed him out for partying all night with his friends? No. Dennis is gone from her life. He was never a puncher anyway. That was the only good thing about him.

****

"Hey, Dee, you got a couple minutes?" Lafferty said after poking his head through Dee's office door twenty minutes later. "Need your opinion on something."

"Something to do with Mary?"

Rick nodded.

"Close the door." After he had, Dee asked, "What do you have?"

Rick pulled the notebook he'd taken from Mary's car from an inner pocket and handed it to Dee. "This. Take a look at it, tell me what you think."

"Where'd you get it?"

"Mary's car. I found it sitting a block from Lukens's place. IA never looked for it, evidently weren't interested in it. Parking Control ticketed it four times, never ran the plates to see if it was wanted."

"Figures." Dee shook his head. "You search it?"

He pointed to the notebook in Dee's hand. "How I found that."

"Let's see what we have." Dee opened the notebook

and went through the pages silently for several minutes then looked up. "You decipher any of this?"

"Most of it." He told Dee what he'd figured out.

"Looks like she spent weeks tailing someone, tracking his movements. Lukens?"

Rick had taken a seat when Dee started reading Mary's notes. "That's my guess. The plate number on the first line comes back to a blue T-bird owned by him. Couple things still have me stumped, though. Like OFP and ofb."

"OFP could be Old Franklin Pike. Market Street going north becomes Old Franklin Pike at the city limits." Dee studied the page for a second. "What's wrhs?"

"Warehouse. She dropped the vowels from words when she was taking notes fast."

"That fits with Old Franklin Pike. There's a dozen or so warehouses on the west side of it a couple miles outside the city."

"I still don't get ofb, dfd, rtb, or ora. None of them work with her way of taking notes."

Dee studied Mary's notebook for another minute. "Got it, I think. Ofb could mean open for business, dfd: done for the day, rtb: return to base, and ora: on the road again."

"How do you figure?"

"Take March sixteenth. Lukens was ofb at three-twenty-five near Lincoln High and dfd at four-oh-five. Schools let out at three-thirty. Lukens set up shop just before school let out and packed it in a few minutes after four. And what do you do at the end of the day?"

Rick hunched a small shrug. "Go home?"

"Right. Return to base, rtb in military-speak. After

Lukens made his last sale, he goes home. The pattern repeats every day except every fifth day. After he's home for a while, he leaves again, so ora—on the road again."

"That makes sense." Rick leaned back in his chair.

Dee laid the notebook on his desk and tapped the cover. "Let's put together what we have here. March sixteenth, Lukens visited a warehouse on Old Franklin Pike where he picked up something, probably drugs. From there, he drove to Lincoln High, set up shortly before classes let out for the day and, in the next forty minutes made twenty-seven sales of assorted drugs. The next day and every day after that, he did the same thing at a different high school."

"Week days only, hitting ten schools in random order every two weeks. Every Monday, he goes to the warehouse to stock up for the week, and every Friday he meets with JD—Joey Day probably—to hand over the money he made."

"Probably Joey. You notice those Friday meets were never at the same place?"

"Yeah."

Dee waved the notebook. "So what do you make of this?"

"It reads like Mary was stalking Lukens before she blew him away."

"It does, but you don't believe that, and neither do I. This looks to me like Mary was gathering intel on him. She believed, or at least suspected, he sold Sam the coke that killed him, and was gathering proof he'd done it before either diming him out or confronting him."

"If she was going to dime him, she wouldn't have gone to his condo, she'd have just made the call. She wanted to confront him, give him a choice: turn himself in or she'd do it for him."

"Only it went haywire on her?"

"Yeah." Rick tamped down the hurt that rose every time he thought about Mary getting shot. He stood. "Can you give me a ride?"

"Where to?"

"Lukens's place. I want to get Mary's car, move it to her apartment's garage."

"It needs to go to impound so Forensics can go over it."

"They don't need to. I already searched it." He pointed to the notebook. "That's all there was. I want Mary's car waiting at her place when she comes home."

"Forensics might find something you missed. Let them have a look at least. Plus Harter, Pryzlo, and the IA guys on Mary's case will shit bricks if you don't." Dee rocked back in his chair. "Make you a deal. Mary won't be coming home for at least a month, maybe longer. Soon as the lab rats have had their look at her car, we'll move it to her place. Fair enough?"

"Fair enough."

Dee rose from his desk and slipped into his suit coat. "Let's go get it."

Chapter 19

Joleen flopped on her couch and giggled. God, she felt giddy. She'd never expected the day to turn out this good. Tim had a big part in it. He'd been so sweet. He'd said he was ready to skip lunch, use his whole meal break to hunt for her, wouldn't eat until he found her. She'd never had a man do that before. She'd offered him the other half of her sub. He'd said he'd get something later, he just wanted to talk.

She'd liked his smile. It made her feel warm all the way through, like snuggling under a comforter on a cold night. She liked, too, that his eyes stayed on her face as if memorizing every detail instead of roaming over her as if he was hunting the best cut of meat in a butcher shop.

Still, Bryce had left her gun-shy about men. McHale had worsened it. So she'd waited warily for Tim to come on to her, feed her some line, but all he'd talked about were Grisham novels, and her guard had slowly lowered. His almost boyish bashfulness had quelled any fears she had that McHale had sent him.

When he had to go back on patrol, instead of asking for her number, he'd given her his and said maybe they could get together some time and talk some more about books. She'd said she would call. And she'd meant it. She loved to read and talk about books she'd read. Bryce never wanted to talk about anything but sex and getting high, and McHale never talked at all except to abuse her. Talking to Tim about books would be heaven.

After he left, she'd finished her sub and read, nibbling on the chips, and sipping Coke. When she'd tired of reading, she stretched out on the blanket and let the sun beam down on her. Late in the afternoon, she'd gathered up her things and gone home. If anything, her walk had even more spring in it.

Joleen hugged herself. Maybe meeting Tim was the start of something good. She was due. She dropped her arms to her lap and reminded herself not to get her hopes too high. She'd had them crushed before. Why not let them soar? She *was* due. She'd had her share of crappy breaks. More than her share. Time for the breaks to go her way for a change.

As much as she wanted to keep basking in the day's goodness, she was a working girl, and tomorrow was a work day. She needed to wash clothes tonight. She hung her light blue dress carefully in the closet. From now on, it would be her lucky dress. She giggled at the idea as she changed into jeans and a tee and banded her hair into a ponytail.

She piled dirty clothes into the laundry basket and lugged it to the basement. She got two washers going then settled into a chair, opened *The Street Lawyer,* and took out the notebook page Tim had given her. She unfolded it and read his number and the *Call me. Please!* he'd written below it. Her heart did a little flutter, and she smiled. Count on it, Tim.

Two hours later, she lugged her clean laundry into her apartment. Even with two washers and driers at her disposal, it had taken longer than usual to finish her wash because one of the dryers was acting up and took forever to dry its load. She hadn't gotten much further in the Grisham book either. Every time she tried to read, her thoughts drifted to Tim and talking with him in the park.

She hung the last piece in the closet and tossed the empty laundry basket in after it. Her stomach rumbled. She glanced at her watch. No wonder she was hungry. It was almost eight and she hadn't eaten dinner. She pawed through her kitchen cabinets. Nothing appealed to her.

She checked in the fridge. Yogurt? Gak! Not today, no way. A frozen pizza? Twenty minutes freezer to table. She'd die of starvation in that time. Plus it was a supreme, loaded with extra everything. She'd be up half the night gobbling Tums.

This was her day to celebrate, to enjoy. She wasn't about to end it cooking dinner for herself. She grabbed her purse and headed for the door.

At Sol's Deli, she ordered a hot roast beef and Swiss on rye with mustard. Sol had the best roast beef, tender and juicy. She savored every bite and every sip of Coke.

****

McHale drove into Swedetown, aiming for Joleen's apartment building. That the bitch had pulled a knife on him still rankled. She was gonna pay for it. And pay big. The image of his fists and boots smashing into her put a big smile on his face.

He might be pushing it coming after her this quick. But teaching her this lesson couldn't wait. You wanted a dog to learn it had done wrong, you punished it the first time it did wrong. You didn't, it thought it could do whatever it wanted.

He hoped to catch her on the street, blindside her, and beat the crap out of her, make it look like a mugging. Less chance of her fingering him that way. He'd give it until eleven then go to her apartment. He didn't want to kick her ass there, but would if he had to. One way or another, she was getting a tune-up. Tonight.

Stopped for the light at Taft, he glanced to his right. He couldn't flippin' believe it. He took a longer look. Joleen sat at a table in Sol's Deli, the old man shuffling toward her with a mug and plate in his hands like she was some kind of friggin' queen. He'd show her she was anything but soon as he got his hands on her.

McHale made a left, cruised the block on Taft, and parked his car on the corner across the street from Joleen's apartment. Leaving the Impala, he crossed the street, lit a Marlboro, and took a slow stroll up the block towards Sol's, just another guy out for a stroll and a smoke. She was still there, sipping coffee and nibbling a pastry. He retraced his steps to the mid-block alley. Joleen would pass right by it on her way home. He scanned the street in both directions as he took a final drag on the cigarette. Nobody in sight. He dropped the butt and slipped into the alley.

****

Sol set a cherry Danish and mug of coffee in front of Joleen.

"Thank you, Sol, but I didn't order this."

"So you didn't. It is for you from me. Today, I see you smiling for the first time in forever. You have a pretty smile, Joleen. You should show it more often." He waved a hand over the dessert. "This is my humble attempt to keep you showing that beautiful smile. Enjoy."

"That's so sweet of you. Thank you, Sol."

He slid into the seat across from her. "I should tell you, too, a police officer was in here today asking about you right after you were in this morning."

She stiffened in her chair and the sandwich, so good tasting a minute ago, soured in her stomach. McHale. She'd never be rid of him. She stammered, "Di-did you te-tell him where I was?"

"I could not. I did not know for sure. I only told him which way you went, towards the park." Sol gazed at her for a second then waved his hands. "Ach, I say this wrong, and I frighten you. I am so sorry, Joleen." He laid an age-spotted hand atop hers. "Please, let this old man start over again. This policeman, he came in not two minutes after you leave, as I said, asking do I know you? I am not the only one who notices your smile." He waved a raised finger. "This policeman was also quite taken by it. That is how he described you: as the pretty young lady with the beautiful smile."

"What did he look like?"

"Young, handsome, red hair, brown eyes, and more freckles than the poppy seeds on a bagel." He waved the raised finger again. "And smitten by you as well as your smile, I am thinking. He turned bright red when he asked about you."

Tim. Her blood thawed, and she let out a sigh. "Yes. He found me."

Gentle pressure from Sol's hand atop hers. "Does this officer want you because you are in some sort of trouble, Joleen?"

"No."

"Then this was a good thing, this policeman looking for you?"

She covered his hand with her own and smiled. "Yes, Sol. I think it was."

"That is good. I know this young policeman from

here. He comes in often for his food. He is a nice young man." Sol pointed to her dessert. "Now enjoy." He stood and stepped away from the table. "Ach, I am getting old. I am forgetting again." He turned back and laid a business card by her hand. "This I found on the floor after you left this morning."

Richard M. Lafferty. Detective. Joleen slid the card toward Sol. "I don't really need it."

He slid it back. "It is always good to have a policeman on your side. You have two."

She bit into the Danish and sipped the coffee. Both were pure heaven. The perfect end to the perfect day.

She was tempted to leave Detective Lafferty's card on the table then slipped it into the pocket of her jeans. After paying Sol, she stepped from his deli into a night as spectacular as the day. It was still warm, and a zillion stars dotted the sky. Joleen strolled toward her apartment, her steps still light and bouncy. Tim. She'd call him tomorrow as soon as she got off work. She pirouetted on the sidewalk, giggling as the world spun around her.

Her steps slowed over the last half block to her building. Today had been so good, so wonderful, she didn't want it to end. Tomorrow with its dull routine loomed ahead. No, she wouldn't think of it that way. Tomorrow was a blah day but there would be other good days to come. She knew it, she could feel it. She had climbed the first rung out of the pit of her life.

A hand grabbed her ponytail. Before she could scream, another hand clapped over her mouth. They pulled her into the alley. She backpedaled frantically to keep from falling. The hands swung her through an arc then suddenly let go. She slammed into a dumpster, and breath shot from her lungs. A fist crashed into her face. She staggered and fell to her knees. Blood dripped from her mouth. "Please don't hurt me."

But he did. With punches and kicks, steel dumpsters and brick walls and paving. Pain burned in her, filled her, overwhelmed her senses.

****

At 2313 hours, District car M-34 entered Taft from Fifteenth. Officer Estevez, driving, and Officer Ketchum, riding, scanned the empty streets and dark buildings for trouble. Both were still a little flushed and sweaty from a quickie in the back seat five minutes earlier. They hadn't set out to have an affair, it just happened. Neither one liked cheating on their spouses but, damn, the sex was flat out the hottest either one had ever had.

They crossed Sixteenth. Ketchum glanced down the alley connecting Taft to Chestnut. Something amiss in the alley registered, but the cruiser was past the alley before he could identify it. "Back up, Raquel."

"What? Why?"

"I saw something in the alley." Other cops had nicknamed Ketchum 'Owl.' He could spot things in the dark no one else could.

Raquel braked, shifted into Reverse, and let the cruiser roll back until Paul said, "Stop."

He flicked on the roof bar's sidelights. The halogen beam lit up a purse ten or fifteen feet into the alley and a body a few feet beyond it. "Raquel."

"I see it." Estevez backed the cruiser up a few more feet, cranked the wheels hard right, and eased M-34 into the alley entrance. She flipped on the car's high beams, her spotlight, and the takedown lights on the roof bar as

Paul keyed the radio to report what they'd found.

Estevez and Ketchum got out of the cruiser, switched on flashlights, and edged cautiously into the alley toward the body, playing the beams of their lights everywhere. A few feet beyond the purse, Ketchum's beam lit up a red smear. "Blood here."

The body was a woman on her back. Blood, vomit, and grime stained her clothes. Her ripped tee exposed a torn bra and bleeding breast. One arm had an extra kink above the wrist. Estevez shifted the beam to head. Dirt, blood, and cuts streaked the woman's face. Swollen purple flesh closed both eyes. Blood oozed from her flattened nose, raw abrasions on her cheeks and chin, and split lips. Her mouth hung open revealing broken teeth. A low moan escaped the woman's shattered mouth. Raquel and Paul said, "Holy shit!" in unison.

Paul dropped to his knees beside the woman and pressed two fingers behind the angle of her jaw. "She's alive."

"Call it in." Raquel said then sprinted toward the cruiser.

Paul stood and thumbed the talk button on the mic clipped to his epaulette, requesting backup, detectives, and a rush on an ambulance. When Raquel returned with the first aid kit, he had his flashlight on the woman's face. "We know her."

Raquel grabbed his arm. "Holy crap, yeah. She works at Nate's."

"Yeah. She's there mornings when we stop for breakfast. Her name's Joan or Joanne or something like that."

"Joleen?"

"That's it." Raquel straightened and ran the beam of

her flashlight over the area around Joleen. Blood smears decorated the dumpster and brick walls of the alley.

****

Rick Lafferty settled in bed and clasped his hands behind his head. Acid sloshed in his stomach, and he doubted he'd sleep tonight. The cryptic stuff in Mary's notebook made it clear she'd tailed Bobby Ed every day for a month before bracing him in his condo.

After he and Dee had decoded Mary's notations, Dee had said Flynn and Schmidt didn't need to see the notebook. He trusted Dee's word that IA wasn't looking to jam Mary up over dusting Lukens. But he didn't trust Flynn and Schmidt. IA guys loved nothing better than nailing cops. They lived for it. If they got their hands on Mary's notebook, they'd use it to nail her for killing Bobby Ed for sure.

Rick's first instinct had been to destroy it, shred every page. His gut had said do it. His mind had said not so fast. He'd thought long and hard about it all evening. Just before eleven, he'd locked the notebook in the gun safe in his closet then switched on his TV. He'd watched the WCBL news, sitting on the edge of his chair, waiting for any mention of Mary. There'd been none. When the news ended, he felt as if he'd been holding his breath for the whole half hour.

Rick wasn't a praying man, but ever since Mary had been shot, he'd fired off a quick prayer for her recovery every time he thought of her. As he waited for sleep, he said another one. He was just drifting off when the phone yanked him awake. He grabbed it. "Lafferty."

"It's Dee."

His gut knotted, and he sat up suddenly. "Something happened to Mary?"

"No. Meet Evans and Steele at the alley on Taft between Sixteenth and Seventeenth."

"Why? What's going on?"

"They'll fill you in."

Rick was in his car and rolling three minutes later. Barry Steele met him at the crime scene tape sealing off the alley five minutes after that. In the alley, Stan Evans watched crime scene techs gather evidence under the blazing blue-white glare of halogen work lights. Rick shook Barry's hand and asked, "What's going on?"

Steele jerked a thumb over his shoulder. "Woman named Joleen Wilson got the crap beat out of her sometime this evening."

"Name doesn't mean anything to me."

Steele pointed along the street. "Home address is an apartment house on the corner. That do anything for you?"

"Nope."

"You sure?"

"Yeah, I'm sure. Why?"

"Found this in her back pocket." Steele held up an evidence bag with Lafferty's business card inside.

It bore his name. "I hand out lots of them."

"You remember when you gave it to her?"

"No."

"She a CI?" Confidential Informants, secret agents in the war on crime, pass things they hear on the street to the police.

"No."

"She tied into a case you're working? Witness? Victim?"

"No. Again." Rick planted his hands on his hips. "Maybe if you tell me something about her, I can tell you something in return."

Steele said, "Uni who found her say she's a waitress at Nate's on Taylor. That help you?"

The nickel dropped. "Yeah. Couple days ago, I was in there for breakfast, and a waitress named Joleen served me. Had a bruise on her cheek, said she walked into a door."

"One with a fist?"

"Mm-hmmh."

"Boyfriend?"

"Probably. Said it was the first time he ever did it, he promised it wouldn't happen again."

"Until next time he pops her one. Which was tonight."

"I gave her my card, told her when he does, call me." Rick glanced up the alley. "How bad is she?"

"Out cold when the unis found her. Probably going to make it, according to the EMTs. But she's gonna be one hurting broad for a while. Got a lotta bruises and cuts, some busted teeth, a broken arm and nose, couple cracked ribs, maybe some internal injuries. She's at University Hospital now. We'll know more when they finish treating her."

"Robbed?"

"Nope. Unis found her purse a few feet from her, untouched. Sort of."

"Sort of? What the hell's sort of?"

"Show you in a minute. She give you the boyfriend's name?"

"Nope."

"Detectives?" A female patrol officer stood a few feet away. She was a curvy Latina with curls of glossy black hair escaping from an untidy bun.

"Yeah, Sweetcakes?" Steele answered.

"Sir, with all due respect, my name is Officer Raquel Estevez. I would appreciate it if you'd address me by my name or as Officer."

Steele shot Rick a 'how touchy can you get' glance. "Oh-kaaay…Officer Estevez. What'dya got?"

"I talked to Sol Tischler, owns Sol's Deli in the next block." She opened her notebook. "The victim was in his place this evening, left just before nine. Arrived alone, left alone, and didn't meet up with anyone outside. Sol says she's a regular, comes in a couple times a week, buys cupcakes, a pastry, or coffee, occasionally a meal. That's what she was there for tonight, a meal."

"Okay. Thanks, do—Estevez."

She shot him a blistering glare. "Sir, there's more. Tischler said she was in just before noon today, too, and right after she left, a patrol officer came in and was asking about her."

"He get the officer's name?"

"I was just getting to that, sir. Sol says he's a regular. Name's Tim Morris. I know the guy. Everyone calls him 'Specks' 'cause of all his freckles. He works mostly day tour out of the One-Nine." District 19 butted against District 7 on the west.

Steele and Rick exchanged 'oh-ho!' looks.

"Sirs, I know what you're thinking." She pointed to the alley. "And I know Morris didn't do this."

"How do you know that, Officer Estevez?" Rick asked.

"I was in the academy with him. There were only six females in my class, and we took no end of shit from the guys. The only one who never gave us any was Morris. Worst of the bunch was a jerk named Rogers, always hitting on us, copping feels doing takedown drills, whispering in our ear what he'd like to do to us and how much we'd like it. About two months before graduation, Rogers shows up at roll call one morning with his face looking like he went ten rounds with Ali. Said he fell down the stairs. Whispers said Morris gave him an attitude adjustment behind the dorms the night before. Never had a problem with Rogers after that."

"We still need to talk to Morris," Steele said.

"Yes, sir, I understand that. I'm just saying doing something like this would be out of character for him."

"Noted, Cu—Estevez."

Another paint-stripping glare. "One more thing, sirs?"

"Go ahead."

"I heard you say a boyfriend might have done this to her." She twirled a finger in the air. "This is Ketchum's and my regular beat. We never handled any Dee-Vee calls from Joleen."

"Doesn't mean her boyfriend wasn't knocking her around."

"Yes, sir, it does. Lotta old biddies in her building always got their noses in everyone else's business. None of them ever said anything about her having a boyfriend, let alone one smacking her around. We'd hear about it from one of them."

"Okay. Soon as your partner's free, you can return to patrol."

"Sir, Officer Ketchum and I usually grab breakfast at Nate's after end of tour. You want, we could talk to her co-workers there, see if they know anything about this."

"Good thinking, Swee—Estevez, good initiative.

Do that, let me know what you get."

Rick handed her one of his cards. "And if you would keep me in the loop, too, Officer Estevez, I'd appreciate it."

"Yes, sirs." She saluted and walked away.

Steele blatantly ogled the sway of her rear in the tight uniform pants. "Mm-mm-mmm. Man, that's prime. Think Ketchum's tapping her?"

Rick said, "I think now would be a good time to show me the victim's purse."

"I was just wondering—" He held up his hands at Rick's growl. "Okay, Lafferty, okay. Cool out." He led Rick to a Crime Scene Services van and took an evidence bag from a crate in the back. The purse inside was small and black.

Stan had understated things when he said it was 'sort of' untouched. The clasp was broken, the leatherette scuffed and torn with a key poked through in one spot. The other side showed multiple imprints of a lug-soled boot. Barry opened the evidence bag and lifted the purse out. "Take a look inside."

Rick did. Everything inside was so smashed, bent, broken, or crushed, he could only guess what they had been. He handed the purse back to Barry. "This isn't a boyfriend smacking her around in an argument. This is somebody sending her a message."

Barry nodded. "Question is who?"

Chapter 20

Saturday – April 25, 2015

Paul and Raquel slid into a booth at Nate's at eight-forty and grabbed menus from the rack at the wall end of the table. A minute later Ramona came over. "Hey, you two. What can I get you?"

"Fruit plate, waffles, sausage links, and coffee," Raquel said.

"Two eggs over easy, toast, hash browns, bacon, coffee, and OJ. And a couple minutes of your time when you can spare it."

Ramona shot a glance across the diner. "It important? We kinda busy this mo'nin' and we one girl short."

"It is, or we wouldn't ask," Raquel said.

"Okay. I'll put your order in right away and see if someone'll cover for me for a bit. Can't promise nothin.'"

"We'll wait," Paul said.

Ramona scooted away as someone called her name.

"How you want to handle this?"

"Play it straight with her?" Raquel said. "We don't want to hold her up longer than we have to."

"Sounds good." He rested his hand on her thigh.

She shifted it off, leaned toward him, and said in a low voice, "We agreed, remember. None of that in public."

"Yeah, I know. It's just...Jeez...I'm gonna be going crazy, not seeing you for two days. All I'm gonna be doing—" He stopped as Ramona delivered their juice and coffee.

"Nate said I can take a couple minutes when your order's up."

"That's great, Ramona. Thanks."

She left and Paul said, "All I'm gonna be doing is thinking about you the whole time, Raquel, and wishing we were on duty."

"You think it's any easier for me?" she asked. "Think I don't think about you when I'm off, too? Think it doesn't drive me just as crazy? But we gotta keep it on the downlow."

He sighed. "You're right." He downed his juice in two swallows. "It just gets harder all the time."

"And I love it when it's hard." She ran her hand along his thigh. "The harder the better."

He loved it when she teased him like that. It turned him on in an instant. He hated it, too. It made it almost impossible for him to keep his hands off her. "Now who needs to keep it in check?"

"Goose and gander." She smiled and took a sip of her coffee. "So, what are you gonna do while we're off?"

He didn't know if he could survive two whole days without her. "The usual stuff. Run errands, mow the yard, fix a dripping faucet, do some painting. Think about you." He put cream in his coffee and stirred. "You?"

"Laundry and cleaning. I gotta run over to my sister Gloria's house tomorrow, water her plants, feed her parakeet." She raised one eyebrow. "She and Tony are away on a cruise."

He wondered if she was giving him a hint. Before he could ask, Ramona arrived with their breakfasts. She set them out along with an extra mug of coffee then sat next to Raquel in the booth. "So what you want to talk about that's so important?"

"You said you were a girl short today. Who didn't show up?"

"Joleen. Didn't call or nothin'. Nate's pissed 'bout it. Couldn't get no one else to come in and cover for her neither. So we all runnin' round like chickens with our head cut off." She took a swallow of coffee. "That ain't like her. She never missed a shift long as she been here."

"She didn't bail on you," Raquel said. "She's in the hospital. She got jumped last night near her apartment, had the crap beaten out of her."

"She what? No! Who done it?"

"That's why we wanted to talk to you. Were you close to her?"

"We all tight here but, yeah, I'd say me and her was a little closer'n anybody else."

"Had she said anything recently about having trouble with an old boyfriend, neighbor, anyone?"

"What hospital she in?"

Paul and Raquel exchanged glances at Ramona's evasion. "University Hospital. So, had she had trouble with anyone lately?"

"How bad she hurt? Can she have visitors?"

Another evasion. "She's beat up pretty good, got a broken arm and nose, concussion, cuts and bruises, going to be in the hospital a couple days," Raquel said. "Ramona, look, you're saying how busy you are, yet you won't answer our questions. The quicker you do, the quicker you can get back to work. So, who was giving Joleen trouble? And don't say you don't know. I know you do or you would have said 'I don't know' the first time we asked."

Ramona sipped her coffee. Her expression told him she was weighing her answer. She set her coffee mug down. "Okay. She was havin' trouble with a cop. Had her jammed up over some dope a year ago. Was makin' her do him in trade for him keepin' mum 'bout it."

"Let's hear the rest of it," Paul said. "And don't say that's all there is. I know there's more."

Ramona took a big swig from her mug, swallowed it slowly. "He busted her twice holdin' her man's blow. Third time, he said she either do him or do hard time. Makes her do him whenever he wants."

"What's his name?"

Ramona shook her head. Her large hoop earrings swung wildly. "I ain't sayin' no more. You tight with him, you tell him I ratted him out, he gonna come back on me."

"You and Joleen are our favorite waitresses," Raquel said. "You think we'd let some guy—cop or not—get away with doing that to her? Or you?"

"You wanna know who done it to her, you go ask her."

"We can't. He beat her so bad, she's in a coma."

Ramona closed her eyes, pursed her lips, and tipped her head forward.

"What if he'd killed her, Ramona?" Paul said. "Would you have given him up then?"

She nodded without raising her head.

"Well, he almost did."

Ramona snapped her head up, her eyes wide.

Raquel held a finger and thumb a millimeter apart. "He came that close. Why would a cop do that to her?"

"She was gettin' tired bein' his for-free ho. He been gettin' mean on her, too, popped her a good one a few days ago, give her a shiner. She was sayin' she was gonna kill herself. I tole her I dint wanna hear none of that. Tole her she had to stand up to him just once, scare him off, that'd be all it took to get him outta her life."

"How did you tell her to scare him off?" Paul asked.

"Told her he be scared of knives."

"How did you know that?"

"I done some bad things in the past. He caught me at it once, made me do him like he been making Joleen. I got tired of it like her, swung a blade at him, he dint never bother me no more." Ramona gazed across the diner. "She must a done it, too." She looked at Raquel and Paul. "That puts her gettin' stomped square on me, don't it?"

"You had nothing to do with it, Ramona. He beat her up, not you."

She shook her head. "I ha'n't tole her to do it, none of that would a happened. It's all on me. Should a took care of it myself."

"You can make it right, Ramona, balance the scales again," Raquel said. "Tell us who did this."

"Unh-unh!" She drained her mug and slid toward the edge of the booth.

Raquel grabbed her arm. "Come on, Ramona. You stood up to him once, do it again. For Joleen. And for yourself. Or he's going to get away with beating the shit out her and go on raping her whenever he feels like it. And any other woman he gets his hooks into."

Ramona glanced around the diner. "He got a lot of

friends. I ain't sayin' his name out loud." She took her order pad from her apron. "You be wantin' anything else?"

Raquel and Paul both shook their heads. Ramona scribbled something on the slip and tore it from the pad, laid it face down on the table, and slid from the booth. "You all have a nice day."

Paul turned the slip over. At the bottom, Ramona had written *McHale.* He handed the slip to Raquel to read. They shared raised eyebrows expressions and finished breakfast in silence.

While Paul counted out money for the bill and tip, Raquel jotted something in a small pocket notebook. She tore the page out, folded it, and slid across the table to him. "I'll be at my sister's about noon tomorrow."

He unfolded the paper and read the address she'd written. He smiled. "I gotta run a few errands about that time."

****

"You wanted to see me?" Rick asked as he entered Dee's office a few minutes after nine.

"Patrol found Enrico Salazar this morning."

"Great!"

"Not great. Restaurant owner in Baltic Heights tossing trash this morning found his body in his dumpster. Medical Examiner's on-scene report said he had over a hundred knife slashes on his body, would have bled out from them if he hadn't taken a knife to the heart. Had the crap beat out of him first."

"Joey Day's handiwork?"

"More likely César Molina's. On Joey's orders."

"Sending a message to Ernesto?"

"A 'Keep your mouth shut!' one."

"Too late for that."

Dee leaned back in his chair. "Maybe word got to Joey that Ernesto had spilled and, since he couldn't get to Ernesto, he took out Enrico."

"A 'You're next' message?"

"Could be. Central Jail put him in segregation as a precaution."

"Evans and Steele get anywhere on the woman patrol found in the alley last night?"

"Nope. Word from the hospital is she's still out. They'll try again this afternoon. Where you headed today?"

"Same as yesterday, talking to cops." One cop in particular. He'd had a call late last night from Sergeant Alvarez asking for a meet. Alvarez had offered no details, just said he had info. They'd set up a noon meet at The Bite Shop on Locust. "I'd better get to it if I want to get anything done today."

"Wait up. I'll walk out with you."

****

Rick's cell phone rang seconds after he started his car. "Lafferty."

"Detective? It's Officer Estevez. From the alley last night?"

The Latina officer who'd put Steele in his place. "I remember. What can I do for you, Officer Estevez?"

"I think Ketchum and I got a lead on who jumped Joleen Wilson."

Rick pulled a notebook from an inside jacket pocket. "You really should be telling this to Detective Steele."

"Yes, sir, I know. But, all due respect, Steele's a pig."

"No argument. But you still need to give him what

you got."

"Yes, sir, I will. You still want to hear it, too?"

Rick opened his notebook. "Yeah."

"Ketchum and I talked to a waitress at Nate's this morning who knows Joleen well. She said a cop had Joleen on a possession charge, but was letting it float in exchange for her doing him whenever he wanted sex. Joleen was getting sick of it, might have pulled a knife on him. This waitress said the cop wets his pants at a knife."

McHale! His absolute terror at the sight of a knife was the best know secret throughout the force. No officer in his right mind ever mentioned it in McHale's presence. Those foolish enough to do so fell victim to sudden accidents. But there might be other cops with the same fear. "This waitress give you a name?"

"Yes, sir. McHale. She thinks he might have put the hurt on Joleen for trying to slice him."

"Thanks, Estevez. I need a number where I can reach you, and I need you to keep yourself and Ketchum available for a meeting in Captain DeAngelis's office in the Oh-Seven this afternoon. I'll get back to you on the time."

"Steele going to be there, hear I gave you first what I should have given him?"

"Nope. This is a separate investigation from his. And, except for your partner, I need you to keep this meeting under your hat."

"Yes, sir. I can't promise Ketchum will be there, but I will."

"Do your best." Rick ended the call and dialed Dee's number.

****

"You're sure it's okay to talk to her?" Dee peered through the ICU cubicle glass at Corinne James.

The surgeon at St. Luke considered for a moment. "As long as you don't tire her out or upset her."

Dee entered the cubicle. Corinne watched him through blackened puffed slits, the whites of her eyes red with blood. Her face was still almost completely purple, but the swelling had gone down some. Butterfly bandages crossed the cuts on her face and a white plastic shield spanned her nose. The ventilator was gone, the tube no longer blocking her mouth.

Dee decided once she healed, she'd be a rather pretty woman. "Ms. James? I'm Captain Marco DeAngelis with the Police Department. Do you feel up to answering some questions?"

She sat still for a moment or two then nodded a small nod.

He pulled a small recorder from his pocket. "Do you have any objections to my taping our conversation?"

She shook her head.

Dee pointed to the chair in the corner. "May I sit down?"

Another nod.

Dee pulled the chair closer and sat. He activated the recorder and noted the time, day, and location, his name and Corinne's. "Can you tell me what happened to you?"

"Two policemen…at door…had questions…let them in." Her voice had a husky, raw rasp as if each word stripped flesh from her throat. "Asked what…I knew…about shot cop…told them I—" She pointed to the cup on the bedside table. "Water, please."

Dee held the cup and guided the straw to her swollen lips. She took several short pulls on the straw, pausing after each one before swallowing. "Thank you."

"Can you describe the officers?"

In the same halting, pause-filled way, she described the two men. It matched the ones Dee and O'Malley had seen on the video tape and the description Chris had given. When she finished, she asked for more water.

After she'd indicated she'd had enough, he returned the cup to the table. "Continue, please."

"Asked where cop was...I didn't know...asked again...said same thing...three times...started..." Tears welled in her eyes, and she shook her head.

Dee offered her more water. After she'd finished, he said, "You want to take a break for a few minutes?"

She nodded. Dee stopped the tape.

****

A uniformed officer passed the seventh-floor nurses' station in University Hospital and started slowly along the hall, checking room numbers. He carried a blue and silver wrapped package in his hand. Outside room seven-thirteen, he took in a deep breath and checked that his uniform was squared away, eased the door open and entered on soft steps. He studied the patient in the bed, recording her injuries in his mind, his heart hurting and beating faster with each passing second. Joleen Wilson didn't move the whole time.

The officer set the package on the bedside table and left. He hated that he'd had to wrap it in Christmas paper, but it was all he could lay his hands on in a hurry during a quick trip home. He didn't think she'd mind. Besides the surprise was the important thing, not the wrapping.

Joleen would get a blast out of it when she opened it.

****

Corinne James took a few deep breaths then powered the head of her bed higher. "Okay."

Dee started the tape again.

In two- and three-word clumps, Corrine said the two men started hitting her every time she said she didn't know where Mary was, hurting her worse each time. That was when she realized they weren't real cops. Tears flooded her eyes at the memory.

"Take your time."

She closed her eyes again and drew several breaths then continued. She'd begged the men to stop hurting her, told them she couldn't tell them what she didn't know. They broke the forefinger on her left hand then the middle. Screaming in pain as it snapped, she'd told them maybe at Northeast Medical Center.

"Why did you say there?"

She said after they broke that finger, she was ready to tell them anything to stop them from hurting her more. They broke her other two fingers anyway. She'd told them a guy she dated, a LifeFlight nurse, said he'd flown a patient there from Jefferson Hospital that night. She'd put two and two together at work. The lady cop hadn't died, she'd been the patient.

Dee hated that Corinne James had endangered Mary, but he could understand her caving in under such torture. He couldn't swear he wouldn't have done the same. "Why didn't you tell them that the first time they asked?"

Corinne said she knew Jefferson could handle anything that came along. The only reason to transfer the lady cop to NEMC was for her protection. She didn't want to put the cop in danger, but the pain had hit the point where she couldn't take any more.

Dee had had broken bones and knew how much they hurt. He could only guess at the overwhelming pain Corinne had suffered having all those bones broken one after the other. "Was that the end of it? Did they leave then?"

She shook her head then raised her right hand. "Slammed me. Into coffee table. Shattered it. Smaller one. Held arm down. Bigger one. Stomped on hand. Last…thing I…remember." Tears poured from her eyes again.

No wonder she'd passed out. Dee plucked a tissue from the box on the bedside table and gently blotted her tears away.

"Thank you." She raised her arms slightly. "Little things. Suddenly. So hard."

Having a hand out of commission made everyday tasks tough. Having both out would make them almost impossible. "I can see." He returned to the chair. "Do you remember anything else about the attack, anything the men did or said?"

"Laughed. Every time…they hurt…me. Every time I…screamed."

Sick bastards. "Anything else?"

"Smaller one…in charge. Asked questions. Told big one…what to do."

"Did either man say the other's name?"

Corinne thought for a moment. "Bigger one. Called smaller one. Otter. Made him mad."

Otter. Dee made a mental note to check with Criminal Intel if they knew the name. "Anything else you recall about the attack?"

Corrine shook her head.

Dee glanced at his watch. "Interview concluded at

ten-twenty-two a.m." He stopped the recorder and dropped it in his jacket pocket. "Thank you, Corinne. You've been very helpful. I know reliving what you went through was very hard for you." He laid a business card on the bedside table. "If you think of anything, no matter how small, let me know."

She nodded.

"Corinne, I'm going to do everything I can to get the jerks who did this to you."

Dee cleared the hospital's front doors, pulled his cell phone out, and dialed CIU He recognized the man who answered. "Art? Dee."

"Hey, Dee! Long time. What's up?"

"It has been. We should get together some time, the four of us, for dinner. Need info on a ganger goes by the street name Otter."

Art laughed. "Hector Otero. Also aka Little O. Member of Los Lobos. Why're you asking about him?"

"Name came up in relation to an attack on a woman."

"Then Músculos was in on it, too."

"Músculos?"

"Miguel 'Músculos' Mercado. Another Lobos. Otero calls the shots, Mercado does the heavy lifting. He's long on brawn, short on brains. Very short. He's so dumb, if he doesn't have someone lead him home, he gets lost."

"Can your guys round Mercado and Otero up for me?"

"Happy to. Where do you want 'em stashed?"

"My house." Dee wanted to interrogate these two worms on his home turf.

"Gimme a couple hours."

"Also, can you put together a couple six-packs with their pictures?" Stiff manila pages that held six photos.

"Happy to. How quick you want it?"

"Soon as I can get there." Dee disconnected then dialed Lafferty's number. When he answered, Dee filled him in on Corinne James, Otter, and Músculos, and their tie to Mary. "You want in on the fun?"

"Absolutely."

Chapter 21

Rick talked to four cops before he headed for the meeting with Alvarez. They'd given him information that convinced him he could cross three more names off his list. At The Bite Shop, he ordered their Fisherman's Sub basket and a Coke.

Alvarez joined him as the waitress delivered his meal. "Sorry I'm late. Big pile-up on the Lincoln Boulevard off ramp had me tied up." He gave the waitress his order.

"Not a problem. So what's up?"

"Rynert's worried IA's gonna jam him up over taking that money."

"Not gonna happen."

"I have your word?"

"Mine, Dee's, and IA's. Rynert did wrong taking that money." Rick raised a hand to stop Alvarez's protest. "He made it right turning it in. Makes it a wash as far as IA's concerned. Most that will land on him is a Letter of Warning in his jacket. That all you want?"

"It's none of my business, but did you do anything yet with those names I gave you?"

"Looked into most of them."

"Mind telling me how you made out?"

"Cleared almost all of them. Have a couple to go yet."

The waitress delivered Alvarez's lunch. He

slathered tartar sauce on a crab cake. "Make sure you look at Davenport, Rynert's patrol sergeant."

"Why?"

Alvarez took a long swig of soda. "He's a slider, for one. Did what he had to, to get by, no more. Every promotion he ever got was for time in rank, not because he earned it. Made sergeant when he did because a bunch of old dogs all pulled the pin about that time. The brass had more holes to fill than qualified people to fill them. So they slapped an extra stripe on his sleeve and dropped him in one."

"That doesn't make him dirty."

Alvarez's expression said he was sorting out how best to say what was on his mind. "I rode with him for a few months when we both worked out of the Three-Three. Besides cutting every corner he could, he took every freebie that came his way. And I'm ninety percent sure he boosted stuff from crime scenes we were at, especially if it was a robbery at some rich guy's place. I'd see something—a watch, a ring, some cash—on a dresser or somewhere. Next day, the victim would call and say Uncle Harry's pocket watch or Grandma's engagement ring or a hundred bucks was missing, too."

Rick signaled the waitress for two coffees. She asked if they wanted dessert. They passed. Rick asked, "You report him?"

"Never actually saw him take anything. Closest was at a rollover crash on South River Drive. Fancy camera the driver had in the car got tossed when it flipped, landed on the bank almost into the river. Spotted it right after we got there, went to get it for the driver before we went back on patrol, and it was gone. Had to be Davenport took it. Only him, me, and the driver anywhere near it. I changed partners right after that. He was going to go down sooner or later, and I wasn't about to go down with him."

The waitress delivered their coffees. Rick took a sip of his. "That why you told Rynert to reach out to you if he had problems with Davenport?"

Alvarez nodded as he stirred sugar into his coffee. "Like I said, kid's gonna make a good cop with some seasoning, the kind you want backing you up when things go sideways on the street. I don't want to see a rookie like that getting involved with the likes of Davenport."

"Where does McHale fit into this picture?"

"Him and Davenport are like this." He held up a hand with the first fingers crossed. "And that's one guy I *don't* trust. Always had the urge to keep one hand on my wallet and the other on my weapon every time I was around him."

"Why?"

"A guy does you a favor, you owe him one in return, right? McHale does you a favor, you owe him ten. And it won't be covering a shift for him. He'll want your blood."

"You got any specifics?"

"I never worked with him, so what I'm telling you is second hand, but it comes from guys I know to be reliable, so I'd stake money on it being true. You know he's a fixer, right?"

Rick nodded.

"Greenie gets himself in a jam like Rynert did, McHale steps in and unjams him. Couple weeks later, McHale wants the kid to do something not really illegal, just on the line. Next day, the kid finds an envelope with a couple C-notes in his locker. Next thing McHale wants from him'll be a little bit over the line. Each time after that, it's a little further over. Couple more jobs like that and the greenie's so far over the line, McHale owns him body and soul. The kid ever balks, all the bad stuff he ever did suddenly lands in IA's in-basket."

The waitress delivered their checks. Rick covered both with his hand. "On me."

Alvarez nodded thanks. "Every District Davenport's been posted to is low-crime."

Department policy was to post new officers to low crime areas to get some seasoning.

"Davenport's McHale's birddog. A greenie screws up, he's right there to hook him up with McHale. McHale's got his hooks in some civilians, too." Alvarez paused for a sip of coffee. "I heard some time back, he popped some girl for coke the third time. It's plain as day each time she's just carrying it for the jerk she's with but she takes the falls, does short time in city lockup first two times. Girl's a looker according to the story, so the third time, McHale tells her she's facing big time in a state facility unless she does something for him."

"Sleep with him?"

Alvarez slugged back the rest of his coffee. "Women don't sleep with McHale, they put out for him. They're just something he uses to get his rocks off, nothing more."

****

Dee entered Corinne James's cubicle again. "Sorry to bother you so soon, but I wonder if you'd be willing to look at some photos and see if the men who attacked you are among them?"

She nodded.

Dee held up the first sheet. Corinne instantly paled under her bruises. She turned her head and took a few deep breaths. Dee lowered the six-pack. She took another deep breath. "Top row. Right. Hurt me."

Dee held up the second sheet. She examined the six photos for a moment. Her voice trembled as she said, "Bo-bottom row. Middle. Told other one. To do it."

She'd picked out Mercado and Otero. Dee laid the sheets on the overbed table and noted the date by each man's picture. "I know this will be difficult, but could you please write your initials under the dates?"

She took the pen he offered and slowly scratched a shaky CMJ on each sheet. Dee took back the pages and his pen. "Thank you, Ms. James. I promise you we'll get these bastards."

****

McHale made his noon call to Joey Day from the corner of Tenth and McKinley.

"*Buenos dias, mi amigo.* Tell me you have fixed the problem I asked you to."

Great. Joe was into the Hispanic lingo shit again. "Not yet, *Jefe*. I told you it would be a day or two."

"No longer, *mi hermano. La policia* must learn the hard lesson that they cannot harm my people without worse harm being visited on them. And they must learn it quickly. That lady cop must die."

He hated trying to translate Joey's cryptic remarks sometimes but, Jesus, to talk openly about killing a cop on the phone was plain dumb. Joey too often let his *machismo* override his common sense. Time to remind the stupid beaner that he had gotten them into this fix. "Haste makes waste, *Jefe*. Had we thought matters through a little more thoroughly the other night, we

288

wouldn't be in the situation we're in now."

Silence. McHale held his breath, and a little trickle of fear slid down his spine. Joey didn't like being told he'd made a mistake. Guys had died for telling him that. Guys had been rewarded for it, too. Joey was too friggin' unpredictable to know which way he'd jump until he did. It did a real number on a guy's nerves.

Finally a sigh. "Perhaps you are right, *mi amigo*."

McHale relaxed. The one atom of common sense Joey owned had won this round.

"Perhaps we should have indeed taken a more cautious approach then." Joey sighed again. "Well, there is no use crying over spilt milk. All we can do is mop it up." Joey chuckled at his own joke.

"Si, Jefe."

"Those errors need to be—what is the word?—rectified. And soon?"

"You have my word, *Jefe*."

"Muy bien."

"In regards to that matter, Jefe, I need something."

"How may I be of assistance, *mi amigo*?"

If Joey was gonna blab about offing a cop, no reason for McHale to hide it. If the shit hit the fan, he could always cover his ass by saying he was posing as a dirty cop to get the goods on Joey. "I need a piece. Untraceable twenty-two auto with suppressor. Fourteen round magazine. Ten will do, but fourteen would be better. And a spare." He wanted to hurt Virgin big before he punched her ticket for good.

A moment of silence. "Talk to Alejandro at the bodega on Thirteenth in an hour."

"Gracias, *Jefe*. And nothing with a tail on it like last time. I want a clean one."

Joey sighed. "As you wish, *mi hermano*."

McHale climbed into his cruiser and fired the engine. As he gripped the shifter, a chill ran through him. Like he was hanging from a rope over a deep chasm, and the rope was fraying fast. He shook it off as he drove away, but he couldn't ditch the feeling it was an omen of bad coming right at him.

****

Rick stands across a room. She is so glad to see him, it has been too long since the last time. She walks toward him. For every step she takes, he takes one back. Why is he doing that? She walks faster, jogs, sprints toward him but he backs away just as fast, never letting her close the space between them. Confused, she asks him why. He says, "Orders."

The darkness comes again.

****

"Harter says the phone call about Mary's shooting is a dead end," Dee said after Lafferty entered his office.

"How so?"

"Came from a cell in the area of Fourth and Birch. Male voice, no name, reporting shots fired inside Lukens's apartment then hanging up. No way to track him down."

"Harter told me the DeSchain is pretty much soundproof. So how did the guy hear the shots? Through an open window?"

"Nope. I asked. Harter says the windows in Lukens's condo were shut."

"So the guy who reported it had to be either the shooter or inside Lukens's place when Mary got it."

"Unless you have another way it could have gone down."

"Can't think of one. We got any good news?"

"Corinne James picked Mercado and Otero out of photo line-ups, and CIU just delivered Mercado to us. Grabbed him at a Wendy's. Guys who rode him in said he bitched the whole way about not getting to eat his 'snack.' Had more food on his tray than the whole squad eats for lunch." He stood. "Ready to go talk to him?"

"Yeah."

Dee handed Rick a thick folder from his desk. "Here."

Rick flipped through Mercado's jacket as they walked to the pit. His arrest record was mostly A and B beefs, many with 'with intent' charges tacked on. "Did a lot of bad stuff, didn't do much time."

"CIU said he tends to plead out quick or give up someone in exchange for a reduced sentence. They say he's sharp as a stick of butter, easy to roll over."

"How'd he last this long in Joey Day's outfit doing that?"

"Good help's hard to come by. Just seeing this guy coming at you would make you give up whatever he wanted."

They entered the observation room and Rick eyed Miguel Mercado through the mirror. His massive frame strained the black track suit he wore. His rap sheet listed him as five-ten and two-fifty-two. Músculos fit him. He was one big lump of muscle. Dee was right. One sight of this guy would have Rambo shaking and quaking. "No kidding."

Dee said, "Ready to see what he'll give up today?"

They entered the pit. Mercado had short black hair and a round face with a wide soul patch under his lower lip. He gazed at them with dull black eyes full of innocence. Dee and Rick sat facing him and Rick said, "How's it going, Músculos?"

"I'm hungry. Can you get me somethin' to eat?"

"In a little bit. You have to answer some questions first."

Mercado shrugged massive shoulders. "Okay."

"You remember what you were doing two nights ago?"

"Yeah."

"You want to tell us what you were doing?"

A moment's scowling thought before he answered. "Oh! Otter an' me ate at McDonalds then we went somewhere an' did somethin'." He flashed a child-like smile. "Can I get somethin' to eat now? 'Cause I'm really hungry."

"I think we can manage that," Dee said. "Candy bars okay? That's all we have in our machines."

"Ones with nuts? I like nuts."

Dee stood. "Nuts it is. But you have to keep answering our questions."

Mercado thought that over. "Okay."

Once Dee left the interrogation room, Rick said, "You remember what you did after you left McDonalds?"

A momentary blank look before he answered. "Oh! Otter had to talk to this lady about somethin' so we went there." He smiled, happy he had remembered.

"Do you remember the lady's name or what Otter wanted to ask her?"

"Otter dint tell me her name. But he wanted to know what she knew about somethin'." A brief scowl followed by a smile. "Somethin' about some lady cop who got shot."

"What about the lady cop who got shot?"

A long silence. "Otter wanted to know where she was. I think he wanted to send her flowers or somethin'." He grinned, proud he'd come up with that.

Dee had Músculos pegged right. Dumb oozed out of the big man like grease from a kielbasa.

"Why did you go with Otter to talk to the lady?"

"'Cause he ast me to." Said as if it was the most obvious reason in the world.

Dee entered the room and tossed a half dozen candy bars on the table. Mercado grabbed a Hershey bar with almonds, ripped the wrapper off, and stuffed it his mouth. He chewed rapidly, swallowed, and picked up a Baby Ruth. Rick took it from his hand. "What did you do while Otter was talking to the lady?"

"Nothin'. Just stood there like he told me to."

"That's all?"

Mercado nodded. "Unh-hunh."

Rick and Dee stared at him with deadpan expressions. After a quarter minute, Mercado started squirming in the chair. He squirmed a little more then said, "And I hit her when Otter told me to, too."

"Why did Otter tell you to hit her?"

"'Cause she wou'n't tell him where that lady cop was. I had to hit her a couple times before she told him."

"You did more than hit her, didn't you, Musculos? You beat her up, broke her arm, her nose, her fingers, smashed her hand."

"Well, yeah. But that's sort of like hittin', kind of." He picked up the Baby Ruth again and tore the wrapper. "An' I dint—"

Rick snatched the bar from his hand. "Finish what you started to say then you can have this. You didn't what?"

A moment of confusion until Mercado recalled what he'd started to say. "I dint do it for no reason. I done it 'cause Otter said to 'cause she wou'n't tell him what he asked."

"And after you hit her, did the woman tell Otter where the lady cop was?"

"Unh-hunh." Another grin. "They always tell Otter what he wants to know after I hit 'em like he tells me to."

"So Otter told you to break her arm and do all those other things?"

"Unh-hunh. He always tells me what to do."

"And where did the woman say the lady cop was?"

A long scowl this time. "It was someplace with a big name I can't remember."

Rick handed him the candy bar. "Was it Otter's idea to talk to the lady about the cop?"

"Yeah." He inhaled the bar.

"He didn't do it because someone else wanted to know where the lady cop was?"

"You mean like Mr. Day?"

Rick stared at him for a moment. The man raised the standard for dumb to a new level. Or dropped it to a new low. "Was it Mr. Day?"

Mercado pointed to the candy bars in front of Dee. "Can I have another one?"

"Answer the question first," Dee said. "Did Mr. Day tell Otter to find out where the lady cop was?"

"I don't know." Mercado shrugged his massive shoulders. "Maybe. Otter does stuff for Mr. Day all-a time." His face brightened. "Sometimes he lets me help."

Dee slid a 5th Avenue bar across the table as Rick asked, "Was it Mr. Day's idea for you to hit the lady when she didn't answer Otter's questions?"

Mercado stared at them as confused as if they'd suddenly started speaking Chinese. Rick and Dee exchange glances and head shakes then Rick said slowly, "Did Mr. Day tell Otter you should hit the lady when she didn't answer Otter's questions?"

Mercado wolfed down the candy then shook his head. "Otter dint tell me nothin' like that. He just said I should go with him to see the lady and when he tells me to, I should hit her."

"What were you wearing when you visited the lady?"

A big grin filled Mercado's face. "Me an' Otter had uniforms just like cops wear. They even had fancy patches here," He slapped a beefy shoulder with a broad hand, "just like real police have. And mine had stripes on each sleeve. Like a 'V' only with the pointy end on top instead of the bottom." Another big grin. "Otter said that made me a corporal."

Dee slid an Almond Joy bar across the table to him. "Where did you get a police uniform?"

Mercado heaved his shoulders again. "Otter had it when he come for me. He gave it to me and said I should put it on, so I did."

Dee said, "Miguel, you are in deep trouble here. We have you on video going into the lady's apartment, and she picked you and Otter out as the men who attacked her. And you just admitted you attacked her and impersonated a police officer."

Mercado scowled for a full minute. "Maybe I shouldn't say no more."

"Too late."

****

Rynert studied the bodega on Thirteenth from the front seat of his Jeep.

McHale had called him a half hour ago and said he had a job for him. Rynert yawned. Man he was tired. He'd been sound asleep when McHale called. He wished he could have told him no and gone back to sleep. No way he could, though. If he had, McHale would see he got kicked off the job, and he'd end up prowling some mall at three in the morning.

He and Kathy could have a good life on her teaching salary and what he made as a cop. If he lost that, they'd be living on peanut butter and hot dogs. Staying a cop was the main reason he'd agreed to do this undercover thing.

His heart thumped hard against his ribs. He blew out a big breath and dried his palms on his jeans, both for the tenth time. He hoped he could pull this off. All he had to do was pick up a package from some guy named Alejandro in the bodega and deliver it to McHale. It couldn't be that hard. So, why was his mouth so dry? He unwrapped a stick of Juicy Fruit gum.

Rynert checked his watch again. Three minutes to one. McHale had said not to go into the bodega before one. Man, this waiting was hell.

He couldn't sit there any longer. He left the Jeep, jaywalked to the bodega, and went in. He'd never been in one before, so he wandered the aisles, checking it out. It was a good way to kill the few minutes until he could hook up with Alejandro. He was a bit surprised to see the bodega wasn't much different than the mom-and-pop grocery on the corner near his apartment. They even had Fruit Loops, his favorite cereal.

He checked his watch. Almost one. Close enough.

He strolled up to the counter. Two small, wiry men, one old, one young, stood behind it, talking in rapid-fire Spanish. Rynert gave them a few seconds to notice him then cleared his throat.

The younger man glanced his way then spat out an annoyed, "What do you want?"

The old man fired something angry-sounding in Spanish. The younger one replied the same way, took in a breath, and said, "How can I help you, *Señor*?"

Rynert said, "I, uh, I'm looking for Alejandro. He has a package for me?"

The younger man faced him. "I am Alejandro." He studied Rynert for a second. "But I know of no package here for you, sir."

"It's, uh, not really for me, I'm just picking it up for someone else."

Alejandro stepped to the counter and folded his arms across his chest. A tatt of a bushy animal's tail showed on his right arm below the rolled up cuff of his long sleeve white shirt. It was a wolf's tail, part of a Los Lobos tatt. Alejandro gave him a hard stare. "And who would this someone else be?"

Another angry Spanish outburst from the old man. Alejandro waved a 'go away' gesture at him.

"Sergeant Michael McHale."

The old man launched a tirade at Alejandro. It rolled off him as he studied Rynert with the same hard stare long enough to make Rynert edgy. "And what did this Sergeant McHale want you to pick up for him?"

"Uh, I don't know. He didn't tell me. Just asked me to pick something up here."

"Could he have meant his cigars."

"Uh, yeah, I guess that's it."

Alejandro smiled. "One moment."

He stepped through a curtain at the far end of the counter. The old man followed, yapping away. Both returned a moment later, the old man still yammering, Alejandro carrying a box of Monte Cristo Churchills. "Here you are."

Rynert took the box. Seemed awful heavy for a box of cigars. "Do, uh, do I owe you anything for this?"

"No. *Señor* McHale paid for them when he ordered them."

"Okay. Thank you. Uh, *gracias*."

"*De nada*."

As Rynert left the counter, the old man lit into Alejandro again. Alejandro lit back. They were shouting by the time Rynert hit the door to the bodega. He could still hear them when he got to his Jeep. He wondered what the argument was about and decided he'd ask Kathy if she knew anyone who could teach him Spanish.

He drove ten blocks south on Thirteenth and pulled to the curb. After shutting off the Jeep's engine, he pulled on latex gloves then opened the cigar box. Inside, wrapped in stained olive drab cloth, was a Browning .22 semi-automatic, a suppressor, and a spare loaded magazine. He ejected the magazine in the pistol. It was full, too. Ten rounds in each. He racked the slide to clear the chamber. No round popped out.

He looked the pistol over carefully. The serial number had been ground off, the spot covered with brush-on bluing. He pried his cell phone from the belt holder and dialed Alvarez's number. After five rings, it went to voicemail. Rynert hung up.

"What do I do now?" Panic surged through him. He wasn't cut out for this undercover stuff. The only reason he'd agreed to it was because his gut told him he'd be better off working with Alvarez and Captain DeAngelis than with McHale. And because Kathy would be so proud of him if he pulled this undercover thing off. It would prove, she'd say, he could do anything he put his mind to.

Easy for her to say. She was smart. Rynert wasn't. He'd spend his whole career in uniform, probably patrolling a beat. Maybe with tons of luck and lots of help from Kathy, he could make sergeant some day. But he'd never make detective. He didn't have the brains for it, even though Kathy was always telling him he could become anything he wanted if he worked hard enough for it.

That didn't help him now. He had to figure out what to do about the .22. He'd never been in a situation like this, and they'd never covered it at the academy. He needed someone to tell him what to do. Now. He'd always gone to Alvarez when he had questions, but he couldn't wait. Who could he ask?

He opened his cell and dialed.

Chapter 22

Dee pulled into the employee parking lot behind the Jacob D. Ferber Memorial Public Pool and scanned the cars. No red Jeep. He backed his Crown Vic into a slot and shut it off. A burly man in a blue tee bearing the pool's name came out an EMPLOYEES ONLY door, nodded once to Dee, got in a white Dodge 'Department of Parks & Recreation' pick-up, and drove away.

Two minutes later, Rynert arrived and parked next to him. Dee opened the Jeep's passenger door and looked at the Monte Cristo box on the seat. "This it?"

Rynert said, "Yes, sir."

"Bring it." Dee grabbed a battered gray briefcase from his own car.

Rynert got out and joined Dee at the metal door. He opened it and motioned for Rynert to follow him inside. The building was tomb quiet except for a muted hum of pumps somewhere. Rynert glanced around nervously. "Where is everybody?"

"On break."

"They all go on break at the same time?"

"They did today."

"Oh?" A pause. "Oh! Okay. Got you, Captain."

"Tell me how you got that piece."

Rynert explained about McHale's call and picking up the .22 at the bodega as Dee led him through the building to a workshop. There, Dee pointed for Rynert to set the cigar box on a metal workbench. He opened his briefcase next to it, took out latex gloves and worked them over his hands. "Let's see what we have here."

Opening the Monte Cristo box, he folded back the cloth, revealing a Browning .22 pistol, magazine, and suppressor. He took out the pistol. "You touch this at all?"

"Yes, sir. I gloved up first."

"Good thinking, Rynert." Dee noted the repaired bluing where the serial number had been filed off. He ejected the magazine and ran the slide to clear the chamber. The action was smooth. He held the pistol up to the light hanging over the workbench and examined the barrel. It was clean. He thumbed all but three rounds out of the magazine, dropped them in the cigar box, and slid the magazine into the pistol's grip.

"Uh, Captain, what are we doing here?"

He threaded the suppressor onto the muzzle. "We're going to test fire the piece, recover the rounds, and take them to ballistics for analysis. We should fingerprint it, too."

"Geez, Captain, no! If McHale finds out—"

"I didn't say we were, Rynert, I said we should." He lifted the suppressor from the cigar box and started threading it onto the .22's muzzle. "Come on."

Dee led Rynert outside to the pool. Walking to the shallow end, he squatted, aimed the automatic at the deep end, and fired into the water. The pistol made only three muted pops, the sound of the action and the splash of the bullets hitting the water louder than the gunfire.

"Okay, Rynert, get the net over there and retrieve those slugs." He rounded up the three ejected shell casings and dropped them into a small plastic baggie he'd taken from his jacket pocket. "Bring them to the workshop."

At the workbench, Dee took a small gun cleaning kit from his briefcase and swabbed the automatic's barrel. Rynert entered the workshop with the slugs in the net as he was reloading the magazine. "Uh, Captain?"

"Yeah?"

Rynert shifted nervously on his feet. "Captain, I gotta get going." He pointed to the pistol in Dee's hands. "McHale's waiting for that. If I take too long getting it to him, he might think something funny's going on."

Dee thumbed the last three rounds into the magazine and slid it into the pistol. "Tell him you got held up in traffic. Or you had to run an errand for your fiancé."

"Captain, I don't know. I mean—"

Dee suppressed a sigh, sure for a second they'd picked the wrong guy for this UC op. Rynert was too green for something this risky. But you worked with what you had. "You can come up with something he'll buy. Use your imagination."

Rynert rubbed a hand over his sandy hair. "You say so, Captain."

"Was there a round under the hammer when you picked this up?"

"No, sir. Chamber was clear. Uh, Captain?"

"Yeah, Rynert. Just a second." Dee rewrapped the pistol in the cloth exactly as it had been, set it in the cigar box, and closed the lid. "Okay. Take off."

As Rynert scampered away, Dee grabbed the net and shook the bullets out onto a small rag he'd laid on the workbench, patted them dry, and put them in a small paper bag. After stowing it in his briefcase, he left the building. Stepping through the EMPLOYEES ONLY door, he pulled the paper plug from the latch pocket in the jamb, letting the door shut behind him and lock.

He dropped the plug in a trash barrel by the door, got in his Crown Vic, and drove away.

****

Rynert raced toward Fairmont Park, cursing traffic all the way. Man, it was worse than five o'clock Friday night. If he didn't get there soon, McHale would screw him royally. He'd be lucky to get a job as a crossing guard at a daycare center. That would deep-six his future with Kathy for sure. She told him every day she loved that he was a cop, said she always felt safe when she was with him for that reason. She'd probably kick him to the curb when his uniform was a Day-Glo orange vest and a STOP hand paddle. He swerved around a taxi and stepped harder on the gas pedal.

****

Dee entered the Police Forensic Science building. It wasn't much to look at from the outside, just an old brick pile the city had picked up cheap years ago. Inside was anything but old. All four floors held modern testing equipment run by the best forensic techs the city could recruit. An ex-Assistant Chief of Police on the city council made sure they never scrimped on the police department budget.

Dee checked in with the receptionist then headed for the Fingerprint Lab on the second floor. There, he made his way to a cubicle where a heavy brunette woman typed on a computer. She glanced up, jumped to her feet, and crushed him in a bear hug. "Marco!"

"Hey, Vicki."

Releasing him, she said, "To what do I owe the pleasure?"

303

"I need a favor." Dee pulled the bag with the empty shell casings from his jacket pocket. "Can you do these fast for me? And off the books?"

She took the bag from him and slipped it into her lab coat pocket. "A couple hours."

"Thanks, Vicki. I owe you one."

"No you don't."

Dee had once convinced a sleazeball by the name of Matt 'Chiller' Wright that continuing his efforts to revive a terminated relationship with Vicki's daughter, Muriel, would lead to an extended stay in ICU. Or a new home in the deepest part of Delaware Bay.

Leaving Fingerprints, Dee took the elevator to the basement. In the Ballistics Lab, he asked Harold McAllister, the secretary, if Chester was working. Harold said he was, dialing his extension. A half minute later, the balding gray-haired paunchy man opened the locked door to the lab proper and waved Dee in. "What can I do for you?"

Dee gave him the bag with the bullets. "I need to know what you can tell me about these."

"How quick?"

"Soon as you can?"

"Couple hours. They from a case?"

"Not exactly. Can you keep them out of the system until I tell you to put them in?"

"Is the mayor a blowhard?" Chester opened a desk drawer and unlocked a small metal box inside. He dropped the bag in the box, locked it, and shut the drawer.

****

Rynert tucked the cigar box under his arm and headed into Fairmont Park at just short of a trot. He

304

hoped McHale wouldn't be too pissed it took him so long to get there. Sweat beaded his brow, trickled along his temples, and dampened his chest. He didn't know if it was from the heat, exertion, or fear.

He took the gravel path to the little clearing where McHale said to meet him. Breaking into that trot, he entered the clearing a few seconds later. McHale sat on a cast iron bench on the far side. He leveled a glare at Rynert. "Where the hell have you been?"

"Sorry, Sarge. I had to drop some dry cleaning off for my girl, and there was a bunch of people ahead of me. And traffic was a bitch."

McHale eyed him for a moment.

"What?"

"Looking for the collar. She's got you on a leash and you ain't married yet." McHale chuckled. "You better shuck that collar quick, before she has you so hogtied you can't take a dump without getting her okay first."

"It's not like that with us, Sarge. We—"

McHale's eyes went cold. "I don't give a shit how it is. From now on, my errands come first. You got that?"

McHale's sudden mood switch scared him more than the glare. "Okay, Sarge. Yeah. Sure. I got it."

McHale snatched Rynert's cell from its belt holder

"Hey! What're you doing?"

"Just want to know who you've been talking to."

"That's none of your business."

"Kid, I own you. I want to know who you've been talking to, you tell me. Unless you'd rather work night security at the mall. Follow me?"

"Yeah. I follow."

McHale flipped Rynert's cell open and tapped several buttons. Cold sweat broke out on Rynert's

305

forehead. Captain DeAngelis's number would show on his phone and McHale would want to know why. He needed an explanation McHale would believe. His mind blanked. Winging it wasn't his strong suit. He could never have come up with the dry-cleaning excuse for being late if the captain hadn't suggested it.

McHale held the phone toward him. "Who you calling at the Zero-Seven?"

"What? Oh! A pal. He called me earlier, wanted to know if my girl and me wanted to get dinner with him and his wife tomorrow. I was calling him back." Rynert had no idea where that had come from. It just popped into his head.

McHale tapped a second number on the phone's screen. "Who's this?"

"Kathy."

"And this?"

Oh, shit. Alvarez. How was he going to explain that? Forget having trouble getting a job as a crossing guard. He was dead. "My old training officer. I had a question for him. I didn't get him." At least that wasn't a lie.

"What did you want to know? Maybe I can answer it."

"Nah, it's nothing serious, just something he told me right after I went on the street I wanted to ask him about. I'll try again later." Man, he was pulling answers out of his ass today.

McHale eyed him for a moment then shrugged. "Suit yourself. Here." McHale tossed him his cell phone then pointed to the cigar box. "You know what's in here?"

"No, Sarge." Captain DeAngelis had told him to play dumb. He could do dumb easy.

"Didn't maybe take a peek on the way over?"

"No, Sarge."

McHale lifted the lid and flipped back the cloth.

"Why are you getting a gun from—"

"None of your business. You're just a delivery boy. Got that?"

"Sure, Sarge."

McHale lifted the pistol and suppressor from the box. "You didn't mess with this did you? Maybe take out the firing pin, anything like that?"

"I told you, I didn't even look in the box."

McHale screwed the suppressor to the muzzle. "You aren't lying to me, are you?"

"No. No way."

McHale pointed the silenced Browning at him.

He dropped to the ground and clamped muscles hard to keep from soiling himself front and back. "Jesus, Sarge. What the hell are you doing?"

"Just checking."

"Che-checking what?" The sweating he'd done before was nothing compared to this. He was drowning in it now.

"If you were lying to me." McHale tipped the pistol toward the sky. "Guess you're not. Get up."

Rynert eyed him warily as he got to his knees and then his feet.

"Relax, kid. I'm not gonna shoot you. But I'm telling you right now, next time it takes you forever to get something to me, your ass is grass and I'm John Deere. You understand me?"

"Yeah, Sarge. I hear you."

"And you ever try to screw me over, you're dead. You got *that*?"

"I got it, Sarge."

"Get out of here."

Rynert didn't need to hear it twice. He took off at a fast walk. Ten feet down the gravel path, he broke into a jog, then a run. He slowed to a walk just before the path entered the heart of the park and strolled from there to the parking lot.

He stopped at a trash barrel and vomited. Then he pulled out his cell phone and dialed.

****

Joleen Wilson didn't know where she was. The bed didn't feel like her bed and the air didn't smell like her apartment. She opened her eyes. They took a second to focus. A stocky dark-haired woman dressed in pink scrubs bent over her. She had kind eyes.

"You're awake. That's good."

"Where am I?" It hurt to talk and her voice sounded thick.

"In University Hospital."

She inhaled then cried out as pain ripped through her chest.

"Easy. You have three cracked ribs."

Joleen took in a shallow breath. "How long have I been here?"

The nurse checked her watch. "About sixteen hours."

"What happened to me?"

"Don't you know? Don't you remember?"

Panic welled inside her. "No." Her nose felt funny. She raised her right hand to touch it and saw the cast covering her arm from elbow to knuckles. She shifted, and pain wracked her body, making her gasp. It all rushed back. The hands grabbing her, pulling her into the alley. The punches and kicks and crashing into walls and dumpsters. She started to cry.

"You remember now, don't you?"

She nodded. "Some-someone beat me up." Her tears came faster.

The woman stroked Joleen's hair. "There, there, honey. It's all right. You're safe now. No one will hurt you here. We'll just make you all better."

The woman's soft voice soothed like her mother's, easing her pain and fear. Her tears stopped, and the woman dabbed the wetness from her cheeks.

"Could I have some water?"

"Sure, honey." The woman took a plastic cup with a straw off the bedside table and held it to her lips. "I'm Nurse Jacobs, but you can call me Donna. I'll be taking care of you today."

Joleen took several sips then pushed the straw from her mouth.

"What's your name?" Donna asked.

"Joleen. Joleen Wilson. How bad am I?"

"You have a broken nose and a cracked bone in your cheek and some damaged teeth along with a broken arm and the cracked ribs. You also have a lot of bruises and some cuts, and you're going to be very sore and achy for a while. But you didn't have any damage inside you. Don't you worry. We'll take good care of you and in no time, at all you'll be as good as new again. Is there anything I can do for you before I go?"

Joleen realized she was hungry. "Can I get something to eat? I'm starving."

"The doctor has to examine you first, now that you're awake. Then we'll ask him, and if he says okay, I'll get you a tray." She told Joleen about the call button and how to use it. "Here's something else that will help you feel better: You have an admirer."

"Who?"

"A policeman. He stopped by this morning and left you a present." Donna picked the bright silver and blue wrapped package off the table and held it toward her. "Here you go."

Panic filled Joleen. McHale. An image of the alley flashed in her mind. She'd never seen her attacker's face but she was sure it was McHale. He'd tried to kill her there and failed. So he'd left something in her room to finish the job. "No! Take it away! Take it away!"

"Joleen, honey, you don't mean that. He made a special trip here to give this to you."

"I don't care! I don't want it! It's a—"

"It's a book, Joleen. I can tell by the shape."

Joleen reached for the package then hesitated. Could McHale kill her with a book? Could he rig a bomb in one? Could he do something—spray a poison or toxic chemical on it—that would kill her days from now? She suspected he could do either.

"He was a very nice young officer. He stopped at the desk and said you liked books," Donna raised the package an inch, "and asked if he could leave this for you."

Tim? Would he have made a special trip just to give her a book? She wanted to believe he'd do something that kind, but her experiences with Bryce and McHale had her distrusting all men. An image of Tim in the park yesterday filled her mind. He'd been almost timid with his words and actions, as if to assure her he had no ulterior motive in mind. And sweet. Yes, she could see him bringing her a book. "What did he look like?"

"Tall, red hair and brown eyes, a chipped tooth here," Donna showed her own and touched an incisor, "more freckles than a Dalmatian has spots."

Tim! Knowing he cared enough to go out of his way to bring her a book lessened her pain. She held out her hand.

Donna gave her the package. She eyed the wrapping—Christmas paper with blue bows and silver ribbons—and laughed, even though it hurt. Then she tore the paper off, revealing Grisham's *The Summons*. A folded paper slipped out. She opened it.

Joleen

I heard what happened. I'm so sorry. I hope you haven't read this, I hope you like it, and I hope it helps you feel better soon.

As much as I couldn't stop thinking about you after I first saw you yesterday, it was even worse after I left you in the park. I really enjoyed talking about books with you yesterday, and I hope we can do it again soon.

I'd like to come see you when you're feeling better, if that's okay. Just tell the nurse and she'll get word to me.

Thinking of you now.

Tim

P. S. Sorry about the paper.

She held the book against her chest, and tears rose in her eyes. The last man to write her a note anywhere even close to that had been a high school boyfriend. Donna handed her a tissue. She blotted her tears and said, "Could you call him for me?"

****

"DeAngelis."

"It's Chester at the lab."

311

Dee sat up in his chair. He'd only left Ballistics an hour ago. "You got something for me already?"

"Yeah. And you won't like it."

"Maybe I will. Lay it on me."

"Those slugs you brought me match ones taken from a body found in an alley off Figueroa two years ago. Kid by the name of Benny Kelsey."

"What do you know about him?"

"Nothing beyond that. I just know bullets and what you all-powerful detectives tell me." Said with a laugh. "Detective Richter in the Two-One was lead."

The name didn't click with Dee. "Thanks."

"Listen, Dee, I can't hold these slugs back now. They gotta go in the system."

"I hear you. But keep my name out of the picture as long as you can."

"Do my best." Chester hung up.

Dee dialed the Two-One and asked for Detective Richter. Moments later a deep voice on the line said, "Richter."

"Captain Marco DeAngelis, District Seven. What can you tell me about Benny Kelsey?"

"What's your interest in him?"

"Case I'm working ties to the bullets that took him out."

"I remember the name but I'm drawing a blank beyond that. Hold on a sec."

A good sign in Dee's book. Richter didn't guard his cases like a pit bull guarding turf. A rumble as Richter opened a desk drawer then clicks as he finger-walked through his files then the soft thud of one landing on Richter's metal desk.

"Let's see. Benny Kelsey. Twenty-three, Caucasian,

five-eight, one-ninety, blond over brown. Found dead in an alley between Willow and Harrison. Shot twice in the back of the head with a .22. What else do you want to know about him?"

"Anything you can tell me."

"Snake tatt on his right arm marked him as a Viper. Had a blood drop hanging from each fang."

"So he made the grade." Had killed.

"Times two. Word on the street was he snuffed a Monarch—Rahmal Whittaker—for poaching Viper turf and a fellow Viper—George Dahl—for reasons unknown. Never got enough to charge him for either one."

"Rarely do. Any idea why Kelsey got iced?"

"Street chatter was Diego Torres, a Lobo, took great offence at Kelsey doing the hump and pump with his main squeeze, one Garabina Vasquez, a Lobas. Other Lobos screwing her regularly was okay. But a Viper banging her once was a no-no."

"Anything happen to Vasquez for getting it on with Kelsey?" Gangs had a strict code of conduct, and violators paid a steep price.

"Disappeared the same day Benny caught lead poisoning. Her body turned up on a vacant lot in Lobos turf two weeks later. Had the shit beat out of her, was tied up, raped, sodomized, and tortured before she was killed. Cause of death was—hold on a sec, let me dig it out."

He pawed through a drawer again and, after a second or two, dropped another file on his desk. "Damn! I forgot what a hot *chica* Vasquez was. She hadn't been a ganger, I wouldn'ta minded hooking up with her." The rustle of pages turning. "Here it is. Official COD was strangulation by wire ligature."

"Who did her?"

"Based on what the ME found, CIU thinks her sister Lobas gave her a hard-core beat down for going outside the clan then dumped her on Viper turf. You can guess what those slimeballs did to her."

Dee didn't need to guess. He'd seen a dozen gang members who fell into the hands of rivals. The result was never pretty.

"When that got boring, they amused themselves by almost killing her—ME says the wire had been tightened around her neck then loosened a dozen times—before they snuffed her and dumped her in the lot. Her last days on earth were probably a living hell."

No probably about it. Gang sister or not, she didn't deserve to suffer and die that way. The desire to see the guilty pay for cruelty like that was one reason Dee became a cop. "Thanks, Richter. I owe you one."

"I don't keep score." Richter would trade favors but not insist on tit-for-tat.

That was good to know. Dee filed Richter's name away. He was the kind of detective Dee wanted on his squad. He'd offer him the next opening he had. His phone rang again almost the instant he hung up.

"Tony and Marie's on Eighth is my favorite restaurant." Vicki.

"Ooh-kay. Why are you telling me this?"

"You owe me a dinner there for getting you answers so fast."

"You're on. What answers do you have for me?"

"Good and not so good."

Uh-oh. "And the good is?"

"I lifted prints from two individuals off the casings

you gave me."

"And the not so good?"

"That's not all the good. Based on a quick peek, I matched the prints to names. And I'm confident a closer comparison will confirm it."

"So what's the bad?"

"One print belongs to Diego Torres."

Dee wasn't surprised.

"The others come back to César Molina. I've seen enough of both of them that I know them almost as soon as I see them. And call me a special TV offer."

"What?" Dee was totally confused.

"But wait, there's more. The prints from that home invasion and assault at Foxcroft Terrace a few days ago came back to Miguel 'Musculos' Mercado and Hector 'Otter' Otero."

Chapter 23

McHale's cell rang as he sat at the light at Melrose and Twenty-third.

"It's McAllister from the crime lab."

"Wha'd'ya want?"

"I got something for you."

Background noise—trucks, horns, cars, a siren—told McHale his caller was outside, away from the other lab rats. Safer for both of them, but the din annoyed him. "Speak the frig up. I can hardly hear you."

A few seconds later, McAllister said, "I'm in my car. This better?"

Not by much. "Super. What do you want?"

"You wanted to know any time certain names came—"

"Cut to the goddam chase."

"Okay, okay. You want to know any time evidence ties to Los Lobos. Some .22 casings and slugs came in earlier today. Prints on the casings came back to César Molina and Diego Torres. Ballistics matched the slugs to ones from an open homicide probably done by a Lobo."

McHale glanced at the cigar box on the Impala's front seat. Shit! No, couldn't be. He was just jumping to conclusions. "Okay. Thanks."

"Wait. I got more."

"I'm listening."

"We got some prints in Thursday from a home

invasion at Foxcroft Terrace, woman by the name of Corinne James."

"That name supposed to mean something to me?"

"I'm just telling you. We matched the prints to Hector Otero and Miguel Mercado."

That wasn't good. "Thanks."

"So, uh, is all that worth something to you?"

"Two Cs."

"Come on, McHale! Two hundred? All that's gotta be worth more than that." An ex-wife getting big alimony and a mistress with expensive tastes had Harold McAllister in a constant cash-flow bind.

"Or nothing." McHale never paid more. "Take it or leave it."

McAllister sighed. "Take it."

"I knew you'd see it my way." McHale closed his phone. He pulled his cruiser into the first parking spot he found. He needed to do some thinking.

Casings and .22 bullets tied to Los Lobos showing up at the lab today didn't mean they'd come from his gun. There had to be at least a dozen .22's in Joey's armory. The slugs and brass in the lab probably came from another .22 César or Diego had used on a job and had just surfaced now. Coincidence pure and simple. McHale shook his head. Nope. Like all cops, he didn't believe in coincidence.

Maybe Rynert had taken the gun to the lab before delivering it. It had taken him a hell of a long time to get to Fairmont Park. Nah, no way. The kid was too scared of losing his job to cross him. And the lab would have kept the .22. Plus the kid didn't have the smarts to pop a few caps from the piece and hand them and casings over. If he had the smarts, he didn't have the juice to get them jumped to the head of the line. Rule out Rynert.

That was good. McHale would hate to have to crush the kid this fast. A greenie like him, McHale could use for a long time. Still, he had to talk to the kid, remind him his career in the department was hanging by a thread and McHale had scissors.

Had to be Tomás, Joey's armorer, had dropped the ball. What was the beaner thinking, giving him a piece with a tail on it for a hit, especially one on a cop? Probably wasn't thinking, had just grabbed the first .22 he came to, never checked if it was clean.

And what was that crap about Mercado and Otero leaving prints all over some broad's apartment? Mercado, he could see. The hippo was too dumb to breathe without reminders. Otero was a different story. He'd been one of Joey's top men for years, he should have known to glove up before hitting a place.

Joey's people were getting sloppy. No surprise. Ninety percent of them shot up, snorted, or smoked something, and maybe half of them had major league habits. Joey needed to get his people straight. Heads would roll for real when he did. Too bad. But needed. Screw-ups like that could bring them all down.

McHale dialed on a new burner. Three rings later a voice snarled, "Wha' chu wan'?"

"Put me through to Joey."

"He can't talk. He's busy."

Which meant he was eating, toking, or banging one of the many women who hung around his penthouse apartment willing to trade sex for drugs. "Then give him a message to call McHale."

"I ain't no secretary."

"Cut the crap. That's why you're holding down the

phone. Now give him the goddamn message or next time I talk to Joey, I'll tell him how you jerked me around."

"Okay, man. Chu don't gotta get nasty. What chu wan' me to tell 'im?"

"Just give him the message." McHale snapped the phone shut.

****

Rick entered Dee's office a few minutes after three and took one of the chairs facing his desk. "Flynn and Schmidt aren't here?"

"On their way in."

A minute later, the office door opened, and the two IA officers filed in. Flynn asked, "So what's up, Captain?"

"Time we had an update on this McHale thing."

Flynn grabbed the other empty chair facing Dee's desk. "You got something new?"

"Yep." Dee flipped back the cover on a notebook. "Talked to Corrine James this morning. She picked two of Joe Day's goons, Hector 'Otter' Otero and Miguel 'Músculos' Mercado, out of photo lineup as the guys who beat the crap out of her. She told them Mary Conner might be at NEMC in Marshville."

"So Day knows where Conner is?" Flynn asked.

Dee nodded. "Looks that way."

"That all you got?" Schmidt leaned against the wall.

"No." Dee gave the young IA man a baleful look. "Rynert called me a little after one, said he'd just picked up a package for McHale at a bodega on Thirteenth. Inside was a Browning ten shot .22 semi-auto, extra magazine, and suppressor. Piece had the serial number filed off. Rynert brought it to me, I fired three rounds, and recovered the brass. The bullets match ones recovered from a Viper named Benny Kelsey. A Lobo named Diego Torres supposedly capped him for knocking boots with Torres's lady, Garabina Vasquez. Prints on the casings came back to Torres and Cesar Molina."

"Where's the .22 now?" Flynn asked.

"McHale has it. After I did the test fire, I gave it to Rynert to deliver to McHale."

"You think that was a smart play?"

"If he hadn't, McHale would have known something was up."

"So we've got a piece tied to the Lobos in McHale's hands. Rynert know why McHale wanted it?"

"No. He asked but McHale blew him off, said it was none of his business. But McHale was suspicious, wanted to know what took Rynert so long to deliver the piece, and asked him if he'd sabotaged it."

"Did he? Or you?"

"Couldn't risk it. If McHale found out the piece was damaged, it would have blown Rynert's cover."

DeAngelis glanced up at the tap on his door and motioned for Officer Estevez to enter. She took one step into his office and froze. Just as crooks could sense cops, cops could sense IA officers, and Estevez instantly pegged Flynn and Schmidt as IA. Rick stood, motioning to his chair. "Have a seat, Officer Estevez."

She eyed Flynn and Schmidt. "Am I in some kind of trouble here?"

Flynn stood and extended his hand to her. "I'm Detective Flynn. You have my word you are not being investigated for any wrongdoing. We're investigating another matter for which you may have pertinent information."

She eyed him skeptically. "What matter would that be, sir?"

Rick said, "What you and I talked about this morning."

****

She knocks on a door. A man answers. She doesn't recognize him, yet she has come to talk to him about something. About what? Something important, something he did, something that hurt her. What? What? It's there in her mind if she can only find it. But before she can, blackness steals over her.

****

Donna took the paper med cup from Joleen's hand. "There are two detectives here to talk to you about what happened last night."

A chill ran through Joleen. McHale had found her. "What are their names?"

"Evans and Steele."

Dumb to ask. Their names didn't matter. Everything she told them would go straight to McHale. He'd told her once he was so wired throughout the police department that if she ever filed a complaint against him, he'd know about it before she signed it. "I don't want to talk to them."

"Honey, you have to." Donna stroked her hair. "How are they going to find who did this to you if you don't?"

"I don't care if they don't."

"You don't mean that. What if that animal that did this to you beats up another woman? What if she's your friend? What if he kills her? Could you live with yourself knowing you could have stopped him but didn't?"

She would have to. She'd learned to live with a lot

321

of things over her years in the city—vanished dreams of success and fame, betrayal by a man she loved, jail time, losing her pride to keep her freedom. This would be just one more.

She wished she had a way out of this mess, had just one person who could help her escape it. Tim? She sensed she could count on his help. But he was young. She doubted he had the muscle to save her from McHale. She was trapped. Nothing would change her fate. McHale would be in her life forever, using her, abusing her, any time he wanted.

It is always good to have a policeman on your side. Sol had said that to her last night at his deli. *Just 'cause Lafferty's a cop, it don't make him like McHale.* Ramona had told her that the other day. She could trust Ramona, but could she trust Lafferty? If she couldn't, she'd be no worse off than she was now.

"Donna, do I have to talk to those detectives? Can I talk to a different one? I mean, if I say I'll only talk to a certain one, do they have to let me talk to him?"

"I don't know, honey. But I'll find out. If you can, who do you want to talk to?"

"His name's Lafferty."

"I'll see what I can do."

****

"So what's our next play?" Captain DeAngelis asked after Officer Estevez left his office.

"I say we grab McHale," Schmidt, the younger IA officer, snapped. "We got him cold on abuse of authority with the Wilson woman."

"No we don't," Flynn, his partner, said. "All we have is hearsay, that waitress's—Ramona's—word that the Wilson woman was doing McHale in exchange for him not charging her with possession. 'Til we talk to Wilson, we got nothing." He looked at Dee. "And you said your friend and her daughter won't file a complaint?"

"Never." Heather Bartlett had been adamant on that. Dee suspected it was partly to protect Ashlee but mainly to keep hubby in the dark about her own extra-marital activities.

"So we got nothing there either."

"We have the Salazar kid admitting he gunned down Ellen Shires on Joey's orders. Maybe he can tell—"

"He's not telling anybody anything right now," Flynn said sourly. "We got word on the way over he got shanked heading to his cell after lunch."

"That was fast. One of Joey's boys?"

"Doer was a Pagan name of Dougie Paulson. Could be he did it for Joey. Could be he stuck Salazar for looking at him cross-eyed."

"Shit," Dee and Rick said in unison.

"Yeah," Flynn said. "It's touch and go right now. Salazar could check out any minute or live another fifty years. He makes it, we see what he knows about Joey Day's organization. He doesn't, we're no worse off than now."

Schmidt ran a hand over his short blond hair. "Meantime we just twiddle our thumbs until McHale screws up big?"

"You give up too easy, kid. We keep looking. Sooner or later, we'll get something. And we need to talk to the Wilson woman. Who's primary on her assault?"

"Evans and Steele," Dee answered.

Flynn shook his head. "As of now, they're off it. We'll handle the notification." He wagged a finger at

Dee and Rick. "One of you talk to Wilson. And the officer—Morris?—Estevez told us about."

Rick said, "I'll do both. What about leaning on Davenport? One sergeant I talked to said he's always taken the easy way. Let him think you've got enough on him to lock him up till he's eighty, offer him a deal if he co-operates, and see what he says."

"Might work."

Dee leaned back in his chair. "It's worth a shot, at least. If he doesn't roll all the way on McHale, he might still give up something you can use."

****

Rick waited by the front desk at District 19's house as the patrolmen dribbled in at end of watch. A young officer stepped toward him. "Detective Lafferty? Officer Morris." He extended his hand. "You wanted to see me?"

DeAngelis had called the One-Nine and told them Lafferty needed to speak to Officer Morris. Rick shook his offered hand. 'Specks' fit him. His freckles had freckles. "It's Tim, right?" He pointed to the break room to the left of the front desk. "Let's go in here."

In the room, Morris faced Rick. "What's this about, Detective?"

"You know a woman named Joleen Wilson?"

"Yes, sir. Did something happen to her?"

Rick leaned against the wall. "She got the crap beat out of her last night."

"I knew that. I meant did she take a turn for the worse or something?"

"How did you know somebody'd worked her over?"

"Raq—Officer Raquel Estevez told me. We were at the academy together. She and Ketchum, her partner, found her. I guess my name came up when Estevez was talking with the detectives, so she gave me the heads-up a suit would be looking to talk to me."

"How well do you know Joleen Wilson?"

Morris got a Coke from the fridge then took a chair at the scarred wood table. "Not real well. I just met her yesterday."

"Tell me about that."

Morris popped the tab on the can and took a long drink. "Okay. I went 10-7, was gonna grab a hoagie at Sol's Deli for my lunch. I'm getting out of my unit, and I see this girl walking. Prettiest girl I've ever seen. Curly brown hair and big brown eyes and a blue dress." He shook his head. "Man, she knocked me for a loop. So, I go in Sol's and ask about her. He knows me, so he tells me her name's Joleen and she might be heading toward Griffin Park."

"And you went there?"

He held the can halfway to his mouth. "Yeah. Forget eating, I was ready to burn my whole meal break looking for her. I just wanted to meet her, that's all. I got lucky, spotted her right away, but I took it easy going up to her, trying to figure out how I could talk to her without her thinking I was hitting on her. Then I see she's reading a Grisham book, so I ask her if she likes him. We talked about him and books we'd read until I had to go back on patrol."

"You ask her for a date?"

"No, sir."

"Ask her for her phone number or where she lived?"

"No, sir. Just the opposite. She seemed a little jumpy, like even though I didn't put any moves on her, she wasn't sure about me. So I gave her my number and said if she ever wanted to talk about books some more to call me. Then I went 10-8."

"What time was that?"

Morris took another hit of soda. "Quarter of one. About then."

"What was she doing when you left?"

"Sitting on a blanket, eating a hoagie, and reading."

"You see anyone approach her as you were leaving?"

"No, sir."

"That the last you saw her?"

Morris took a big swallow of soda. "Well, I kinda saw her this morning."

"How did you 'kinda' see her?"

"After Estevez told me what happened to her, I swung by my place for a Grisham book I thought she'd like and took it to her in the hospital. She was out or sleeping or something, so I didn't talk to her. I just left the book in her room."

"Account for your time after you left her yesterday."

"Am I in trouble here? Do I need to call my PBA rep?"

"I'm not accusing you of anything. I'm just asking how you spent your time after you left Ms. Wilson."

Tim drained the last of his soda. "I patrolled until four, worked out at the Y for an hour, had dinner with my mom and dad starting at six, left about eight-thirty, got home about nine."

"Anybody see you, call you after you got home?"

"Lady in my building knocked on my door fifteen, twenty minutes later, said the tenants on the other side of her were having a screaming match, could I do something about it. So I go talk to the couple. The wife's an actress, and she and hubby got a little carried away rehearsing her lines for a play she's in. They apologized to the neighbor and me for causing a problem, said they'd keep it down."

"What time did you get back to your place after talking to them?"

"I wasn't down there too long, so maybe nine-thirty."

"Give me their names and numbers."

Morris read him the information out of a small notebook. "Detective, I swear I didn't hurt Joleen. I just, like I said, when I saw her on the street, I had to meet her. That's all I did in Griffin Park. I didn't pressure her to go out with me or anything like that. Just gave her my number and said if she wanted to get together and talk books some more to call me. I let it all up to her. I didn't even try to touch her. Closest I came was handing her her book when she dropped it."

He paused for a second. "I wrote her a note I put in the book I gave her today. I said I'd like to see her—not I *wanted to* or *had to* see her, just I'd like to—after I got off duty today and if that was okay with her, to let me know. Nurse at University Hospital called me maybe a half hour ago and said Joleen wanted to see me. If I'd beat her up, you think she'd do that?"

He had a point. Everything Morris said rang true to Rick. No evasion in his words, the way he said them, or his tone. And Morris displayed none of the tells—glancing away, saying too much, nervous tics—that gave away lies. Rick's cell rang.

"It's Steele. What's this shit about pulling me and Evans off the Wilson assault? You got the hots for the Estevez broad or something?"

He gave Morris a 'hang on' sign and stepped out of

the break room. "Pulling you wasn't my call. Came from Flynn in IA. You got a problem, bitch to him."

"I will. Meanwhile, the Wilson woman's awake and asking for you, says she won't talk to me or Evans."

"Gee, I wonder why." Probably because Steele had called her Sweetcakes like he had Estevez last night. "Okay. I'll be there in fifteen, twenty minutes."

"More like forty. Got a major bitch-up on Expressway southbound. City trash truck hit the ass end of a semi, two dead."

"Great. I'll get there fast as I can." Rick closed his phone. "Get yourself signed out, Morris, then meet me back here."

"What for?"

"I'm heading to University Hospital. Joleen wants to talk to me. You want to go along to give her moral support?"

Morris stood. "I do, Detective. But I'll follow you there. I'm staying after you leave."

****

McHale's cell rang as he sat at the light at Melrose and Twenty-third.

"It's Osborne."

His contact in the Public Information Office at police headquarters. "What do you want?"

"I got something for you."

Osborne was talking so low, McHale could barely hear him. He was stuck at his desk in the PIO bullpen. That didn't stop it from pissing McHale off. "You got friggin' laryngitis? Speak the hell up."

"I can't. I'm at work, got people all around me."

"Then go where they ain't and call me back." He thumbed the END button on his phone.

It rang a minute later.

"Me again. I'm in the john."

As if the echo coming through the phone hadn't told McHale that. "I'm happy for you. What do you want?"

"IA dragged Davenport in ten minutes ago, took him right up to thirteen."

So IA had Davenport. That was his problem, not McHale's. The light changed, and he gunned his cruiser across Melrose. "Okay. Thanks."

"Wait. I got more."

"I'm listening."

"Hochner and Kauffman pulled him in."

That could make it his problem, and a big one. Regular cops feared IA cops. IA cops feared Hochner and Kauffman. Attila the Hun would fear Hochner and Kauffman. Still, no reason to panic yet. Maybe this was just an IA fishing expedition.

"So, uh, is all that worth anything to you?"

Osborne was into Vinnie Scarfone for thirty large. McHale helped him pay it down a little every time Osborne passed him info. "Two Cs."

"Two hundred? Come on, McHale! It's gotta be worth more than that."

"Take it or leave it, Wendell."

Osborne sighed. "Take it."

It would be good to know if Davenport was singing and what songs. "You do more for me, I can do more for you."

"Anything. Name it."

Christ, the dweeb was easy to play. Or Vinnie had sent one of his gorillas to remind Osborne he still owed Vinnie a bundle. "Get your ass up to thirteen and find out what Davenport's telling IA."

329

"I don't know if I can. I mean I don't have any reason to go up—"

"Make one." McHale closed his phone. He couldn't shake the feeling he was standing on a frozen lake and the ice was cracking under his feet. He could keep going and hope he moved fast enough to outrun it and not land on a thin spot on the way. Or he could get the hell off the ice now. That idea was feeling better and better all the time.

Nah, it was just this thing with Virgin spooking him still, wigging him out. No way would Davenport rat him out. The guy knew which way the wind blew. If he kept his mouth shut and took his lumps, everything would be dandy. He rolled over, he was a dead man.

And speaking of Virgin, it was time to close that play. McHale fired the cruiser and eased into traffic. As soon as his tour was over, he would head to Marshville.

Chapter 24

Thanks to rush hour, Rick and Tim took almost an hour to reach University Hospital. Tim jabbed the up button for the elevator then jabbed it again and again and the button for the seventh floor the instant they stepped in. Rick said, "In a hurry, Morris?"

"Yeah. I can't wait to see her. I've been thinking about her all day in the back of my mind and sweating she wouldn't want to see me. Best news I got all day was that nurse saying she did." A pause. "You mind if I ask you something, Detective?"

"Go ahead."

"You ever meet a girl that was so…perfect, you wanted to do everything right with her right from the get-go? Be a really good guy, prove to her you're interested in her as a person, not just hoping to get laid?"

Rick hadn't thought about it that way before, but yeah, the more time he'd spent with Mary, the more he'd started feeling that way toward her. "Yeah."

"That's how it was with me about Joleen yesterday. There was just something about her from the minute I saw her made me want to do everything right, not mess up the least little thing with her."

As they entered room seven-thirteen, Morris brushed past Rick, making a beeline for the bed. "Hey, Joleen. How are you?"

"Tim!" She croaked and held out her uninjured

hand. "Glad you came."

"You think I'd miss a chance to see the prettiest girl I ever met?" He took her hand in both of his and a goofy look filled his face.

Rick settled a shoulder against the wall. *He's got it bad for her.*

She said, "Not so pretty now."

"Still the prettiest girl I ever met." Morris touched a swollen, bruised cheek under a black eye lightly. "Even if you did get a little carried away with the purple eye shadow." He touched the plastic guard over her nose. "And I don't think this will ever be a hot fashion trend."

Joleen smiled. Rick could see it hurt.

Tim smiled back, a big broad one. "Your call made my day. How are you?"

"Sore. Hurts to talk."

"So do you like the book?"

"Didn't read much. Can't stay awake. So tired." She nodded. "Good so far."

"I'm glad. Anything you need while you're in here, let me know, and I'll get it for you."

She nodded again.

Rick straightened. "Excuse me, Ms. Wilson. I'm Detective Lafferty."

Morris and Joleen stared at him as if he'd suddenly materialized in the room. She said slowly, "Gave me card...Nate's...few days ago."

"That's right. You said you wanted to talk to me? Why?"

"Don't trust...cops here earlier...asking about...last night."

Rick glanced at Morris. "Give me a couple minutes with Ms. Wilson, Officer."

"Yes, sir. I'll be right outside, Joleen. Yell if you need me, and I'll come running." Tim left the room, almost walking into the door, gazing at her instead of where he was going.

Oh, yeah, he's got it big for her. Rick pulled a chair close to her bed. "Why don't you trust the police?"

"Bad experience…with them lately."

"So why do you trust me?"

"Ramona…work with her…at Nate's…says I can."

"What kind of bad experience did you have with the police?"

"Dated a guy…used coke, had me…carry it. Cop stopped us…three times. First two…did thirty days…city jail. Third time—" She closed her eyes for a long stretch of seconds then took in a deep breath. "Third time, he said…sex with him…or prison…for long time"

"When did this officer stop you the third time?"

"Last spring. Made me do him…twenty times since."

Her story echoed the one Dee had told Rick about his friend and her daughter—a cop offering to bury a crime in exchange for sex. Although, the tone in Dee's voice had hinted that his friend had made the offer to the cop, not the other way round. "Did you ever report the officer to the police department?"

She shook her head slowly. "Said if…I did, he'd know." She paused a second. "And…kill me." Tears welled in her swollen eyes. "So tired of it…didn't care if he did."

Rick handed her a tissue. "You let that happen, and you'll leave one very heartbroken young cop," he pointed to the door, "wondering forever what he could have done to save you."

"Really?"

"Really. How long have you known Officer Morris?"

"Met him in Griffin Park yesterday."

"How did that happen?"

"Eating lunch, reading book. He came up, asked…if I liked author. Talked until…he had to…go back on patrol."

"Did he ask you out or make any advances that you said no to?"

"Opposite. Never tried anything…gave me *his* number, said call him if I wanted."

"Tell me what happened last night."

"Walking home…man grabbed me…pulled me into alley near my home." She cycled a few deep breaths. "Beat me…punched me…kicked me…threw me…against walls…and dumpsters."

"What time was this?"

"Little after nine."

"It was definitely a man?"

She nodded.

"Did you get a look at him?"

"Big. All in black. Mask over face."

"Can you tell me anything else about him? The color of his eyes? The sound of his voice? Anything?"

A slow head shake "Happened too fast. Didn't say anything. Just beat me." Tears filled her eyes again.

Rick sensed she wasn't telling him everything. "Joleen, you know who he was, though, don't you?"

She nodded.

Rick pointed to the door. "Officer Morris?"

Another head shake.

"So who attacked you in the alley?"

A long silence. "Cop making me have sex…with him."

"How do you know it was him?"

"Said if I ever crossed him, he'd kill me."

"Did you cross him?"

"Was doing same…to Ramona," She paused for several breaths. "She swung…knife at him. Left her alone then." Another pause for a breath. "Two nights ago…came after me again. Did like Ramona. He ran away. Then said he'd kill me."

"Tell me his name."

She looked down at her cast-covered arm for a few seconds then shook her head. "Don't want to die."

"You stood up to him two nights ago all by yourself. Stand up to him again, this time with me and Tim," he pointed to the door again, "and a lot of other good cops standing with you. Don't let him get away with this, don't let him do to another woman what he did to you."

She looked at the ceiling and tears leaked from the swollen flesh around her eyes. She drew in several deep breaths, wincing at the pain each one loosened. "McHale."

****

McHale's phone rang moments after he entered his apartment.

"You wished to speak with me, *mi amigo*?" Joey.

"Yeah! The tools Tomás gave me today were used! I wanted new ones." Christ, he hated speaking in code. It made getting the message across loud and clear a crapshoot. No way to know for sure if it got through. Especially with Joey.

"They were? I am shocked. I will speak with him about this immediately and have him deliver new ones to you later this evening."

Hoo-friggin'-ray! He got it. "No time. I'm on my way out of town in a few minutes."

"You have not forgotten solving that problem for me, have you?"

Joey's chiding voice grated on McHale's nerves like a file on sheet tin. No, he hadn't forgotten about killing Virgin. "Where do you think I'm going?" He entered his bedroom. Time to give the taco muncher a little wake up. "This is the second time Tomás has sent me used tools. Little screw-ups like that can take you down. Hard."

"He will not make that same mistake ever again. I will see to it."

Can't make any mistakes when you're dead. McHale wondered how long Tomás had to live. Hours probably. "He's not the only one who's fucked up lately, *Jefe*."

"Who else of my people do you know have failed me?"

"Otter and Músculos. They left fingerprints all over some woman's apartment when they worked her over. Your boys need to get their shit together. Fast."

Silence. McHale wondered if he'd come down on Joey too hard. After long moments, a deep sigh. "You are right, *mi amigo*. I will attend to the matter immediately."

"Just use your—" He said "head" to a dead line.

McHale took two days' worth of clothes, including a blazer tailored to conceal a shoulder holster, from his closet. He folded them neatly and packed them in a duffel along with his shaving kit. He was on his way to kill Virgin, just not as fast as he'd led Joey to believe. He was driving to Marshville tonight and spending tomorrow thinking things through.

He hadn't dwelt on the standing-on-thin-ice feeling he'd had earlier. He didn't really believe in omens or karma or any of that woo-woo shit, but that feeling nagged his mind all afternoon like a stubbed toe he kept stubbing. Maybe the time had come to bail out of Joey's organization.

But first, he owed Joey a finished job on Virgin. He took the cloth-wrapped .22, suppressor, and magazine from the cigar box, slipped them into a large plastic bag, and stowed it among his clothes in the duffel. He started to zip the duffel closed then stopped. If he was going to bail on Joey, he'd need money to live on, at least enough to tide him over for a while.

Opening his safe, he took out forty grand in rubber-banded bills. That should do it. He changed his mind and grabbed another twenty grand. A moment later, he changed it again and packed all two-hundred thousand in another duffel, zipped it shut, and left his apartment.

****

Rick Lafferty entered the Communication Center and crossed the bullpen to the supervisor's station. Madge Grumman looked up as he approached. "Rick. Long time, no see. What can I do for you?"

"Need to listen to a tape." He gave her the date of Mary's shooting. He wanted to hear the call about her shooting for himself.

"We changed the way we do things since you were here last." Madge led him to a storage room lined with shelves holding racks of ten DVDs in plastic cases. "Everything's digital now." She walked down an aisle on the left side of the room, scanning the dates and times on shelves. "Here we are." She pointed to a shelf dated

4/19/15. "What time frame are you interested in?"

"Eight-thirty to nine that evening."

"Do you know who took the call?"

"Nope."

She handed him a rack marked 2000 – 2200 hours, offering him a pitying smile. "Hope you have lots of time."

"For this, I do. The listening station still next door?"

"Yep." She led him to it. "Load the disc and hit 'enter.' It'll be like watching a movie. You'll hear the caller and operator's voices as well as see the information the operator entered into the terminal. Let me know when you're done."

Rick set the first disc in the player, settled the earphones on his head, and touched PLAY.

****

The phone rang just as Dee picked up the sports section. A moment later, Gina called his name. He laid the paper aside and stepped into the kitchen, taking the phone from her hand.

"You owe me a second dinner at Tony and Marie's." Vicki from the fingerprint lab.

"I do? Why?"

"Because I've got some superhot news for you."

"About?"

"The condo where Detective Conner was shot."

"What about it?"

"Latisha just finished processing the prints from there. Lots from Bobby Ed Lukens, the owner, of course, several from KAs of Joey Day, and a few from Mary. But that's not the superhot news."

Dee waited a second or two for Vicki to say more then realized she wanted him to prompt her. He loved her flair for the dramatic, it always made hearing from her a bright spot in any day, but sometimes he wished she'd just spill what she knew. "So what is it?"

"Latisha matched prints from a thumb and three fingers on Lukens's shirt and Mary's weapon to...drum roll please...Sergeant Michael McHale."

****

"9-1-1. What is your emergency?"

"Is this 9-1-1?

"Yes, it is, sir. What is your emergency."

"Somebody...somebody just got, got shot in, in the DeSchain Building."

Finally, after three hours of listening to an endless string of calls for fire, ambulance, and police assistance. Rick pressed the headphones tighter to his ears.

"You say someone was shot in the DeSchain Building?"

"Yeah, yeah. Twice."

"Are you sure someone was shot?"

"I heard it. Pop-pop. Two shots."

"I'm dispatching a patrol car right now. Where was this in the DeSchain Building?"

"Third floor. Apartment 3-C, I think."

"Did you see the person get shot?"

"No. I was just walking by and heard the shots."

"Do you know who lives in apartment 3-C?"

"No, no. I just moved in. I don't know anybody here. I just heard the shots."

"Are you in the building now, sir?"

"No. I'm out-outside behind, behind the building in my car."

"Okay, sir. Please remain there until—"

The hum of a hang up.

Rick replayed the call. The video of the 9-1-1 terminal showed the time as 8:35 p.m. Male caller, gravelly voice, no accent. A touch of panic in the voice, but something about it didn't ring true, as if the caller wasn't really panicked but wanted to sound as if he was.

He replayed the call a third time. The gravel in the caller's voice sounded forced, too. Trying to disguise it? Criminals sometimes reported their crimes using a phony voice, one reason Communications recorded all incoming calls. But there was something in the voice's timbre that stirred a memory in Rick's mind. He'd heard that voice recently.

He backed up the video a short distance and played it again. Yep, he had definitely heard that voice in the last few days. He spotted Madge Grumman leaning over a dispatcher's workstation. When she straightened, he waved to get her attention then beckoned her to the listening station. "I know this voice from somewhere. See if it rings any bells with you."

Madge listened, her head tipped to one side. The pose reminding Rick of a dog hearing something beyond human ears. A few seconds later, she said, "That's Mike McHale."

Rick stared at her. "You sure?"

"Absolutely. I've been listening to him for twenty years."

Rick sprinted from the Emergency Communication Center, dialing his cell as he ran. "Dee. I got something."

****

Darcy Brown slammed the hatch on her Land Rover. That was all of it. Everything she wanted to keep was stowed in the SUV. She took the elevator from the basement garage to her twelfth-floor penthouse apartment and crossed to the antique French desk in the living room, picked up the single sheet of paper from the surface, and skimmed it. Only one unchecked item remained on her to-do list. She picked up the phone and called *Paraiso,* dialing the number any one on staff would pick up at any time. It rang seven times before Gary answered.

"It's Darcy. I hate to do this to you on such short notice, but I won't be in tonight. I have to go out of town for a few days, and I'm leaving as soon as I hang up with you. My stepdad had a major heart attack and has to have bypass surgery." It was a lie, but it would fly. She'd never told anyone at the club about her past. "I don't know how serious it is, so I can't even tell you when I'll be back." That part was true.

"No sweat, Darce. Stay as long as you need. I got it covered."

"Thanks, Gary. You're the best." He was, no lie. From the moment she took over managing *Paraiso*, she could rely on him. He'd been her right hand, more like an extra right hand, doing whatever needed doing without being told, and her ally, knowing when to jump to her aid and when to stand back.

She said good-bye and hung up. She would miss him. They'd made a great team at the club. She doubted she'd ever get lucky enough to work that well with someone again. And it hadn't been all work. The couch in their office was perfect for things besides sitting.

She crossed that last item off her to-do list then read it again, just to make sure she hadn't missed any. She hadn't. Only one more thing remained for her to do before she left town, and that one wasn't written down anywhere.

Crumpling the paper, she tossed it in the wastebasket then retrieved it a second later. Maybe she was being paranoid, but better to be safe than sorry. She carried the paper to the kitchen, held it over the sink with a pair of tongs, and set it burning with a match. As the flames consumed it, she practiced opening her switchblade quietly. When black flakes of burned paper littered the sink, she turned on the water and sprayed them into the garbage disposal. She poured herself a glass of Cabernet and sipped from it while the water ran for five minutes after the last flake had swirled down the drain. Then she switched off the light and left the kitchen, taking the wine with her.

Chapter 25

Sunday – April 26, 2015

Ann Hendershot wrapped the blood pressure cuff around Mary's—there she went again—Miranda's arm. She had to stop thinking of her as Mary or she'd tip her hand. Then Allison and Caitlin would know she knew her patient was really Mary Conner and take her off the case. She couldn't let that happen. She'd promised Rick she'd take care of her.

She owed Rick that. She would always owe him. For saving her from going to jail for a long time.

After one too many 'bad boys,' she'd started dating a good guy, Ben Estes. Just over a month later, Rick had stopped them outside the movie theater and insisted she come home. He'd been so adamant about it, she'd finally relented just to shut him up. On the way, he'd told her Ben was headed for big trouble but not how he knew. She'd ripped into him, telling him he was crazy, that Ben would never do the kinds of things past boyfriends did.

The next morning paper carried a story that rocked their hometown. Ben—senior class secretary, three-sport letterman, salutatorian, and on his way to Princeton— had been arrested just after midnight for murdering a local doctor after he caught Ben stealing jewelry and money from his home safe. If Rick hadn't gotten Ann away from him, she'd be in prison for life just like Ben.

Ann pumped the cuff up and noted Mary's— Dammit!—Miranda's blood pressure was holding steady, a good sign. She hooked her stethoscope into her ears, slipped the head under Miranda's—got it right that time—gown, and timed fifteen seconds on her watch. Heart rate was up, the beat strong and regular, also good. Ann slid a probe cover on her digital thermometer and inserted it in her ear. She shifted her gaze to her face and almost dropped the thermometer.

Hazel eyes looked at her.

Ann quickly covered her mouth to stifle the gasp rising in her throat. Miranda's eyelids fluttered for a moment then slid closed. Ann raced through the rest of her check on Miranda and hurried from the room. She had to notify Dr. Nicopoulos.

First, she had to tell Rick.

****

A man is kneeling in front of her. She can't make out his face yet she knows him somehow and something about him fills her with dread. He pulls a gun and points it at her. She knows she should run, yet she can't. He says, "Orders." Then he fires.

****

Rick caught up with Captain DeAngelis on the steps to the District 7 house. Both carried take-out cups from the coffee shop on the corner. Rick asked, "Anything?"

Dee shook his head. "Not so far. Nothing on the BOLO. Flynn and Schmidt swung by McHale's apartment last night. No sign of him. The super says he hasn't seen him in two or three days. He says sometimes weeks go by between them crossing paths."

"They search his apartment?"

"Not properly. Judge wouldn't sign off on a warrant.

Not enough probable cause." They started up the stairs to the second floor. "But the super likes cops, so he let Flynn and Schmidt in for a look-see just in case McHale was deathly ill or grievously injured." His tone hung quotes around the last five words.

"And?"

"Nothing jumped out at them. Super let them have a peek in the apartment's garage, too. McHale's car is gone." Reaching the second floor, they crossed toward Dee's office. "Flynn kicked the BOLO to the state police, asked them to issue it statewide. He's anywhere in PA, someone will spot him." He opened the door, motioning Rick in.

Rick took a chair facing Dee's desk. He wondered if Mary had come awake for good. No, Ann would have called him back if she had. "He could have gone to Jersey, New York, Maryland, or Delaware. Or be halfway to Florida by now."

Dee settled behind his desk. "PSP said they'd pass the BOLO on to surrounding states."

Both sipped coffee. Dee set his cup on his desk and leaned back in his chair. "Davenport gave a few things up to IA. McHale has two cribs not in the honey file."

Department regulations required officers to register any place they slept on a regular basis and the phone number there. A holdover from the days when landlines were the only game in town, the list was called the honey file because in those days, many officers had a girlfriend on the side and often spent as many nights with her as with the wife.

"The officers who went to those addresses found both front doors jimmied open." Dee smiled. "They entered to secure the premises in the absence of the owner."

Rick smiled back. Thieves weren't the only ones who could bypass a lock. He wondered if Flynn, Schmidt, or someone from Special Response Unit had done it. "They find anything in any of them?"

"A new low for crash pads. Both were just places to sleep. A sleeping bag and a beat-up mattress, and that's it. Oh, and there also was one black SRU uniform, one black balaclava, one pair black lug-soled boots, and one pair black leather gloves in both."

Rick knocked back some coffee. "Jwakeen Phillips said a cop all in black boosted his piece from his car while he was parked under the Hoover Street Bridge."

"McHale's one pad is in the Easthill Projects a block off Hoover. Something else interesting turned up. Narcotics reported a street dealer named Luis Herrera was found beaten to death in an alley off Cherry Street Wednesday. Word on the street was Luis had been shorting Joey Day a fifty here, a hundred there every week." Dee paused for a slug of coffee. "He'd also been maced with department-issue pepper spray. McHale's other crib is only a couple blocks from Cherry. And Crime Scene Techs found traces of pepper spray on the gloves they found there."

"That adds up to McHale working Herrera over on Joey's orders."

"It does. Got some more news for you. You know Narcotics Strike Force took down Deuce Doucette and Rosie Ames in the middle of a drug deal Wednesday night?"

"Yeah, I heard." Not knowing what was going on with Mary was driving Rick nuts. He had to call Ann as soon as he got out of here.

"Two of the city's biggest dealers gone like that." Dee snapped his fingers. "Guess who brokered the deal."

Rick smiled. "Gee, that's a tough one. How many guesses do I get?"

"Three, but the first two don't count."

Rick drained his cup. "Joey?"

"You should be a detective. Deuce and Rosie both swear Joey contacted them, said he got a deal on two hundred kilos of product and would split it with them for what he paid for it. Kicker was there wasn't even fifty kilos in the building."

"A set up?"

"One Rosie and Deuce were too dumb or too greedy to figure out. No dealer's gonna sell product to another dealer when he could sell it on the street himself at a discount and put the other guy out of business." Dee tipped the last of his coffee into his mouth and dropped the cup in the trash. "Ownership of the warehouse traces back through about four layers to Joey."

"Smart. He loses fifty kilos of dope, but he gets his two main rivals off the street with no bloodshed. Probably sees it as a good deal."

"One that may come back to bite his ass off. Rumbles on the street are Rosie's *and* Deuce's boys both want his head. I have a feeling Joey Day's days are numbered."

Dee's phone rang. He answered it then covered the mouthpiece and said to Rick, "It's the hospital. About Mary."

****

Mike McHale woke shortly after eight, feeling groggy and out of it. He hadn't slept well. The frigging mattress had all the give of an oak plank. That wasn't all of it, though. The feeling he was standing on ready-to-crack ice had stayed with him the whole way to Marshville then tainted an otherwise very good roast beef dinner. Even a couple glasses of scotch neat from the bottle he'd packed hadn't driven it away.

Hadn't helped having Osborne call him in a panic last night, saying IA was dragging in his guys like there was no tomorrow. None of them stayed long, and none of them left happy. Could be IA was just fishing. Still, it couldn't be good. Davenport didn't worry him. He was stand-up. Some of the other guys, McHale wasn't so sure about. If one came down with a case of diarrhea mouth, he'd be a dead man. Either at McHale's hands or the legal system's.

McHale rolled out of bed, did some stretches and bends to work out mattress-induced kinks, and ran through a calisthenics regimen to get his blood moving. Then he started the two-cup brewer before he ordered the Farmer's Breakfast from room service. He showered while he waited and thought some more.

He still hadn't decided whether to head back to the city or keep going after he iced Virgin. Moving on meant losing his connections and power and steady influx of untraceable cash. He'd be just another ex-cop living out his life on pension in Nowhereville. The up side was he wouldn't get pinned by a falling beam when the roof caved in on Joey's organization. All he'd have to worry about was some goon showing up on his doorstep one day to deliver Joey's 9-mil retirement package.

McHale tipped the kid a five for delivering his breakfast then sat down and dug in. He wondered if Joey was losing it. Sure seemed that way. He'd been all over the friggin' map on this Virgin thing. Wanting her dead in the next instant one day, telling McHale to take his time the next. Hell, later the same day. Wasn't like Joey at all. And if Joey was going hinky, one day the roof would fall in on him and everybody working for him, for sure. Yep, moving on was feeling better and better.

He wondered what would happen to his goldfish. He'd paid some serious coin for them, their tank, and all the stuff to go with it. He laughed aloud at the absurdity. He was worried about Joey losing his grip, and he was just as bad. Here he was, thinking of doing something that could get him blown away by Joey's thugs, and he was sweating what might happen to some goddamn goldfish. Jesus!

McHale tipped the last of his breakfast coffee down his throat then filled a throwaway cup with coffee from the brewer. After spreading the complimentary newspaper on the table, he dug the twenty-two out of his duffel and disassembled it for cleaning.

****

"What?" Rick asked as Dee hung up the phone, a big smile plastered on his face.

"Good news. That was Mary's doctor. Looks like she's coming around."

Rick let out a whoop of joy then hoped he hadn't overdone it. Dee's news wasn't news. Rick had just stepped out of his apartment that morning when his cell rang. Before he'd finished saying, "Hello," Ann blurted out Mary had opened her eyes.

"So, pack a bag and hit the road." Dee flashed another smile. "That's an order."

"Yes, sir." He threw Dee an exaggerated salute. "Don't need to pack. Had a bag in my car since you told me she was alive." He bolted from his chair and yanked open the door to Dee's office then slammed on the brakes. He'd almost blown it. He turned, hoping his grin looked sheepish. "Uh, Dee, where am I going?"

"Northeast Medical Center in Marshville. Take the Schuylkill to the turnpike north to I-80 west to Marshville."

"Gotcha!" Rick gave a thumbs-up and raced out of the District house.

He sat in his Mazda, sucking in deep breaths, his heart hammering his ribs so hard his hands shook. He couldn't remember the last time he'd been this excited. Not when he got his gold shield, not when he'd passed the detective's exam, not even when he'd been accepted into the police academy. Shaking hands or not, he had to get to Mary. He gunned his Mazda toward the Schuylkill Expressway.

****

Darcy Brown slept late, took a long, hot shower, groomed herself carefully forehead to feet, and dabbed her favorite Oscar De la Renta perfume on her breasts and in the hollow of her throat. She loved its heady, sultry scent, and it drove Joey crazy with lust. Then she slipped on a black lace bra and panties, a black silk Dior dress guaranteed to finish the job the perfume started, and four-inch stilettos. The rest of her clothes were in the back of her Land Rover.

She glanced around the apartment. Even though much she owned remained, it looked so barren stripped of everything dear to her. She would miss this place. It had been her home for eight years and she loved the location, the view from her windows, everything about it. She hoped she could find a place as nice wherever she finally landed, maybe close to the ocean. She took one last look, then closed the door and walked to the elevator.

Crossing the garage to the Land Rover, she cast a longing gaze at her summer car, the red Corvette convertible parked next to it. She hated to leave it, too, but the SUV trumped it in carrying capacity. She could always buy another Corvette. Money would never be a problem for her. She started the Discovery and drove out of the garage.

Chapter 26

Rick got out of his car in a McDonald's parking lot forty miles short of Marshville and stretched. After a trip to the head, he grabbed a coffee. When he opened his wallet to pay, the girl at the register said, "Are you like a cop, too?"

"Too?"

She pointed to the miniature of his shield pinned inside his wallet. "You're like the second guy that's come in here with a badge like that."

"Oh? When was the other guy here?"

"The first time was like," she looked past Rick toward the front door for a moment, "three days ago. Like Thursday? Then he was in here again last night."

"What time was he in both days?"

"Thursday, it was like just after noon, 'cause I'd just come on. And last night it was like just before seven, 'cause I was like getting ready to punch out."

"What did this guy look like?"

"He was a big white guy and old, like maybe your age?"

Thanks a lot. Well, maybe to a teen, nudging forty was old. "What about his hair and eyes? Any scars? Anything else you can tell me about him?"

She pursed her lips for a few seconds. "He had like brown hair but not real dark brown and light eyes, like blue or maybe gray." She touched her chin. "And he had a dimple here."

McHale. "Did he say where he was going?"

"Yesterday, I'm like, 'I remember you from the other day,' and he's like, 'Yeah, I'm on my way to visit my friend in the hospital,' so I'm like Northeast Medical Center and he goes yeah."

"The one in Marshville?"

"Well, yeah." The girl rolled her eyes. "It's like the only one around."

And McHale was headed there. Rick's gut said it wasn't to wish Mary a speedy recovery.

"Is he like a friend of yours or something?"

"Yeah." Or something. "Thanks for the info. Maybe I can catch up to him there." Rick sped for the door.

The girl called out behind him, "Good luck."

Rick crossed the lot to his car almost at a trot. Every cop in the state was looking for McHale, and he'd found him by pure fluke. Rick got in his car and fished out his cell. He had to let Dee know so he could get troops up there to protect her. He started to dial then paused with his thumb over the last numeral. No. He wasn't calling in the cavalry. Going it solo was wrong, but he wasn't trusting Mary's safety to some stranger.

Rick closed his phone and tossed it on the seat. He picked it up a second later. He'd let Ann know McHale was on his way.

****

"Mr. Day, Darcy Brown is here, says she wants to see you." The guard outside Joey's penthouse apartment eyed her top to bottom, practically drooling all over the intercom phone in his hand. "She is *muy caliente* today."

With good reason. The Dior—skin-tight with a deep plunge in front, almost no back, and a very high hem with a slit on the left leg—was her best 'fuck me' dress.

The guard raked a slow glance over her. "I'll be happy to search her before—" He straightened to attention, and his face paled. "No, *Jefe*. I'm sorry, *Jefe*." He looked away from her. "*Si, Jefe*." He racked the phone and opened the apartment door.

Darcy strutted across the foyer, her heart thumping in time to the sharp pops of her heels on the hardwood floor. Machismo and marijuana scented the air. Four muscled bodyguards in gray suits and white tees sprawled on sofas flanking the door to Joey's office. All four locked eyes on her as she approached. One toked a joint, passed it to his buddy and blew her a kiss. One licked his lips, one flicked his tongue, and the smoker rubbed his crotch. Kiss blower rose and took a step toward her, holding out his hand. "Purse."

Her heart thundered, and her mouth dried up. She couldn't hand it over, couldn't let him peek inside it, see the switchblade. He'd confiscate it or kick her out. He might even kill her. All three options sucked. She had to get the knife next to Joey.

The other bodyguards slipped their hands inside their suit coats, grasping guns. Her hesitation flagged her as a danger to their boss.

"That won't be necessary, Pepe." Joey stood in the door to his office wearing a white suit and black tee.

Darcy exhaled. Saved.

"I am sure all the lovely *señorita* has in her purse are the cosmetics she uses to enhance her already considerable beauty."

"Thank you, Mr. Day." Joey was prime stud for sure, all dark hair and eyes and brilliant white teeth in pale olive skin over a lean, hard body. She fought the urge to lick her lips. Damn, he was fine. Killing him would be easier if he was fat and bald.

"But, *Jefe*—"

Joey silenced him with a wave of his hand. Pepe nodded and backed away. Joey took Darcy's hands in his and kissed the back of each. "Such a beautiful woman should not suffer such inconsiderate treatment. My men only have my safety as their uppermost concern. Alas, they sometimes let their dedication to me overcome restraint. Please accept my apology for Pepe's behavior."

"It is nothing, Mr. Day. You are lucky to have such loyal people."

"Yes, I am." He slipped an arm around her waist. "Now tell me, beautiful lady, what can I do for you today?"

"May we talk in private?"

"But of course." Joey steered her toward his office. At the door, he slid his hand down to the curve of her ass to usher her through.

Good. He was putting her plan in motion without realizing it. She'd decided on one last wild romp with him before she killed him—a going away gift for both of them. Hot sex would be the easiest way to get him to let his guard down.

He closed the door behind him. "Now, my beautiful Darcy, how can I help you?"

"It's been too long since I saw you, Joey."

"It has indeed." He shrugged a 'what can I do' gesture. "The pressures of running my businesses take much of my time."

"So much that you couldn't find an hour or two for me?" She undid the button on his suit jacket and ran a hand over his hard flat chest. "I've missed you."

He traced a finger slowly from the hollow in her throat into her cleavage. "And I have missed you, too, *mi enamorada*." Hooking his finger in the neckline of her dress, he drew her closer. "Very, very much. And you are indeed, as Benito says, *muy caliente* today."

Lust filled his eyes. She had him.

He lowered his head and inhaled her scent. "And you smell so *deliciosa*, I could just eat you up." He nuzzled her ear and caressed her breast through the silk. "Perhaps I should take the afternoon off."

She rubbed her hand over his growing arousal. "Perhaps you should."

He opened the door to the living room. "Go. All of you."

Pepe said, "But Jefe—"

"Do not question me, Pepe. Do as I say. Leave Benito and Manuel on the door. They will be enough."

Shuffling and muttering, the bodyguards rose and left the living room. Joey shut the door and pulled Darcy against him. "Now, *Querida*, how shall we spend the afternoon?"

"You decide."

"I have." Gripping her ass, he pulled her tighter against his hardness. "Do you approve of my choice?"

She nibbled his ear and whispered, "*Muy mucho!*"

****

Mike McHale slid his plate back an inch from the edge of the table. Good food for a budget chain hotel restaurant. The burger had been thick and juicy on a perfectly toasted Kaiser roll, the big heap of fries crispy, the corn fresh. His cute blonde waitress dropped his bill on the table as she scurried past on the way to another table. He tipped the last of his coffee down his throat and picked it up. Eleven-ninety-five. The same meal in the city would have run him twenty bucks at least. Living in a small town definitely had its pluses.

He signaled the waitress for more coffee. Refills were free, so why not? He pulled a twenty from his wallet and laid it atop the bill.

He could live like a king for a long time in a Rubeville like this on what he'd amassed over the years working for Joey Day. Provided he stayed alive to live it. He'd have to find a burg so small it wouldn't even show on a map, let alone Joey's radar. Otherwise, one day two Lobos would show up at his door wearing icy smiles below cold eyes. They'd be there anywhere from five minutes to two days, depending on how much Joey wanted him to suffer. When they left, he'd be dead. Unless...

What if he stomped Joey's shit first? He'd never considered that before. The beaner'd been acting so loco lately, it was just a matter of time before the world fell in on him. Why not nudge it along, make it fall a little sooner? Nah, stomp shit, and some always ends up on you. Better to walk away clean, let others get dirty.

The waitress filled his cup, giving him a perky smile as she did. He handed her his check and the money. "Keep the rest."

Her smile got even bigger. As she scooted away, he wondered what she'd be like in bed. Probably pretty good judging by the sexy sway in her walk. Be fun finding out. He scrapped the idea. No time now. He was hitting the road, running hard for places unknown as soon as he whacked Virgin. It wasn't like this was his last chance ever to shag another piece of tail. Wherever he landed, even if he holed up in a monastery, he could find broads to bang.

He sipped the coffee. Even it was good here. Time to run through his plan one last time. Enter the room, pump Virgin full of .22 rounds, split. Simplicity itself. McHale shook his head. What a friggin' mess a simple hit had turned into.

He'd tried to tell Joey icing a cop was a bad idea. Ditto phoning 9-1-1 after he popped her. But the taco eater's cojones had overruled his *cabeza*. He'd wanted Mary's body shoved in the cops' noses to show them they couldn't screw with Joey Day. Dumber than dumb. You wave a red cape at a bull, he's gonna charge, not back away. Same way with cops hearing one of their own had gone down.

The cruiser that had been coming down the street toward Bobby Ed's building as McHale made the call was pure bad luck, nothing but. If it hadn't been there, Mary would have been in Corpse City long before anyone found her. And McHale wouldn't be here in Hicktown cleaning up a mess that never would have happened if Joey hadn't insisted he make the call.

It all added up to Joey losing it. Only thing it could be. All the more reason to get his own ass clear now before the greaser went down in flames, setting everybody working for him on fire on the way.

Maybe he should forget about punching Virgin's ticket, just blow town. Nope. He'd promised Joey he'd cap her. And cap her he would. But this would be the last thing he ever did for Joey.

He chugged the rest of his coffee and headed for his car. Why couldn't he shake the feeling he was heading into the biggest mistake of his life? Pre-hit jitters? Nah, he'd made this play before. Too much coffee? Yeah, had to be that. He got in his car. He had a job to do.

He had a woman to kill.

****

She remembers. The condo. The drug dealer dead on his sofa. Calling McHale. The small automatic in his hand. Shots ripping into her belly. Pain and shock filling her. Asking McHale why. Him saying, "Orders."

Whose, she wonders. Who is McHale working for? And why do they want her dead? For shooting the dealer who sold Sam the dope that killed him?

****

Rick stepped off the elevator on the sixth floor, turned right, and sped on long strides to the nurses' station. Ann must have sensed him coming because she glanced up, spotted him, tipped her head a fraction to the left, pulled a chart from the rack, and headed that way. He followed her into a stub hall. "How's she doing? Is she awake?"

"Not yet, but it could happen any time now."

"Where is she?"

Ann pointed over her shoulder. "Last room on the left."

"You alert security about McHale?"

"Of course."

He stepped back and glanced both ways along the main hall. His cop radar didn't blip. No one in sight looked like security staff. "So where are they?"

"They—" Ann hesitated. "They're watching the lobby for him."

"Goddammit! They should be here, too!" He jabbed a finger downward. "Guarding *this* floor."

"Rick, stop it! They only have so many men. They can't leave the rest of the hospital unguarded just to search for one person."

"Bastards." He took two long steps toward the elevator.

Ann grabbed his arm and pulled him back into the hallway. "Getting mad won't accomplish anything. And I'm not letting you see Mary until you calm down. So chill out."

She was right. He inhaled a deep breath and exhaled it slow, did both a second time. "Okay. I'm cool."

"Good. You don't have anything to worry about. The policewomen with Mary aren't going to let anyone get to her. And now that you're here, she's safer than if a company of Marines were guarding her."

Rick nodded. "Yeah, you're right."

"I know I am. Come on." She grabbed his hand and almost dragged him down the hall to the last door. She tapped on it and, when it opened, said to the face in the gap, "Could I talk to you out here for a second?"

A woman in nurse's scrubs stepped out. She eyed Rick top to bottom, her gaze pausing for a moment where his Colt rested under his blazer, a sure sign she was a cop. Ann said, "Caitlin Burke, my brother, Rick Lafferty. Rick, Caitlin Burke of the State Police."

He held out his hand. She shook it. "On the job?"

He nodded.

"You mind showing me some ID?"

He pulled his badge wallet from a blazer pocket and handed it to her.

She eyed it, returned it, and glared at Ann. "You want to tell me why he's here?"

Rick said, "I came to see Mary Conner."

She gave him a puzzled look. "Mary who?"

"He knows, Caitlin." Ann glanced down for a

moment. "I told him. He's been dating her for over a year. He told me she'd been shot the day before Janice pulled me up here to care for Miranda." She bracketed the name in air quotes. "The minute I read her real name in the chart, I started keeping him posted on her condition."

Caitlin glared at Ann. "Do you realize the danger you put her in?"

"I know I should have told you, but I was afraid if I did, you'd have me replaced. I wanted to take care of her. For Rick. He's the only one I told and only because he was worried sick about her."

"Mary's my partner, Burke," Rick said. "If you think I'd do anything to put her in jeopardy, you're way off base."

"And if you think I'm going to let you waltz in there without checking you out," she replied, "you're not even in the ballpark."

"Fine." Rick took a card from his badge wallet and handed it to her. "Call Captain Marco DeAngelis at the number on the back. He'll vouch for me."

She handed it back. "I verify through my own sources." She stepped into the room.

Rick paced ovals in the hall. Burke would learn he was legit, but having Mary ten feet away yet as distant as the moon scraped on his nerves. Twenty minutes now. What the hell was taking Burke so long? If she didn't come back soon, he'd...

Burke opened the door. "Okay, Lafferty, you're cleared. You carrying?"

"You know I am. You spotted it the second you saw me. Left side under my jacket. You got a problem with that?"

"No. But it stays there unless I tell you otherwise. Got that?"

"Got it."

Caitlin nodded. "Come on in." She swung the door wide.

She said something as he entered the room but it didn't register. All he saw was Mary. He crossed to her bedside in two steps. She was so pale, almost waxy, he couldn't believe she was alive. His throat tightened, and he had to force himself to swallow. He took her hand, held it against his cheek, relished the warmth in it, and his heart thumped in his chest. He leaned down, kissed her cheek, and said, "I love you."

The monitors connected to her went crazy. Her eyes opened, widened for a moment, then slid shut. She whispered something. Rick leaned closer. "What? What did you say?"

"McHale."

****

"*Ay, mujer*! You are amazing." Joey Day lay naked beside Darcy Brown on his king-sized bed, gasping in huge breaths.

Darcy panted equally hard. "As are you."

Both were still coming down from a massive climax that had them shouting the ecstasy of release. She leaned in and gave him a long probing-tongue kiss. "I hope there's more where that came from."

"For you, *mi amante*, I always have more." He held her breast, running his thumb over the nipple. "But you must give me a moment to recover."

She shuddered at his touch. She'd had some incredible lovers over the years, but for wall-shaking, window-rattling, bed-busting sex, no one delivered like

Joey. She would miss that. She wished she didn't have to kill him.

Darcy rolled atop him and planted kisses all over his chest. "I don't want to wait." She pulled the baggie from her purse on the bedside table and opened it. Wetting her finger in her mouth, she dipped it in the coke and offered it to Joey. "Maybe this will speed things up."

"Ah, *carino*, you know what I like." He opened his mouth like a little bird.

She slipped her finger into his mouth and spread the white powder along his gums. She coated her finger again and wiped that on his tongue. Returning the baggie to her purse, she took out a pair of handcuffs, and held them before Joey's eyes. "I brought something else you like."

"Oh, *mi corazon*!" He raised his arms above his head, familiar with the game they'd played many times. "You will be the death of me."

If he only knew. She cuffed his wrists with the linking chain over a rail of the metal headboard. Then she gave him another long kiss and said, "Now I'm going to torture you with pleasure. Close your eyes. I want you to just feel everything."

He did. She kissed his chest for a minute or two then slipped a hand into her purse for her switchblade. Holding it the way she'd practiced to minimize the noise of the blade snapping out, she touched the release. She kissed slowly down his chest for another minute then raised the knife high and slammed it down hard and fast.

Joey's eyes shot open and his body arched as the blade punctured his chest and sank in to the hilt. He stared at her with confusion in his eyes. "Why?"

"I'm done being your whore, Joey." She rocked the

knife side to side to make sure he would die.

He groaned, and a narrow stream of blood ran from the widened wound across his chest and down his side, staining his blue sheets purple. Climbing off him, she stood by the bed, her arms clamped across her body to still her trembling, and waited until the death rattle sounded in his throat, his body slackened, and his eyes closed. Part one of her plan was done, time for part two. Escape to a new life somewhere far away.

She showered in the marble and gold bathroom off Joey's bedroom, washing away her old life as she scrubbed his blood and the scent of sex with him from her skin. She dressed, unable to take her eyes off his body the whole time, not quite believing she'd killed him, afraid he might come back to life.

Time to run. At the door to the bedroom, she stopped. Maybe she should pull the knife from his chest. No. It was a part of the life she was leaving behind. She wouldn't need it in her new one. But she took a moment to wipe her fingerprints from the handle.

She set the lock on the bedroom door and closed it behind her. Crossing Joey's office, she sat behind his maple desk, opened the bottom left drawer, and scooped the forty grand Joey kept there into her purse. Call it a bonus for screwing all the losers he sent her to over the years. Hell, just for the five times he sent her to McHale.

Darcy cracked the door to the living room and peered out. It was empty. She stepped into the living room, pulling the locked door to Joey's office shut behind her. At the front door, she stopped, smoothed her dress along her thighs, and adjusted the bodice to barely contain her breasts. She took a deep breath and opened the door. The two guards turned toward her.

She flashed a smile. "I have a message for you from Mr. Day. He is resting and says you are not to disturb him for at least two hours." She leaned toward them and winked.

The guards, their eyes fixed on her breasts welling out of her dress, smiled and nodded. Benito—or was he Manuel?—said, "Two hours. Yes, *señorita*."

"See you next week." Let them think she'd be coming back. She walked to the elevator, putting extra swing in her hips. She wanted Manuel and Benito to focus on her, not think about Joey or his nap at all. She stole a glance at them as she waited for the elevator. Both men had their gaze locked on her. She waved and they smiled.

The elevator doors closed. As it started down, her knees tried to fold, and she leaned against the wall, forcing deep slow breaths to quell the rising fear. Was Benito checking on Joey right now? Would he or Manuel be waiting in the lobby when the elevator doors opened? Would he kill her there? Or would he drag her back to Joey's apartment? She didn't want to think what might happen to her then. She needed three minutes to get to the street, just three minutes. She'd be safe there. She willed the elevator to drop faster.

She stepped onto the street. Five blocks to her Land Rover. She had escaped Joey's clutches, now she had to escape. She traveled the sidewalk on long, fast strides, a busy woman in a hurry with places to go and things to do. Each click of her heels on the paving sounded like a gunshot. Her heart hammered in her chest, and her stomach burned with fear. She hoped she'd bought herself two hours lead time with her lie.

Midblock she passed a building with a deeply

recessed front door. A hand grabbed her arm, yanking her into the dark alcove. Massive arms circled her, drawing her tight against a hard body. "Hello, *chica*."

She recognized Pepe's voice. Fear filled her. Had Joey's men found his body? Would Pepe kill her? He could crush the life from her with those thick arms as easily as she could crush a gnat. "What do you want?"

He pinned her against the wall with his bulk and grabbed her ass. "What any man wants from a *puta*."

"I'm no whore!"

"You are. Just like all the others." His growing erection pressed against her abdomen.

"Let go of me." She tried to shove him away. He didn't budge. "Joey will kill you for this."

He grinned a cold smile. "You think you are special, *chica*? You think he cares for you? You are nothing, just another *puta* he fucks." He gripped the hem of her dress, started hiking it up. "Now it is my turn."

She'd gut the bastard before she'd let that happen. She fished in her purse for her switchblade and realized with dread she'd left it buried in Joey's chest. There was only one way out of this. *What was one more guy after a hundred?* "Okay, Pepe, okay, you can have me. But not here. Take me somewhere private, and I'll do you like you've never been done before."

He grabbed her wrist and lunged through the door, dragging her with him across the lobby to the elevator. He pulled her into it, punching the button for the top floor. The doors closed and the elevator lurched then rose. Pepe crowded her into a corner, kissed her hard, and wedged his hand between her legs. She fought the urge to chomp down hard on his tongue as he forced it into her mouth.

No way would she let Pepe take her. She had to find a way out. Until then, she had to play along. She ran her hands up his chest. "God, Pepe, you're all muscle."

"You ain't seen my biggest one." He guided her hand to his crotch.

The guys who bragged the most usually had the least. Pepe, she had to admit, could back it up. At a different time and place, she'd have enjoyed hopping his bones. But not here, not now. She rubbed his erection. "I can't wait."

She slipped her arms inside his suit jacket and her hand brushed the edge of his pistol. That was her way out. She slid her arms around him. The elevator made its slow, steady climb. Floor nine. Ten. Eleven. She had to time this carefully. She pulled her arms back so her hand was just above the pistol. The elevator chimed twelve and lurched to a stop. Now.

She jerked the pistol from its holster, jammed it into Pepe's side, pulled the trigger. The BOOM filled the small car, driving spikes of pain into her ears. Pepe gasped and dropped to the floor, shock filling his eyes. Blood welled from his wound, blackened his suit, and pooled on the floor. Pepe grabbed her ankle as the elevator doors opened. Darcy jerked free and ran.

Clattering down the fire stairs as fast as she could, she realized she still had his pistol in her hand. She dropped it without slowing. She burst through the door to the lobby then slowed her pace. She paused at the front door and peeked out. No one lingered in the alcove. Four blocks to go. She stepped onto the sidewalk, scurrying away on long strides.

She expected to hear the crack of a gun, feel a bullet slam into her back with every step she took. Would she hear it? Would it be the last sound she ever heard? Would it hurt, or would she feel nothing beyond it tearing into her, spilling her face first to the sidewalk? Three blocks to go. She broke into a trot. Two blocks. One.

Two cars away from her Land Rover, she thumbed the remote. Getting in, she jabbed twice before hitting the starter button, her eyes searching the street for Manuel and Benito. She buckled her seatbelt, yanked the shifter into drive, and bulled her way into traffic.

Nine blocks later, Darcy steered the SUV up the ramp to the interstate. Her heart finally slowed as she accelerated toward the sun.

Chapter 27

"You're sure this McHale character is coming?" Trooper Burke asked.

"A hundred percent? No. Maybe ninety-eight." Rick had spent the last hour telling Burke and Sheehy everything he had on McHale. "Day's sending someone to finish the job McHale botched in Bobby Ed Lukens's apartment. McHale's the logical choice since he's Joey's go-to hitman. And he dropped the ball on Mary's hit."

"Info we got wasn't that he botched it, but that help got to Mary before she bled out."

"Same thing in Joey's eyes. He told McHale to ice her and she's still alive, doesn't matter why or how. He'd expect McHale to fix his mistake."

****

Twenty minutes later, Rick looked up at the first tap on Mary's door. Burke and Sheehy were on their feet by the second, both drawing their weapons. Rick stepped between Mary's bed and the door, hand under his jacket on his Colt. Sheehy took the door. Burke took up position behind her to her right. A third tap. Sheehy and Burke had their automatics down by their sides when Sheehy opened the door a sliver.

A soft finger snap. Sheehy jerked then dropped. Rick pulled his Colt from its holster. Another snap and Burke fell. The door swung wider. McHale stepped into the room, a small silenced automatic held waist high.

How did he get past hospital security? McHale fired again. Pain exploded in Rick's shoulder and his pistol slipped from his hand. Another pop and pain filled his chest. He fell, heartbroken he'd failed to save Mary.

****

Ann Hendershot stepped into the hall leading to Mary's room. A man stood at Mary's door. His build was too tall and stocky for Dr. Nicopoulos, the only physician treating Mary, and he had seen her an hour ago, he wouldn't return this fast. The man wasn't a nurse either. Only she, Denise Sholes, and Linda Allington were treating Mary.

A muted pop and his arm twitched. Gun! He slipped into the room. Ann sprinted down the hall and charged through the door. She barreled into the man just as he fired again. A bright red spot appeared on Rick's chest, and he dropped like a stone.

The man swung at her, catching her in the face with the pistol. Ann hit the floor, the impact driving air from her lungs with an explosive whoof. Her head smacked the tiles, rattling her brain and making everything wonky.

****

McHale glanced back. The woman who'd plowed into him, spoiling his shot at Lafferty's head, was the nurse he'd run into first time he was here. He should put one in her for that. He pointed the silenced .22 at her then lowered it. She was out cold. Almost as good as dead, but not quite. She was no threat now. He'd finish her off, maybe bang her first, maybe snuff her while doing her, after he'd offed Virgin. He'd save four rounds for her, the two women, and Lafferty. The other twelve were going into Mary.

He was going to shoot her eleven different places, really make her hurt, before planting the last one in her brain. But where? He waved the pistol over Virgin's still form.

****

Ann's head cleared. Pain from her smashed nose filled her face and blood flooded the back of her throat. She fought the need to cough it up. If she made a sound, the man would kill her, just as he had killed Caitlin, Allison, and Rick. They couldn't stop the man from killing Mary. It was up to her.

She eased her head slowly left then right and almost gasped from the surges of pain in her face. She bit her lip to stifle them. Near her right hand on the floor was a gun. Sheehy, stretching her hand toward it, sucked in a sharp breath at a spasm of pain. Ann froze. The man turned at the sound, shot Allison again, and turned back to the bed as if shooting her was no different than swatting a fly.

Ann bit her lip harder to stifle a scream as Sheehy stilled. She slid her hand to the pistol and gripped it firmly. She couldn't have it slip from her hand when she picked it up. Any noise would be fatal to her and Mary. She lifted the gun carefully and slowly brought it to her chest. She didn't want any sudden motion catching the man's attention.

Ann knew guns. Her late husband, a competitive shooter, had taught her to shoot. She'd enjoyed it and had been good enough to give him a run for his money. She eyed the automatic in her hand for a safety. There, the little lever by her thumb. It was off. And the hammer was cocked. She was good to go. She held the pistol the way Dean had taught her—right hand holding it with it resting on her cupped left palm—extended her arms, and pointed it at the man.

After a second, she lowered the automatic. She didn't know if she could kill someone. Her whole adult life had been devoted to healing, not hurting. She couldn't think of that now. Allison, Caitlin, and Rick were dead. She and Mary would die, too, if she didn't stop this man. She had to stop him for Mary's sake. For her sake. An icy calm settled over her, and she raised the gun again.

****

Rick opened his eyes then blinked twice to clear the blur. Ann was on her back on the floor, a pistol in her hands pointed at McHale. He had his silenced automatic aimed at Mary. No! Rick had to get his weapon, had to save them. His right arm wouldn't move. He'd have to do this left-handed. He grasped his pistol and raised it, clenching his teeth against the pain knifing through his chest. His vision blurred, his arm trembled, and his Glock wobbled.

"Stop!" Ann shouted.

McHale shifted his aim to her.

Rick had only one chance to get this right. There would be no do-overs. Either McHale would die or he, Mary, and Ann would. He shut out the pain spearing from his right shoulder, focused everything he had into steadying his left arm. He inhaled, held his breath, and squeezed the trigger.

****

McHale turned toward the sound of a sharply inhaled breath. Shit! Lafferty wasn't dead, and he had his gun pointed at him. Lafferty's pistol boomed, and time shifted to hyper-slow mode. McHale saw the muzzle flash, saw the action cycle, saw the casing whirl away.

He saw the bullet coming toward him and knew he was going to die. No ducking it. He felt the bullet smash through his cheek. Killed by tha—

****

The man's head exploded in an upward spray of bone, brain, and blood.

He toppled forward onto Ann, and a piece of his shattered head dropped onto her cheek. She shrieked and slapped it away. Then she thrashed and wriggled and shoved her way from under his corpse and scrambled toward Mary's bed.

Mashing the big red button above it, she shouted, "Emergency! Emergency!"

Epilogue

One year later

Rick's arm still moved a little stiffly, and his shoulder ached on cold, damp days. Sitting at his desk, he opened the cover of the final report on the scandal the media had dubbed 'Cops for Crime.'

He knew some of it. McHale had been pronounced dead in Mary's room. Trooper Allison Sheehy, shot in the stomach and chest, had died on the way to OR. Trooper Caitlin Burke, also shot in the gut, had undergone eleven hours of surgery to repair her stomach, liver, and spleen. He'd needed surgery for his shattered right shoulder and sternum. A plastic surgeon had reset Ann's broken nose and cracked cheekbone. Mary had come out of her coma three days after his surgery. He'd been by her bed, holding her hand, when she'd opened her eyes for keeps.

A search of McHale's home the day after the shootout in Mary's room had uncovered accounts in six banks holding over two million dollars and a notebook recording work he'd done for Joey Day. The biggest find, however, had been a list of police officers in Joey's pocket. In the next three months, four-hundred-fifty-eight policemen and women—from nine rookie officers to a senior division commander and the Commissioner of Personnel—out of a force of over nine thousand were arrested for crimes ranging from accepting bribes to murder for hire. Davenport and eleven other officers ate their guns to escape prosecution. The rest struck deals, turned state's evidence, or were toughing it out. The DA guaranteed all would do hard time.

The same day McHale died, Joey Day was found stabbed in his bed and one of his bodyguards, Pepe Lopez, was found murdered in the elevator of a nearby apartment building. Suspicion for both deaths fell on Darcy Brown, manager of *Paraiso*, a club Joey owned. The knife in Joey's chest was one co-workers at the club said she carried in her purse, and her fingerprints were on the 9mm Colt used to kill Pepe. No one had seen Darcy since she waved goodbye to two Lobos gang members standing guard outside Joey's condo two hours before his body was found. Police were not exactly moving mountains to find her. Rick wondered if Darcy was living happily somewhere or decomposing slowly in a landfill.

He laid the report aside and picked up the latest gang intelligence update.

Joey's organization had imploded after his murder. César Molina stepped into his shoes but lacked Joey's charisma, and his even more brutal way of dealing with dissent pissed everybody off. Two months later, he was dead, his body ripped apart by a grenade tossed in the open window of his new Bentley Arnage. With him gone, Joey's lieutenants went to war over control of the organization. Four bloody months later, Pedro Ramirez sat on the throne. His reign had lasted all of six days, ending when his main squeeze emasculated him after she caught him screwing a Las Lobas in their bed. She wouldn't have cared, except the Loba in their bed was her fourteen-year-old sister.

Criminal Intel easily rounded up the disorganized and leaderless survivors. Six months after his murder, his organization was as dead as Joey.

The Vipers, Monarchs, and Kings charged into the void. Instead of agreeing to share the drug trade, however, each one had gone after the whole pie. The slaughter that followed gutted all three, and the only winners had been the city's funeral directors. Gangs in the city—except for a few lame, weak wannabees—had ceased to exist.

Rick clocked out early and left the station house. Tomorrow was going to be the biggest day of his life.

****

A few minutes before one, Rick stood in a gazebo in Rosemont Park, looking past the rows of chairs flanking the runner atop the grass. Mary made her way slowly along the runner to a scratchy tape of *Here Comes the Bride*, a spray of baby roses in her free hand. She was still too pale and too thin, but her color was improving and her face had lost most of its former gauntness. She still used a cane to walk but more for peace of mind than necessity. His heart still swelled every time he saw her, even more so today. He was the luckiest guy in the world. Twice over.

Her maid of honor, his sister, steadied her as she climbed the three steps into the gazebo then took her cane. Mary smiled at him—setting off that funny flutter in his gut—as she slipped her hand around his arm. "Last chance to back out, Lafferty."

He smiled back. "Not happening, Conner."

They faced the department chaplain, who cleared her throat and said, "We gather today to unite Richard

Lafferty and Mary Conner in the bonds of holy matrimony."

****

An hour later, at the reception at Fanello's, as the guests hoisted a champagne toast to the newlyweds, Tim Morris leaned toward his date and said, "Will you marry me?"

Joleen Wilson almost dropped her flute.

A word about the author...

I have always had an interest in writing but only dabbled in it for my own amusement until 1995 when the desire to do more infected me. After retiring in 2009 from an almost 40-year career as a pharmacist, I had even more time to devote to writing.

I also enjoy auto maintenance and detailing, woodworking, photography, videography, and of course reading.

I am a father of two grown and successful children, married to the same terrific woman for 45 years, and an elder and deacon in my church.

You can follow me on my Facebook page – David A. Freas – Author – and feel free to contact me at quillracer@hotmail.com.

Reviews are the lifeblood of any author and I would love to read yours, so please share your thoughts.

Thank you for purchasing
this publication of The Wild Rose Press, Inc.

For questions or more information
contact us at
info@thewildrosepress.com.

The Wild Rose Press, Inc.
www.thewildrosepress.com

www.ingramcontent.com/pod-product-compliance
Lightning Source LLC
Chambersburg PA
CBHW070806030726
47504CB00003B/722